CW00701209

WOR

THROUGH

IT

WORKING THROUGH IT

KAY SILVER

Acknowledgements

Writing 'Working Through It' has been a challenge. 'Double Dilemma', my debut novel, was meant to be a stand-alone book. However, so many readers asked me what had happened to the family, and whether Sam ever realised his ambition to become Chief Rabbi, that I felt compelled to write a sequel.

Rabbi Sybil Sheridan, despite her incredible work load, took the time to discuss the religious difficulties Sam had to overcome, and for this I thank her.

Rimma Lerman, from the Hall of Names at Yad Vashem, provided the information I needed about the register of those murdered during the Holocaust. I very much appreciate the swiftness and accuracy of the reply.

The Amazing Mr Silver once more did the technical work necessary to publish the book. Without his superior knowledge, 'Working Through It' would remain buried deep in the computer and I cannot thank him enough.

My thanks also go to my family, who listened patiently when I outlined some of my ideas.

Finally, thank you to everyone who took the time to tell me that they wanted a sequel. It would not have happened without you.

Foreword

'The only thing worse than being blind
is having sight and no vision.'

Helen Keller

All the characters in 'Working Through It' are fictitious;
products of my imagination who became very real to me.
The novel is set partly in England, partly in Germany and
partly in Israel. It refers to a harrowing time during the
twentieth century, so I have endeavoured to use accurate
descriptions of events. The Holocaust, death marches,
camps in Cyprus and the inhumanity shown to the six
million Jews who were murdered during World War Two,
is true.

I have included a glossary at the back of the book so
that readers can look up any unfamiliar words.

CHAPTER 1

Sam crossed the road, head down, oblivious to the Berlin traffic. Several cars swerved to avoid him but he ignored the angry sound of their horns. The day had darkened, and lights shone out from the café where he'd left his family. Daniel and Esther were sitting on red leather stools at the table in the window. Eva and Helen were further back, in a booth with high sides.

The doorbell jangled as he pushed through and stood, eyes sweeping the room. He spotted where his wife and mother were sitting and joined them. The twins got down from their seats and slid in behind him.

"So?" asked Eva tremulously.

"I don't want to talk about it…I can't talk about it. I just want to get back to the hotel." Sam rubbed his eyes and there was an awkward silence as Helen and her mother-in-law exchanged glances.

"We're all done here, so we can leave. Maybe I should drive?" Helen asked.

She looked at Sam. His face was pale and drawn; the worry lines on his head seemed to have magnified during the last hour and his shoulders drooped. He was diminished in size – the interview had not gone well, although sadly it had turned out as Sam had expected.

Keys rattled as Sam handed them over. The women gathered up their handbags and the whole group moved outside and into the car. The journey back to the hotel was short and no-one spoke.

"Can you eat, Sam?" Helen asked but he shook his head wanly.

"No. I need to think over what I'm going to do now. We leave early in the morning, so I'm going to our room. Why don't you all have dinner – I can always get room service if I want something later."

"Come on, granny, I'll help you get ready. Daniel, we'll meet you in half an hour in the dining room." Esther took charge and pressed the button for the lift. Helen followed uncertainly, not sure if Sam wanted her to go with him, but he had already reached the stairs and was striding resolutely up them. She followed Esther and her mother-in-law.

Their room, which before had been a welcome haven, felt hostile and threatening. Sam crossed to the small desk and looked for the headed notepaper. His brain was whirling, as he tried to process the conversation he'd had with Rabbi Langer and his colleagues. He poured himself a glass of water and picked up the pen. He was about to write the hardest letter he'd ever attempted. He would have to give his resignation and leave behind everything he'd ever wanted, and everything he'd ever worked for.

Then he paused. What exactly had the three rabbis said, once their initial shock was over? Had they asked him to resign? Not specifically but the idea was there in the room, hanging like a limp flag on a flag pole. He groaned and rested his head in his hands, remembering how difficult it had been to tell his story.

The three rabbis had welcomed him, offering coffee or tea, even a glass of wine but Sam refused everything. He had loosened his collar and slackened his tie, trying to prolong the moment when he would have to speak. Rabbi Langer started first, enquiring gently if Sam was all right. The astute rabbi realised that there was something Sam had to tell them; something he didn't *want* to tell them. The old rabbi had wondered if there was a problem between Sam and Helen, and whether Sam thought it would affect his chances of being appointed the Chief Rabbi. He had known Sam practically all his life and knew he was an upright and ethical man but that didn't mean his marriage was in a good place.

Rabbi Zimmerman had interrupted in his usual impatient way.

"Look here, Sam," he started. "Whatever's going on…we ought to know. For the last few weeks you've behaved in a very strange way. You haven't explained why you couldn't make your first interview. You haven't given us the courtesy of knowing what the problem is, and now you're sitting there like a…like a…" He paused, searching for a suitable word, and gave up. "I have enough tsuris in my own life without you adding to it. Speak up, man, and tell us what your problem is, before I plotz."

Still Sam was quiet. Rabbi Brauman added his suggestion.

"Whatever it is, Sam, we need to know. Just start at the beginning and tell us." A thought struck him. "Are you ill? Is that what the problem is?"

Rabbi Langer looked up sharply,

"Maybe it's Helen...or the children?"

Sam cleared his throat and wiped his forehead where the sweat was beginning to gather.

"None of those, unless you count my state of mind! Helen is fine and Daniel and Esther have almost finished university." He looked directly at the three rabbis, who were waiting for him to speak. "I have no doubt you will find what I am going to tell you difficult to understand. *I* found it difficult to understand – I still do." There was a heavy silence before Sam started again.

"I was here in Berlin, ready for the conference. I wanted to succeed; I wanted to go forward to the final interview. I'd done my homework and I knew I was as prepared as I could be. And then..." his voice faltered, "I got a strange message to meet a man in the hotel coffee shop. Of course, I didn't know what it was about and I wasn't going to go but I was curious so, in the end, I did. The man I met looked like me – it was weird, I almost felt I knew him. He referred to my interview and said I should talk to my mother. That's why I flew home so rapidly. I knew there was something very, very wrong.

"Ma didn't want to talk to me about it and that made me even more determined to find out what was going on. When she told me I couldn't believe it, but her distress was so apparent that I knew it was true." Sam turned to look at Rabbi Langer. "The baby you first met in that basement room just before the end of the war was the child of Ernst Hoffman, commandant of the camp where my mother was kept and where her sisters died."

Rabbi Langer shook his head in disbelief. "You mean, you are not the child whose brit I performed? No, of course you are. So what you're telling me is that Hoffman was your father."

The rabbis looked at each other in consternation and Rabbi Brauman spoke up. "Your poor mother; how brave of her to keep you and, of course, this doesn't affect your Jewish status – your mother is Jewish, therefore you, too, are Jewish."

"Not so," Sam continued. "Eva is not my birth mother. I am the child of Hoffman and his wife – one of twin boys. I was never adopted, never had a conversion, therefore I am very definitely not Jewish, which means I cannot be a rabbi. Fortunately, Daniel and Esther are Jewish because of Helen, but me – what am I?" By this time, Sam was red faced and shouting and Rabbi Langer put a restraining hand on his arm.

"Calm down, Sam, calm down."

"Easy for you to say, rabbi," retorted Sam. "You can have no idea what this means. Everything I've done over the years means nothing. All the weddings, the funerals…everything! As a non Jew, I wasn't entitled to do any of those things…But I did! I did them all! Unknowingly, but it doesn't make it right."

Sam subsided back into his chair and reached for a glass of water. The three rabbis looked at each other.

"So the man you met was your twin brother. Where is he now?" Sam explained that Hans had run into the road, been hit by a car and died. He said that, as far as he knew, there were no other relatives.

"No doubt about it," Rabbi Zimmerman looked sadly at his colleagues. "This is a mess and something I have no experience of. What do you want to do, Sam?"

"What do I want to do? Do I have any choice? All these things I've done have to be put right, I know, but how? All my life I only wanted to be a rabbi. I wanted a community to serve." Thinking of this made him groan even more. "Now, obviously, I'll have to inform them and resign. I cannot bear it but what else can I do?"

Rabbi Langer turned this thought over in his mind.

"You will have to talk to the synagogue board but please don't be hasty, Sam. Let's think about your options."

Sam was still not calm.

"Options," he shouted. "I don't have any options. All my life I've never thought about whether or not I was Jewish. I *am* Jewish...I *was* Jewish." His voice was ragged as he took deep breaths, trying to control his emotions. "Now I find out that's not true. How do you think I feel? Everything I've done, everything I've achieved is reduced to nothing," he said bitterly, "and you're telling me not to be hasty." He subsided back into his chair and buried his face in his hands.

The rabbis looked at him in consternation. They had never seen Sam so distraught. This situation was something they had no experience of, but they all knew that Sam needed help. They exchanged glances, recognising that they also needed help.

Rabbi Langer spoke for all of them when he said,

"We will need to consult a higher authority. I'll telephone the Chief Rabbi tomorrow and arrange a consultation."

Sam's shoulders heaved as he realised that this was the man whose shoes he had hoped to fill. There was no possibility of that now.

"Before that, though, is there anything else we need to know?" Rabbi Brauman asked gently. "We should have the whole picture, nu?"

Briefly, Sam went through the story, realising as he talked, that this was the first of what would be many explanations. The rabbis sat very still, sometimes interrupting to clarify something but mainly listening until, eventually, Sam stopped. His voice was hoarse and he had no tears left. He waited for Rabbi Langer to say something.

"There is no way around this, Sam," the old rabbi said carefully. "You cannot continue as a rabbi, certainly for the immediate future, but there may be a solution." Sam shook his head despondently but didn't speak. "First of all, I must ask the question. Do you want to remain a rabbi?"

There was the light of hope in Sam's eyes as he nodded.

"What is important, now, is for you to become Jewish, yes? I think the best thing you can do, after you've spoken to your community, will be to take a sabbatical in Israel. There you will be able to complete a conversion course – a formality, I'm sure, and then we can consider the next step. Think about what I'm saying and we'll speak tomorrow."

Sam had left the room, knowing how shaken the rabbis were and understanding that they needed to talk about his revelation.

As he sat on the gilt chair in his hotel room, going over and over in his mind what had been said, be began to formulate some sort of plan.

Since he had found out that he was the son of Frau Hoffman and Ernst Hoffman, the commandant of the concentration camp where his mother had been imprisoned, he had only had a short time to become accustomed to the fact he was not Jewish, despite being brought up in a Jewish family and experiencing all the life cycle events.

Initially he had thought there was no way he could remain a rabbi, despite his total conviction that this was his life's work. He took another sip of water. What had Rabbi Langer said? Something about taking a sabbatical from the community while decisions were made about his future.

Sam groaned again. His future! What future? Whichever way you looked at it, he wasn't Jewish and therefore he couldn't be a rabbi. What good would a sabbatical be! His head was aching but he was beginning to put his thoughts in order.

A six month sabbatical, or more properly, six months away from his community, would give him a breathing space, even though he knew that it would have to be unpaid leave. There was no way his congregation could or should continue to pay his salary when they were told he wasn't a rabbi...wasn't even Jewish. He considered his bank balance – not wonderful, but probably enough to keep him for six months. He might be able to find some work – maybe he could repair Torah scrolls; then he stopped himself. Of course he couldn't. He wasn't Jewish, so not allowed to.

The most important first step would be to go through a form of conversion to ratify his Jewish status. How ironic, he thought, that this was a journey he'd taken with many conversion candidates over the years.

Rabbi Brauman had suggested that Sam went to Israel; it would make the whole process easier – more kosher, the old man had said with a pale imitation of a smile, and he would take his advice. There could be no doubt that he would be accepted for conversion; he had lived as a Jew all his life so the customary learning period might be shortened – even abandoned. He would still need to go through the Beth Din but Rabbi Brauman had snorted,

"A formality, Sam. Just a formality. Once you've got an official conversion, everything else will fall into place."

Wearily, Sam accepted this would be a complicated process. He couldn't imagine that this was a situation that had ever occurred before. But what of the rest? All the ceremonies he'd performed in good faith; all without authority and all now in doubt as to their validity. He knew he had nothing to reproach himself for, but how would his community deal with the knowledge that their rabbi, their leader and teacher, was not even Jewish.

The old rabbis were right. He needed some breathing space. He would go to Israel and regularise his position. Helen would go with him and Daniel and Esther would finish their studies. Both were set to take good degrees. Daniel would go into medicine like his grandfather and Esther would become a lawyer.

He put the cap back on the pen and replaced the writing paper in the drawer. Now was not the time for resignation. Now was the time to make concrete plans.

CHAPTER 2

Sam was staring out of the window when Helen came up to bed. She could see by the set of his shoulders that he was very tense. Wordlessly, she moved to stand behind him and kneaded his neck. He sighed in appreciation, enjoying the feel of her hands.

"I'm sorry I was so abrupt before," he started and Helen shook her head.

"I should think, after the day you've had, you need to have a few quiet moments. Are you ready to tell me now what happened?"

Swiftly, he outlined the rabbis' suggestions and waited for Helen's response.

"It's a big ask," she said, "but I think they're right. I know you, Sam. I've lived with you for half of my life, and I understand there is no way you want to turn your back on what we've got. Daniel and Esther will be all right if we leave them for a while. In fact, it may even do them good to become a bit more independent. As soon as you've spoken to Anthony Bloom at the synagogue, we can start to organise our journey."

"What about the house, Helen? And what about money? I have some savings but not a lot."

"I don't think we need to worry about money, darling. I still have the legacy my uncle left me, and as for the house – I suggest we offer it to whoever takes over from you. We can charge a reasonable rent and that will go towards our living costs in Israel."

Sam's face fell. He hadn't thought about the rabbi who would take over from him, and what that might mean for his future. He voiced his concerns to Helen.

"Maybe the board will want to keep the new rabbi. There might not be a place for me when we come back."

Helen looked at him sternly.

"I think you're running away with yourself, Sam. You've served this congregation for a very long time and I don't think they will jettison you over something which is not your fault. And, anyway," she added consolingly, "even if they were stupid enough to do that, there is always a shortage of rabbis. You would find a job anywhere."

Sam wasn't so sure but let it drop. Helen's face was animated; her dark hair almost standing on end as she made her points forcefully. Sam turned round and buried his face amongst her curls. He breathed in the familiar smell; shampoo and soap and a floral perfume, and thought once again how lucky he was to have her for his wife.

They stayed silent for a few minutes and then Helen broke the spell.

"We should pack; we have an early flight in the morning. Your mother is almost ready and the twins will need to be chivvied a bit but they'll be on time. We can leave the hire car at the airport and we should be home mid afternoon."

Helen slipped into sleep quickly. Once she'd made up her mind to do something she didn't dwell over it so she was soon breathing heavily, her face turned into Sam's back, an arm flung carelessly over his chest.

It was different for Sam, though. The events of the last few weeks had caught up with him and his active mind wouldn't release him from the thoughts which crowded into his brain. He lay still, not wanting to disturb Helen, going over and over what Eva had said, what the rabbis had said, what Helen had said. So far 1990 had been a year of ups and downs and he definitely felt he was sliding further. Eventually, he pushed the bedclothes back carefully and went to sit on the chair by the window.

He watched as the pale light of dawn broke through the low clouds and Berlin began to come to life. The trams clanged along their rails and workers queued for spaces inside. People in Germany started work early and there were already crowds at the tram stops and a few mothers with children in prams, taking them to the kindergarten before they began their shifts.

Helen stirred and Sam looked across. She pushed the hair off her forehead and sat up and, as Sam looked at her with new eyes, he thought once again how lucky he was to have her as his wife.

"What time did you get up?" she asked sleepily. Sam didn't reply but crossed to the bed to hug her.

"It doesn't matter what time; but you should be on your feet, Mrs Goldman."

Helen stretched and swung her feet onto the floor.

"You're right. I'll go in the shower first while you shut the cases and then we'll meet the others for breakfast. I told them seven thirty, so we'd better get a move on if we want to be on time."

The dining room was busy. Helen looked at Eva and suspected that she, like Sam, hadn't slept much. Eva looked older somehow, more fragile, although she was smiling bravely at her grandchildren who had piled their plates high. Nothing seemed to affect their appetites but the rest of them made do with coffee and toast. Eva carefully tore hers into minute pieces but seemed unable to swallow.

Sam drove carefully but quickly to the airport and handed the car keys to the waiting valet. Formalities over, they boarded swiftly and settled into their seats. The tension Eva had felt on her first flight had reduced somewhat and she lay back, eyes closed, unwilling to talk. She held Sam's hand on takeoff and landing and was obviously relieved to be back on terra firma when the plane taxied into its parking place.

They waited in line for a cab, still quiet, each with their own thoughts, and when they arrived back at the house Sam said firmly to his mother,

"I think you should stay with us for a while, ma. You've had a difficult few days and it would save me worrying about you."

Suddenly, Eva was too tired to argue. Exhaustion washed over her, and she allowed herself to be taken indoors. She found herself with a cup of tea in her hand, a stool under her feet and a blanket tucked over her knees.

"Daniel," called Sam. "Will you go next door and get Tess. That dog will think we've deserted her. No need to discuss what we've been doing, son. Just get the dog."

Leaving Eva to rest, Sam went into the kitchen and took a mug out of the cupboard.

"I think I need strong coffee for what I'm about to do now. I can't leave it any longer. I'll have to call the synagogue chairman and set up a board meeting. It might take a bit of time to find a date which suits everyone but I'll stress how important it is. I'll go upstairs and ring from the study."

Sam listened to the sound of the phone in the chairman's house. Just as he was about to give up, he heard Anthony Bloom's deep tones.

"So, it's you, rabbi. You're back. Did you do well?" Anthony Bloom had been the only person in the synagogue who knew that Sam had gone to Berlin for an interview. He had said,

"Much as we'll be sorry to see you leave us, Sam, it's a wonderful opportunity for you and I'm sure you'll always have a soft spot for the East Lane shul, and come back often to see us and give us an occasional sermon." Sam had felt warmed by this comment, knowing how well loved he was in the community. That was all to change now.

"Anthony, we need to call a meeting of the board as soon as possible."

"So, you've got it, then Sam. Mazaltov!"

"No, Anthony, I haven't got it but we still need to have a board meeting."

There was a stunned silence on the other end of the phone as the chairman tried to process what his rabbi was saying. There had been no doubts in his mind that Sam would come back successfully as the candidate for Chief Rabbi. He had said to his wife, 'they would be meshugga not to take Sam.' He had even cast his eye over possible candidates for the soon to be vacant position. Rabbi Stanford could be promoted and there were one or two student rabbis who had promise.

"What happened, Sam?"

"I can't talk about it now. I would be grateful if you could call a meeting as soon as possible, and I'll explain everything then. In the meantime, can you find someone to take services this weekend? I'm really not up to it." Sam thought that was the understatement of the year, but could think of no other way to explain his need to pull back from synagogue life.

Bewildered, Anthony tried to press Sam a little but it was obvious that he wasn't going to say anymore.

"I'll call you, Sam, as soon as I have a day. Maybe after the weekend? Monday or Tuesday?"

"Any day suits me, the sooner the better." And with that, Anthony Bloom had to be content.

"Good," said Helen. "You've finished on the phone. I need to make a few calls but before that, I think we need to talk to the kids and your mother. They're still very much in the dark about what's going on."

Daniel and Esther had tried to work out what was happening but Eva was too drained to even think. They all sat round the table and waited for Sam to speak. No one interrupted; no one commented, as he outlined the tentative plans he and Helen had made.

"But the house, dad," Esther finally said. "We won't have anywhere to come home to."

"I realise that will be difficult for you, but we will need the money from the rent. Israel won't be cheap, you know. You will be able to stay on at university for the holidays if

15

you want. It won't be for long – probably only six months. And, don't forget, you'll be able to visit granny and Aunt Rachel. They might even let you stay sometimes."

Eva nodded. Even though she felt her whole world was crumbling around her, she knew that visits from Daniel and Esther would give her strength. She would miss Sam and Helen and, at her age, she knew how precarious life could be, but she could see this was the best solution all round.

"I'm waiting to hear from Anthony. I've asked him to set up a meeting where I'll be able to explain what's happened and then, after that, Helen and I will be on our way."

"So quickly, Sam! Why so quickly?"

"Ma, it needs to be as speedy as possible. I can't stay here; I'm not the rabbi anymore. They'll need to get someone to take over from me and I need to leave them to it. Things will be easier for the community if I'm not here."

The phone rang and Sam went to answer it. They could hear him saying, "Yes, yes, that's fine. Monday it is. Seven o'clock. Thank you, Anthony. I realise this is difficult but I would rather talk to everyone together. See you on Monday." He rejoined the family,

"There's a lot to do, now. I think we could probably leave for Israel next Thursday, if we can get a flight." He looked at his twins. "You two can stay with granny until it's time to go back to university. You might want to sort your rooms out so that whoever moves in won't have to worry about damaging anything. Put away stuff you wouldn't want people to use and clear a couple of cupboards out – that sort of thing. And get your washing done," he added with a faint smile.

The phone rang again. This time Helen answered it and came back into the room to tell Sam that the Chief Rabbi wanted to speak with him. When Sam returned to the kitchen he had tears in his eyes.

"I didn't have to say anything to Rabbi Hershell," he said. "Rabbi Langer had told him everything. He agrees that going to Israel is the best way forward. He even said there's a hardship fund if we need any financial help but I told him that it wasn't necessary. However, he wants to see me as soon as possible; tomorrow in fact, so we may have to delay travelling for a week or two. He's going to give me a list of accommodation – flats to rent, that sort of thing, at reasonable prices and he'll write to the yeshiva outlining what's happened. He has no doubt that everyone will be sympathetic and make it as easy for me as possible." He wiped his eyes. "You have no idea what that means to me."

Eva's shoulders shook. At that moment she realised the implications of what she'd done. For over forty years she'd kept the secret of Sam's birth locked inside her and now it was coming out into the open, she felt as if her heart would break. What had she been thinking of? If only she had told Rabbi Langer the truth, Sam would not now be dealing with the aftermath.

"I'm so sorry," she said brokenly. "I don't know what I can do to make amends. I never thought this would happen. You know, I think I put all this to the back of my mind but I could have put it right! I could have explained! I could have done something!" She looked woebegone and Sam and Helen wrapped their arms about her.

"I couldn't have had better parents, ma," said Sam. "What's past is past; now is the time to move on. Don't upset yourself anymore; it'll all work out in the end. What's important now, is to ask Helen to start making one of her lists."

Everyone smiled. Helen was the queen of list making and the best person to organise the next steps. She found a notepad and paper and started to make her calls. There was no immediate need to book seats on the Tel Aviv flight but she checked availability anyway. The next few weeks looked good; plenty of availability, so she put that on hold. Sam's sister and husband were due back from their holiday so she left a message on their answer phone, inviting them to dinner. This was a meal she wasn't looking forward to.

Tess moved over to where Sam was sitting and gently pushed her nose into his hand. Absently, he rubbed her head, thinking this was another complication. Maybe Rachel would have the dog while he was away. It would be too much for Eva to manage.

He made a concerted effort to pull himself together.

"I need to go out for a while," he said. "Rabbi Hershell wants some information and I'll have to look in at the synagogue office." He took a deep breath. "He wants the name of everyone I've married or buried. Anything which requires a genuine rabbi to preside over; plus the conversion candidates and so on. In the meantime, he's going to work out which is allowable and remains halachically correct, and which will have to be re-done." His face was bleak as he added, "I don't know how I'm going to explain all this to the people I've married." He looked directly at his wife.

18

"There's also something we haven't considered. You and I were married in shul and I don't think our ceremony was valid, under present circumstances."

Helen gasped, then said staunchly,

"As far as I'm concerned, you're still my husband. Nothing will take that away. Hopefully, Rabbi Hershell will have some answers tomorrow."

CHAPTER 3

It was only a short drive to the synagogue. Sam unlocked the car park and then closed the gates after he'd driven through. It was deserted; the building was in darkness. Once inside he switched the alarm off and hung his coat up in the cloakroom. The familiar smells filtered into his nostrils; furniture polish, candle wax and old books.

Everything was the same as it had been before he left for Berlin. The box of spare yarmulkes was still in the foyer, and in the sanctuary the pews, in serried rows, waited for the members to sit on them. The Ladies Gallery, bounded by fretwork railings, was empty too, although a faint aroma of perfume lingered in the air.

There was a pile of post on his desk and a note from the synagogue secretary on top of the letters, telling him that there would be a visit from a prospective proselyte. His diary was clear on that day, so Annabel had taken the liberty of fixing a time, and she hoped that would be ok.

Sam smiled wryly. 'Not anymore', he thought. 'Not now'. He was no longer the rabbi, and a feeling of sadness washed over him.

The filing cabinet was locked. He fumbled for the key and slid the top drawer open. There was a slim folder labelled 'Conversions' and he took it out and placed it on the desk. There were files labelled, 'Deaths' and 'Marriages' and he pulled them out, too. By the time he'd finished it was a substantial pile, and he wondered how he would trawl through it to find the information Rabbi Hershell needed. There must be an easier way of doing this, he thought, and then realised that the synagogue diaries would tell him everything he needed to know. He replaced the files, located the diaries and sat, carefully copying out all the details.

Contacting everyone was going to be a monumental task. Some people would have moved; he knew of several families who had made aliyah. A few of the couples had divorced and, once again, he groaned. This was going to be even more complicated than he'd thought. He was not on the Beth din, whose responsibility it was to sign gittin, but he had done a lot of preparatory work. As a non Jew would this be acceptable?

He rapidly scanned the list of couples he'd married. Several had divorced but since they hadn't actually been halachically married, a divorce was unnecessary. The civil side was to comply with the legal requirement – nothing to do with him.

The room began to whirl around as he tried to work out the complications. He could see now why the Chief Rabbi needed to see him as soon as possible. He decided he would have to prioritise. He would compile a list so that the most urgent cases could be attended to first. He switched on the lights and, armed with pen and paper, began to write.

Altogether, there were just over thirty couples he'd married, although other couples in the community had been married by his assistant rabbi. Sam was so glad that he'd always had a junior rabbi. If he'd been the sole incumbent of a large community, the numbers could have been huge!

There were few conversions, each posing an additional problem. Any children born would not be considered Jewish if the mother was the one who had converted. Of course, if it was the father, there wouldn't be a problem; the child of a Jewish mother is halachically Jewish. He looked again through his list and put a line through the names of the men who had converted. They would have to be told, of course, but that could wait until the more urgent cases had been dealt with. He hoped his signature on the initial papers wouldn't be considered ineligible.

There were a fair number of deaths but eventually, Sam was finished. He looked around the room, wondering how many more times he would be able to work in what was, in effect, his second home.

Helen was in the kitchen when he got back. There was an enticing smell coming from the pans on the stove and he realised how hungry he was. The table in the dining room was set and Esther and Daniel came downstairs as Helen was carrying the food in.

"Ma?" asked Sam.

"Gone to bed. This has all been too much for her so I took soup up on a tray but she couldn't even manage that. I don't think she's had a proper meal for days," she added with a worried expression.

"I don't know what to say," started Sam.

"There's nothing to say, dad," said Daniel. "You'll get through this."

"Maybe, but it's going to take some time. People will feel let down and all the apologies in the world won't help."

"Wait and see what Rabbi Hershell says tomorrow," Helen said soothingly. "You can't make any decisions until you know what he has in mind."

"We'll clear up," said Esther. "You and mum go and sit down. You both look all in."

"I think I'll just go to bed," said their father. "It's been a long day, and I need to sleep."

But, once again, there was no sleep for Sam. How he wished that Eva had told Rabbi Langer the truth of his birth. Even though he understood Eva's reasons, her decision was going to affect, not just life, but the lives of many, many people.

He felt hot and ran his hand over his forehead, wondering if he had a temperature but his temples were cool. He couldn't settle, and carefully pulled the sheet back so he could easily get out of bed. Helen murmured in her sleep but didn't wake, and he gently tucked the bedclothes round her shoulders.

Downstairs, there was a light on in the kitchen. Daniel was busy investigating the contents of the fridge and looked up as his father came into the room.

"Join me, dad?" He asked, waving the juice bottle.

"Not juice, maybe some milk."

They sat at the kitchen table in silence until each began to speak at the same time.

"I can't believe this of granny," Daniel started, while Sam was saying pretty much the same thing.

They looked at each other; father and son, the same clear blue eyes and dark hair; Sam bearded and Daniel needing a shave and a haircut.

"It's a bit of a mess, isn't it?" Daniel said. "But it's not your fault. I'm sure it can all be sorted out."

Sam ran through all the problems and Daniel's face became more solemn.

"I hadn't thought of the consequences, dad," he finally said. "I can see now why you are so worried."

Sam tried to lighten the atmosphere.

"I can think of only two couples who might be happy not to be married," he said with a slight twinkle in his eye and Daniel laughed.

"I think I know who you mean, dad, but let's not go there. You need to get some sleep. Go back to bed and I'll straighten up."

Things must be bad, Sam thought, if Daniel was offering to wash dishes.

His side of the bed was cool and he moved closer to Helen, who muttered something in her sleep. She curled against him and he relaxed, feeling her familiar shape giving him comfort.

Sam dressed carefully the next morning and left the house before anyone was up. He used the drive to the Chief Rabbi's office to try and put his thoughts in some sort of order. Rabbi Hershell had undoubtedly been kind when they had spoken, but Sam knew what faced him was a monumental problem.

Rebbitzen Hershell opened the door and directed him to the office.

"I'll bring tea," she said, moving down the hall.

Rabbi Hershell was sitting behind his desk in his shirt sleeves, patterned braces on show. The fringes of his tzitzit were visible and his yarmulke was slightly askew, suggesting he had been absentmindedly scratching his head. He stood up and embraced Sam warmly.

"What a to do! What a to do! But we'll find a way out. We're not going to lose a wonderful rabbi because he's not Jewish."

Sam looked at him in astonishment.

The rebbitzen brought the tea and left the room, smiling sympathetically at Sam.

Rabbi Hershell continued,

"We have to regularise what's happened. I've been up all night, Sam, looking for precedent and I have to say that nothing like this has happened before. So, we need to work through the problem in stages.

"First of all, most importantly of all, you need to become Jewish – such a strange thing to say to a man who has been Jewish all his life."

When Sam heard this he almost broke down; he tried very hard to keep a grip on his emotions and listened as Rabbi Hershell went on,

"I've already spoken to the Beth Din in Jerusalem and they understand the problem. As soon as you get to Israel, you will have an interview and then you will be given a certificate of conversion, which will ratify your position. As to your continuing as a rabbi, I did wonder if you should go to Hebrew University again. It might refresh you."

He looked at Sam, eyes twinkling, "but I don't think that is necessary. The yeshivah may wish you to write a paper on something or other, but twenty years of good work will not be disallowed.

"However, before that, we need to attend to the congregants whom you married – in good faith, I know, but whose marriage is no longer valid in Jewish law. Every couple will have to be contacted, told of the problem and offered a ceremony to correct matters. They may wish to do this as soon as possible or they may wish to wait until you return. That will be up to them.

"I can see from your notes that there are some who have divorced and for whom you signed the initial papers. All I can say about that is thank goodness you weren't on the Beth Din. I'm meeting with them later but it looks as if that side of it is okay.

"Now we move on sadly, to those people whose funeral you conducted.

"There is precedent here and, although it will no doubt be difficult for the families of the deceased, it is not such a halachic problem for us. I looked at the way in which soldiers were interred during the war, often by clerics of another faith. In those cases, the deceased were disinterred, the bodies moved to a Jewish cemetery and a Jewish funeral service completed. We only need to have prayers for those people whose funerals you conducted. As you are aware, you don't have to be a rabbi to conduct a funeral – you just have to be Jewish." He paused, seeing how much his words upset Sam. "I would be happy to do that for you. It would be a real mitzvah.

"Conversion is a bigger problem because if the conversion of a woman is null and void, it means that any children born will not be Jewish. That's the bit I'm still working on."

Rabbi Hershell took his yarmulke off and before replacing it, scratched his head.

Sam had been unable to speak, acknowledging all the work that had been done on his behalf.

"Have you spoken to Anthony, yet?"

"Only to ask him to set up a board meeting."

"Mmm. I think you need more than a board meeting, Sam. You will need to speak to the whole community. If you would like, I will come along to support you. You may have need of it. Get Anthony to check my diary with my secretary."

Sam got up to leave, but before he could shake hands with Rabbi Hershell, he was told,

"Sit, Sam, there's one more thing we need to think about. Your dilemma is a huge one and I don't think there is any way we can keep it out of the media."

Sam went white. He hadn't considered this.

"Once we have sorted out the various meetings you need to attend, we will have to put out a press statement. There are too many people involved to keep this quiet, even if we wanted to. This in no way detracts from your abilities, Sam, but you may need to be prepared for some adverse comments."

"I can manage whatever's thrown at me but what about my mother?"

"This is something you need to think very carefully about. In fact your whole family needs to consider what might happen. Your twins are at university, I think. How will this affect them?"

Sam felt as if he was falling into a pit of despair. These were all questions he'd never considered. Maybe he should take the whole family to Israel?

The tea had grown cold in the pot; neither man had wanted any and so Sam shook Rabbi Hershell's hand and left, not looking forward to yet more problems.

"Anthony's been on the phone," Helen said as he let himself in to the house. "The twins have organised accommodation and Eva is in the garden, deadheading. She says it's keeping her mind off things."

"We have a lot to talk about. I'll call Anthony and then we need to get everyone together."

Helen listened with one ear as Sam spoke to the synagogue chairman.

"No problems," he told Helen "Rabbi Stanford is happy to lead the services this weekend, although he was surprised I wasn't doing so myself. He was curious, but Anthony said he couldn't tell him anything – he told him he was in the dark, too. There's a full attendance for the board meeting, but a letter has been sent out saying there is to be an extraordinary meeting. I need to address the whole community and stop any rumours."

"Rumours," questioned Helen. "What do you mean?"

"Rabbi Hershell raised the possibility that the press might…actually, he said the press *would* get hold of this. It's going to make a great story, isn't it? I can just see the headlines, 'False rabbi' at East Lane synagogue. 'Many marriages null and void'." he said bitterly. "If it was just me, I could deal with it but it affects so many people. Not just our family but everyone I've ever…" he stopped, choked with tears, unable to continue.

Helen sat down abruptly. "Oh, Sam," she said. "Whatever are we going to do?"

CHAPTER 4

The gates of the synagogue were already open when Sam arrived for the Monday meeting. Anthony Bloom was sitting at one end of the long table in the office, hand outstretched. Annabel had left a tray with thermos jugs of coffee, mugs, a plate of biscuits and a bowl of grapes and he was helping himself to a drink.

"So, rabbi. What's the mystery all about?"

Sam didn't want to reply. He knew it was going to be a complex meeting.

"I'd rather wait until everybody's here. I really don't want to say the same thing over and over again."

Anthony had to be content with that but pretty soon, people began to arrive. They found their usual seats, poured coffee, took biscuits and waited for Sam to speak.

He had rehearsed what he was going to say over and over again but when he looked at the expectant faces of the waiting men and woman, all his carefully thought out words disappeared. With a catch in his throat he began, not letting anyone interrupt to ask questions.

There was a stunned silence when he'd finished and several of the women were crying.

There were questions, of course, and incredulity, as well as a degree of anger from those who realised that they were particularly affected by Sam's words. Sam answered as best as he could, passing on the information that there would be another meeting for the whole shul, as well as individual meetings for anyone who wished to discuss their circumstances privately.

"I just want to clarify something, rabbi," one of the women asked. "Are you telling me that my conversion will not be recognised and that therefore my children are not considered to be Jewish?"

"Sadly, I have to tell you that may be the case if I signed any papers. As you know, conversions are agreed by the Beth Din, but Rabbi Hershell assures me that everything can be put right. He will be at our extraordinary meeting and will set out a way of resolving all the issues you've raised. Will you contact his secretary to fix a date, as early as possible Anthony?"

The synagogue chairman nodded, trying to process what Sam had said.

"You haven't told us your plans. Have you decided what to do?"

"What can I do?" Sam replied wearily. "It's been suggested I take a sabbatical but I am well aware that is not possible."

"It sounds a good suggestion to me. You'll be able to do whatever is necessary..."

The treasurer intervened.

"I think I know what Sam is getting at, when he says it's not possible," and he looked along the table. "We can't, as a community, consider Sam as our rabbi anymore. He is no longer an employee and therefore not entitled to a paid sabbatical."

"Exactly," said Sam. "It would be wrong for the synagogue to continue to pay me while I'm on leave. In fact," he added, "it may be that I've been receiving a salary unlawfully."

"Let's not go there," said Anthony hastily. "You've served the community well and, since you didn't know that you weren't...Jewish," he stumbled over the words and cleared his throat, "we certainly will not be asking for any repayment of salary."

Sam was relieved at that. He had wondered if the synagogue would decide to claim all his back salary, and he had been unable to sleep, thinking that his house would have to be sold, or worse still, repossessed in order for him to meet the cost of nearly twenty years back pay.

"I know I can't take a paid sabbatical but it has been suggested I go to Israel for six months at least. I can go through a process of conversion there and after that I can decide what to do."

Mrs Leibowitz who, until now had said nothing, became vociferous in her praise of Sam, and then asked, "What about your mother? She must be in a terrible state. How is she coping?"

Sam was grateful for her sympathy. There was no doubt that he was not responsible for the predicament he was in but the same could not be said of Eva, and once again he wished she'd dealt with his situation in a better way.

"She's not too good," he answered slowly. "I don't think she's eaten properly for a week. Helen can only get her to take some soup. She spends a lot of time in her room and we are very reluctant to let her go home. There are times I'm really worried about her…"

Mrs Leibowitz interrupted him.

"I can understand why what happened, happened. You know, I came to England after the war like Eva. We became friends right from the beginning. You were just a baby, Sam. I wish she'd felt she could confide in me but I can see why she didn't. You were such a lovely little boy. She would have been worried about losing you."

There were tentative smiles all round as they visualised Sam as a baby.

"We mustn't judge. What we can do is work together, yes?

"Obviously, then, once everything about your status has been sorted, you'll come back here and be our rabbi again."

There were nods but also a couple of doubtful faces.

"Will that be possible?" Ted Cohen asked. "Will your qualification still stand if it was awarded to you when you weren't Jewish?"

"At this moment, I don't really know. I'm hoping that by next week I'll have some answers. There's only one more thing for me to say. Until we have our main meeting, I would ask you all to keep this to yourselves. Rabbi Hershell has already said he thinks the press will have a field day with this news – it is a bit of a bombshell. He wants it kept within the synagogue and says he will put out a press release when everyone in the community knows what's going on."

Helen was eager to hear what had happened at the board meeting when Sam got back home.

"How did it go?" she asked.

"How do you think? Shock, horror, disbelief! You name it, every emotion that is possible. All I could do was ask everyone to refrain from talking about it and to organise a meeting for the whole community. I think we can do that in two days time."

"So quickly?"

"Yes, there was agreement that it should be done as soon as possible. Anthony is going to call everyone, stressing that it's important to attend. I've also given him the 'urgent' list and I will make personal appointments for them.

"There's not much else I can do now, so tell me about your day."

Helen produced her list and Sam smiled at the normality of it all.

"Right; if you want, I can book us on flights in a couple of weeks. There are plenty of seats available. The twins have sorted out their own accommodation. Esther is going to share with a couple of friends," Sam looked up sharply but said nothing.

"Daniel is going into halls while he looks for somewhere better.

"While you were out there was a call from the Chief Rabbi's office. His secretary has managed to find us a flat in Jerusalem and he's also found someone to replace you, temporarily, he said. You might know him? Elliot Lansdown? Apparently he took semicha about ten years ago; he was a lawyer before then. He has a couple of teenagers and would be happy to live here. He can stay for up to a year if needed and then, after that, he's taking a pulpit in Canada. I suspect that the Chief Rabbi thought it would leave the way open for you to return.

"Rachel and Ivor are back so they're coming to dinner on Saturday night, not for shabbat. I thought it was better they should come as soon as possible; so many people already know and it's important we tell them but I didn't want it to spoil the Sabbath for them. I've spoken to Eva because I wondered if she would come to Israel with us but she was very firm that she would rather stay here. I'm worried about that but I couldn't persuade her otherwise. She says her friends will rally round. What do you think?"

Sam recounted what Mrs Leibowitz had said and Helen let the subject drop.

"I also sent Esther out to stock up with biscuits. I don't think there will be time to bake, and I suspect with the number of people you will be seeing that catering quantities will be needed."

"You've achieved a lot. You don't know how grateful I am, and I'm sorry if I've left all the organising to you."

"It's not a problem. I'll do anything I can to make it easier. And, Sam, a little bit of me is excited to be going back to Israel even under these circumstances. It's so long since we've been and I miss it."

Sam looked searchingly at her and saw she was smiling.

"You're right. It will do us good."

Sam spent the next couple of days poring over books to try and find resolutions for his problems but it seemed that nothing like this had ever happened before. He could find no precedent. The phone rang constantly and he made what seemed like hundreds of calls himself. The extraordinary meeting had been attended by almost all members of the synagogue and the presence of the Chief Rabbi had kept the proceedings more subdued than they might otherwise have been. Mrs Leiberwitz was a staunch supporter, saying over and over again that the situation had not been a decision that Eva had made; it had been thrust upon her and Sam should not be castigated for his birth.

In the main, people were sympathetic and, strangely, the ones who were more affected were the more consoling, thinking more of him than their own situations. There was a steady stream of congregants; some wanted advice, others brought gifts of food and offered sympathy, and he worked far into the evenings. In many ways, he felt as if he was sitting shiva, and had to remind himself frequently that what had happened was not a death. Even so, a small part of him felt he was in mourning for the man he had been, and the life he had enjoyed.

By the end of the week he was exhausted but comforted that he had made referrals for those congregants who needed them. There were some who were prepared to wait for him to return from Israel, and were already planning celebrations. Others agreed that they would have private marriage ceremonies with whichever rabbi was available.

All through those difficult days, Eva withdrew more and more into herself. She made the effort to get up each morning and shower and dress but after that she stayed in her room, refusing to come down for meals and letting Helen care for her. This was so unlike the strong mother that Sam remembered all his life and he could not work out how to help her. He felt helpless, faced with what he saw as a decline in her mental health. All the reassurances he gave her, the hugs he thought would comfort her, didn't help. Each day she became quieter and quieter.

35

In the end, he told her that he would call her doctor if she didn't come downstairs and help Helen.

"Ma, Helen's exhausted. For the last week she's been doing all the organising so today it's your turn. It's shabbat and we need a good meal so, please, come downstairs and start cooking."

Eva looked at Sam and saw the pleading in his eyes. There was kindness and love there and she realised that no judgement had been passed on her. Sam loved her, she was sure of it so she had better do as he asked.

"All right, Sam. I'll come downstairs and I'll cook the meal. Did Helen manage to do the shopping? Did she get the challah, the chicken...? Are the candlesticks polished?"

Sam hugged his mother again and they stood together for a few moments before Eva said,

"Enough, enough! Stop. There's work to be done."

Helen was relieved, too, when Eva came hesitantly into the kitchen. There had always been a strong bond between the two women and Eva often said that Helen was like a second daughter, and how lucky she was to have two wonderful girls.

"It's okay, Helen, I know I've behaved badly. I've been sorry for myself but that's stopped now. Sit down and I'll start cooking. Take some tea with you and have a rest."

Helen did as she was told, and leaned back in her armchair. It had been a hard week, there was no doubt about that. She couldn't see the end of it, either. Tonight they would celebrate the sabbath and tomorrow they would see Rachel and Ivor and the whole story would have to be told again. There would be a lot for Rachel to come to terms with, and then there was Ivor to consider.

She leaned her head back against the chair and allowed herself to drift off. She was barely aware that Esther and Daniel had come downstairs and were in the kitchen, doing what Eva was telling them.

Friday evenings were always special for the Goldmans. Not just because Sam was a rabbi but because it was a time when the family could get together, and follow the familiar traditions. The tablecloth gleamed white, the candles were waiting for Helen to light them and the wine and challah were part of the ritual.

Eva looked around at her family and realised how lucky she was. Would she still feel the same after tomorrow, she wondered.

CHAPTER 5

Saturday was usually a quiet day; synagogue, a cold lunch, maybe a little visiting but today Sam was restless. He sat looking out of the window, watching people walk slowly by; mothers with children, chivvying them along; dog walkers, pulling reluctant animals past the enticing smells around trees and lampposts. An occasional car went past but no one Sam recognised was driving.

Eventually, he pulled himself together and wandered into the kitchen. Helen was busy counting out knives and forks for the evening dinner.

"We'll have lunch in here, because I want everything set up in the dining room. Give me a hand with the tray – you might like to set the table?"

Sam knew she was trying to make life seem normal but he knew that life would never be normal again – for him, anyway. He did as he was asked and when everything was to Helen's satisfaction, they sat at the kitchen table, enjoying coffee.

"Why didn't you go to synagogue?" Helen asked.

Sam looked at her, almost unable to comprehend her question.

"Helen," he started, "you must realise why."

"No, I don't," she said decisively. "Please tell me."

He looked at her to see if she was joking.

"You know why, Helen. How can I?"

"Ah...you're not the rabbi anymore? Well, you don't have to be a rabbi to attend services. Next – maybe because you're not, halachically, Jewish. Ah, no again! Anyone is welcome in our shul. You know that, Sam. Perhaps you feel you couldn't follow the service? Well, I think you're perfectly able to do that, don't you. So what is it, Sam. Are you afraid? Do you think people will turn on you, maybe shout at you."

Sam wouldn't look at her.

"Sam," she started again but gently this time. "You can't hide yourself away. You've told the community but at some point you will have to be able to talk to them as individuals, not just see them in a meeting. Most people will understand. I'm sure about that. Look at the way the older members have dealt with it. Not one person has been unkind; not one person has been anything other than supportive. If you were to get a move on, you could get to shul in time for the Torah service. Esther and Daniel are already there and I'll come with you. Come on, now," she coaxed. "Get it over with. There are a couple of weeks before we leave for Israel and I don't think you could manage to miss services for that length of time."

Sam knew she was right. His tallit was already in the synagogue, waiting for him to wear. He stopped, reminding himself he wasn't Jewish so not entitled to wear his tallit, but he was able to wear his kippah. A small consolation; so many things to think about. He went upstairs to see if Eva would come with them, and was pleasantly surprised when she replied that she would.

39

Helen adjusted her felt hat until it was to her satisfaction, and took Sam's arm for the short walk to shul. Eva's face seemed to have acquired more lines but she bravely took her coat off its hanger, shrugged it on and waited by the front door.

The synagogue doors were closed but there was the sound of singing coming through the open windows. The women paused, giving Sam the opportunity to walk through but he ushered them in front of him. The senior warden was sitting at a table in the foyer and looked up as they came in.

"Lovely to see you, rabbi," and Sam flinched briefly. "Yes, I know all about it. I was at the meeting, you remember? But, as far as I'm concerned, you are the rabbi...or at least you will be when you come back to us."

"In the meantime," Sam said carefully, "You should just call me 'Sam'." Levi looked disconcerted. It was not something he'd ever done...call the rabbi by his given name, but he nodded and decided he wouldn't call him anything at all.

Sam went into the sanctuary, feeling very alone, as Helen and Eva went upstairs to the ladies gallery. Men turned to see who the late arrival was and he welcomed their smiles. He was discreetly beckoned to a seat beside old friends but he couldn't bring himself to move along the rows. Instead, he sat at the back and it was a very strange experience. He was used to standing on the bimah, looking at the congregation and now the positions were reversed. Even so, he could feel the warmth of the community surrounding him.

When the last prayer had been said, when the last hymn had been sung and Anthony had thanked those who had led the services, and given out the notices for the week, people moved into the kiddush room. The tables were laden with the usual shabbat treats; dainty sandwiches, bowls of fruit, tiny tartlets and cakes. Mrs Leiberwitz was busy, passing round small glasses of wine and she smiled over at Eva, telling her she'd catch up with her in a minute.

Sam raised his glass and the tears which these days were very near the surface of his mind, threatened to spill out of his eyes. He caught Eva's glance and took a deep breath before joining in the blessing. He watched as Mrs Bloom picked up the two challah loaves and blessed the bread, and when the portion he took melted in his mouth, it was as if some of his worries were melting away.

Afterwards, he was surrounded by people. They shook his hand; one or two of the men hugged him and suddenly he knew he was where he belonged. They were eager to talk to him and anxious to tell him that he would always be their rabbi.

"Hurry up and come back to us," a young couple said. "We want to get married next year and you must be here for the chuppah."

Sam was too emotional to reply and because his future was so uncertain, he knew there was no real answer. All he could say was,

"I'll do the best I can."

Mrs Leiberwitz was in close conversation with Eva, and Sam was relieved to see that she was answering her friend, nodding her head. Other women came over and put their arms round his mother and he saw that her expression had lightened and she seemed more relaxed.

41

Anthony crossed the room to get to Sam and waited patiently until the conversation was finished.

"A word, Sam" he said. "I must talk with you before you go."

Sam had a sinking feeling in his heart as he wondered what Anthony wanted to talk about – nothing good, he felt.

The two men stood in the office and Anthony cleared his throat.

"This is not easy, Sam. The Chief Rabbi called me yesterday. He has spoken to the editors of the Jewish Chronicle, the Jewish Telegraph and the Jewish News, and he's called a press conference for tomorrow afternoon. His secretary has informed the dailies, and also the BBC and ITV newsrooms. He expects you to be there and feels it would be a good idea if Eva, also, was present. He is in no doubt that this is going to be headline news. You will have to talk to the press; in any event, you must talk to your family. Whatever happens at the conference will have an impact on them."

He was very quiet on the walk home and Helen left him to his own thoughts. She didn't ask him what the synagogue chair had wanted to speak to him about; she knew he would share it with her when he was ready. The twins had followed them home and they made short work of the soup and sandwiches.

"Do you think all this will be a problem for Rachel and Ivor?" Sam asked as they waited later that day for them to arrive.

"I don't think so, although Ivor can sometimes be a bit...mmm...outspoken. The good thing is that he thinks the world of ma so he'll probably make an effort."

Helen could tell that Sam was anxious. When he heard the car arriving she saw his hands were shaking and she smiled encouragingly at him.

"Rachel's your sister, Sam and she loves you. It will be alright, you'll see."

Eva, too, was shaking. She moved to hug her daughter and waited while Rachel rummaged in her bag.

"Something we brought back for you, ma", she said. "A Statue of Liberty," and looked astonished as Eva bolted out of the room.

"Can't say I've had that impact on ma before…"

She looked closely at her brother. "There's something going on here, isn't there? Come on, Sam, tell us what's happened. Is ma ill? She looks as if she's lost weight."

"No, nothing like that. But you're right. Something has happened. Sit down, both of you. I was hoping we could eat first but we need to talk. It's probably better for ma that she's gone upstairs."

He took a deep breath and launched into the explanation of his birth, and how Ernst Hoffman had given him into Eva's care. He finished by telling them that there would be a media briefing the following day, and he saw Rachel's face whiten.

There was no doubt she was shaken. She had prevented Ivor from interrupting several times and it was hard to tell what he was thinking. His face was grave as Sam related the story.

"So there you are. The whole story and the problems we have. We plan to go to Israel for a while and, hopefully, after we come back, things will be more in order."

43

"You said…the press…Does this mean everyone will know about you? How will this affect us? You know I have a business to run."

Ivor was very outspoken and he waited for Sam to answer.

"I have no idea. The Chief Rabbi said it would be better to have everything out in the open, and I think he's right. People are people and they will talk amongst themselves. The truth is difficult enough, but if it's distorted because there is gossip it will be worse. I can see that everyone in the family will be affected – even your parents, Ivor. I think you need to tell them before they find out for themselves. They didn't go to the meeting this week, and I have to admit I was glad about it but someone is bound to mention it and they would be in a bad position if they knew nothing."

"You're right, Sam. They need to know, especially as they are survivors themselves. We'll call on the way home."

"What about ma?" Rachel asked. "She looks dreadful. Will she go to Israel with you?"

"She doesn't want to. Daniel and Esther will be around to help her and I'm sure you'll keep an eye on her."

Rachel, practical as ever, said,

"I'm going upstairs to talk to her. I'll try and find out what she really wants to do but if she's determined to stay here, she should come to us."

"And you have plenty of room," added Sam.

Rachel and Ivor looked at each other and smiled.

"Not for much longer," he said.

Helen looked closely at her sister in law. Rachel had put on a little weight since they'd last seen each other. Her

44

face was more rounded and her dark hair shone with health. The trip to New York had obviously agreed with her. But there was something else...something which was making her look so happy.

"Rachel," she gasped. "You're not...?"

Rachel and Ivor clasped each other's hands.

"Yes," they said in unison. "In about four month's time."

Rachel laughed. "I think I'll be the oldest new mother in the hospital but it's what we've always wanted. We had hoped when we got married that we'd have a large family but we eventually had to accept it wasn't going to happen. I know I'm not going to see forty again but the doctor is very positive that there's nothing wrong. He can't explain why, after all these years, there's a baby on the way but we are both so, so, glad. And ma will have someone special to care for. Under the circumstances, I can't imagine her going to Israel with you."

Sam shook Ivor's hand and the two men grinned at each other, waiting for Rachel's return downstairs. They heard a scream of delight and then Rachel came back into the room.

"I think you heard. Ma is absolutely delighted, refuses to go anywhere with you and will stay with Ivor and me until you get back. So that's sorted. I expect the baby will be born when you're away but we can bring him or her to see you, or you could make a short trip back. Nothing's impossible these days."

The meal became a cause for celebration and first of all, the baby's health was toasted in apple juice, then Rachel's and Ivor's, and finally they all raised their glasses to new beginnings.

"That was a remarkable evening. Who would have thought it? I could never have imagined Rachel and Ivor having a child after all these years but how wonderful for them."

"You're right, Sam," Helen said thoughtfully. "Of course, it's wonderful for Rachel and Ivor but it will be so good for Eva. A new baby, a new life and she'll have her hands full, looking after Rachel. Who would have thought it! So, tonight wasn't as bad as you expected. I think you will still have to talk to people every day before we leave, but tomorrow I intend to start sorting out the things we need to take with us. After the press conference, that is. We will all be there."

Sam knew he was fortunate. However difficult it was, they would get through it and then he groaned. He hoped that he wouldn't have to help with the packing, other than getting the suitcases out of the loft.

CHAPTER 6

The newsroom was busy. The background noise was increasing as more people came in to start work and switched on their computers. Most of the reporters preferred the new technology, but there were still a few who liked the old ways and used decrepit electric typewriters. In Mason's office there was even an old Underwood with battered keys, kept as a reminder of how newspaper reports were worked on 'in the old days'. It sat on top of a filing cabinet and the youngsters were amazed at the time it took to bash a report out on it.

Now, with a flick of a key, they could erase whole paragraphs and replace them in a few seconds. The story went that the boss himself had used the old machine when he was a trainee reporter, although his desk was now equipped with the latest in computers.

Mason came out of his office, wearing his old blue cardigan, scarf wrapped tightly round his neck despite the warmth of the room. He was holding a sheaf of papers and there was silence as he started to speak.

"Today's tip off," he said. "There's been a report that a building's been evacuated in the City. No reason given, so get down there as quick as you can." He handed the information sheet over and added, "it could be a gas leak…or a bomb! Take a taxi and get some pics."

Must be serious, Alan Carmichael thought as he shrugged his jacket on and left at speed.

"Now, some traffic stuff. You can take that, Mike. The police will be there a while, so you can get the bus. Phil, you go with him and get some close up shots if you can. Looks as if it might be a hit and run."

He continued handing out assignments, until he came to the last one.

"Now, this one. Not sure we need to bother, really; the Chief Rabbi's office has issued an invitation to a press conference at five o'clock this evening. He's due to retire this year so I expect he's going to announce his successor. Short notice and no overtime, so if anyone wants to volunteer…? If not, we can call his office and they'll give us the details over the phone."

There was silence until Carl Hendry raised his hand.

"I could go. I'm not doing anything this evening and it would be a good opportunity to do some writing, instead of just proofing the copy."

Mason smiled at the intern's enthusiasm.

"Okay, Carl, it's yours. Since it'll be a late finish and not exactly heart stopping news, you can file in the morning."

The Chief Rabbi's office was preparing for the press conference. Chairs were brought in from various rooms in the building and arranged in rows. Two men carried in a long table and placed it at the front. Someone produced a carafe of water and glasses and set them out.

"Will we need better lighting?" the secretary asked.

"Probably," was the reply "but the BBC are bringing their own and possibly ITV as well. They're getting here before four o'clock, to set up and do a sound test. The Goldmans will be here before then – I don't want them to see anyone from the media before we start so they'll stay in my office. Sam is very anxious – I've spoken to him already today and he's not sure he can go through with this press conference, but I've no doubt he'll manage.

"He said Esther and Daniel wanted to come but I've told him not to allow them. Eva and Helen will be here with him; that's important, but I don't think it's a good idea for the youngsters to be around. Much better if they stay out of the limelight. They have to go back to university soon, and I don't want them identified if I can help it."

Sharon Mosson looked at her boss.

"Are you all right, rabbi?" she asked sympathetically. "I know this is difficult for Sam but it's hard for you, too. You look awfully tired. Will you take a little rest this afternoon? I could bring you some tea?"

Rabbi Hershell smiled at her. How lucky he was to have such loyal staff. Sharon had been his secretary for forty years and had wanted to retire when he did, but he'd persuaded her to stay on, to help the new Chief Rabbi to settle in. He sighed. This would be more important than ever as the news of Sam's birth became common knowledge. Whoever took over would have a huge job, keeping the community on an even keel. He had even considered delaying his retirement and then thought better of it. He would go as planned but be there in the background, of course. It was right that his successor, whoever that was going to be, should take office as planned.

He decided he would take a short rest and sat down heavily on the sofa in his office. It was time for afternoon prayers, so he took his well thumbed siddur off the shelf and flicked through the pages till he found what he was looking for. Soon he was lost in the age old traditional words, which gave him great comfort. He added a prayer for inter faith peace…there didn't seem anything which included the media. He wondered how long it would take for some enterprising rabbi to compose one as he slipped gradually into a light doze.

Sam, on the other hand, was pacing his sitting room floor. The twins were adamant they were going with their parents to the press conference. Sam was just as firm that they were not.

"Have you any idea what this means?" He said loudly. "I am going to be identified as an 'illegal rabbi'. My name is going to be in the papers. The Chief Rabbi has said that can't be avoided. I have no doubt there will be an anti-semitic back lash. Old memories die hard and there are still people around who feel that Hitler didn't do a good enough job."

The twins looked confused, and Sam continued,

"Everyone is going to know the name of Goldman. You are going back to university and I don't want you to be targeted."

"But we want to support you, dad."

"You will be supporting me if you do as I ask. I shall have mum and granny with me and I want you to stay here. Apparently, there is going to be television coverage. You can watch it on the tv."

He raised his hand.

"That's final, and I don't want to talk about it anymore."

Helen had been listening from the doorway and she came fully into the room.

"Dad's right. Once you go back to university it would be better if there was no publicity around you. I think when we get back from this media thing we'll need comfort and you can do that for us."

Esther and Daniel looked at each other and reluctantly nodded their heads.

"We'll be here but we'll be thinking of you."

"Are we all ready, then?" Eva asked. "Time to go. The traffic might be bad and we don't want to be late."

They were all silent on the short drive. Eva was wrestling with her own demons, thinking back over the years and the opportunities she'd had to put things right. She gave herself a mental shake. No good dwelling on the past, she thought. What's done is done. What she needed now was a way through this problem and the first step would be to speak to the press about it. She had been rehearsing in her head what she could say but she knew that her response would depend on the questions asked.

Helen, sitting beside Sam in the front of the car, could feel his nervousness. She knew he had overcome his feelings of anger toward Eva, realising she was the only mother he'd had or ever wanted. Undeniably, though, things could have been different if she'd spoken to someone...Rabbi Langer maybe, years ago.

Sam sighed. He couldn't change anything and now he realised that, more than anyone, he wanted Rabbi Langer to be with him but the old man had returned to his congregation in Belgium.

There was a lot of activity at the Chief Rabbi's office but Sam, Helen and Eva were able to slip in the back door unnoticed. Sharon took them to where Rabbi Hershell was waiting and they all stood awkwardly, before he ushered them to seats.

"This is how it will be," he started. "It would be better if you let me begin by outlining what's happened. Apart from the Jewish papers, there will be representatives from all the major dailies, and the BBC & ITV are also here. In fact, they're already putting lights up, etc.

"We will all sit at the top table and I've asked Dov Aaronsen to be with us. He's the senior partner in a law firm and represents my office. He'll be able to answer any legal questions. Once I've said my piece, we will throw the floor open to everyone. I fully intend to control this as tightly as I can but I think it may be a free for all." He looked around.

"Don't forget, there has been a degree of curiosity as to why we're having this conference at all. I'm sure they think I'm about to announce the name of the person taking over from me, and when they see you, Sam, they will think their suspicions have been confirmed.

"I would advise you very strongly against mentioning anything to do with Israel. I really want to keep this as discreet as possible; we don't want the press to follow you abroad."

He looked at Eva, absorbing some of her anxiety.

"Eva, I have no doubt there will also be questions for you."

She looked ill and trembled in her seat.

"Helen, you may be asked if your relationship to Sam will survive. Are you prepared for that?"

Helen nodded dumbly, as Rabbi Hershell continued.

"I have every intention of deflecting questions away from the family. Sam, you're going to be in the hot seat, even though realistically you can't defend any of this. All you can do, is to say you were unaware of your background until you were contacted by Hans."

There was a knock at the door and Sharon came in to tell them the Press was waiting.

The room seemed very hot, possibly the extra arc lighting or, more likely, their accumulated worry. They filed in and the Chief Rabbi shook hands with Dov, who rose from his seat. There was silence, and the reporters sat, pencils poised for the Chief Rabbi to speak.

He welcomed everyone, thanking them for coming at such short notice for what was a very important event. He asked them to keep questions until he'd finished speaking and then he cleared his throat and launched into his prepared speech.

It was obvious he'd put a great deal of thought into what he was saying. No one spoke, until he explained that Sam's birth father had been Ernst Hoffman, a Nazi war criminal. Hands went up immediately and there was a clamour of voices.

The Chief Rabbi waited until there was silence again and said,

"No questions until I've finished speaking, please."

There was a gasp, when they heard about Eva being blackmailed, and a further sharp intake of breath when they learned of Hans' death.

"And now, ladies and gentlemen, you may ask your questions."

They came thick and fast, firstly to Eva, who answered as clearly as she could. It was obvious that she was in torment when she described how her own child had died, and she had been given Sam without realising he wasn't her baby.

A young woman at the back of the room raised her hand.

"Why didn't you hand the baby in at the end of the war? Were you taking revenge on the commandant because of what he'd done to you?" she asked.

Eva flushed. "I couldn't hand him over. By then he was my son," she said.

"But he wasn't your son," the reporter followed through. "You were not entitled to keep him."

The Chief Rabbi intervened, telling the room that Eva had received a letter from Mrs Hoffman, giving the baby into her care. He was interrupted by a bearded young man, who said angrily,

"A letter! How legal was that? Did you not think that this child had a family somewhere in Germany who was missing him?"

"I didn't think. I couldn't think," Eva continued bravely, although tears were raining down her cheeks. Sam put a protective arm around her and she leaned against him.

"Sam was my son. I had forgotten everything about his background. I just knew he was mine."

"Very convenient," responded the reporter scornfully.

Attention was turned to Helen. As the chief rabbi had expected she was asked in detail about her relationship with Sam. She was able to answer in a dignified way, saying her relationship wasn't affected at all because love was the most important emotion she felt.

Somewhat chastened, the reporters let the matter drop.

Sam had been waiting for a verbal attack. He was the last to speak and his hands were clenched tightly together. Surprisingly, the questions seemed kinder, once it was confirmed he had been unaware of his parentage until contacted by his twin, and he gradually relaxed his fingers.

"What will happen now, Mr Goldman?" the young intern asked. "I understand that you are no longer a rabbi – not even Jewish," he added. "What do you intend to do?"

Sam took a deep breath and then described his intention to complete a conversion course. After that he would work towards becoming a rabbi and having a pulpit again.

Another hand was raised, a BBC interviewer this time.

"What are your feelings towards your mother...or should I say 'Eva' now? And will you go back to Germany to try and contact any relatives you might have left?"

Before Sam could say anything, Dov Aaronsen intervened.

"Since we learned of his," he cleared his throat, "rather unorthodox background." There was a little ripple of laughter through the room, and he smiled too. "Yes, unorthodox, we have been in contact with the war records department in Germany and we have learned that there is no one from the Hoffman family left alive. Hans was the only survivor and sadly he died in a car accident as you have been told. Sam will be spared having to trace anyone."

"I think we can draw proceedings to a close now. If you have any further questions, please contact my office. In the meantime, thank you all for coming." The Chief Rabbi stood up, signalling the conference was at an end but before anyone could leave, there was a slight commotion at the door. Heads turned to see who was coming in. Several uniformed policemen pushed through the crowd and found their way to the front.

"Mrs Goldman. I am Inspector McQueen of the Metropolitan Police. I am here to ask you to accompany me to the Police Station to answer a charge of historic child kidnapping. You are not under arrest and you do not have to say anything, but it may harm your defence if you do not mention when questioned something which you later rely on in court. Anything you do say may be given in evidence."

The room went into uproar; the flashes from a multitude of cameras ricocheted off the windows. The young intern, conscious he had the scoop of a lifetime, rushed to find a phone before any of the other reporters. Eva was led out, supported by a woman officer, closely followed by Sam and Helen.

CHAPTER 7

The noise in the room ceased. Heads turned as Eva was hustled through the door and Dov Aaronson, moved to stand in front of the inspector.

"Excuse me," he said. "Could you please tell me what's going on. Why are you taking Dr Goldman into custody?"

"Who are you, sir?"

Dov explained he was the lawyer to the Chief Rabbi's office and the policeman said how fortuitous this was, and asked if he was Mrs Goldman's solicitor. Eva looked bewildered and shook her head.

"I'm happy to come with you to the police station, and represent you should it be necessary," affirmed Dov and Eva, looking over towards Sam for advice, nodded. The inspector continued,

"We've received a report that she is involved with a kidnapping, dating back to 1944, and we need to clear this up. Mrs Goldman is not under arrest; she will be helping us with our enquiries. There's no problem with you coming along, Mr Aaronson, if you are representing the lady."

Sam moved forward.

"I'd like to come with my mother, too."

"You're free to do so, sir, but you won't be able to be with her in the interview room. You'll have to wait outside while we go through the details of what's occurred."

Helen put a restraining hand on Sam's arm as he was about to reply.

"It's ok, Sam. Leave it for now. Better if we just go with Eva and wait until she's had her interview, then we can take her home afterwards, when all this has been cleared up," and she glared at the officers.

The reporters were listening avidly to the conversation, making brief notes in their pads and, once the police had departed with Eva and her family, racing to file their reports. Carl Hendry had managed to get to a phone first and was dictating rapidly to a colleague in the news room.

"Will I get a by line for this?" he asked.

"I should think so," was the reply. "Lucky you, to get the scoop of the year – maybe the scoop of the century! Well done, lad."

Eva arrived at the police station in a state of disbelief. On the drive, Dov had advised her to stay silent until she heard what the charges were likely to be but in any event she was so shocked she couldn't speak. She was escorted to a bleak interview room, and Sam and Helen shown to seats near the reception desk.

"Please confirm your name and address," she was asked, "and state your relationship to Samuel Goldman."

"I'm his mother."

"Now, Mrs Goldman, that's not strictly true, is it." was the response.

Eva looked at the policeman.

"I've always thought of Sam as my son," she faltered.

"Yes, I'm sure, but the truth is that you stole him from the Hoffman family and brought him to England, where you raised him as your own child. I understand that you arrived in England with false papers."

Dov interrupted,

"Officer, my client was a refugee after the second world war. Her original papers were lost in the Holocaust and she was issued with a replacement passport and other documents by the government of what was then Palestine. She came to England in 1946 and became a British citizen after the birth of her daughter, Rachel. Her husband, also a refugee, and Sam achieved British status at the same time."

Eva was surprised that the solicitor knew all this, then realised that the Chief Rabbi's office would have briefed him before the press conference.

Dov continued,

"Dr Goldman qualified as a medical doctor and has run a very successful practice…"

"That may all be true," responded the officer, "but it doesn't explain why Samuel Goldman has false papers."

Eva looked directly at the officers sitting across the table from her. Some of her innate strength returned and she was able to reply firmly,

"You are correct when you say I brought Sam to England as my son. However, I had not abducted him. When I left the concentration camp, just before the end of the war, I thought the baby I had been allowed to take with me was my son. I had no idea that my child had died. I was shocked when I realised that the child in my arms was the son of the commandant."

She turned to look at Dov, who nodded encouragingly at her.

"Do any of you have any understanding of what Berlin was like towards the end of the war? There was total anarchy. Ernst Hoffman had left me with a child, amongst burnt out buildings. Bombs were still raining down, and then the Russians arrived, it was a struggle to survive."

"But, Doctor Goldman, why did you not hand the baby to someone in authority?"

"Can't you hear what I'm saying? There *was* no one in authority, and besides, how could I...a Jewish woman, hand in a German child. I would have been shot."

Dov Aaronson prompted Eva,

"You have a letter?"

"Yes. I have a letter from Mrs Hoffman, giving Sam into my care. She said..."

The policeman interrupted her.

"There's no need to tell us what's in it. Do you have it? We will need to see the actual letter itself."

"Of course I have it," Eva responded hotly. "But I don't carry it in my handbag. It's at home."

"In that case, we can clear this matter up to our satisfaction. I will expect you to return to the station at nine o'clock tomorrow morning with the letter, and we will see if you are telling the truth."

There were two spots of red high on Eva's cheeks as she retorted,

"I am not used to having my word doubted. However, I will return tomorrow. I assume I'm free to go now?"

"You are, but please remember you have been cautioned. If you do not return I will issue a warrant for your arrest."

Sam and Helen sprang up from their chairs as Eva came into the reception area, her elbow held by Dov, who spoke quietly to Sam.

"I would get your mother home as soon as you can. You'll need to bring her back tomorrow but I have no doubt that this matter will be resolved when she produces the letter that proves you were given into her care."

As Helen put her key in the lock, she could the sound of footsteps racing down the hall.

"Is everything all right? We watched the conference on tv and we saw granny being taken away by the police. Where is she? Is she all right?"

Sam was helping Eva out of the car. Suddenly, she had become overcome with despair. The adrenaline which had kept her going had evaporated and she became aware of every one of her years.

Esther urged Eva into a chair and the old lady rested her head on a cushion.

"Helen, darling, I just want to go to bed but before I do, will someone get the letter out of the sideboard. I taped it to the underside of the top drawer in case someone came looking for it. I won't rest until I have it in my hands."

She was clutching it as she went up the stairs, closely followed by Helen who turned the bed down for her.

"What about something to eat, ma?"

"No, I just need to sleep, and you need to talk to the twins."

The Goldman's kitchen table was the family meeting place. Esther had put mugs of tea out, and Daniel had found the whisky.

"You might need this, dad. You managed those questions very well, even though some were near the mark. And what about granny?"

"Let me have a drink, and then I'll tell you." Sam swallowed and set his glass down. "All I can say is that it was worse than I thought it would be. It's a good job you weren't there. There weren't any questions about family so your names might have been protected. I don't understand why the police arrived…"

"I should imagine that a reporter rang the news in."

"Yes, probably, but it has made everything worse. I understand why this had to come out into the open but it's opened a real can of worms."

"What now, dad?"

"In the morning we'll take granny to show the letter to the police and hopefully, that will be the end of that problem. As for the rest…well, you saw the news broadcast? I expect the papers will be full of it tomorrow."

There was no real sleep for anyone; Eva tossed and turned, Sam and Helen talked in whispers, trying to plan the way ahead and Daniel did what he always did when worried – he raided the fridge. Esther got her books out and tried to do some revision but the words on the page blurred in front of her eyes and eventually she gave up, and lay wide eyed in the dark.

They heard the thwack of the newspaper on the floor early the following morning, and at the same time the phone and the doorbell rang. Sam pulled on his dressing gown and went to answer the door. He was faced with a barrage of people outside, all holding microphones and asking him questions.

"What does it feel like to be the son of a Nazi?"

"Did Eva Goldman steal you to take revenge?"

"Are you going back to Germany where you belong?"

Sam slammed the door shut, shaken. He hadn't foreseen this. The phone rang again and he picked it up. A harsh voice said,

"Nazi," and he slammed it down again.

He unfolded the paper and the headlines jumped out at him.

'Prominent rabbi seeks conversion. Sam Goldman, ex rabbi, has been outed as the son of Nazi war criminal Ernst Hoffman. Stolen from his birth family by Doctor Eva Goldman, he has lived with a false identity all his life.'

Sam couldn't bear to read anymore and pushed the paper into the rubbish bin to prevent anyone else seeing it. He turned the radio on, to find his situation was the lead story on the news. Breakfast television was worse. There were pictures of him, wearing tallit and kippah, officiating at a ceremony in the Town Hall. He remembered it. It had been a special memorial service to mark the 25th anniversary of the liberation of Auschwitz concentration camp. How ironic that this particular photograph had been in the archives.

The phone rang again, and he let it ring on. It stopped and started again, until eventually he lifted the receiver and laid it on its side. A moment later, he checked himself and dialled Rabbi Hershell's number.

His secretary answered and when she realised it was Sam, said she would put him through straight away.

"How are you Sam?" the kindly voice asked. "I didn't want to ring too early but I see you're up already. I suspect you've seen the papers?"

"Yes, and the radio and the television, and the phone doesn't stop ringing. I have to take Eva back to the police station and, after that, I don't know what to do."

"Have you got things to settle before you go to Israel?"

"Some, but not too much. Helen's booked flights in about ten days so we need to survive this until then."

"I have a suggestion, Sam. Why don't you borrow my flat in Bournemouth. You'll just drop out of the picture and might get some peace."

"Isn't that tantamount to running away? I feel I should face this; perhaps if I talk to the reporters it will help?" There was a question in his voice. "Maybe the rest of the family should go away, though. I don't want the twins hounded, or Helen and Eva. Let me think about it, and thank you. I appreciate the offer."

Eva came into the room as he was finishing the conversation. She had obviously made an effort and looked very calm and elegant. Her white hair was neatly brushed and she had even put on a little lipstick. Her handbag was clasped closely to her chest, as if protecting what was inside.

"If you could run me down to the police station, I would be grateful Sam. Leave the others here." She caught a glimpse of a face peering in at the window. "I wondered if we would be harassed. It's okay, I can deal with it. I had worse than this during the war."

Decisively, she crossed to the window and pulled the curtains across, thwarting the reporter who thought he would get a story.

"I've already been out in the garden and the people next door are appalled at the way the press have gathered here. They suggest we go through into their garden and borrow their car. It's in the garage so we can drive out without anyone seeing us. They're such nice people, Sam."

Eva was right. The press were too busy looking at Sam's house to notice the 'next door neighbours' driving off. Eva was still gripping her bag tightly. In it was Frau Hoffman's letter – the proof that she hadn't abducted Sam.

Dov was waiting on the steps outside the police station and they all went in together. Again, Sam had to stay in the reception area but he was relieved when Eva came out of the room smiling.

"The Inspector agrees the letter clearly says I was to care for the Hoffman's child. He says no further action will be taken and acknowledges you were unaware of all this until recently and have been well cared for all your life. I feel free at last, Sam, even though there will be hard days ahead. Let's get home and tell the others I'm not going to be put in prison."

Sam wondered how Eva could be so relaxed, knowing that there were still so many problems. They got into the car and he sat a moment before letting his head drop onto the steering wheel. He buried his face in his hands, wishing he could disappear.

CHAPTER 8

The Thompsons next door were a great help to Sam and Helen. They offered the use of their car at any time, brought in shopping and invited them in for coffee.

"We've seen the news, Helen," Mrs Thompson confided, "and we think the way the newspapers are behaving is just dreadful. Anyone with half a brain could understand Sam's mum doing what she did. Please do whatever makes things easier for you. We're retired, so we don't need the car much – you can use it whenever you like."

She poured coffee into Helen's cup.

"I can see how this is affecting you all. Has Sam decided what to do?"

"Yes, we're going to Israel in a few days. Everything's organised and there'll be a family moving in the day after we've gone. You'll like them. He's a rabbi, and his wife doesn't work but I understand she's hoping to get a job in the school."

"I'm sure we'll get on but it won't be the same as having you next door, dear," was the staunch reply.

There was the sound of running feet, and Mrs Thompson looked out of the window.

"There's someone rushing down your path; a lad with a baseball cap on. And your Sam's come out after him."

"In which case, I think it's time to go. At least the reporters have all gone home now so I'll go out the front door."

Sam was standing on the path, looking aghast and when Helen followed his eyes she saw why. A large swastika had been daubed in red paint on the front door. Drips were slowly coursing down the panels and pooling on the ground.

"Leave it, Helen," Sam said as she moved towards the door. "I'll get some turps and a rag, and I'll soon have it off."

"I'm going to call the police. Did you get a good look at who did this?"

"No, just a blur as he ran off. I could see he wasn't very tall – probably a teenager, but I have no way of identifying him."

"It's all right, Eva, no damage done." Helen tried to prevent her mother-in-law from seeing outside but it was too late.

"I can't believe it. It's like Germany all over again. I never thought this could happen here in England." She shivered, not wanting Sam to see how affected she'd been. When the police had hustled her away, for a moment – just a brief moment, she was back in the camp at the mercy of the uniformed soldiers. The swastika on the door had brought memories to the front of her mind. Things she didn't want to think about.

Sam put a protective arm around his mother. "You know, ma, the more I think about it, the more I feel you should go to Bournemouth. The twins will go with you to keep you company, and we'll come and visit. It's only a hundred miles and won't take long to drive. All this will settle down…"

Eva interrupted him,

"But, Sam, you're going away. I need to see you before you go."

"And you will, don't worry. Come on, now, Helen will take you home and help you pack a bag and then we'll drive you down and settle you all in."

Esther and Daniel couldn't bear to see their grandmother so upset and readily agreed to go with her. They sorted out what they needed and Helen put some groceries in a large carrier bag, handing Esther some money.

"For shopping," she said firmly, adding, "sensible food," as she saw Daniel's smile.

The police advised them not to do any cleaning but to leave the swastika on the door for them to see. They arrived shortly after Helen called.

"I'm sorry this has happened, Mrs Goldman," said the sergeant. "We'll take a couple of pictures and then you can get it cleaned off. I think it's unlikely we'll catch the culprit as no one actually saw his face, but we'll record this as a crime and someone might report in that they'd seen it happening. Unless you recognise the blighter who did this, we can't do anything. You've made the right decision to get your mother and kids away, though. Pity you couldn't go with them."

"We have a lot to do before we leave next week. There'll be a new family coming in so could I ask you or your colleagues to keep an eye on the place. The man who's coming is going to be the rabbi at the East Lane synagogue, and I wouldn't want him to be targeted."

"Yes, sir, I'll make a note of it," and with that Sam and Helen had to be content.

The drive to Bournemouth was a sombre affair, and there was little conversation; they were all lost in their own thoughts. Sam felt only able to stop briefly at the flat before driving home even though Helen offered to take the wheel. He said he needed to concentrate on something – anything, in order to clear his head and Helen wisely stayed silent. It was dark when they let themselves in their house. The graffiti was still on the door, and they both felt uncomfortable with it there, but there was nothing they could do until the morning.

They made another couple of trips to Bournemouth and each time saw a sadness in Eva which hadn't been there before. She had seemed so cheerful, once matters had come into the open but they began to realise how traumatised she had been underneath a veneer of confidence. Sam was tempted to stay in England but the whole family stressed how important it was for him to have an Israeli conversion. They pointed out that a conversion granted outside of Israel might not be accepted, so reluctantly, he agreed. The last visit before his departure had a degree of poignancy, as he knew he would not be there when his nephew or niece was born; he would miss the joyfulness of the occasion and the celebration after the birth.

On the morning of their departure, Helen handed the house keys to Mrs Thompson. The two women hugged each other and said they would keep in touch. Sam was leaving his car for the new rabbi to use so they called a taxi and arrived at the airport in good time.

The aeroplane was fairly empty; not many people were flying to Israel and the flight was relatively quick. As it taxied along the runway at Ben Gurion airport, Helen grasped Sam's hand.

"It's a long time since we've been here and I have to admit I'm excited. I'm looking forward to seeing old friends and making new ones."

"We need to get settled in first. I should make an appointment to go to the Beth Din offices and see what I have to do," he paused, considering his words, "to regularise my position. I know Rabbi Hershell said it would be a formality but I can't help feeling anxious."

Helen squeezed Sam's hand again.

"You'll be all right, dear. He wouldn't have suggested we come to Israel if there was going to be a problem. I expect the Chief Rabbi has outlined everything in advance of our arrival – that might help?" She looked hopefully at Sam.

"You're right, as usual," he said with a laugh. "What would I do without you?"

They appeared to have a lot of luggage but Helen defended this, when Sam complained they had brought too much. They would be in Jerusalem for at least six months and, of course, one of the heavy suitcases was full of Sam's books and papers.

There was a shout from across the barrier and a burly figure pushed through the crowd.

"Shalom, shalom, Sam. Ma hamatzav?"

"We're fine," Sam replied.

The two men greeted each with bear hugs, slapping each other on their backs.

"And Helen, as beautiful as ever. Come, come, I have a car. Is this your luggage? You have so many cases…maybe you're making aliyah?" And he laughed at his own joke.

Helen was overcome. "I wasn't expecting anyone to meet us. Who told you we were coming?"

"I have my sources," was the enigmatic reply, "so come, come!"

Darkness was falling as they drove from Tel Aviv to Jerusalem. As they left the city, street lights were coming on, spreading a yellow glow into the inky blackness. Helen was tired, and happy to sit in the back seat, listening to the men catch up. It took well over an hour before they arrived and they got out of the car stiffly.

The flat was on the third floor and, of course, there was no lift. Between them, they hauled the luggage up, the men making a couple of trips each. Helen was already in the tiny kitchen, opening the door which led on to the balcony, letting in the remainder of the warmth of the day.

She could smell the bougainvillia trees growing in the courtyard below and breathed deeply, enjoying the familiar sweet scent of the flowers, as well as the aroma of fried onions and hummus which was wafting in.

There was iced lemon juice in the fridge and a bowl of salad, chopped finely, Israeli style. Helen pottered around, opening cupboards and drawers, discovering where everything was. She kicked off her shoes and felt the cool tiles beneath her feet, looking up to see Bernie smiling at her.

"It's been a while, hasn't it" he said, "but I can see you're happy to be back, whatever the circumstances. Get settled in and come for dinner on Friday. You'll be able to see the kids – Arye's on leave from the army; I'll ask Ben to come home from the yeshivah and Sofia and her husband will also come, I think. Karen will be pleased to see you, I know. She's missed her chavera. Letters are good, no doubt about that, but no substitute for the real thing."

He put their door keys on the table, and then he was gone, the sound of his footsteps on the stairs fading as he took them two at a time.

In the bedroom, it was clear someone had made sure everything was in order. The bed was made and the curtains had obviously been kept closed all day because the room was pleasantly cool. Sam crossed to the window and pushed the shutters to one side. Even though it was nearly midnight, there were still people in the streets. Most of the restaurants were closing down and youngsters were calling goodnight to each other. The buses had stopped running, of course, but a walk home would mean nothing to them.

Helen moved across and watched with him. They could hear the faint sounds of singing, and a few irate shouts of, 'shut up and go home,' as the last few left Zion Square.

"I'll unpack tomorrow," Helen said tiredly. "All I need is sleep now."

They came awake early, light flooding in through the uncovered window. Helen groaned as she realised it was only five thirty.

"We forgot to close the shutters," she said, "but actually I feel rested. Shall we just get up and start the day?"

"Really?" asked Sam.

"Really," said Helen, smiling. "I'm desperate to get out. I think the market should be open soon so let's go and get some fruit and vegetables. Actually, I just want to be there to listen to the sounds of Jerusalem and breathe in its unique smell." Sam smiled indulgently at her, realising he felt the same way.

Helen was right. The Mahane Yehuda market was opening for business. Fruit and vegetables were piled high on the stalls, and the smell of bread wafting out of the ovens, made them feel hungry. The loaves were still warm, as Helen put them in the shopping basket she'd found on the back of the kitchen door. Soon it was full of fat tomatoes, their skins shiny and red; small cucumbers, large white onions and purple figs.

There were several stalls selling only sweet juicy dates. Stallholders called out to passersby, inviting them to try and then to buy, and of course they did, helping themselves from the mounds of beautifully arranged fruit. They walked round the market, dipping their fingers into the brown paper bag, enjoying the soft taste, taking their time to explore the rest the shuk had to offer. They stopped only when hunger captured them and they decided to have breakfast. They drank strong fragrant coffee and ate flaky borekas standing at the counter of a small café, remembering the taste from times past.

Finally, they took their shopping back to the flat, with Helen remarking that she would be able to eat whatever she wanted; there was no way she would gain weight with all the stairs she was going to climb.

"We're lucky there's a phone here, darling. I won't have to go out to find a call box so I'll ring the Beth Din now and make an appointment."

Helen left him to it, and went into the kitchen to put everything away. She could hear the murmur of his voice but not what he was saying and waited to hear what the outcome was.

"I spoke to Dayan Freedman. He can see me next Tuesday so he suggested we use the time before then as a little break. He seems to have plans for me once everything's settled and says there won't be any time for sightseeing after that. I have to take all the paperwork; fortunately, I photocopied the letter from Frau Hoffman because he says that's very important. He was very kind, and just said that he'd never come across a situation like this before." He stared into the middle distance.

"Actually, I don't think anyone's come across anything like this before. I suspect there'll be a few research papers written about it."

Helen wasn't sure if he was joking or not so didn't respond, and Sam continued,

"It's beginning to drizzle a little, so get your raincoat and we'll go down to the kotel. It should be the first place we visit, don't you think?"

Buses were running down Jaffa Street but they decided to walk. The rain was light and surprisingly warm, and they wanted to absorb Jerusalem before serious meetings would begin. The pavements were uneven so they stepped carefully, looking in the shop windows; at the jewellers, where Magen Dovid's were carefully displayed; at the fabric shop, where rolls of material were propped up outside, covered in plastic to protect them from the weather; and at the street vendors selling fresh juice.

The traffic increased as they reached the road junction before the Old City. They crossed over carefully, taking in the sights of arab ladies in hijabs and long dresses, and orthodox men in black coats and fur trimmed hats.

The sloping path down to the Jaffa Gate was slippery with the rain. Helen held on to Sam's hand and, when they walked through, they saw to their left, the café they'd always used when they were last in Israel. They were content for a moment to sit there, under the stripy awning, drinking glasses of pomegranate juice and watching the world go by.

CHAPTER 9

A school group passed by, the children in pairs, holding hands.

"On the way to the Wall, I think," said Sam. "Come on, we'll follow behind. We may get through to the Kotel easier if we stay close to them. Tourists will let a line of kids go by and it'll be better than forcing our way through the crowds."

They left shekels to pay for the drinks and moved on into the souk. On each side of the narrow alleyways, shopkeepers called their wares. There were piles of scarves, tallit bags and tallits. One of the stalls was selling bowls and salad servers, candlesticks and chopping boards, all made from olive wood. There was a cacophony of languages from all over the world – American, French, German and over the top of it all, a mixture of Ivrit and Arabic.

Sam and Helen hurried on through, past the spice market and the clothes draped across the tops of the stalls. Helen hung back a little and Sam urged her on, saying,

"We have six months here. Plenty of time for shopping," and she acquiesced whilst at the same time casting her eyes over the different goods on display. Once through the Cardo, they reached the stairs which led down to the Wall. Sam went towards the men's section and Helen towards the women's area. She pulled her scarf over her head and picked up a prayer book from the table at the entrance.

It was still fairly early, so not many women were there. She was able to stand close to the weathered stone, made shiny from the touch of millions of hands. As far as the eye could see, little pieces of paper had been inserted into crevices where the mortar had eroded; hand written prayers for those unable to get to the Wall, brought by friends or relatives; prayers from those who were leaving Jerusalem; many, many prayers. Helen took a moment to compose her thoughts before she was able to pray herself and she put all the longing and heartache she felt at Sam's predicament into her own words.

They met up at the bottom of the steps and Helen looked at Sam with a worried expression on her face.

"How do you feel?" she asked.

"I feel calmer; I feel that there will be a good outcome; I feel better all round, and I feel I'd like a good Israeli beer." They both laughed, and Helen tucked her hand into his arm.

"Come on then and we'll find somewhere to eat and you can have your good Israeli beer."

It was steamy in the little restaurant. The tables were close together; they had red formica tops, where plastic covered menus were leaning against jugs of water. The cutlery, wrapped in paper napkins, was piled high in woven baskets. A steady stream of people came in until eventually every table was full. The waiters bustled round, taking orders, bringing salads and warm bread.

"I'd forgotten the amount of food that arrives before you actually order your meal. Do you remember last time we were here we often couldn't eat everything, until we started ordering one meal between the two of us." Helen reminisced.

"Yes, and how embarrassed we were, until we realised everyone was doing the same."

"One meal and two forks," they said in unison.

"For old time's sake, Sam? Hummus for two, then shakshuka, chicken schnitzel and chips."

"And cold beer!"

While they were waiting for the food, Sam pulled a guide book out of his pocket, pushed the salt and pepper to one side and opened out the map on the centre pages.

"I brought this from the flat. I know that, strictly speaking we're not tourists – I think we did all the sights when we were here in the seventies, but things may have changed. There are a couple of places I'd like to revisit, too; Yad Vashem for one. There was some mention of collecting the names of all the survivors and ma asked me to put our family details there."

The salads arrived, bowls of chopped tomatoes, cucumbers and peppers; pickles, and the hummus with hot bread. Sam tore off a piece of pitta and dipped it into the hummus, closing his eyes in ecstasy.

"I don't know why we haven't been back to Israel."

"Well, I can think of a few reasons. Work, kids and cost! Still, however this has happened, we're here now so we need to make the most of it. Do you think the Beth Din will find you a job? Once you're back to being a rabbi again there might be something you can do in Israel."

The waiter interrupted their conversation, putting down a huge plate of schnitzel and a big bowl of chips. Sam continued speaking.

"Possibly, but I want to get this conversion procedure over first. I'll take it from there once I'm properly Jewish again, but I don't think I can be re-instated quickly. I suspect it won't be so easy."

There was silence as they enjoyed the food and Sam had another beer. When all the plates were clean, they paid the bill and went out into the cooler afternoon air.

The walk back to the flat was uphill and they took a slightly different route, approaching from the back of Zion Square.

"Have you noticed anything that's different to home, Helen?" Sam asked as they reached the entrance to the flat.

Helen shook her head.

"There's no McDonalds, no fast food at all. In fact, the only fast food in Jerusalem is the falafel on the stalls."

"Not for long. I should imagine that as soon as McDonalds get agreement that the food they cook is kosher, they'll be springing up all over the place. Not while we're here, though. We'll just have to overdose on felafal, hummus and shawarma. I suspect that won't be a problem."

Helen set about turning the little flat into their home for the next six months, and by early evening everything was put away, suitcases resting on the tops of the wardrobes and, surprisingly, they both felt hungry again.

"It's all that walking, but I'm ready for dinner," said Sam, checking the contents of the fridge to see what there was and discovering only salads and cheese. "Would you rather go to a restaurant or buy food in the supermarket?"

"The supermarket. We need more than just food, although that's important, too. I've made a list already."

"You and your lists," Sam said teasingly, "maybe you should make a list of all the lists you've made."

Helen swatted him on the back of the head with the shopping bag. "Enough! Come on, or everywhere will be closed."

The neon lights illuminated the inside of the supermarket and Helen and Sam walked up and down the wide aisles, choosing all sorts of food. In many ways, this was similar to the shopping Helen did at home; she even recognised some of the labels on the jars, but there was a difference. There was very little convenience food, and piles of fresh vegetables and salads were stacked on low counters. There was shelf upon shelf of bottled water and a huge variety of juices. Busy housewives pushed infants in buggies, while their older children manoeuvred the trolleys, occasionally bumping into the legs of other shoppers.

Pretty soon, Helen had accumulated a basket full of everything they needed, and joined the queue at the checkout. Payment made, she and Sam strolled back to the flat, each carrying a heavy bag.

"Maybe in future," Helen laughed, "we'll not buy so much at one time. These stairs..." and she set off resolutely to climb them.

Sam was determined to organise the next few days before what he considered to be 'the real work' started. First on the list would be a visit to Yad Vashem, where he wanted to make sure that the names of everyone in his parent's families who had died in the Holocaust, would have their names recorded.

There were several museums and galleries to visit, and perhaps a day at the beach at Haifa. The phone rang, disturbing his thoughts and Helen looked up sharply.

"Even here," she said thoughtfully, "even here, people want you."

Sam picked up the receiver, telling Helen it might be for her but she shook her head and, of course, she was right. It was from Rabbi Hershell. She waited as Sam spoke to him, noticing his face become very grave, and she mouthed,

"Eva?" at him but he shook his head and, content with that, she waited until he'd finished the call. She watched him opening the sideboard drawer and then scribbling on a piece of paper.

"I don't know whether or not I told you a couple of families had made aliyah? They've been told of their 'irregular marriage' status and they want to see me. I'm to meet them and go through their options. I'll call them now," he said, busy dialling.

This was something Helen had not anticipated. The reason for the trip to Israel was to give them breathing space, as well as the opportunity to clarify Sam's position. All of a sudden, they had been jerked back into the world of doubt and uncertainty. Sam finished the call and related what had been said to Helen.

"Apparently, they're still close friends with each other and when I spoke to Deborah, she said she and her husband had been talking to the other couple and would prefer if they could come together." He ran his hands through his hair. "To be perfectly honest, it suits me to have them here at the same time so they'll come in the morning. They don't want to wait until after shabbat before meeting; they want to know as soon as possible how things can be resolved."

"It looks as if more biscuits will be needed, then," Helen said, trying to lighten the atmosphere.

"I think we'll need more than biscuits," Sam said wearily. "Probably strong drink."

The next morning they waited expectantly for the knock at the door, trying to work out what to say and failing miserably.

Deborah and Martin Levy arrived first, closely followed by Natalie and Warren Stein. There was a brief flurry as jackets were removed and Helen invited them to sit on the balcony, while she made tea.

The conversation was stilted; it was difficult for them to find the words, and when Helen put the tray down on the metal table, she could see that Sam was struggling.

Grasping the bull by the horns, she said steadfastly.

"We all know why you're here. Sam has already spoken with all the others he's married. I think you are the last two." Turning to Sam, she continued, "maybe you need to run through what's already been discussed with the others."

When he'd finished, Sam said softly,

"I am so sorry this has happened but I want to make it right. Have you any idea what you would like me to do?"

"We have talked about it, as you know. We realise that our civil marriage in England means we are legally married but we would all like to be religiously married." The women nodded their heads, "and as soon as possible."

Sam outlined what he was about to do.

"The conversion first, then I need to get my status as rabbi confirmed. Would you like me to see if one of the Israeli rabbis could marry you?"

"If it's all right with you, rabbi," Natalie began, then stopped. "I mean, Mr Goldman, Sam, oh, for goodness sake. You've always been my rabbi and I shall continue to call you that."

Her husband added,

"That goes for the rest of us, too. What happened was really nothing to do with you. It certainly wasn't your fault. We'll get through this and you'll be back in a pulpit very soon."

Martin Levy spoke carefully,

"We'll leave it to you then, rabbi, to get yourself sorted out and then you'll call us and we'll arrange a short ceremony." He was interrupted,

"A short and meaningful ceremony," his wife added.

"Yes, indeed. And then, no reception, just a little dinner for our families and you and the rebbetzin, of course."

Deborah's parting words as they left were, "couldn't you have found a flat on the ground floor?" The atmosphere was more cheerful after they'd gone; Sam was light headed with relief that a solution had been found and could see that the Chief Rabbi's input was making it as easy as possible for him.

The next morning they set off for Yad Vashem. Sam was thoughtful, knowing that to see the family's names in black and white would confirm Eva's knowledge that she was the only one left alive. The last time they had been there, the museum had been open barely twenty years so there would be additional exhibitions to see. The main reason for going, of course, was to see that Eva and

Friedrich's family were listed amongst those murdered by the Nazis. As far as Sam knew, Eva was the only survivor of the Frankenburg family and he knew that every member of Friedrich's family had died in various concentration camps.

Eva had been very helpful before they left, giving him a list of all the names.

"You know, darling," she had said. "When I left Palestine, Yad Vashem did not exist. It only came into being in 1953 and, although I could have sent the names in, I hesitated. I thought if I wrote their names down, it would mean they really were dead. I couldn't come to terms with it. My sisters were so young, and Reuben not much more than a child. What you are doing for me is such a good thing and perhaps, one day, I will go back to what is now Israel and see for myself."

Mother and son had looked at each other, acknowledging the loss and accepting it was part of the healing process. And now, Sam and Helen found themselves walking up the path and into the great halls. There would be plenty of time to look properly at the information from the past. For now, the important thing was to record the family's details.

They were directed to where the pages of testimony were stored, original documents describing the names and lives of those who had been murdered.

Sam started with Eva's family name, moving swiftly through the alphabet until he reached the letter 'F'. There were several similar names until Frankenberg jumped out of the page. He really hadn't been expecting to see anything at all; Eva had been the only one left alive and she had never sent the details of her family to Yad Vashem.

Sam scanned the pages, reading about his grandparents and Reuben and his mother's sister, Leah. There was no mention of her other sister Anna but there, in black and white, Eva's name was recorded among the dead.

CHAPTER 10

Sam reread the page, incredulous. How could his mother's name be amongst the dead? It would be too much of a coincidence for another Frankenberg family to have the same two children, Reuben and Leah, who had perished in a camp. Maybe Anna's and Eva's names had somehow got mixed up. His hands were shaking and he laid the book down on the desk.

Helen could see that his face had paled and she leaned over to take the volume from him. She had expected him to show some emotion when he saw that the family was not listed, but not this severe reaction.

She too went white, as she saw what had upset Sam.

"This can't be right. It must have been put in by a family member who got the names confused. Don't worry, Sam, we'll get this sorted out at the enquiry desk."

Sam shook his head.

"As far as I know, no one was left alive after the war – only Eva."

The woman working behind the desk looked up as they got nearer.

"Can I help you?" she asked with a pleasant smile and then, noticing Sam's demeanour, suggested he sit down.

"A lot of people react like this," she said gently. "Somehow, seeing the names makes it seem more real – more final. Who were you looking for?"

Sam explained that there had been a mistake. He didn't know what had happened to his Aunt Anna but his mother, Eva Frankenberg, now Goldman, was very much alive and well. His mother and his two sisters had been in the same camp, but the younger girls had been separated from their sister, who had assumed they'd both died.

"Would you be able to tell me who had put the details in?"

The clerk looked doubtful.

"I don't think that's allowed," she replied. "In fact, I don't know if we even keep the names of people who've given us information. We keep here the names only of those who were murdered." Her voice, faintly accented, faltered slightly.

Sam leaned forward to read the name tag on her blouse.

"Look, Shulamit, if there is any chance that the names have been confused, it could mean that my mother has a sister who also survived."

Helen added,

"It would be wonderful for my mother-in-law to find a member of her family, when for the last forty years she has assumed everyone is dead."

Making her mind up, Shulamit turned the sign on her desk to the 'Closed' side and asked them to wait while she spoke to her manager.

It was a long twenty minutes before she returned. Sam was unable to sit still and constantly fidgeted, while Helen twisted the hands of her bag round and round.

Shulamit came through the door behind her desk, a tall bespectacled man following her.

They both sat and Shulamit introduced him as the 'Keeper of Names'. Sam outlined the problem, finishing with,

"So you see, Mr Morris, this would be wonderful for my mother."

"I am sure you appreciate I can't just hand over information. I will need you to confirm your name, your mother's name and any details you have about your grandparents and family. If I think this is genuine, and, you must understand, I'm not doubting you – it is just our procedure, I will get in touch with the person who listed the Frankenberg family. I will ask if he or she would like to make contact with you. Do you have those details?"

Sam thought carefully. He had his passport, of course, but that showed Goldman, not Frankenberg. Then he remembered the list Eva had given him.

"I'm afraid that is not conclusive enough. Is it possible you could ask your mother to give you her birth certificate? Maybe she has some pictures of the family? That would be a great help, especially if we can match them to our records."

Sam looked directly at Mr Morris.

"I understand you have to be sure that the information is correct but I can assure you that it is. My mother is in England but I will ask her to fax the details to me, as long as you are prepared to accept documents which were issued to her at the end of the war, and not the originals. I'm sure you appreciate that much paperwork was lost and duplicates issued," he added stiffly.

"Mr Goldman, I suspect you feel I'm being less than helpful, and I don't mean to cause you any further distress. I think you know we have to make sure that people are who they say they are. Even after all this time, there are imposters; those who would try to have a Jewish identity and hide their...shall we say dubious origins. I would ask you to be patient and I will do what I can."

Helen and Sam left Yad Vashem very disturbed.

"How on earth can I ask ma for her papers? She will wonder why, and I wouldn't want to raise false hopes that someone from her family is alive."

"Could you tell her that you can't list the family without proof of the relationship?"

"I suppose so," Sam replied doubtfully. "In a way it's kind of true. Until I give Yad Vashem the right documents, I can't progress any further. Oh Helen, if someone had survived...how wonderful for ma."

Helen, ever practical, told Sam he needed to restrain himself.

"Even if Anna survived the war," she said thoughtfully, "she might not be alive today."

Sam's face fell. He hadn't considered that. His sole thought had been that a living member of the Frankenberg family had been found.

"I suggest we go back to the flat and you make that call, Sam. You might find it easier than you think."

The phone rang for a long time before it was answered and Eva's familiar voice came on the line. When she heard Sam, her immediate response was,

"What's happened, Sam? Are you all right?"

Sam, laughing, replied, asking her why she always thought there was a crisis when he rang.

"Can't I call my own mother, without there being a problem?"

Sam could hear the catch in Eva's voice as she answered him.

"Of course you can, darling. It's just calls are so expensive…so, of course, I thought maybe you were ill. Or Helen," she added.

"Nobody's ill, ma, and we're enjoying the sunshine but, you're right, calls are expensive so let me tell you what I want. I've been to Yad Vashem and, of course, we can list both sides of the family but we need to prove we have a right to do that. So could you please fax your birth certificate, and dad's too if you have it. That will put the wheels in motion."

Eva didn't seem to think this was an unusual request. Sam also asked for any photographs and Eva had to reply sadly, that there were none.

"Nothing survived from the war." She thought a moment then added.

"Actually, there might have been a photograph in the stuff we rescued from my parents' garden. I'll look for it and fax everything I can find. This is so important to me, Sam. It's a real mitzvah you're doing. If my family's names are not included in the list of people who were murdered by the Nazis, it will be as if they've never lived. There are no gravestones for them, nothing."

"I expect you could use the photocopier in the Post Office. Wait a minute, and I'll give you the number at Yad Vashem to call. Ask one of the twins to give you a hand and don't forget to write the name of the sender on every page. We don't want to get mixed up with another family," he said lightly.

"The twins are out at the moment, Sam, but I've written everything down and I'll do it first thing in the morning."

Sam took a little time to make sure Eva was all right and she was happy to tell him that the Bournemouth flat was very comfortable and they were able to walk down to the seafront. She'd met a couple she knew and they were intending to set up a bridge game.

"I'll call you again, soon, ma," Sam finished and he clasped Helen's hand for some comfort. It had been difficult to keep the real reason for his call a secret. He sighed. There had been so many secrets in his life already.

They waited until the afternoon of the following day before going back to Yad Vashem, and asking to speak to Mr Morris. He came out of the office and when he saw who it was, he smiled broadly.

"Mr Goldman," he said, extending his hand to be shaken. "I have good news for you. You'd better come into my room and sit down, as I think you may be going to get a shock." His eyes were twinkling, though, so Sam was quick to realise it would be a pleasant surprise.

Sam sat on the edge of his seat, while the other man brought a file out of his desk drawer. Helen's hand searched for Sam's and they waited while Mr Morris cleared his throat.

"The fax from your mother, Eva Goldman, came this morning. In fact, it was on my desk when I arrived at work. I think it must have been sent last night." He looked over his glasses and said that he thought Eva was anxious to get the matter resolved.

"Actually," Helen said, "We didn't tell Eva that it was possible she had a relative alive. We didn't want to raise her hopes."

"I realised that by the way the accompanying letter was written, but no matter. I ran a quick check through our records and it seems very likely that your mother's name was added incorrectly by her sister Anna when we started our record keeping in 1953. She has listed the whole family as perished. Furthermore, I'm pleased to tell you that Anna is still alive and lives in Haifa with her husband."

Neither Sam nor Helen could speak. Mr Morris waited patiently, until eventually Sam asked if he could have Anna's address.

"I'm not sure how we can deal with this, Mr Goldman. The majority of our survivors have suffered great trauma after their experiences."

Helen was about to speak but he raised his hand gently and continued.

"Don't worry, I'm not saying she shouldn't be told, or you shouldn't go to see her." He smiled benignly, "I'm only saying we need to be cautious, and we should be aware of the impact it will undoubtedly have on her."

"Do you know if she is in good health? Does she have children? Where exactly does she live?" The questions came tumbling out until Mr Morris put a stop to them. "I can't tell you anymore. What I suggest is that we give you the address and one of my staff comes with you. Anna will be in her sixties now and this is going to have a great effect on her. She might be reluctant to speak to you and she will certainly need to know exactly who you are. Shulamit has already offered to accompany you and she can make the introductions. Now, how does that sound?"

Sam and Helen saw the wisdom of this suggestion. In his eagerness to make contact with Anna, caution had flown out of Sam's window. Of course it would be difficult for Anna, and taking someone with them would break the ice.

Mr Morris went on. "It's shabbat tomorrow so travel will be difficult. All the buses and trains stop early, as you know. How would it be if Shulamit collects you first thing on Sunday morning? We'll rustle up a car from somewhere for her, and she can drive you to Haifa. It might take a couple of hours but it'll be better than public transport."

Sam and Helen were very grateful. They accepted nothing could be done until shabbat was over and so continued with their plans to have dinner with their friends.

"Sam, I need to do a little shopping before we go to Karen's & Bernie's. I'd like to take them a basket of fruit, or something sweet. Could we go into Mea Shearim and get something there?"

Erev shabbat in the ultra orthodox area saw housewives doing their last bit of shopping for shabbat. Young men could be seen rushing around, flowers in their hands, to give to their wives. They hardly looked old enough to be married, Helen thought. The popcorn sellers were busy filling bags, and selling them to grandparents who were taking them to give the grandchildren. Helen bought a bag, unable to resist the warm sweet smell. The fruit shops caught her attention, and she bought dates and almonds, some large oranges and strawberries, nestling amongst tissue paper. Finally, at the bakers, the cheesecake and kichle begged to be put in her bag.

Karen and Bernie were amazed when they heard what Sam had to say.

"You certainly know how to lead an exciting life, Sam," said Bernie slapping him on the back. "When you were in Israel last, you were such a quiet studious sort of chap. Now look at you. Sit down and meet everyone. Do you remember the children? They were small, of course, but they tell me they do remember you. You made quite an impression on them. A quiet one, of course," he said smiling at the idea.

All the family was there. The young men shook hands with Sam and Sofia smiled brightly. He stood back and looked at her. "I can't believe you're married…"

"And expecting, too, I think," Helen chipped in.

"Not just expecting; I have an older one fast asleep in the bedroom."

It was a warm family occasion, just what the Goldmans needed after the events of the past few weeks. They sat drinking in the atmosphere, eating the good food, and it was almost midnight when they left to walk back to the flat.

Stars twinkled in the dark blue velvet sky, and the streets were free of traffic. Other couples were out in the streets, some pushing buggies, despite the lateness of the hour. There were men in high black hats, women in dark, modest clothing, and a feeling of warmth as strangers wished them 'shabbat shalom'. There was an air of peace around the city; an air of tranquillity, an air of welcome.

CHAPTER 11

Saturday in Jerusalem is like no other day of the week. The streets are empty, markets are closed and the shutters of the shops are firmly fastened. Most of the people who are out are on their way to synagogue for morning prayers or they are tourists, marvelling at the silence.

Helen and Sam dressed carefully as they prepared to go to the service. Helen pushed her toes into shoes which were a little tight and Sam raised an eyebrow.

"It's the heat," she replied in answer to his look. "My feet are a bit swollen but they'll settle down. I know people are a little more relaxed here but I'm going to wear my navy suit anyway, and the hat!"

"And you'll look beautiful, as always."

Helen blushed, as she always did when Sam paid her a compliment.

"Why are we going to the Great Synagogue? I'm curious, because there are so many different shuls. I thought perhaps you'd want to go to one in the Old City."

"In view of what we've just discovered, I thought it was a good first shul to attend. And, besides, I don't think you'd manage the walk to the Old City in those shoes!"

"First shul?" queried Helen.

"I am going to find this very difficult. You remember how I struggled at our own synagogue once the news was out? Well, here I am in Israel, going to services on shabbat morning…still not able to wear my tallit because I'm not Jewish. Until my status is sorted, I don't think I'll be able to settle. I'm mindful of the Chief Rabbi's advice and I don't want another media storm like there was in England. I think I'll visit different synagogues until the conversion is completed. If I went regularly to the same synagogue, and wasn't wearing a tallit I would stand out like a sore thumb. People will think I'm a curious tourist if I only attend a shul once!"

"I see you've got it all worked out and now I understand, but tell me, Sam, with all the shuls to choose from, why this one?"

"This synagogue has an interesting story. When we were last here, I don't even think building work had started. Men and women met in all different venues although, as the number of congregants increased, the space became tighter. Eventually, it was decided to build a bigger place of worship."

He turned to look at Helen, with a glint in his eye. "And who do you think was the biggest benefactor? It was Sir Isaac Wolfson. Do you know who he is?"

Helen shook her head.

"He must be in his nineties, now, but he was a great philanthropist and he wanted to build this synagogue in the memory of the six million who died in the Holocaust. How appropriate for us, and another reason for choosing this shul."

Helen moved closer to him. Words couldn't help, she thought, but human contact might. She put her arms round him and they stood together for a few moments as Sam adjusted his kippah.

"At least I can wear this," he said with an awkward smile. "Even men of different faiths are instructed to cover their heads at a service as a mark of respect."

The streets were fairly quiet although there were a few family groups obviously going to attend services. St George's Street was only a short walk from their flat and they reached the doors to be greeted by young men on duty at the door.

"Is this your first visit?" they were asked. "Can we explain anything? Show you where the Sanctuary is and the stairs to the ladies gallery?"

Helen thanked them, and said they would be alright, with Sam adding it was their first visit to the synagogue but not to Israel.

They stood in the foyer for a moment, breathing in the atmosphere before separating; Helen to go upstairs where the women were, and Sam joining the men downstairs.

Helen could see, looking down over the balcony, that Sam had found a siddur and was leafing through it. Men who hadn't seen each other since the previous week were obviously catching up. The noise was dense, floating up from the Sanctuary and it comforted Helen. It was all so familiar…yet different.

The magnificent voice of the cantor soared up to the ceiling and the congregation joined with him in singing the opening psalm. Helen kept glancing at Sam and saw that, after a while, his shoulders relaxed as he lost himself in the traditional liturgy.

At the end of the service there was a surge towards the main hall, where people mingled. There was silence as the prayers were said and kiddush made. Helen pushed her way through the throng to Sam's side, and waited until he'd finished his conversation with a man whose back was facing her. He turned and she recognised him. It was a contemporary of Sam's. They had been to yeshivah together and had kept in touch spasmodically.

"Do you remember Avram?"

"Of course I do. What are you doing in Israel, Avram? I thought you'd gone back to America once you'd qualified."

"I did, I did. I'm just here on holiday. My congregation offered me a sabbatical so I grabbed it with both hands." He looked around. "Yes, here she is. I'm with Miriam, my wife. We left the children stateside with their grandparents. They're both in school so it would have been a shame to disturb their education, and it's given Miriam and me the opportunity to spend time together. Sam tells me you've just arrived. Sadly, we go home next week. Ships that pass in the night, eh Sam? Maybe we'll have a chance to get together before we go back?"

"Did you manage all right, Sam?" Helen asked as they went down the steps into the street. "You looked a little uncomfortable when you were talking to Avram."

"I was waiting for him to ask me why I wasn't wearing my tallit. I remember showing it to him before the graduation ceremony and telling him how special it was, so I was sure he would ask why I didn't have it on." He shook his head slightly. "Maybe he knows. Maybe everyone knows. Maybe that's why he didn't ask."

"And maybe you're getting paranoid about it. So what if people know. This problem isn't of your making. Nobody is going to think badly of you."

"You're right, why should they?" but Sam's face belied his cheerful words. "Come on, beautiful wife, time for lunch. Back to the flat, where I know you have everything under control for a meal of gigantic proportions. After that, a walk and an early night. Tomorrow is going to be a challenge, don't you think!"

They took their lunch on to the balcony and looked out onto the shabbat streets, quietly stretching in all directions. They knew that things would liven up in the late evening, when shabbat was over and the restaurants and cafes would open again. They were content though, and, as they sat together, Helen asked,

"Have you decided what to tell Anna? She's going to get a shock, isn't she!"

"I think in the beginning, we should leave the introductions to Shulamit. From what I can gather, she's had a great deal of experience, talking to survivors. After that I think I'll just play it by ear."

The walk they enjoyed later served two purposes; they were able to revisit some of their old stamping grounds when the streets were almost empty, and they were tired when they got back to the flat.

The doorbell rang promptly at nine am the following morning. They had been ready for well over an hour, Sam pacing the floor and Helen trying to calm him down.

"Shulamit, I just remembered something," was Sam's greeting. "I should have asked you to bring the photograph my mother faxed over so I could show it to Anna."

"Done," she replied with a smile. "All the papers are in the folder but before we go, please remember that Anna is no longer a young woman. I don't think I ever met her but Mr Morris seems to think she is not very tall. Tiny, he described her, and when I looked at the photo I could see what he meant. I don't know how old she was when it was taken, of course, but she looks very young and very anxious. Anyway, we shall talk on the way there. Please get in and make yourselves comfortable."

She coughed the engine into life and turned the car onto the main road, narrowly missing a couple of people who were trying to cross the street.

"You are not, I think, strangers to Israel but things may have changed since your last visit. Our roads are improved, yes? We have more traffic lights but I suspect no one takes any notice of them."

Sam and Helen exchanged glances but, wisely, did not respond.

"It will get hot, I think today," Shulamit remarked. "Do you have hats with you? I brought water and I am sorry that there is no air conditioning in the car. It is an old model. The best I can do is open the window for you." She wound a window down, and muttered to herself as it stuck halfway.

Helen cleared her throat before she spoke.

"Does Anna know we are coming?"

Shulamit nodded. "I called this morning, very early, in case she had left for work."

"She works?"

"As far as I know – maybe – yes, of course. Most women here work, although she may have retired. Living is expensive in Israel so two salaries are needed. Anna is a teacher, I think, or if not a teacher she maybe works in a kindergarten – something to do with children anyway. Mr Goldman, Mrs Goldman, I cannot give you answers to your questions because I do not know them. I am just guessing. I am sorry. Mr Morris said that there was little about Anna on the form."

She took her eyes off the road for a moment and the car swerved crazily to one side. Helen blanched as a driver furiously pressed on his horn and then she looked at Sam who had his eyes firmly closed.

"The information we need for Yad Vashem is really only about the people whose names we wish to remember. We record who gave that information to us, and their relationship to the deceased, but that's about all. There are plans to extend the way in which the names are displayed but they may have to wait a while until we raise some more money."

The car was slowing down at the approach to Haifa. Shulamit was driving along the bottom road, past the railway station and then she made a sharp turn into Ben Gurion Street. They saw in front of them the steep hill leading to Stella Maris and what looked like a construction site starting at the bottom.

"Anna's home is not far now but I think we should stop for a coffee before we visit her." She parked outside a small café which had tables set on the pavement. "You will be able to maybe decide how you tell her your mother is alive and you can also visit the bathroom."

"We have no idea how to tell her. We hoped you might be able to introduce us."

"Of course, I will introduce you. The name 'Goldman' might be a way in. She knew your father, I assume?"

"Yes, she was at the wedding of my parents. Shulamit, do you know if she's in good health? I wouldn't want to give her such a fright that she has a heart attack!"

"I don't know about her health but I think she will be robust enough to deal with this, especially as she spent time in a camp. For a survivor to find a family member is the most wonderful thing. I think it will make her very happy."

She looked at her watch, the Hebrew lettering telling her the time.

"Okay. I said we'd be with her at about eleven, so time to go."

Sam and Helen held hands on the last little bit of the drive. They pulled up on a patch of gravel outside Anna's home and saw a wooden gate and through it a paved garden where there were lots of pots containing brightly coloured flowers. Shulamit rang the bell and they waited while footsteps tapped on the tiled floor inside the house.

An elderly couple stood framed in the doorway. Shulamit had been correct. Anna was tiny – probably not even five foot in height. The man standing beside her was tall but seemed taller because Anna was so small.

They were both smiling and looked pleased to see them. The man moved forward to shake hands and introduced himself.

"I'm Yaacov Brendel and this is my wife Anna. It's good to meet you but your reason for being here is a bit of a mystery. So, come inside. Anna has made biscuits and there is fresh coffee on the cooker." He ushered them into a spacious lounge, with comfortable chairs set around a carved coffee table. Under the window, there was a low settee covered in brightly patterned fabric. It was piled high with cushions and a black and white cat was sitting on one of the arms, washing its face industriously. It paused in its ablutions to look curiously at the visitors, before resuming its grooming.

In the corner of the room, Sam saw an easel, with a canvas resting on it. Yaacov's eyes followed Sam's and he said proudly,

"They are Anna's. She is a talented artist and much of the work in our home has been created by her." He turned as Anna tugged his sleeve.

"What is it, my darling?"

Anna's fingers flew, as she spelt out the words she wanted to say.

"Anna says you are very welcome. Please to sit." Yaacov saw Helen's shock, as she realised that Anna was not speaking but signing.

"You are wondering why my wife doesn't speak?" He put an arm protectively round Anna's shoulders. "She has not said a word since she came out of the concentration camp. She speaks only with her hands, although she hears perfectly."

CHAPTER 12

When Sam saw Anna, he wanted to rush across and put his arms around her. The similarity between her and his mother was striking; the white hair, the smiling face, even the way she bustled into the kitchen, bringing out the coffee and strudel. She was much smaller than his mother but other than that, there was no doubt that they were sisters.

He kept himself in check, though, not wanting to scare her, and waiting while she poured the coffee, raising her eyebrows at each person in turn and pointing to the sugar and cream jug. They knew what she was asking, though no words were said.

When they were settled, Sam looked expectantly at Shulamit who, in turn, was looking at Anna and Yaacov.

"Yaacov, you said our visit is a mystery so I'm here to try and explain why we've come. First of all, let me introduce Sam and Helen Goldman. They're English and here in Israel for a few months. They very much wanted to meet you." She paused, as Anna's fingers flashed, along with her smile. Yaacov patiently relayed what she was signing.

"Why would she want to meet us? I don't think we've ever met them before. In fact, the only Goldman I've ever known is Friedrich, who has never been heard of since the war."

Shulamit continued, choosing her words carefully.

"What I'm about to tell you will, I think, come as a shock but a pleasant one, I hope." She looked at Sam.

"There is no other way to say this. Friedrich Goldman was Sam's father."

Sam didn't correct her. There would be time enough for that later, when Anna had absorbed some of the information.

Yaacov was watching his wife's hands intently, making sure that he didn't miss a word. He looked stunned.

"Does this mean that Friedrich is alive? He was married to my sister Eva, who was murdered in the camp."

Sam took a deep breath. He could see that Anna's hopes had been raised so he chose his words carefully.

"Friedrich died some years ago," he watched as some of the light disappeared from Anna's eyes. "But…"

He was unable to continue.

Helen moved across to Anna, knelt on the floor, and took her hands. The older woman was trembling.

"Anna, I am so happy to tell you that my mother-in-law, Eva, is alive."

There was absolute silence in the room; Helen's words hung in the air. Even Shulamit, who knew that Eva had survived, was moved to tears. No one spoke, no one moved until Yaacov told them what Anna's fingers were saying.

"She says this cannot be true. She was told that Eva had died just before the camp was liberated. Bombs were dropping as the allies attacked, and there were many, many dead. Eva was working for the camp commandant and she was killed along with his whole family. She was told this by someone who had seen Eva amongst a pile of bodies. There is no doubt it was her, because the kapo identified her before she herself died."

Shulamit passed over the photograph Eva had faxed and Anna looked closely at it.

"Yes, there is no doubt it is of my family. See, here is Leah and Reuben, and Eva too. I am the little one in front. Where did you get this picture?"

"Eva retrieved it from the garden of your home in Germany, where your father had buried it. She also has everything else that was there…candlesticks, menorah and so on. Do you remember them?"

Tears were cascading down Anna's cheeks and she was shivering uncontrollably. Yaacov pointed to a blanket on the corner of the settee and Shulamit wrapped it around the slight figure of, undeniably, Eva's sister who was still holding Helen's hands as if they were a lifeline.

"Yes, I remember them. I remember everything but I cannot talk about it. I cannot say the words out loud." Her fingers became still and she rested them in her lap for a few moments, before resuming the rapid movements again. She was looking at Yaacov with a hopeful expression on her face.

"She wants to know if you are Eva's son, and if you have any brothers and sisters."

Even though Sam knew this was a question that would be asked, and even though he knew it would be one he would have to answer truthfully at some point, the words would not come. Helen pressed his hand and her smile was encouraging but he could only say,

"I have one younger sister, Rachel. She is home in England, expecting a baby later this year."

"A child! Does this mean that Eva will be a grandmother...or do you have children, Sam?"

"I have twins – a boy and girl." He fumbled in his wallet. "Here is a picture of them with my sister and her husband. I'm sorry," he stuttered, "I should have thought. You'll want to see photos of my mother. I only have this one," and he passed her a picture of Eva in her graduation gown. "It's an old picture, taken many years ago."

Anna looked carefully, taking in the mortar board, and the black robes.

"So I can believe Eva is alive – and she completed her studies. How wonderful. Is she happy? Does she know about me?" Anna sank back, exhausted, on to the settee.

Helen took over, telling them that they had gone to Yad Vashem to have the Goldman and Frankenberg family names put into the records and how astonished Sam was to see Eva's name included.

"I can understand what a shock it was," Yaacov said. "As much of a shock for Sam, as finding relatives is for Anna. What can we tell you? Anna is unable to speak with her voice but her hands are very eloquent."

He turned to his wife.

"Do you feel up to talking?" he asked.

"I don't know," was the answer. "I never, ever thought that anyone was alive and that I had relatives." When she had finished signing, Yaacov said she had told him to speak for her. He knew all that had happened to her so she didn't need to sign it herself, although she might add bits in.

"Sadly, we do not have any children so meeting you is wonderful for us," and he embraced Sam. "Anna's story is complicated. I don't think I could tell it all at one time, and I can see she needs to rest. Would you be able to come back? I think it would be better."

"I think that would be a good idea," Helen said soothingly. "Sam is tired too. I can tell. We should perhaps plan a longer visit. Maybe we could come next weekend? Shulamit has told us that Anna still works. What about you Yaacov?"

"Yes, I work as a sculptor. Anna and I complement each other very well but during the week she takes care of the deaf children in the school, and they all love her. The weekend is a good idea. We have a spare bedroom so you could stay with us." Sensing a refusal, he added firmly, "It would be such a pleasure for us to have Anna's nephew to stay. Come on Friday, before shabbat."

"That would work well for us, as we have some things to do in Jerusalem."

"Good. That's settled, then. I'll write our phone number down, and maybe you'll give me yours?"

Everyone could see how tired Anna was but the smile on her face as Sam kissed her goodbye was beautiful. She clutched his hand and kissed his palm, folding his fingers over.

"There, take that with you and remember me until the weekend. And you may both call me 'Aunt Anna'," she added, smiling through even more tears. She stayed on the settee as Yaacov took them to the door.

"I can see why the children in the school love her," said Shulamit as she revved the engine rather violently and accelerated rapidly out onto the road, just missing a large wagon. Sam and Helen closed their eyes.

Anna and Yaacov were discussing the visitors.

"I can't believe my sister is alive. That kapo was so sure she had died. And how awful for Sam," she lingered over his name. "How awful for my nephew to see his mother's name on the list of the dead. We must prepare for the weekend, I think. I will not know how to explain everything to him. When he finds out what I did, he may not want to know me at all."

"I think that is very unlikely, my dear. I could see from his eyes that he is a very kind man, and I liked his wife, too. Whatever you did or didn't do during the war was because of circumstances. And it kept you alive. If it hadn't been for that, we would never have met and we would not be so happily married."

Anna reached for him as she signed, "You always know what to say, Yaacov. You are the most wonderful, caring man I have ever met."

On the way back to Jerusalem, Shulamit suggested they stop for a meal but neither Sam nor Helen could face food.

"You must eat," she said reprovingly and, as much for her benefit as their own, they agreed. She turned sharply off the main road, swerving energetically, shortly before they arrived at the outskirts of the city.

"I know a little restaurant near here. It's very small, very simple, but the food is good and it's not expensive." The owner came out, almost before the car had stopped and led them through to a small room behind the main restaurant. Without asking, he put plates of salad and

109

aubergine pate, bread and hummus on the table; bowls of soup appeared and he sat with them while they ate.

"We were in the army together," Shulamit said, "but now Yuval is the proud owner of his own place. And the food is good, isn't it."

Faced with the simple fare, Sam and Helen found their appetites and did justice to what was in front of them, and when Shulamit explained why they had gone to Haifa, she was told the meal was 'on the house'.

"It's always a miracle when someone is found. So many were exterminated; some families were completely wiped out. Your mother and aunt are lucky," Sam was told and he smiled unconsciously. Only a Jew could say a fellow Jew was 'lucky' after they had lost most of their family in the Holocaust. A parcel of food was pressed into his hand.

"Take this in case you're hungry later. You can rest tonight as you won't need to cook."

Shulamit stopped the car outside the block of flats and reached across Helen to open the door, which seemed to have stuck a little. They unravelled themselves onto the street and waved as she drove off, leapfrogging along the road. Sam looked at his watch.

"I'm glad it's still fairly early; there's time to try and dissect what Anna said. There were so many questions I wanted to ask...I still can't get over how like ma Anna, sorry Aunt Anna is. If it wasn't for the difference in height, I would say they were twins."

"We did the right thing, Sam, letting her get some rest. She'll have time to process what's happened. Strange, though, she didn't ask if ma had a telephone. I would have thought she would want to speak to her."

"Perhaps she was in such shock she didn't think of it. I'm glad, really, because it will give me time to work out how to tell her what happened to ma. In the meantime, I still have the appointment at the Beth Din to worry over. You'll come with me, won't you?"

Surprisingly, after the emotion of the meeting, and despite their feeling that they would be awake all night, they slept well. Dawn broke and the birds singing outside their window brought them back into the world. They had left the balcony door open all night, trying to keep the bedroom as cool as possible but were still hot and sticky, and extremely glad the shower worked.

"Should we take a taxi?" Sam wondered. "Or would you prefer to walk?"

"I'm so enjoying being here that I think a slow walk would be good. I'll put sandals on, though!" smiled Helen. "Smart ones, of course."

It took them almost an hour to walk from the flat to the offices of the Beth Din.

"It's amazing," said Sam. "It's a long time since we were last here, yet I remember as if it were yesterday, how to get around."

"And that's without all the new building to confuse you. You're a bit like a homing pigeon, aren't you! Or you have an elephant's memory. We're here, anyway, Sam. Deep breath and then we go in."

The offices were built of white stone and very unassuming, considering the responsibilities the Beth Din had in agreeing conversions and marriages. The double doors kept opening and shutting as men wearing the traditional large black hats, their peyot shaking in the wind, moved swiftly up the steps. Modestly dressed women, some holding the hands of children, walked more sedately into the foyer. Sam and Helen pressed their fingers onto the mezuzzah on the door, then followed behind and went up to the desk.

"I have an appointment at ten thirty with Dayan Berthold. Could you tell me where I have to go, please?"

The receptionist looked at her list and asked Sam to give his name. She ran her finger down the column of names, then said,

"The dayan will come for you when he's ready. Please take a seat."

Sam sat, very conscious that his whole future depended on the decision Dayan Berthold and his fellow judges were going to make.

CHAPTER 13

They didn't have long to wait. A heavily built man with a serious expression on his face emerged from a door halfway down the corridor. Sam was already on his feet, and Helen stood up too, as the man stopped in front of them.

"Mr and Mrs Goldman, I assume," he said slowly and carefully. It was obvious that English wasn't his first language. "Follow me please, and we'll go into the office. The others are waiting."

He ushered them in and they saw two other men wearing white shirts and black jackets, kippot placed firmly on their heads, sitting behind a long wooden table. Several large books were already open and a notebook and pen were placed ready by each man. Dayan Berthold took his place between his colleagues; it was clear he would be in control of the meeting.

"Please take a seat, and we'll see what we can do to sort out this problem." He cleared his throat noisily and said, "first of all, I should introduce my colleagues; on my left is Dayan Cohn and on my right, Dayan Lintz. They are both very experienced in conversion conundrums." He chuckled and then resumed a serious expression.

"I think we're all clear about Mr Goldman's position. As far as I know, we've never had to deal with a situation like this before. Of course, we have been talking to Rabbi Hershell in England, who has given you a wonderful reference, and has outlined some of the difficulties. We think there are two major problems; the question of your religious position, and whether or not you are able to continue as a rabbi. The latter has caused a whole host of issues..."

One of the other men interrupted.

"The first problem we can deal with quite quickly so let's leave the other until later. Agreed? Under our normal procedure, we would expect the rabbi of a community where a candidate has expressed an interest in conversion, to explain exactly what is involved. I imagine you have done this in the past?"

Sam nodded, "many times."

"And then, if you felt the candidate was sincere and knew exactly what the process entailed, you would outline what was expected; attendance regularly at services; a course of study; circumcision for men, of course; learning about our life cycle events and then a final meeting with the Beth Din."

"Indeed, indeed," interjected the third man. "However, in your case, we have deliberated how we can achieve this. First of all, we will ask you if you wish to become Jewish."

Sam felt the blood rushing to his face. He had always thought he was Jewish but he realised that the three judges were as much at sea as he. He answered firmly,

"Yes, I do wish to become Jewish."

114

Dayan Berthold continued. "You understand we had to ask the question. We cannot take it as a given."

Turning to Helen,

"I need to be assured that you, Mrs Goldman, have not in any way forced him into this decision."

Helen's face, too, flushed. This was not something she was expecting. Nonetheless, she answered steadily, telling the three judges that she had not in any way pressured or coerced her husband in his decision to accept the Jewish faith. She was breathless when she finished speaking but was grateful for the sympathetic looks the men were giving her.

"Now we have determined that, we can move on. Will you take notes, please, Dayan Cohn?" He continued,

"I don't think that any of the normal requisites can be in any doubt. You have, since you were born, fulfilled everything we would ask of anyone wishing to convert." He looked at Helen,

"I am sure you know that it is not common practice to have a relative of the proselyte in the room whilst he or she is being interviewed. This is such an unusual case, that we felt it was important you confirmed your husband's wish to become Jewish."

Rabbi Cohn chortled.

"We did not expect anything else, other than the answer you gave."

Dayan Berthold rustled amongst the papers on his desk.

"I have a fax here…somewhere…from Rabbi Langer. It confirms your brit milah." He muttered to himself as he flicked through the pile of documents.

"Ah, here it is. There is no doubt of its accuracy but I'm afraid it is not valid. Rabbi Langer is a rabbi of great standing and there is no doubt that he did carry out your brit, even though he is unable to confirm the actual date, saying it was shortly before the end of world war two. We are prepared to accept that; there were so many hardships at that time and accurate records were difficult to keep. However, at the time of your circumcision you were not halachically Jewish, and this does present a problem. Before your arrival we consulted with each other and have come to the conclusion that you should undergo hatafat dam brit, like all other male candidates for conversion who have previously been circumcised."

Sam had been expecting this; it was only right and proper and he would have a certificate to prove its legitimacy.

"We have taken the liberty of making an appointment for you, provisionally of course, with Doctor Lambert on Thursday. Will that be convenient for you?"

"The sooner the better."

All three judges smiled with relief. They had conferred before the meeting but they hadn't met Sam, and didn't know if he would be happy to agree to their suggestion. It had been made quite clear to them that Sam would be a great loss to the rabbinate; he had, after all, been in the running for Chief Rabbi. They would do whatever they could, whatever was halachically correct, to ensure he continued as a rabbi.

Dayan Cohn passed a slip of paper over to Sam.

"This is the telephone number you need to confirm the arrangements to see the doctor. Maybe you would like to call now?" he added, pushing the telephone across the desk.

Sam spoke briefly and replaced the receiver carefully.

"That's all sorted," he said. "Nine o'clock on Thursday morning. I will need a rabbi with me; would one of you come along?"

"I would be honoured," said Dayan Lintz. I don't have any classes on Thursday morning so I'm free. As you know, this is just a small procedure, a symbolic letting of blood. I am assured that there is no discomfort. Afterwards, we will all meet again here, and you will receive your certificate of conversion. You will need to also make an appointment at the mikvah – it gets very busy on erev shabbat." He looked at his colleagues.

"I think we are all of the same mind; if you have completed everything which is necessary, and the small...er...incision has healed, you will be able to attend shul on shabbat morning wearing your tallit. There are many synagogues you can choose for your first visit as a Jew." All three men leaned over the desk to shake Sam's hand, and greatly daring, Helen kissed him.

"Thank you so much, gentlemen," Sam responded. "I'm not sure you are able to understand what this means to me. I have lived all my life as a Jew and I was devastated at first to discover I was not entitled to be Jewish." He looked at Helen. "But this has reinforced how important Judaism is to me."

"We can relax a little now," said Dayan Berthold, "and discuss the way forward for you."

"You mean the rabbinate."

"Not exactly, I was thinking of this week only. By shabbat you will be able to take your place in shul, wearing your tallit. Now, I understand from the Chief Rabbi that there was a media frenzy in England. It could happen here also. I assume you would not wish this."

"Indeed we would not," Sam replied, including Helen in his answer. "It is a great occasion, of course, but it is confirming my status...not just conferring it. I would like the whole thing to be carried out as sensitively as possible."

"That won't be a problem." He looked at the others who were nodding their heads. "We can do that but would you like an aliyah? I suggest you come to services at my shul and that way there'll be no fuss."

"I would like that. However, we," he hesitated over the words, "that is Helen and I, have one further problem."

Helen's face reddened as she realised what Sam was about to say and she looked away, embarrassed.

"It is many years since our chuppah but, since the discovery of my rather...unorthodox background, we realise that we are not married in Jewish law. We need to put that right."

Dayan Berthold smiled at them both.

"I'm glad you raised the subject. My colleagues and I have already talked about this and we suggest that, after you visit the mikvah, you come to my office in the synagogue and we will do whatever is necessary. There will be a chuppah and a new ketubah ready. Under normal circumstances, we would ask if you would like anyone present but I suspect you just want to put matters right with as little fuss as possible."

"You're right," said Sam. "We have felt very uncomfortable since we learned we were not, strictly speaking, married. Thank you for dealing with this so sensitively. Until Thursday, gentlemen."

"Do you think it would be unseemly if I did a little dance out here?" asked Sam as he and Helen went out into the street.

"Unseemly? Well maybe a little, but feel free, darling. You did so well."

"And so did Rabbi Hershell and the dayanim. They have really made this as simple as possible. Let's celebrate. How about a special lunch?"

"You know what, Sam, I think it would be better to wait until after we're married," Helen said with a mischievous glint in her eyes.

"And, talking about the weekend…we were supposed to go back to Haifa on Friday. You'll need to contact Anna."

"I'd forgotten about that. Should I postpone the hatafat dam brit?"

"I don't think you should. It's the gateway to your new life and I know you are on tenterhooks. It would be much better if it was all done before you next meet Anna. I'm sure she'll understand. But do it sooner, rather than later. If she's anything like ma, she'll already have started to prepare food."

"What now, Helen? What would you like to do?"

"I'll tell you what I would really like to do. I've thought for a while that your tallit was getting a bit shabby. I'd like to buy you a new one." She smiled winningly at Sam.

"New tallit, new life! What do you say?"

"I've had my tallit since my father gave it to me on my barmitzvah. I can't get rid of it. When I wear it I feel connected to him."

"And I wouldn't want you to; keep it for special occasions. This is a kind of rebirth for you so let's go into the Cardo and see what we can find. You don't have to decide straight away."

It was wonderful for them to walk slowly back into the centre of Jerusalem. The city wrapped itself round them and they were content in the knowledge that they were on the right path.

"Let's go back to the Wall, first, to give thanks and then have a look at these wonderful prayer shawls you want me to have."

"I don't think I've ever been here when the shuk's been quiet," said Helen, "and why is Jerusalem a city of stairs?" But she was laughing.

There was excavation work going on in the Cardo and they leaned over the railings to see what had been discovered. A group of young people, students probably, were brushing sand away from broken shards of pottery and leaving them neatly in a pile for their teacher to look at.

"We're walking the streets that our ancestors walked thousands of years ago. When I see what the archaeologists are discovering, it brings home to me that we are a continuation of that line." Helen saw Sam's face fall.

"Oh Sam, I didn't mean…I'm sorry…that was thoughtless of me."

"No, you're right and I'm going to have to stop being so sensitive. I feel the same as you; we do all share a common heritage. That's the way I'm going to look at it in future."

The shops in the Cardo had baskets outside, with piles of Judaic ephemera; kippot, tallit bags but no tallitot. A large grey cat was preening itself on a stone platform and when Helen looked over at it, it came across and wound itself around her legs. She bent to stroke him and he purred loudly, enjoying the attention. It waited outside the shops, seeming to know it wasn't allowed in, as Sam and Helen looked at all the tallitot on offer.

"I can see one I like." The shopkeeper smiled in anticipation of a sale and handed the prayer shawl for Sam to feel.

"Hand made and good quality. Pure wool, not like the cheaper imitations you can see at other places."

It was indeed a beautiful prayer shawl; a creamy white with blue stripes and, on the collar, hand embroidered, a dove.

"This is the one I would like. Simple but special, with the dove of peace."

"Would you like to try it?" asked the shopkeeper but Sam shook his head. "It's for a special occasion, so I'll keep it till then. If you could wrap it, please, and perhaps there is a matching kippah?"

"Indeed, indeed and I'll include that in the price, along with the tallit bag. I can see this tallit will have a good home," and he smiled impishly.

It had been a long day and Helen urged Sam to call Anna as soon as they got back to the flat.

"You call, and I'll make a start on getting the meal ready."

Sam sat in an easy chair, and took a deep breath before dialling the number. He wondered how Anna would manage a conversation but of course, it was Yaacov who answered. Sam explained he would have to re-arrange their meeting and he hoped a different date could be arranged. He didn't say why – just that there was something which needed his attention. He waited while Anna signed her answer.

Sam could hear the murmur of Yaacov's voice but not what he was saying, and then Yaacov came back on the line.

"I'm sorry Sam, she doesn't want to see you. She was prepared to talk to you this weekend. In fact, she was looking forward to it, but if you can't make it, she says not to bother coming back at all."

Sam protested that something had cropped up, something he couldn't re-arrange, but Yaacov interrupted him.

"Anna can hear what you're saying, Sam, and she says if you can't be bothered to keep to our arrangement, that's it."

Helen heard Sam's response as he replaced the receiver.

"What is it, Sam?"

"It's Anna. She says she doesn't want to see me again."

CHAPTER 14

Helen came through from the kitchen, wiping her hands on a towel.

"What did you say, Sam? It sounded like you were telling me that Anna doesn't want to see us."

"That's exactly what I'm saying. Yaacov said if I didn't go this weekend, she didn't want me to go at all. Do you think she's realised who my birth father was, and doesn't want to have any more to do with me? I can understand that. She was in the camp, too, and by all accounts he was a cruel man. I'd just like the opportunity to explain everything to her. I wanted to make arrangements for her to see ma, too. Surely she would want that?"

"Something's happened to make her like this, I'm sure. And I don't think it has anything to do with you. I noticed when she was talking, that her hands were shaking even while she was signing."

"You didn't say anything about that, Helen. Why?"

"Because we ended the visit on a positive note, and because it was obvious that she really did want to re-connect. You were worried about meeting her, too, and *you* were trembling." Helen rubbed her eyes before continuing, "I can't imagine why she would want to cancel."

"I'm going to postpone my appointment with Dr Lambert. This is more important. She's an old lady. What if something should happen to her, and I'd never had the opportunity to put her in the picture?"

"Sam, Sam, calm down. Let's look at this logically. She must have had a huge shock when Shulamit told her who you were. Maybe she just needs time to process it a bit more. Remember, Eva told us a little about what happened to her in the camp, and she won't have any idea that we know. She might feel she has to tell you and she might be embarrassed or ashamed or…I don't know. But you mustn't cancel your appointment. Anna is important but so is your future. Leave it for tonight, and I'll ring her in the morning; she might feel easier if it's a woman calling. I can tell her that you didn't know about the appointment when we went to see her but it's vital that you attend. Don't worry, I won't tell her what it's about."

Sam was still concerned; he could see where Helen was coming from but he couldn't understand why the smiling woman he'd met a few days ago should be so angry with him and never want to see him again.

In Haifa, Anna was listening to Yaacov, her fingers flying in response. He was doing his best to persuade her to see Sam.

"He's come a long way…"

"Pshaw. I don't think so. He didn't know I existed so what difference will it make to him. He didn't come 'a long way' as you put it to see me. He came here for some other reason."

"He went to Yad Vashem…"

"He went to Yad Vashem to put family names on the list. Why now? Why never before. And, come to that, why did Eva not come to Israel to do it. Answer me that, Yaacov – if you can."

"Anna, Anna." He tried to put his arm around her and she shook it off.

"Don't try and placate me Yaacov Brendel. I know what I feel and there is something strange going on."

"Anna," Yaacov started again. "Could it be that you don't want to be open with Sam?"

Anna's eyes flashed. She didn't need to sign anything because her expression told Yaacov exactly what she was thinking.

"There's no need to bring that up. What's past, is past. I had no intention of telling Sam anything. What he doesn't know won't harm him."

She sat very still on the settee, hot tears coursing down her cheeks.

"You have no idea how I feel about what happened to me. No idea at all."

Yaacov looked reproachfully at her.

"Anna, my darling, we have been married a long time and I know everything about you. I know what you look like when you fall asleep and I know what you look like when you wake up. I know how you taste the raw gefilte fish to make sure there's enough sugar in it, and I know how you always add a pinch of salt to everything you cook – even when it doesn't need it. I know how you were when you first came to Israel and I know how you are now. And I know that your past is always there but if you let it out, maybe it won't have this effect on you."

"You want me to see this Sam, then, don't you?"

"I do. We all have demons, Anna, some more than most but if you see Sam, and after that your sister, maybe the big dybbuk will become a little golem – one you can deal with?"

"You and your stories, Yaacov." Anna was calmer and she sat more upright, using her fingers to tell Yaacov,

"Okay. If he calls and if I haven't put him off forever, I'll talk to him and, maybe and only maybe, I'll see him another time. It all depends on what he says, and I'm not promising you anything."

Sam and Helen were trying to get used to the Israeli heat. The humidity was high and the flat didn't have air conditioning so each morning they woke up hot and sticky. The first thing they wanted to do on waking was to stand under a cool shower before dressing for the day. Helen emerged from the bathroom with a towel wrapped round her, shaking drops out of her hair.

"I'll call Anna after breakfast. Oh, no, I can't. She'll be at work...unless I talk to Yaacov. Maybe that would be better. What do you think?"

"Call this evening. I think she might not like it if you spoke to Yaacov when she wasn't there. I think underneath it all she's a feisty lady, even though I saw a lovely person. I think her lack of speech might make her more assertive in some ways. After all, she can't really speak for herself, can she? Now, plans for the day. I want to sort out my books. What about you?"

"I'd like to go to the school to see if they need any volunteers. I know we're not allowed to do paid work but, much as I like being a tourist, I need something to focus my days on. When we walked to the Beth Din yesterday I

126

saw a kindergarten on the way, so I thought I would see if they needed any help."

Sam looked fondly at his wife. He wasn't surprised she was looking for something to do with her time. In all the years they had known each other, they had always been busy. Their home had been a hub for the community and Helen had helped at the religion school as well as the local playgroup.

"Looks like we've both got ideas, then. How about we do our own things and meet up for dinner at around six o' clock."

"Great, then I can call Anna before we eat."

Sam was already immersed in his books as Helen let herself out of the flat and onto the street. She decided to walk; there was something very pleasant about the Israeli sunshine and the way in which people smiled at her.

If only people didn't smoke so much, she thought, as she went in through the gates of the little kindergarten. Several members of staff were outside, all smoking and chatting. This wouldn't happen at home.

The headmistress was delighted to hear that Helen was looking for something to do with her time.

"I'm not a qualified teacher but I think I'm capable of helping with the little ones."

The headmistress wanted to know why Helen was in Israel and how long she would be available. This was difficult to answer so, in the end, Helen just said she would be around for a few months and that she and her husband were here on personal business.

The tactful headmistress didn't press any further. The good character of the woman in front of her shone out and she could see that Helen would be a welcome asset for her team. They arranged that Helen would come in for three days every week, giving her time to see more of Israel and catch up with old friends.

Back out in the sunshine, the afternoon stretched ahead. Helen had no intention of going back to the flat while Sam was working out where to put his books. She knew he would be better on his own, so she decided to do a little people watching.

A café nearby had placed wicker chairs, and tables covered in lacy cloths on the pavement and Helen realised she was hungry. The menu was tempting; different filled pitta breads and a wonderful variety of pastries. She ordered tea, sandwiches and a selection of little biscuits and sat with her back to the restaurant observing the world walking by.

It was that time of day when housewives had finished their chores and went out to meet friends. Every woman seemed to have a baby in a buggy, many with one or two other little ones holding on to the pram handles. Most of the women were wearing sleek wigs or snoods which restrained any elusive curls and kept their hair hidden. Despite the heat, they were dressed fairly sombrely, in darker colours, longer length skirts and long sleeved blouses. There were some girls in bright colours and shorts but Helen knew they would be tourists, and when they walked past she could hear snatches of their conversations. There were many Americans and some Europeans sidestepping the pushchairs and trying to avoid stepping into the road.

By contrast, most of the men were wearing dark trousers and white shirts, some open at the neck. They all had their heads covered – black kippot or wide brimmed hats; there were some wearing overcoats despite the heat, and the strings of their tzitzit could be seen hanging below their jackets.

A tour group came past, the leader holding up an open umbrella with a dozen or so holidaymakers following. They were Japanese, busily taking pictures and chattering excitedly. Helen thought the guide looked very tired. She looked at her watch. There was time to browse the shops before going back.

Sam heard her steps on the stairs and rushed down to help her carry the bags back up.

"You've been busy," he said with a smile.

"Some lighter clothes which I think we both need and a couple of scarves for my hair. I felt a bit out of place last shabbat wearing a hat. I'd forgotten that few women wear hats here, even though they keep their hair covered."

"How was your day?" She looked around; Sam's books were neatly arranged and she said,

"You've been busy, too. Let me put this stuff in the bedroom and I'll call Anna."

There was a short delay while Helen heard the phone ring and, just as she was about to put it down, she heard Yaacov's voice.

"Shalom. Who is that?"

"It's me, Helen, Sam's wife."

"Wait a minute till I get Anna." She heard footsteps and his voice calling, and then he was back, waiting for Helen to speak.

"Yaacov," she began, "this is so very difficult for us. We didn't know that Anna was alive when we came here and there are some things we must do. This appointment is something we have to keep. I'm so sorry that Anna was upset but we really do want to see her. I wonder if there is some way we could re-arrange our visit for the following weekend. I promise we won't let anything stop us from coming."

She had to wait while Anna signed her answer.

"Anna is sorry she was so sharp with you yesterday but she was very disappointed that you can't come as planned. However, she's had time to think and she is happy for you to come when you say. She very much wants to hear about Eva and all the family and hopes you will bring some photographs."

Helen and Sam breathed a sigh of relief. It seemed that it was the disappointment speaking and nothing else. Arrangements made, they said goodbye and Sam hugged Helen.

"Thank you for that, my darling. I'm not sure how I would have managed if she had said again we couldn't see her."

"Now all you have to do is visit the doctor on Thursday and we're back on track."

"Um, well, let's not talk about that for now; time for dinner, I think."

Thursday came around quicker than they'd expected. The surgery was very near the flat and they were there punctually. Dayan Lintz was waiting for them and raised his eyebrows at Helen's presence. She was quick to assure him she would be in the waiting room while Sam had his procedure.

The two men went through to the surgery and Sam was shown where to undress. He lay on the couch with a towel placed strategically. He felt the alcohol wipe and then a brief pressure and then the dayan was saying the customary prayer.

"All done now, my boy; that all important drop of blood. Come to the office and we will give you your certificate of conversion. I know we usually do this during morning service on shabbat and we can still do this if you prefer…"

"No, you're right, I would rather it was given privately. After that I will go to the mikveh and feel whole again."

Dayan Lintz patted him on the back.

"This whole situation is unusual, isn't it, Sam, but necessary. I suggest the next step for you will be to talk to someone at the yeshivah, but let's wait a bit. Once you have that all important piece of paper you'll be in a better position to discuss your future. So now, go and get your wife and celebrate."

CHAPTER 15

"Do you think the days are passing very quickly?" Sam asked as they walked slowly back to their flat. "It's amazing that we've only been here a couple of weeks or so, and already the conversion process is over and by this shabbat I will be able to have an aliyah."

"Are you saying that because, under normal circumstances, a conversion takes a long time?" Helen responded.

"Possibly, but we seem to have done an awful lot since we arrived."

"Could that be because there is an awful lot to do?"

"True. And the next step is to make an appointment at the yeshivah. Do you think it's possible that the rabbi who ordained me is still here?"

"It's possible. I don't think he was especially old. You could ask for him when you make that call."

"I seem to spend as much time on the phone here as I did at home," Sam grumbled, but he smiled as he said it. He was experiencing a sense of euphoria as he knew the first hurdle had been overcome.

Sam was in luck. When he asked for Rabbi Eliazar he was put through immediately.

"Sam," said the voice he knew so well. "I've been waiting for your call."

"Why am I not surprised?" Sam retorted. "I suppose you've been talking…"

"Yes, to Rabbi Hershell, who has explained your somewhat unusual problem. I have a space in my diary on Sunday morning at ten thirty. Come along then and we'll see what can be done. Bring your wife, and we'll go back to my home for lunch. I know that Estee would like to see you and Helen again. It will be good to catch up on what you've been doing. Okay, that's arranged then. Sunday morning. Ten thirty, and lunch afterwards. Good. See you then."

Sam put the receiver back on its cradle and stretched out on the settee. Suddenly, the adrenalin he'd used that morning had left his body and he was feeling very tired.

Helen moved to put a cushion beneath his head and urged him to have a sleep. "You've used up all your energy. Rest now and then in the morning we can start to prepare for shabbat."

"Good advice," Sam thought as he drifted into a light slumber.

Helen woke him after a couple of hours and they ate a light meal before Sam again said he was tired and they decided to have an early night. The singing of the birds in the early morning woke them as usual, and they lay a while enjoying the chirruping before beginning their day.

The city of Jerusalem slowly closed down. Public transport stopped early afternoon, followed by shops and cafes. The streets became quiet and it seemed as if everyone was at home preparing for the sabbath. Sam and Helen dressed carefully and walked to the synagogue.

"I almost can't believe it," Helen said. "Today is our wedding day!" She had found a light cotton dress, with a matching scarf and Sam smiled his appreciation when he saw her waiting for him.

"I know what you mean," he replied somewhat sadly, and Helen looked sharply at him.

"Of course, it's a wonderful thing to do but I can't help thinking of people who are missing from our lives. My father, for example, was so proud when you and I were standing under the chuppah together." He stumbled over the words, and Helen nodded.

"I know, darling. It's happiness and sadness at the same time. This is no consolation but at least he died with the knowledge you were his son. Perhaps that's for the best."

Helen went inside the synagogue while Sam found the mikveh. A small wooden door was discreetly placed at the back of the main building. He pushed it open and went into a small waiting room where the faint astringent smell of the water reminded him of home. The attendant came out and spoke to him.

"I have everything ready for you. No one else is coming until later so you will have time on your own."

He handed Sam a towel and a small plastic bag of toiletries.

"Everything you will need is in there, including nail clippers. Please undress and use the shower and make sure your beard, hair and nails are absolutely clean."

He handed him a small bell. "You can ring this when you are ready and I will accompany you into the mikveh. I have been told this is a very special occasion so I will do my best to make sure it is an enjoyable experience. Dayan Lintz will be here for you when you have finished." He nodded to the dayan, who was waiting patiently, sitting on a chair in the corner.

He left Sam alone to follow his instructions, returning only when he heard the bell. Sam was wrapped in the towel and when he got to the top of the steps leading down into the water, the attendant reached for it, keeping his eyes lowered in respect of Sam's nakedness.

Sam wondered how many times he had accompanied a convert and watched as the process was gone through. He had never thought that he would be in the same position himself. Even though he did attend the mikvah, it had never been because he was in the process of converting.

The attendant turned around when Sam was in the water, and watched as he submerged himself, said the blessing and then submerged again. Sam smiled as he saw that the text of the blessing was fixed on the wall.

"Blessed are you, O Lord our God, King of the universe, who has sanctified us with Your commandments and commanded us concerning the immersion." He had said those words so many times in his life and yet never had it been as important as it was now.

"Mazaltov," said the attendant, and shook Sam's hand.

"Mazaltov," said Dayan Lintz. He had a sparkle in his eye as he added, "welcome, welcome. We should go to the shul office and you will be given your certificate of conversion, and then we will marry you and Helen. After that, the evening service will start soon and I expect you want to attend it?"

"I do. And Helen too, and we will come to the morning service tomorrow."

Sam and Helen had been to many weddings but none like this. They stood together under a tallit held by the three dayanim and the assistant rabbi of the shul. They answered the questions when asked and drank from the cup of wine. They signed the ketubah and then Sam stamped firmly on a glass securely wrapped in a napkin, to the somewhat discreet cries of 'mazaltov'. The rabbis withdrew so that Sam and Helen could share a private moment together.

"I remember our first yichud," Helen said. "How young we were and a little scared, I think."

"And I remember the cheers as we rejoined the family after we'd shared our first meal."

"Snack, more like," retorted Helen. "And look, they've left some wine and biscuits for us. There's a note on the tray," She picked it up and read it out.

'We all wish you mazaltov on this special day. May your future be assured and your happiness guaranteed.'

"How do you feel?" asked the dayan later. "I think you are only at the beginning of a long road but at least you've started your journey."

Sam thought carefully before he replied. They were sitting in the rabbi's office with small glasses of whisky in front of them and a plate of kichel. His appetite had returned with a bang and he realised how hungry he was, as he crunched a sweet biscuit.

"To be honest, I didn't think I would feel very different – if different at all. As far as I was concerned, I have always been Jewish, even if not halachically so. However, I do feel different. Once I knew about the circumstances of my birth, even though I kept saying it wasn't important, I knew deep down that the conversion would go a long way to correcting the past. More important, though, was the mikveh. That moment when I came up out of the water, and said the brocha was very definitely a rebirth. And now Helen and I are properly married again it feels as if things are coming together. I feel strong enough to try and get myself re-instated as a rabbi."

There were approving nods from the rabbis in the room, who completely understood what Sam was saying and how he felt.

"So, Helen, how do you feel now that you know your husband is glatt kosher?" Sunset had come early, and they were walking back to the flat.

"To me, my darling, you always were, so nothing's changed for me. What I do see, though, is that the big black cloud that was hovering over your head has disappeared."

"Black cloud," mused Sam. "I didn't know there was a big black cloud over me."

"Indeed there was. Maybe you haven't realised just how tense and worried you've been. Admit it, Sam. You were more worried than you thought you'd be."

"I may have been…just a little" Sam admitted reluctantly. "I did worry about whether or not they would accept this very irregular process."

"Oh Sam, how could they not. Please put all these thoughts out of your head. Tomorrow we'll go to shul, you'll put your new tallit on, you'll get an aliyah and you can start to look forward."

Helen had prepared a cold meal for their return, so there was little to do when they got back to the flat. Sam found his chumash and looked up the parasha for the following day. He decided to prepare in case he was asked to read the Torah portion, and when he arrived at the synagogue the following morning, he was glad he had.

"Would you leyn for us this morning?" asked Dayan Lintz. "I have no doubt that you're able to and it would be a good start for your new life. I also think it will be an unusual experience for you."

"What do you mean, unusual?"

"I expect in England you were never called up – you would be reading the parasha anyway," and the Dayan smiled at his own thought.

"That's true, so I'd better do a good job."

"Indeed, indeed."

Sam sat in the sanctuary, in a fever of anticipation. The dayan had been right. This was a completely new experience for him. He remembered before he'd been ordained, that he had been called up many times but as a rabbi...none. He wrapped his new prayer shawl around his head and shoulders, saying the special prayer, then leaned back in his seat as men trickled in and found their places.

He glanced up to the ladies gallery and saw Helen smiling happily as she chatted to a woman sitting on her right.

The service flowed and it all had special meaning; each psalm, each song brought a resonance which was new and refreshing to Sam. And then he heard the warden call out his name, and he made his way along the row of seats to the bima. The seated men leaned back to allow him to pass by, smiling their approval. He said the prayer before reading the Torah, waiting for responses from the congregation, echoing their words.

The scroll was unrolled, the cream parchment in contrast to the deep black lettering. The yad waited for him, inviting him to start reading. He kissed the fringes of his tallit and touched them on the margin of the scroll, and then began, slightly hesitantly at first, and then more confidently as the ancient words sprang to life.

When he had finished, there were cries of 'shekoyach' and the scrolls were paraded round the synagogue again. As he made his way back to his seat, shaking outstretched hands, he could see Helen, wiping her eyes discreetly with a lace handkerchief as he sat down.

Afterwards, they mingled with others. They were introduced as Mr and Mrs Goldman, which sent a pang round Sam's heart. Helen glanced at him, reading his face and squeezed his hand.

"It won't take long," she murmured. "Not too many hurdles to jump over now," and he smiled whilst inwardly still worrying.

They were invited to lunch at Rabbi Lintz's home. It was a short walk from the synagogue and pleasant in the afternoon sun. The rebbitzin made them welcome and they sat round the big table, with other guests and several children of all ages and sizes. There was a little curiosity about why Sam was in Israel but nothing he couldn't answer. They left with a warm invitation to come again.

By late evening, though, Sam was becoming more tense about his interview the following day.

"I feel more nervous now than I did when I went for my initial interview," he confessed. "I really don't know what to say."

"Just be yourself," Helen advised. "You've been a rabbi for a very long time. You should know all the answers," she chided gently. "Think about what you would do if a rabbi you knew came to you with the same problem. How would you guide him? What would you say? You know, this isn't a question about whether or not you are you suitable for the rabbinate; it's more a way of making sure you continue."

Sam listened to Helen but he wasn't convinced that what she said was right.

"We all know this is a situation which has never before arisen. The yeshivah dean will be as much at sea as me. He may have to take higher advice."

"From Hashem?" asked Helen. "In that case, there won't be a problem at all."

Sam wasn't so sure and tossed and turned all night, thinking ruefully to himself that insomnia was now part of his life.

The yeshiva was in the densest part of the old city but the twists and turns of the alleys were familiar to Sam, who had spent his final year of study there. He was slightly out of breath when he arrived at the top of the worn stone steps leading up to the ancient wooden door. He pushed through it and his nostrils were immediately assailed by the well remembered smells of old books, and strong cigarette smoke.

Through an open door he could see engrossed students debating with each other, their books propped on book rests. He could hear the murmur of chanting from a room at the end of the corridor and there were several students walking briskly, peyots moving in the slight breeze from an open window.

"Reb Eliazar?" he asked one of the young men who had his head in a book despite the fact he was walking along the corridor. Without pausing in his reading or looking up from the pages, the boy pointed to a door and continued on his way.

Sam knocked. It wasn't the study as he recalled it, but Reb Eliazar looked much the same – a little greyer of hair and beard possibly, but other than that the same rotund teacher who had been Sam's mentor all those years ago.

"Come in, my boy. Come in. Sit. Where is your wife? No matter," he said without waiting for an answer. "I expect she's meeting us later, or is she downstairs?"

Sam tried to be still but his shaking hands gave away his nervousness.

Reb Eliazar looked shrewdly at Sam.

"You're worried, I think? Yes, yes, of course you are. We have much to talk about Sam. Would you like some tea? Coffee?"

Sam was inwardly impatient to hear what Reb Eliazar's suggestions were but knew there was no point in hurrying the other man. Tea had been suggested so tea they would have, then a little chat before the older man got to the point. Finally Reb Eliazar cleared his throat.

"We have a conundrum here, my boy. Indeed, a conundrum. There is no doubt of your abilities but I have to tell you that some of my colleagues have raised the issue of inherited traits. There are a few who think that the son of a Nazi war criminal may have inherited some of his ideals. They feel that conversion is one thing which you are entitled to, but leading a community is another."

Reb Eliazar paused, waiting for his response but Sam was unable to speak.

The words stuck in his throat and he just shook his head, the ever present emotion not far from the surface of his mind.

141

CHAPTER 16

Sam and the rabbi walked back to his flat for lunch. Sam was thoughtful, trying to absorb what Rabbi Eliazar had said and he was relieved when he saw that Helen had already arrived. She was talking animatedly to the rebbitzin, who was putting finishing touches to the meal.

They became a serious group. Helen started to ask Sam how the meeting went, but he could only say quietly,

"Not now, Helen. I'll tell you later." Neither of them tasted the food and as soon as they could, they said goodbye. The rebbitzin embraced Helen warmly and told her to call if she needed to talk. The two men shook hands and Helen and Sam went out into the street. It looked the same as it had before lunch but there was an infinitesimal change in the atmosphere. Maybe Israel wasn't going to solve all the problems.

Once in their flat, Sam flung himself on the settee, put his head in his hands, and gave way to despair. Helen spoke gently to him.

"You need to tell me what happened, Sam. My mind is racing. What on earth did the rabbi say that's made you like this?"

Sam looked up despondently. "I don't know whether I'm sad or angry with the yeshiva, or angry with ma, or just plain depressed."

Helen had wondered if Sam would suffer from repressed feelings of anger towards his mother. So far, he'd been very understanding, comforting and reassuring her, but it seemed that whatever had been said at his meeting that morning had woken up deep feelings.

"So tell me," she said soothingly. "Nothing is so bad that we can't work through it."

"All right. Apparently, there are some rabbis who think that, because my birth father was a Nazi war criminal, I will behave as he did."

Helen gasped, unable to believe what she was hearing.

"How ridiculous! You've been a community rabbi all your adult life, so where's the evidence?"

"No evidence, just that they're saying now I know about Ernst Hoffman, I may decide to 'follow father's footsteps.' After all," he added bitterly, "I wasn't born a Jew. That must make all the difference, even though we're not supposed to refer to a conversion! Helen, I don't know what to do. All my life I've been a rabbi and now it looks as if that's lost to me."

"Did Rabbi Eliazar have any ideas?"

"He did. His colleagues suggested I do a further course of study," he broke off to wipe his eyes, "I can't believe they said that. As well as study, they want me to work with a community in Jerusalem and be a kind of teacher. The senior rabbi is one of the men who doesn't think I should be a rabbi at all. He will observe me and if he is happy with my attitude and the way I conduct myself, he will confer with the others. The whole group will have to agree that I can be reinstated. All of this after I've written a paper at the end of my studies, of course. A satisfactory paper," he added sarcastically.

Helen looked sternly at him. "Are you feeling like this because your pride is hurt?" she asked. "After all, you were in the running to be Chief Rabbi and now it seems you are relegated to student status again. Does it really matter what you have to do if, at the end, you are going to be Rabbi Goldman again? If they ask you to jump through hoops, you ask them 'how many'."

"Oof, Helen. Straight to the point!" he said ruefully. "You may well be right. I do feel as if I'm being treated as a naughty boy…"

"I think you need to turn this round. Maybe they just want assurances that things haven't changed. Do you know who this 'supervising' rabbi will be?"

"It's Rabbi Chasky."

"I've heard of him," Helen said slowly. "He wrote a piece in the Jewish Chronicle about what it was like for him after the war, when he realised he had no relatives left because of the Holocaust. He had escaped death in one of the camps only because it was liberated and some British soldiers managed to revive him. He was young, just a teenager, and he told how they had dribbled water into his mouth because he was so dehydrated. He went from the camp to an orphanage before he came to Israel. I suspect you have your answer there, Sam. So many people have invisible scars after the Holocaust."

"I didn't recognise his name but I can see what you mean. And, you're quite right, my dear, as you always are. My pride was hurt that I should need to be supervised. I shall do as they suggest and prove that my past will not affect my future."

Helen heaved a sigh of relief. It wasn't often that Sam became upset and she was glad he was able to put matters in perspective now.

"So, when do you start?"

"Whenever I like. I have to let them know what I want to do."

"Oh, Sam! You mean you didn't tell them already?"

Sam looked a little shamefaced. "I said I needed to think about my future. I'll call now."

Helen felt she was getting a little tired of only hearing one end of a telephone conversation but she was relieved that Sam was smiling, at least.

"You start at the school tomorrow and I will start at the synagogue. Rabbi Chasky will meet me at the shul office and tell me all about the community. In the afternoons I'll go to the yeshiva to do some advanced study. I will be able to lead services and some teaching but mornings only."

"I heard you tell him that we were going to Haifa at the weekend to see your Aunt. How did he take that?"

"He said family was important and I should go. After what you told me about him, I understand why he was so accommodating, even though he has doubts about me. Just as well, as I think if I'd had to cancel again, there would be no chance of seeing Anna."

By Friday morning, they had established a routine. They left at the same time each morning and came together for dinner in the evening. Helen found the children delightful. They were interested in her, and where she came from and asked innumerable questions. By

Thursday, when she'd completed her first few days as a volunteer, the children all knew her and were relaxed in her presence.

Sam said the same about the students he was teaching but he added how strange it was- to teach in the morning and then go to a class in the afternoon.

"Strange but enjoyable," he commented as he spread his books out on the table each evening.

"I've been thinking," he said as they queued for the bus to Haifa on Friday morning. "A car would help us to get around. I'm hoping that we'll be able to see Anna regularly and there are places in Israel I'd like to visit, or re-visit. What do you think?"

Ever practical, Helen asked if they could afford it, and did they need it as they would only be in Israel a few months.

"I think so. We don't need anything extravagant; just a little run about that will save us time. I'll see if there's anything for sale at the garage near the station when we get back. I did think about hiring a car but when I added up the cost over six months, buying something seemed like a good idea. We can always sell it before we go home."

The bus was crowded with a mixture of passengers. Housewives getting off in the suburbs before the bus started its longish journey to Haifa, their shopping bags full of treats for shabbat; the ultra orthodox, mainly young men going home to their families after a week of studying at the yeshiva, and a fair number of soldiers in full uniform, still carrying weapons, on the way back to parents.

They stood for a while, swaying with the movement as the bus stopped and started. Once they left the city limits of Jerusalem behind them, seats became available and they were able to sit together. The landscape never failed to fascinate them and they passed the time looking out of the dusty windows. The driver pulled up with a jerk at the bus station and they got out, Sam adjusting his sunglasses against the ferocious afternoon heat.

Before they could ask for directions to Anna's house a tall, skinny man uncoiled himself from the lamppost he was leaning against and they realised that Yaacov had come to meet them.

"Shalom, shalom, Helen and Sam. Welcome, welcome. Anna will be home from shopping by the time we get back. She's looking forward to seeing you again. You know, she felt bad after last week. She is so thrilled to have family at last but her disappointment got the better of her. She can sometimes be a bit…"

"Feisty." Sam completed the sentence. "Like ma. I think we'll find they have a lot in common."

The two men established an easy camaraderie and Yaacov leant over to take the basket from Helen.

"Let me help."

"Thank you," said Helen gratefully. "It is getting heavy, even though there's just fruit in it. We are so pleased we're here this weekend. Sam will have a lot to tell you, I'm sure."

They were at the gate to the front garden and Yaacov pushed through, holding it open for Helen and Sam. Anna was standing at the door, aproned and waving a wooden spoon. She moved forward and hugged Sam spontaneously, fingers as usual flickering back and forth.

"She says she wishes she could use her own voice to tell you how much this weekend means to her. She's been worried all week in case you didn't come, after she was so rude."

Helen and Sam shook their heads and Helen moved forward to take the older woman's hands.

"We understand how you felt. Sam's been worried all week too. I think there is a lot of catching up to do."

"Supper I think, and then talk. Let's get you settled in first." He was leading them up the stairs to a small white room, where the bed was covered in a blue patchwork quilt. "One of Anna's creations," he said. "She's very talented. Okay, come down when you're ready."

Sam stared critically at his face in the mirror. "I don't want to tell her straight away. Do you think she'll look at me and realise I'm not ma's son? I don't look like her, although I suppose the beard hides a multitude of sins?"

"There's no point in worrying about it. Come and eat. I think she might have been cooking all week!" They smiled at each other, each thinking of Eva.

Enticing smells were coming out of the kitchen and the table was simply set with bowls and dishes. A small vase of pale pink flowers was in the centre and matching napkins rested by each plate.

Anna flapped her hands at them and they understood she wanted them to sit.

"Help yourselves," Yaacov urged and looked at Sam, who was looking around for the shabbat candles.

"Ah, you've noticed. We don't light shabbat candles. We don't go to synagogue and we don't observe any of the festivals – not even Yom Kippur."

Sam looked from one to the other, watching Anna's hands.

"She asks, what do we have to thank God for; what do we have to atone for? For being in a camp? Where was God when that happened? And why did God leave us there?"

Yaacov watched again. "Does Eva light candles?"

Sam nodded, and Anna continued bitterly,

"How has she come to terms with what happened to her? Of course, she has a son. I have no children. There is no one to care for me or Yaacov in our old age."

There was silence around the table. Sam and Helen had not been expecting such a diatribe. They realised that the room, in fact the whole house, was devoid of any of the traditional trappings of Judaism. No menorah, no candlesticks, nothing.

Yaacov spoke on his own account.

"We don't want you to feel uncomfortable but you should know that we decided that God had deserted us in the Holocaust. We live a good life, but not a religious life."

"But you live in Israel – the Jewish homeland. How can you not…"

Yaacov interrupted him to tell him what Anna was signing.

"We are here accidentally. We did not apply to come here, it was offered to us. After the war we were brought here and it's a good a place as any to stay. Neither of us could face going back to Germany and there was nowhere else that would take us. But please, eat and we'll speak later. Anna wants to know about Eva and your children so let's talk about them."

It was the first time Helen and Sam had eaten on erev shabbat without lighting candles and saying the blessings, but they managed to get through the meal. Sam said the prayers under his breath. He would have felt ungrateful if he hadn't thanked God but he did it discreetly and if Anna and Yaacov noticed, they didn't say anything.

The dishes were cleared and a tray brought in. They moved to the more comfortable chairs and waited.

"It's time to tell you what happened to me in the camp, Sam. If you wish to leave after you've heard my story, I will understand." She poured tea, and then warmed her hands on her glass, despite the heat of the evening.

Anna settled in her chair and began to sign, "I was very young when I was taken to the camp. Not only young in years but young in outlook. I was the baby sister, although Reuben was actually younger than me. I had been loved and yes, maybe, mollycoddled all my life. When we were unloaded off the lorry at the camp, I was terrified, and when Leah and I were taken to one side, I wanted Eva to come also. She was the oldest – the most sensible, I suppose and married. But, as you know, we were separated, and Leah and I went one way and Eva the other."

CHAPTER 17

Anna ran a hand through her hair, then signed furiously. She looked beseechingly at Yaacov, who came to sit beside her. Sam and Helen waited for what seemed a long time before Yaacov finally spoke.

"Anna has been unable to speak properly since she left the camp. She uses her hands, as you know, but she has asked me to tell you everything. She will correct me if I get anything wrong, of course." Anna flashed him a look from below her lowered eyes and then signed again furiously.

"She says she is worried what you will think of her." He looked directly at his wife and said,

"What happened during the war, happened! You survived; it doesn't matter how, and no one can blame you for the actions of others." He took her hand and stroked her fingers. "You are precious to me and I'm sure your family will feel the same." He cleared his throat and started slowly.

"Anna was very young...She was the one who was more nervous than the others and when the soldiers came that night she was terrified. Reuben had already left to go to the partisans and she worried constantly about his safety. She hoped – they all hoped, that he would survive in the mountains but we know now he did not. In fact, he didn't live for long because he was caught in an ambush. Anna thinks that someone informed on the resistance and that is why they were found and killed."

Anna nodded furiously in agreement, and Yaacov went on,

"It was a small village and everyone knew everyone else, so it must have been obvious that the family who could afford to buy extra food was getting the money from somewhere. After the war ended, Anna learned that a group of local men were hanged in the market square. Rough justice, I think, but that is what happened. Anna was told this by someone who came to Israel with her. But I'm getting ahead of myself." He coughed and drank some tea.

"Eva and Leah were very protective and did their best to shield Anna but when they got to the camp there was no choice; the sisters were separated. The last memory Anna had of Eva was her screaming; she wanted to go with her sisters. She heard the camp commandant laughing as he pulled Eva away. There was no choice; no opportunity for the girls to say goodbye."

By now, there were tears in Helen's eyes and she looked sympathetically towards Anna.

"The sisters, along with a dozen or so others, were taken to a large stone building. It seemed different from the low wooden huts the other prisoners were taken to, and she didn't know why. They stayed there for two whole days, without food and water. Several of the other girls died. It was very cold and Anna and Leah were only wearing nightclothes, but they huddled together and somehow managed to stay alive.

"On the morning of the third day, a tall officer came in, followed by a small group of men who removed the bodies of the dead. They dragged them out by their hair and Anna says she will always remember the sound of their heads hitting the floor. Even though they were dead and couldn't feel the pain, Anna felt it for them. The officer saw her crying and pulled her away from Leah, asking her why she was wasting her time, crying for a dead girl. She couldn't answer. She says there *was* no answer. She knew that there would be no dignity in death for the young woman and cried even harder.

"The officer looked over at the door and a woman, dressed in prison uniform, came through carrying a pan of food. She set it on the floor and the girls rushed towards it. Anna says she and Leah did the same. The officer laughed as he saw them scooping the porridge out of the pot with their fingers."

Anna's hands were moving swiftly and Yaacov picked up the story again.

"She says they were all like animals, fighting for something to eat, while the officer just laughed. When the pot was scraped clean, he ordered the girls outside. Anna was shaking with terror and Leah whispered to her,

'They won't kill us after they've fed us. It would be a waste of food, so be brave little nightingale. Keep strong and maybe we will find Eva.'

"But, of course, they didn't find Eva. Eva was dead to them and, in fact, they were told later that she had been sent to the wrong side in the selection and had gone straight to the gas ovens.

153

"They were taken to a shower block and herded under the water. It was hot and they were given a small amount of soap and rough sacking to dry themselves on. Anna and Leah had never undressed in front of anyone before. In fact, they hardly ever saw each other naked. They were modest girls, well brought up…"Anna nodded her head, "but they had no choice. The officer paraded around, occasionally touching one of the girls with his riding crop, moving them to one side.

"He spent a long time, standing in front of Anna, even removing the cloth she was trying to wrap around herself. He used his crop to lift the hair up from the back of her neck, then shoved her roughly towards the door. Leah caught hold of her hand and the officer looked again at her, then shoved her also with Anna. The two girls held hands until they were pushed outside.

"No one took any notice of two naked girls standing outside on the barrack square. Their breath steamed in the cold air, and they tried to cover themselves with their hands. They were forced to walk across the parade ground until they reached another stone building and forced inside. They stood in line with other women and girls until they reached the end of the queue. Their names were taken and they were given a number.

'If you forget that number, there will be serious consequences,' whispered the clerk. 'Do not forget it. It is worth more than your life.'

"Once again they were manhandled across the stony ground and then pushed through the wooden door of one of the low huts. It was warmer out of the wind, and a couple of the young women who were there, came over to them and gave them blankets to wrap themselves in. They

154

were too shocked to talk and the other girls, who were lying on their bunks, didn't try to make them; they were listless and just lay there, until the door was pushed open and two numbers were called out.

"Two of the girls climbed down off their bunks and went to the door, waiting while their numbers were checked off against a list the officer was holding. They did not resist, just followed the men.

"Anna says that she couldn't work out what was going on but she was exhausted and when someone pointed to an empty bunk, she and Leah climbed on it, lay down and fell into a deep sleep. They didn't hear the girls returning, only waking when two more girls were selected and went out into the cold atmosphere. This continued all night but Anna and Leah were left alone.

"Hot porridge arrived in the morning and there were bowls and spoons. The girls were orderly, carefully dishing out equal portions and making sure that Anna and Leah got their share but still there was silence. Eventually, Leah ventured a question. She asked why they were there, and one of the older girls laughed bitterly.

'We are here for the officers,' she said.

"Anna was too young and sheltered to understand, but she says that Leah realised straight away. She kept asking her sister what the girl had meant but Leah wouldn't tell her."

Anna signed rapidly, telling Yaacov to say that she hadn't been so innocent. She should have known because the other girls in her hut, though all wearing the camp uniform, had make up on and their heads had not been shaved. All the other inmates had shaven heads and pale faces but these girls looked better fed and more 'normal', if living in a concentration camp could ever be called normal.

Yaacov looked directly at her. "I think maybe you didn't want to think about what that girl meant," and Anna signed 'yes.'

"The days went by and Anna and Leah were left alone. Every time the door opened, Anna would shriek with terror and Leah would tell her not to draw attention to herself but, of course, fear is a terrible thing and Anna could do nothing to control herself. Food came at regular intervals; porridge in the mornings, a watery soup at midday and in the evening something more substantial. Occasionally, there was even a little meat, but there was no way the girls could know what was in the stew; they just knew it wouldn't be kosher.

"At first, Anna wouldn't eat and Leah began to worry that she would die of starvation. She implored her to pick up the spoon and told her that the most important commandment was the one to save life. Reluctantly, Anna began to swallow and, although her stomach rebelled at first and she was sick, eventually she managed to keep the food down.

"They began to be lulled into a sense of false security. Perhaps they had been forgotten about. They tried to fade into the background whenever the door opened, and hung back when the food was brought. The other girls said little, only telling them,

'Your time will come.'

"And then one evening, it did. They were lying on their bunk when the door was flung back and the tall officer appeared. He called out their numbers and at first they didn't heed his voice. He called again, more roughly, and they scrambled to their feet. One of the girls whispered 'good luck' to them, as they were led out of the door."

By now, Anna was crying soundless tears.

"Do you want to stop?" Sam asked. "Is this too much for you?"

She took a deep breath and shook her head, and Yaacov carried on.

"They were taken to the officer's quarters and pushed into a bathroom.

'I will come back in thirty minutes,' they were told, 'when you have bathed and washed your hair. Make sure you are clean or there will be repercussions.'

"The girls hadn't washed properly for over a week so they took advantage of the hot water and soap. Leah didn't know how she was going to talk to Anna about what was going to happen. She was humming gently as she washed her outstretched arms, enjoying the soap lather and the feeling of being in hot water.

"Leah looked at her sister and began,

'Anna, little nightingale, do you know why we are here?'

"The humming grew louder.

'Anna, listen to me. We are here so that the officers can take their pleasure with us.'

"Anna was so innocent, even though she was over twenty years old. She asked Leah what she meant and, faltering over the words, Leah told her.

'I can't. I won't,' she told her older sister.

'Listen to me, Anna,' and Leah shook her. 'Listen. If you want to live, you will do whatever they want.'

"Anna said she told Leah that she would rather die. Leah told her that she could not die. She was to live, so

157

she could see her parents and Eva and Reuben again. She was to live, so that she could tell the world what had gone on during the war.

"She told her that whatever happened she had to imagine she was in the garden of their home, smelling the flowers and listening to the birds. She was to think of her family, and not what the officer was doing. And then the door was pushed open, and one of the kapos came in carrying a bundle of clothes. The girls were told to put them on. They were shocked. The dresses were red with black lace, and there were stockings and suspenders, and shoes with very high heels but there was no underwear.

"They did as they were told and Leah encouraged Anna. 'Remember,' she kept saying. 'The most important commandment of all is to save life. You will live, little nightingale. You must live.'

"Anna looked behind her as she was pulled into one of the rooms. There was a bed in it and an officer sitting on it, with his head lowered. He motioned to Anna to pull off his boots and then he unbuckled his belt. She thought he was going to beat her with it. Afterwards she wished she had been beaten. Those bruises would heal, but the mental scars of her experience remain. She cowered as he laid his belt on the bed before unbuttoning his tunic. Turning round, she saw it was Ernst Hoffman, the camp commandant, the man who had signalled which way she should go when she first arrived at the camp."

Sam let out a strangled cry of horror, and Anna and Yaacov looked at him.

"We should stop now," Yaacov said. "This is all becoming too much for us. Let's call it a night and get to bed." Sam agreed weakly, and he and Helen went up the narrow stairs to their room.

CHAPTER 18

Yaacov's voice floated up behind them.

"You can use the bathroom first. We'll just finish off the dishes and see you in the morning. Sleep well."

Sam was extremely agitated. He paced the floor until Helen told him to stop before he wore a path on the carpet, or Yaacov came to see why there was so much noise. They got into bed and put the light out. Speaking in whispers, they discussed Anna's revelation.

"I knew that Hoffman was a monster but not that he would have done anything like that. Ma said he was devoted to his wife…"

"You're very naive Sam, if you think that husbandly devotion means that men don't stray. Some do – the ones who think their wives won't find out. And, I don't suppose Hoffman had any emotional attachment to the girls he abused. They were prisoners, they were under his control and they were available."

"But for there to be this connection! It's more than a connection! How can I ever tell them that Hoffman was my birth father? I can't do it. Helen. I can see that Anna is still affected by what happened to her. This might traumatise her further. And I think it could colour her relationship with ma...not to say me!"

Helen turned on to her side, propped herself on her elbow and asked Sam why he hadn't told Eva that Anna had survived.

"You've had plenty of time. What's held you back?"

"I don't know, really. I was going to call her, but Anna reacted badly to postponing our weekend. I thought it would be better to get to know Anna a little before I told ma. I'm glad I did because this would have been too much for her."

"You'll have to tell her sometime and I think she may well be annoyed that you didn't tell her sooner."

"That's as maybe, Helen, but I want to take things slowly. It looks as if there's a lot more for us to discover. I think it will be better if Anna continues talking to us and then, afterwards, I'll have to find a way to talk about ma's experiences. It won't be easy – I'm only delaying the inevitable, I know, but let's leave it at that."

Helen knew that Sam would find it difficult to sleep. She put her arm around him and they lay together in silence. They heard Yaacov and Anna coming upstairs and the rush of water in the bathroom. They heard the toilet flush and the click of the bedroom door as it was closed.

Anna left the bedside lamp on so she could sign to Yaacov. The glow was comforting and cast long shadows into the corner of the room.

"What do you think upset Sam so much when I told him about Hoffman? Did you see his face...and Helen's, too? Do you think he was disgusted with me for allowing Hoffman and the others to use me like that?"

"First of all, you did not allow anyone to 'use' you. You were a prisoner and there is no doubt that what you did saved your life. You should always remember that. Secondly, I don't think Sam is the kind of man who would judge anyone. You can see how good he and Helen are together. What is a little strange, though, is that they haven't really said why they are here – only that they will be in Israel for around six months. What does that tell you?"

Anna thought a minute, shifting a little on the pillows.

"Maybe he's a teacher and he's here on sabbatical," she signed after a moment. "Or maybe he's thinking of making aliyah and wants to see what it's like by staying for a while. You know, a lot of people have this idea that Israel would be perfect for them but find the reality a bit different."

"A teacher? Yes you could be right. He seems a studious sort of person and religious too, I'd say, so maybe, yes, a trial aliyah. No doubt they want to go to the synagogue tomorrow morning."

Anna thumped her pillow hard. "*They* may want to and *they* can, but they'll be going without me. I think I made my feelings perfectly plain about religion. As far as I'm concerned, it's caused a lot of heartache and it certainly doesn't interest me." With that she turned her face towards Yaacov for his goodnight kiss and switched off the light.

"Do you think they were talking about us?" Helen murmured into Sam's ear.

"Very probably…in the same way we're talking about them. It can't be easy for either of them. Let's wait and see what the morning brings."

The morning brought rain – a heavy persistent downpour that soaked the garden and made the windows steam because of the humidity. Despite the deluge, the atmosphere was hot and the kitchen windows were opened to try and draw some air inside.

Anna was at the stove, stirring scrambled eggs and Yaacov was at the table, eating dark rye bread. He looked up as Helen and Sam came into the room. Noticing the dark shadows under their eyes, he decided not to ask them if they'd slept well but contented himself by smiling and inviting them to sit.

"Anna is not a morning person," he told them. "She is always uncommunicative, but she'll make up for it later. Breakfast first and then perhaps a walk?"

Sam and Helen exchanged glances and Sam spoke,

"We usually go to shul on shabbat morning. Would that be alright?" Anna kept her back firmly turned against him and Yaacov spoke,

"Of course, as long as you don't want us to come with you. I can walk with you to show you the way and then we can meet afterwards. And, look, the rain is stopping so you won't need to carry an umbrella."

The synagogue was only a few blocks away and it was only when they were in the foyer that Helen and Sam realised it was a progressive shul.

"A new experience, I think," Helen said with a smile. "You and I will be able to sit together."

Sam looked startled. It was against all his principles to worship in a progressive temple. In fact, it was the first time he had ever been inside one. He turned to leave, as a young man approached to welcome him. Sam stumbled over his words,

163

"I thought this was...I'm afraid we have to leave."

The young man smiled a little at his discomfort.

"You're Jewish," he said, "welcome."

Sam moved towards the door, telling the young man he'd made a mistake. He had meant to attend an orthodox synagogue.

"There isn't one within walking distance," was the reply.

Sam was still intent on leaving until Helen tugged at his sleeve and said reproachfully,

"This looks as if it's the only possibility, then, darling." Reluctantly, Sam allowed himself to be led into the sanctuary.

They had never sat together in any synagogue and this was the first time they had ever been inside a progressive temple. The service was familiar, though, but Sam, after his initial surprise, was still tense. Helen had tied a scarf over her hair but when she looked around, there were few women with their heads covered. Altogether the atmosphere was more casual – more open necked shirts for men and summer trousers, rather than the dark suits she was accustomed to.

The enthusiasm was there, though, and there seemed to be less chatter. Sam had occasionally rapped on his reading desk at home in order to hush his congregation, but there was none of that here. The dress code might be casual, Helen thought, but the prayers were not.

They were invited to stay after the service finished but they made their excuses. That was maybe a step too far and besides, they could see Yaacov outside and didn't want to keep him waiting.

"Is everything ok?" he asked. "Anna's been thinking all morning that you despise her for what she had to do. She had no choice, you know," he added mildly.

Sam was dismayed that Anna had felt that. He chose his words carefully,

"We very definitely do not think badly of Anna. Ma has told us something of what happened and we know how appalling the situation was. I'll tell Aunt Anna more later but I am beginning to feel that she wants to get what happened to her out in the open, so let's start with that!"

"Are you happy to continue telling us your story, Aunt Anna?"

Anna's face flushed with pleasure, as she heard Sam call her 'Aunt' for the first time.

Yaacov nodded approvingly as she inclined her head and led them through into the large back garden. He poured wine for them and they filled their plates, waiting for him to speak. Anna shook her head, and Yaacov looked at her hands before telling them what she had said.

"Anna wants to tell you this in her own words. She doesn't want me to explain and make it sound better than it was." He watched again, "she says it was raw and obscene and you deserve to know the truth." He looked at his wife and held her close, saying,

"You are so brave my darling. I will do as you ask, and then maybe later I can continue the story for you?" He raised an eyebrow and Anna smiled and made a 'thumbs up' sign which they all understood. They waited for Anna to begin, with Yaacov turning her hand gestures into words.

"It wasn't just Hoffman, of course. All the officers had their turn, and when the girls got too worn out to do their 'work' they were passed on to the ordinary soldiers. When there was nothing left and they were just the husks of the beautiful young women they once were, they were sent to the ovens. At night, Leah would encourage and cajole, to make sure Anna kept as bright as she could be, and they felt lucky that they had each other.

"The weeks went by, and some of the girls who had gone to the officers' quarters were not in their bunks any more. They disappeared and no one knew where they were but, of course, they guessed. The ovens were on day and night, pouring black smoke into the air and giving off a smell which Anna can't describe because it was so awful. Anna and Leah were called for frequently and by now they were grateful for that. It kept them alive.

"They knew the end of the war was near – they had overheard snippets of information from the officers. It was obvious that the camp would be destroyed, probably with all the prisoners. There were bombardments every night and, when they were in their bunks, they were terrified. They clung together shaking, thinking how ironic it would be if they were killed by a bomb from the allies.

"Trucks began to arrive and soldiers carried wooden boxes full of documents out of the office. The vehicles were piled high, and the trucks drove off. All this time the girls were still 'working'. It seemed that the officers needed their services more, as the danger increased.

"And then, one night as they were crossing the parade ground, a low flying plane dropped its load. They ran for cover but Leah was hit by some shrapnel. Anna crouched by her side and saw her gasp for breath as she told her, 'little nightingale, you have to live. Live for me.'

166

"A piece of metal was sticking out of Leah's stomach and she was bleeding profusely. Anna didn't know what to do. She tore a piece of her dress off and tried to stop the bleeding but she couldn't. Hoffman was walking across the parade ground and Anna begged him to help her sister.

'I will help,' he said, 'sie nützt jetzt nichts – she is no use now,' and he drew his pistol out of its holster. He took aim and fired. Leah convulsed before lying still.

"One of the officers dragged Anna away but there was no life left in her sister. Her eyes were glazed and staring at the sky and it was obvious she was dying."

Yaacov clutched at his wife, trying to calm her.

"Anna was lucky not to have been shot also, because she screamed at that officer and pummelled him on the chest. It excited him even more and he just grinned at her."

Anna choked but shook off Yaacov's protective hand.

"She couldn't grieve for her sister. She wanted to stay – she wanted to die with her. She knew that the rest of the family was dead and she wanted to be with them. She felt so alone; she felt there was no point in living anymore."

Yaacov could see that telling her story was taking its toll on Anna and he intervened.

"I can carry on from here. Sit back and rest, Anna, you look drained."

Anna obeyed, closing her eyes as Yaacov continued.

"The night of the big bombardment was the beginning of the end. There were all sorts of rumours afterwards; Hoffman had been killed; Hoffman had run away; no one knew where Hoffman was. She hoped and hoped that he had been killed but there was no way she could find out.

"The following morning, those officers who had survived the bombing forced everyone out of their barracks. All the prisoners thought they were going to be killed because the soldiers were so angry. Anna says she was glad she was going to die, because she wanted to be with Leah and Eva and Reuben. But they didn't kill all of them. Some, the old and the weak, were shot but the rest were organised into a long procession and marched out of the gates of the camp." Yaacov's eyes were wet and he brushed his hand over his face.

"The weather was atrocious; very, very cold, with sudden flurries of snow. The ground they marched on had a hard crust, but underneath it was soft. Most of the prisoners were without shoes; their feet were wrapped in rags, and as they trudged along, sank through the top layer of earth into the soft mud. If someone who was wearing shoes died, they were quickly taken by another prisoner. Walking was very difficult, and many people fell and were shot by the soldiers. After a while, the soldiers stopped shooting and just left people where they dropped. They knew the freezing conditions would soon finish them off.

"And now there was a shift in how she felt. When Leah died, Anna had wanted to die too. Now, she was determined to live. She made up her mind to survive and go back to the camp after the war had ended, to find her sister and give her a proper burial."

Helen was weeping and Sam held her hand, as Yaacov continued.

"Of course, that was impossible. Anna soon realised there was no way she could identify Leah. There had been so many bodies, piled high against the barracks, in heaps against the wire fences and in rows on the parade ground. She would never have been able to find her.

"Anna looked back as she walked through the gates for the last time, and saw that flames were leaping from the barracks into the dark night. Sparks, like fireworks, shot into the sky, illuminating the camp. A series of bonfires burned, as the wooden huts were torched. It looked like a painting of hell. The camp was Leah's funeral pyre."

CHAPTER 19

No one could speak. They sat still, holding their breath until Anna signalled she wanted to continue. She shook off Yaacov's comforting arm and sat up straighter in her chair.

"The long procession of prisoners continued to walk, and Anna says that it was Leah's words which kept her alive. She repeated them over and over in her head. 'I'm going to live. I must live'. She became an automaton, putting one foot in front of the other. There were times when her heart beat so fast with the exertion that she thought it would burst out of her chest; there were times when she could see herself trudging along, as she hovered above her own body, but that was an illusion, of course.

"And then they stopped outside a large barn. There was total panic, as people told each other that they would all be killed. They were reluctant to go inside. Some of the women were screaming and the men were trying to shield them. The soldiers forced them through the big doors at gun point so, of course, they had to do as they were told.

"They were all hungry...starving, even, and hadn't been given anything to eat on that long march. One of the men found a pile of potatoes in a corner – mostly black and frozen, but those who could, gnawed at them and that went some way to keep them alive. Some of the prisoners couldn't eat and just lay down to die.

"The following morning, they were herded out on to the road once again and had to continue marching. No one knew where they were going and why. There was some furtive whispering in the column and there was a general feeling that they were being sent to another camp while they were fit enough to work. If the guards saw them talking, they were beaten with the handles of the rifles.

"And that is what happened. Anna has no idea how long they walked. The days blurred into each other and they felt fortunate if they were able to scoop some snow up to suck, because no water was given out. They felt lucky if they stopped to sleep in a barn; some nights they just lay by the roadside and when they resumed their march, there was always a fewer number. Anna tried to put Leah's death out of her mind while she was walking and came to the conclusion that because she had seen her sister's last moments she, at least, knew what had happened to her. She had no idea where the rest of her family was, and that has been a continual sorrow all her life."

Anna signed rapidly, her white hair standing out against her head.

"She says this is why it is so wonderful that Eva is alive and she wants to see her as soon as she can, unless you think Eva wouldn't want to see her."

Sam immediately reassured her that Eva would be overjoyed to see her little sister, adding that Eva had been a doctor until she retired and was a very compassionate woman.

171

"But I don't think you have told her Anna is alive," Yaacov said questioningly. "Why is that?"

Sam felt awkward, searching for the words which would put his aunt's mind at rest.

"Because I want to tell her gradually. She will be thrilled to know Anna is alive but I thought if I heard the story first, I could relay it and maybe it wouldn't be too much of a shock."

Yaacov seemed happy with that and Anna smiled her agreement. She went into the kitchen to make more tea and Yaacov followed. Sam and Helen looked at each other as they heard Yaacov's slow voice speaking soothingly to his wife.

Once settled with the tea tray, Anna resumed her story.

"There were hundreds of people in the line when we set out and when it arrived at the next camp, the numbers were hugely reduced. Maybe only ten percent were left, all starving and most with cracked and bleeding feet. They were herded into a barracks and had their first meal in days – a thin, watery soup with cabbage leaves floating in it."

Anna smiled impishly and Yaacov laughed out loud.

"Strange though it sounds, it was the best meal she had ever had and she made sure that she ate every drop."

Sam looked at Helen and knew what she was thinking. How could Anna look back on this awful journey and still have a sense of humour. Helen caught his eye and acknowledged his thoughts.

"Of course, when they arrived there was another selection, but Anna was sent to the right side. She began to realise that, although her experiences with the officers had been demeaning, they had kept her alive. She was in better physical condition than many of the others so she was set to work breaking stones.

"Every morning she joined the labour gang and hacked and broke the chalk in the nearby quarry, and every evening she returned filthy and exhausted to eat her bowl of soup and hard dried bread. Anna has no doubt she would have died if this back breaking work had continued but one day she collapsed. The soldiers knew she was a good worker so they dragged her off to the hospital.

"There were doctors in the hospital; Jews who had been captured and put to work to make sure the rest of the prisoners were able to continue. The beds were always full. Whenever possible, the doctors tried to extend the lives of the prisoners by taking them into the hospital and giving them a few days rest from the hard toil, but often the hospital was their last resting place before they died.

"The doctor took one look at Anna and realised what the problem was – she was pregnant. Anna hadn't realised – she'd had no idea, but she knew she couldn't have the baby. She begged the doctor to help her get rid of it but the doctor said there was no need – she was losing it anyway. That was why she had fainted. They had to keep it a secret, of course. The doctor told the officer that Anna would be fit for work in a couple of days. The officer wanted to know why she had collapsed.

'She does not get enough food, sir,' he was told. 'People doing hard labour need more substantial rations than they are getting,' the doctor added daringly. 'If you want good work, you need to feed the workers better.' Surprisingly, the meal that night was more generous and it continued that way."

Yaacov broke off from his translating to say,

"I know that the food ration was very poor because I, too, was in a camp. I think we were given around four hundred calories a day – not enough to survive for very long. But there was no need to feed the prisoners more; there was always another transport arriving with more people on it. The prisoners were replaced frequently.

"Sadly," he resumed Anna's story, "after what happened, there would be no children for Anna. She was fortunate to survive after the miscarriage but it had damaged her."

He looked fondly at her. "She makes her life now with the children from the school, as do I. Usually, at the weekend, we invite some of the families over to eat with us but this weekend we kept for you."

The fingers flashed again.

"Anna says she will see them all on Sunday. Some of the children she works with are the children of the first ones she met when she first arrived in Israel, and they have become her surrogate grandchildren – mine, too.

"So! Anna recovered and went back to work. Prisoners coming in from other camps were able to say what was happening and everyone knew the war couldn't last much longer. There were still some children in the camp and they were protected by all the prisoners, who gave them extra food when they could. It took a while for her to understand why the little ones had been kept alive. There had been talk of a doctor who was making experiments on children and, every now and then, some of the children would be taken away and never returned.

"Anna managed to gather as many as possible together and was able to watch over them, helped by one of the nurses in the hospital. There were no books, of course, so she told them stories and taught them songs; she tells me she had been a wonderful singer, but she couldn't stop some of them being taken away. When the soldiers came in to the barracks, there was always screaming and shouting as the children were removed. If they didn't obey, they were shot. There was no difference in treatment between adults and children. The soldiers were in command and could do as they pleased.

"Food supplies, which had improved a bit for Anna, started to diminish. An air of apathy took over the camp and work ceased. The prisoners noticed there was a smaller number of soldiers guarding them, until one morning, they woke and there were none there at all. Most of the prisoners were too weak to do anything, but Anna got her children together and they went foraging. The cookhouse had very little food in it – some turnips and carrots but there was a fire so they set to and made a kind of soup. Anna says there were so many times in her life where she was saved and this was undoubtedly one of them.

"No one knew what to do. They didn't know where they were; were they in Germany or Poland? Should they attempt to leave the camp; would there be friendly people outside the gates or would there be soldiers waiting to shoot them?

"Some of the stronger men broke up the bunks and they made fires to keep warm and then they stayed in the camp, waiting to see what would happen. Many, many people died; the old and worn out and some of the little ones. And then, one morning, they heard the sound of tanks approaching. Anna took the children into one of the barracks and kept them close.

175

She had no idea if the vehicles were full of Nazis, or whether they were being liberated by the allies. No one knew if the war was over and, if so, which side had won. And then she heard voices speaking English. Still scared, she stayed in the barracks, until the door was flung open and she saw, silhouetted against the light, a man dressed in American uniform.

"She sat where she was, with a dozen or so children huddled around her. The sergeant approached them cautiously and squatted down beside them. The children were hiding their faces and there were tears falling unchecked down the soldier's face. Anna couldn't understand what he was saying – she couldn't speak English, and when he put his hand in his pocket, she flinched. He was fumbling for a bar of chocolate, which he handed to one of the little ones, who immediately gave it to Anna. The child had never seen chocolate before and didn't know what it was.

"Anna slowly unwrapped it and placed it under her nose. The rich smell brought back many memories – of birthdays and hot chocolate on cold nights. She held it there for a moment before carefully breaking it into squares and handing a piece to each child. The children took the square of chocolate and then imitated Anna, holding it under their noses and sniffing, until Anna put her piece in her mouth. The children copied her and couldn't believe the sensation on their tongues as the chocolate slowly dissolved. They looked optimistically at the soldier, holding out their hands for more.

"He yelled at his fellow soldiers and the children screamed, not knowing why he was shouting. A couple of men came running and when they saw what the sergeant had discovered, they too handed out chocolate, until Anna stopped them. She knew that too much food, too soon, would have an adverse effect and, although the children begged for more, she was firm. She promised they would have some later, as more men came in, handing over their rations.

"The sergeant spoke to her but she shook her head. Eventually, one of the prisoners came over to help. He could speak some English so he translated what was being said. He told Anna that the men were American Army, there to liberate the camp. The war was over.

"Anna cried; all those years of occupation – the German soldiers who had been in her village; the journey to the camp in the truck and the separation from her family; the selections and what she had done to keep alive. It all became too much for her and she wept without pause for a long time. She was conscious of what she looked like and how she smelled and when the soldier tried to put his arms around her she shrank away from him and shouted.

"She was expecting him to behave like the German soldiers in the camp, and she tried to run into a corner of the barracks…and she screamed…and screamed. He waited patiently until she'd stopped, and then tried again to put his arms around her. He pointed to his chest and said something which she thought was his name. Then he pointed at her and she understood he wanted to know her name. She opened her mouth and tried to speak but nothing came out. He pointed to his ears because he thought she might be deaf but she shook her head, trying to say something, but she couldn't. Since that day, Anna has never spoken a word."

177

CHAPTER 20

The room was alive with unspoken words. The atmosphere was heavy until the sound of the traffic outside brought them slowly back into reality. The smell of the honeysuckle was sweet and Sam and Helen sat, breathing it in and looking at each other, trying to make sense of what Anna had told them.

Yaacov tried to lighten their feelings and suggested they should go for a walk.

"We could go down to Ben Gurion Street to see the work going on at the Bahai Gardens," he said. "The day is drawing on, but we should still be able to see what's developing. It's a work in progress, of course; they started it about three or four years ago and when it's finished it will have the best viewpoint over all Haifa. They are making a series of terraces from the road at the bottom to the temple. What do you say, Sam? A walk before we eat?"

It was still warm. The air was soft and balmy, so they went out without jackets and turned down the main street. The lights in the restaurants were coming on, ready for the after shabbat diners. Sam suggested they should have dinner in one of them and asked Yaacov for his recommendations. A quick glance at Anna and Yaacov agreed, telling Sam they had a favourite near the end of the street.

They were given a table under a tree whose overhanging branches dripped blossom, and they had a good view of the building work going on. Sam cleared his throat and looked directly at Anna.

"Thank you for sharing your story with us. It can't have been easy. So you managed to get to Israel after the camp was liberated? Eva was here, too."

"At the same time as me?" Anna rocked back and forwards in distress. "We missed each other! We could have been together all these years."

The waiter put glasses and a jug of water down and took their orders. No one felt like eating much but, even so, they asked for sandwiches and tea and waited until it came out from the kitchen.

Anna was busy, telling Yaacov what to say, and when finally, they were alone, he started again.

"Coming to Israel wasn't so simple. The American soldiers had to decide what to do with the emaciated men and women, and they had grave concerns about the children. Anna couldn't speak and she couldn't sign in those days, but she could write and she asked for paper and pencil. When it was her turn to go to the administration block, she handed the officer the notebook. Of course, he couldn't understand what was in it – he didn't speak German, so he called for an interpreter who read out what was written. She told them her name and how she had been taken to her previous camp but she didn't tell them she had worked in the officers' brothel. There was no way she could have talked about that.

"The officer thought she was one of the children; you can see how tiny she is and, of course, she was very thin. He didn't ask her age and she didn't think to tell him. He asked about her family and she told them they were all dead, killed by the Nazis; she was the only one left.

"He looked away from her and called over to the doctor who was standing by and they had a conversation. She didn't understand a word and then the interpreter asked if there was anywhere she could go. Would she want to go back to Germany? She banged her fist on the desk violently. Her reaction obviously convinced him that wasn't a good idea and so he asked if she would like to go to Israel. Apparently, she nodded her head furiously and she remembers him smiling at her enthusiasm.

"The interpreter said that, although it was difficult for adults to get to Israel, there had been a special dispensation for children like her. Anna knew in that moment she would not admit her age. Britain was not allowing many refugees to go to Israel. A lot of boats had been turned back but children could go, as long as the monthly quota wasn't exceeded.

"It was explained to her that she and the other children would have to remain at the camp for the time being, but they were no longer prisoners. They would be well fed and their strength would return. As soon as possible, they would be allowed to leave.

"Even though she couldn't speak, Anna was seen as the spokesperson for the little ones. Some of them were not old enough to remember their parents or siblings and they clung to her. She went back to the barracks and, with the help of the interpreter, explained what was to happen.

"In the meantime, the American soldiers organised the clearing up of the camp. They were appalled to see the extent of the horrors which had been wreaked upon the prisoners. They saw the gas ovens where bodies were burned; the hospital, which was no more than a place where people went to die, and the piles of bodies left in the open by the retreating Germans.

"Grown men cried, and many became angry and threatened harm to any German they might meet. The American captain was a principled man and good to those who served under him. He offered to reduce their hours of working so they could deal better with the atrocities they were seeing. Anna knows this, because the sergeant who had initially helped her became a friend, and he told her that no soldier accepted his suggestion. To a man, they worked longer shifts in order to make the camp as habitable as possible.

"It took weeks to clear the worst away. The captain brought in a rabbi to say kaddish over the death pits, but Anna wouldn't go with the others to the service. She and the children stayed back, watching from a distance, and listened as the familiar words were said. No one cried. They stayed dry eyed, although the soldiers were visibly upset.

"Eventually, the Americans started to ship the prisoners out. They were helped onto trucks, which drove out through the gates to the sound of cheering. When it was Anna's turn, she was terrified. She says that the rational part of her mind knew that nothing bad was going to happen, but the other side of her brain took her back to her first journey on a truck. At first she resisted and wouldn't get on but the children tugged at her hands and she climbed up reluctantly. The tail gate was closed and she was left alone with the youngsters and her fears.

"They drove through the morning until they reached the nearest town. Ordinary German citizens, going about their business, kept their eyes averted. Orders had been given to them that they must donate clothes to the hospital so the Jews would be able to wear something other than the prison uniforms. This was not an order that was obeyed easily. Many people refused; they didn't want to give away their good things to 'dirty Jews'. Eventually, the Captain did a house to house collection with a group of his soldiers. They were ruthless in what they took, and jubilant that there would be warm clothing for the survivors.

"Anna and the children were taken to the hospital for a thorough check up. They were weighed and the nurse shook her head at how underweight they were. She gave out vitamins and then sent them to the town hall, where beds had been placed in rows. Anna kept the children close, waiting to be told what to do next.

"The friendly sergeant came over and sat beside Anna and, as he leaned forward to speak to her, she noticed a glint of gold under his tunic. He followed her eyes and undid his top button to show her what was underneath. He was wearing a small Magen Dovid, suspended from a chain around his neck.

"Anna says she couldn't believe her eyes. She pointed to it and he understood she was asking him why he was wearing it but she didn't understand his reply. The interpreter had wandered over and he told her the sergeant was Jewish. Anna was amazed and wanted to know how he could be Jewish – he was American.

"At that he roared with laughter and told her that many people in America were Jewish. His parents were Jewish, his wife was Jewish and he had two Jewish children.

"He took the Magen Dovid off, and carefully placed it around Anna's neck."

Anna leaned forward and Helen and Sam could see what she was pointing to.

"She's never taken it off. Of course, she was very curious as to how a Jewish American could find himself in Germany. He explained that he had volunteered to work with the liberating forces. There had been a lot of press coverage about the conditions in the camps and he wanted to do his bit. Anna understood – how could she not and, to this day, they keep in touch. Ben is a grandfather now but he has visited us here with his wife. Anna has often said that he was kind of the only family she had...until now!"

They walked back to the house in thoughtful mode. Sam turned to Anna.

"I think you need a rest and I am sure there is still a lot more to tell. Would you come and visit us next weekend in Jerusalem. There is still a lot we don't know about each other."

Helen nodded agreement. The flat had two bedrooms and she was beginning to feel a great warmth for this new aunt by marriage and her sculptor husband.

"As long as we don't have to go to synagogue on shabbat," Yaacov said with a broad smile.

Helen and Sam were already feeling like locals as they climbed aboard the Jerusalem bus. They had abandoned the concept of queuing and pushed their way, like real Israelis, to seats at the back. Helen's bag was filled with left overs. How alike the two sisters were, she thought, and how wonderful it would be when they were together.

Jerusalem was alive as they walked down to their flat, although the Mahane Yehuda market was closing down. The shopkeepers were sweeping the floors and piling rubbish outside, ready for the refuse collection. The smell of strawberries and melon hung in the air, and Helen darted in to the last open stall and bought a large bag of soft fruit.

"Supper," she said. "Easy and healthy."

The air in the flat was slightly stale and they opened the windows and sat on the balcony, the bowl of strawberries in front of them.

"Have you decided when to tell ma about Anna?" Helen asked cautiously. "I think we've heard the worst."

"I'm going to call her now. It would be better if she had someone with her, but the twins aren't there now they're back at university. She's going to get such a shock, but hopefully a good one."

Two and a half thousand miles away, the phone rang in the Bournemouth flat. It was a few minutes before they heard Eva's voice and her usual enquiry,

"What's the matter? Are you all right?"

"We're fine, ma," replied Sam, "and we have some wonderful news for you. Please sit down before we tell you."

"Tell me, Sam. What is it?"

"Sit, ma!"

They heard the sound of a chair scraping across the floor as Eva pulled it near to the hall table, and the whoosh of her breath as she sat.

"So, okay, Sam. Now tell."

As gently as he could, Sam explained what they'd discovered at Yad Vashem and waited for Eva's response. He omitted to tell her that her name was amongst the dead; only that Anna's name was not on the list.

"I don't understand, Sam. How could the family names be there but not Anna's? Who put them there?"

"Anna put them there, ma. It was Anna."

"It can't have been Anna. She and Leah died in the camp. Someone has made a mistake."

"No mistake. I've met her. She's married and she lives in Haifa. We've just come back from there. She and her husband are coming to stay with us next weekend."

"Sam, is it really true? You're sure? You don't know her – what she looks like. Are you sure it's her?" Eva's voice trembled. "I've heard stories of concentration camp guards passing themselves off as prisoners to avoid prosecution. This person you met might have been one of them. You must be careful."

"No one could doubt that she is your sister, ma; a smaller version – you might almost say pocket size, but she is the image of you. Not only does she look like you, she also cooks like you. Believe me; it's Anna all right."

"Where has she been all these time? Why didn't she look for me? All those missing years," and Sam could hear the grief in her voice.

"She's been in Israel since she was liberated from the camp and she didn't look for you because she thought you were dead. Apparently a kapo told her. And that's the reason why you didn't look for her, isn't it. You thought she and the rest of the family were dead."

"It's true, it's true. I did. I thought they had all gone into the ovens. What kind of a life has she had? Is she happy? Does she have children? And Sam, have you told her about…?"

"So many questions, ma. I can't give you every answer now. She's started to tell me but I know there is much more. As yet, I haven't said anything about Hoffman – that's for later."

"In that case, I'm coming to Israel."

CHAPTER 21

Sam started to tell Helen what Eva had said, and then the phone rang. He shrugged his shoulders.

"It'll be ma, I expect. She's probably regretting she said she would come here – you know how she feels about flying." But it wasn't Eva. The clear tone of Esther's voice came down the line.

"Esther," said Sam with delight. "How good to hear you. How's things? Did you do your exams?"

"That's why I'm ringing, dad. It seems that I've got a first. Professor Ingram told me, but it's not been posted yet so I shouldn't really be telling you. I was just so thrilled!"

Esther paused as Sam relayed the good news. She held on and heard her mum shout 'Mazaltov'.

"What now? A pupilage with a good chambers?"

"That's why I'm calling, dad. I really need to talk about what I do next. Term's finished so I wondered if you'd like to have some visitors. Daniel's finished for a while so we could come out soon. Maybe even next week, if you have room for us?"

Helen was nodding emphatically so Sam said, of course. They would find somewhere for them. There was a spare room and a couch in the lounge, but could they come after the weekend, as they already had people coming.

"Who's coming, dad? You've settled in well if you've made friends already."

"Esther, I was going to call you as I have some news that I think you'll be amazed to hear." Sam went on to tell her about Anna and that it was she and Yaacov who were coming.

"Dad, are you telling me that granny's sister is alive? How long have you known?

"Not that long, but I wanted to meet her and make sure she was who she said she was, before I got granny's hopes up."

"And you're sure?"

"Yes, there's no doubt in my mind that it is Anna."

"Why were you going to call?" Esther interrupted. "Was it to tell me about Anna?"

"Not exactly. I've just spoken to granny and she says she's coming to Israel. You know how frightened she is about flying so I wondered...I was going to ask you...would you travel with her? And don't worry about the money. Your mum and I will cover the cost of tickets for you and Daniel."

"I'll call granny now," Esther said. "She can tell me when she'd like to travel and we can all come together."

Sam replaced the receiver thoughtfully.

"Esther wants to talk to us in person. Whatever it is, she was a bit mysterious."

"She's got a first, so she can't be worried about her exam results. Do you think she's met someone? Maybe she wants to get married? Maybe he's not Jewish? How would you feel about that, darling? She wouldn't come all this way to talk if it wasn't something serious."

"Helen, you're running away with yourself but, how would I feel if my prospective son-in-law wasn't Jewish? To be honest, I would rather he was, but I would want Esther to be happy so, as long as he was a good person, I would have to accept it."

Helen hugged him. "You're such a fine man, Sam, and honest, too."

"Even so," Sam responded. "I think we're getting ahead of ourselves. We should wait until Esther's here before we jump to any more conclusions."

The phone rang again.

"What is up with the phone tonight? Your turn to answer, I think," Sam said passing the receiver to Helen, who took it and then passed it back.

"It's the Chief Rabbi for you."

"Hello, Rabbi Hershel. What can I do for you?" And then there was silence, punctuated only with the occasional 'yes' or 'no' or 'I see'. It was a lengthy conversation and when it ended Sam went into the kitchen for a glass of water.

"What is it?" Helen asked, alarmed.

"Nothing to worry about. Rabbi Hershell has just outlined what is happening with my...the...congregants. In all the excitement of Anna, the yeshiva and so on, I'd clean forgotten to call him and ask. He's also up to speed with what's happening here so I didn't need to tell him anything." They both laughed.

"Spies in high places," Helen said and Sam nodded. "You're not wrong! So, to put you in the picture; all the couples I married, who need to go through a ceremony again, have arranged dates and times. If you remember, there were a few who wanted to wait until I returned but since Elliott is in post, he's going to do whatever is necessary.

"There are two couples in the process of divorcing who will only have to do the civil bit. They won't need any intervention because I wasn't involved in the proceedings. Those couples who were already divorced, have been to the Beth Din and, as long as I didn't sign anything, that's okay too. The conversion issues are still ongoing but the Chief Rabbi seems to think it will be ok, and there is to be a ceremony in the cemetery to take care of those people whose funerals I officiated over."

Sam's whole demeanour seemed lighter as he explained all this to Helen and she remarked to him,

"You know, Sam, this has been pressing on your mind more than you think. I know I'm relieved, and you must be too."

"Relief cannot describe how I feel. A very heavy weight has been removed from my heart. I know that this wasn't of my making, but it has had horrendous repercussions."

"What a weekend we've had. And tomorrow is the beginning of another week. What have you got planned?"

"Yad Vashem is more urgent now that ma's coming. Can you imagine how she would feel if she saw her name on the list of the dead? Something has to be done about that as soon as possible. I shall go tomorrow and talk to Shulamit and see what she can suggest. I might also ask her about buying a car," he said with a grin.

"I don't think so," said Helen indignantly. "If we're getting a car, I would prefer one with a complete engine and no bad habits."

Helen enjoyed walking into the school on Monday morning. The children were pleased to see her and at lunch time she stayed in the staff room, chatting to the teachers. They were curious about her life in England but she was able to tell them truthfully, that at home she had been doing much the same as now.

"Different country, different school, different kids, same job." And there was general laughter at that. At the end of the day, she left with one of the other staff and they chatted about what Helen and Sam would like to do in their spare time. Helen described meeting a relative and travelling to Haifa on the bus.

"Yes, our buses are almost always crowded. Soldiers are either going home to family or going back to base. It's rare for our very orthodox families to have a car so they, too, travel by bus. Mostly, they have a lot of children so an average sized car wouldn't be much use."

"You're right," said Helen. "We're thinking of getting some sort of a vehicle but we're not sure where to get one from!"

"As it happens," said Raffi, "I know someone who wants to sell their car. Would you be interested?"

"Maybe," said Helen, "but I'll have to ask Sam." Raffi scribbled an address and telephone number onto a piece of paper and handed it to Helen.

"If you feel it would be worth a look, just call. It's my cousin so you can say I told you about it."

Sam wasn't sure about buying a car from someone they knew – or even a friend of a friend.

"It could cause all sorts of problems. I think I'd rather not. I had a look at the adverts in the paper today but couldn't see anything. We'll just have to keep an eye out for something that might do."

"How are you going to tell Anna and Yaacov about your connection to Hoffman?" Helen asked on Friday morning. Sam flushed.

"I don't think it's a connection," he said. "It was an accident of birth but I have been thinking about it. I'll know what to say when it's the right time."

"Before Eva arrives, I hope. I think it would be better coming from you. Shall we meet them off the bus? Yaacov said they would be here around one thirty."

Jerusalem bus station was crowded. Soldiers with heavy packs, getting off buses; soldiers with heavy packs getting on to buses, and people milling about everywhere. Sam and Helen stood by a pillar until they saw Yaacov, so much taller than the people around him. Anna was lost...her tiny frame not visible, until Yaacov waved and then there were hugs all round.

Helen and Anna walked together but conversation was one sided, of course. In front of them, Helen could see that Sam was talking animatedly to Yaacov. When they turned the corner into their street, he smiled at Helen, signifying that he thought everything was all right. They sat a moment in the living room and the silence was awkward, until Anna started to tell Yaacov what to say.

Sam interrupted, telling them he had some news; Eva was coming to Israel. She wanted to see her sister as soon as possible. Anna's reaction was startling. She stood up, as if she was going to run away, and then went out onto the balcony. Yaacov followed her, waving to Helen and Sam

192

to let him deal with his wife. Anna was nodding when they came back into the room and indicated that Yaacov should speak.

"Anna is worried that Eva will think badly of her. I think you know that already, and I have tried to reassure her. You know your mother. Please tell Anna that Eva will not have a problem."

This was the moment, Sam felt, when he should be more open and he took a deep breath.

"Aunt Anna," he began. "You suffered terribly during the Holocaust I know, and so did Eva, but not just in the way you might think. I had hoped that ma would tell you herself but maybe I should speak for her. You are worried that she will have a problem with what you had to do, but I can assure you that is not the case. It's possible that she is thinking that you might have a problem with her."

Anna raised her eyebrows, and Yaacov asked why Eva would worry about what Anna would think about her.

"There are things in ma's life which are difficult and painful for her..."

"In that case, she should talk to Anna privately. I know Anna wants to finish telling you how she got here. Let's put Eva's story to one side and continue with Anna's."

While they had been speaking, Helen had put food on the table and she urged them to eat.

Anna picked up a slice of bread and crumbled it in her fingers. Yaacov nodded and she started to sign.

"They stayed in the Town Hall for quite a while; they had no idea of the passing of time. The children grew stronger and began to play. Anna was so pleased to see them running around and when some of the refugees began to get irritated with their noise, she was very happy.

193

They were becoming more like normal children. They played tricks, and got dirty and were constantly hungry."

Yaacov paused, then added,

"I think Anna had been worried about the memories they would take with them but she could see they were recovering…at least a little.

"They didn't understand, of course, why she wasn't able to speak but they soon learned some of the gestures she developed; if she held a finger to her mouth they knew she wanted them to be quiet and if she shook a finger at them, they knew they had been naughty."

Anna laughed and signed, "Pretty much what I do at school today, really." and everyone smiled.

"Sergeant Ben came often to see Anna. He would bring a little extra food and some chocolate. It seemed that Anna had become a kind of…a kind of….mascot."

Yaacov had searched for the word until Anna interrupted, telling him what to say.

"The soldiers all donated their chocolate rations to the kids and Anna felt that the children were becoming used to seeing men in uniform without fear. She thought that would be very important in the recovery process. She wasn't to know that the next stage in her journey would undo most of the good work started by the Americans.

"There was always gossip in the Town Hall and, because Anna was so small and people thought she was a child, she was able to move around freely, listening to what was said. She learned that most people were transferred to displaced person camps elsewhere in Germany before they set off for Palestine. She did not find this prospect appealing so when the sergeant came to see her one morning, and told her that the children had received special dispensations to emigrate to Palestine, she was delighted. The sergeant embraced her and gave her his address in America and she promised to learn English so she could write to him."

Yaacov looked fondly at her.

"And she kept her word, although it is much easier for her to write Ivrit.

"They were told they would be travelling by ship and they should get their things together." Anna grimaced, and her hands moved rapidly, as she signed angrily.

"Get our things together? What things? We had very little but I had my magen dovid and I was determined to hang onto it."

"She marshalled the youngsters together and they travelled by train to the port. There were several ships at anchor, some large, which looked comfortable and one run down rusty boat which looked as if it was a cargo ship. That was the ship which had been organised to take them to Israel – a journey of around fourteen days.

"They were herded onto it, and taken into a large bare area, which had obviously been used to transport animals. The smell was appalling and already a couple of the smaller children were coughing and retching. There were no beds, no blankets and no comfort."

CHAPTER 22

"On a cargo boat? You went to Palestine on a cargo boat?" Sam recalled Eva telling him about her journey on a refitted cruise liner but refrained from mentioning that to Anna, who continued signing.

"Not only a cargo boat, but a filthy cargo boat; one which had poor sanitary facilities, no bedding and very little food. The children were upset and Anna did her best but she didn't know what to do. The journey was horrendous. They slept on the floor, the children curled up like puppies and the adults did what they could to comfort them.

"Many of the passengers were sea sick and the smell in the ship made it worse. The crew did their best, but there was no spare water for washing and a general air of apathy overtook everyone. Some of the children stopped eating, and Anna did what she could to encourage them to swallow the hard bread but they resisted her efforts.

"There was a retired teacher amongst the refugees and she took over, telling them stories about how wonderful Palestine would be and how they would have ice cream and chocolate – as much as they would like. She cajoled and chivvied the reluctant eaters into forcing some food down and praised them when they did. They began to look forward again to their arrival in what she called 'The Promised Land'.

'Not long now,' she kept telling them. 'Not long now. Maybe another day or two.'

"They had been at sea for almost two weeks when the coastline came into view. They saw the buildings at Haifa Port and a great cheer went up. Everyone was on deck, and they were jumping up and down and waving. And then they heard a loudspeaker. It was coming from a ship which was anchored in front of the harbour, preventing any vessels from getting in. Someone was talking in an unfamiliar language and suddenly everyone was quiet as those who could understand told the others.

'The ship has been turned away from Palestine. We cannot land. The British will not allow us'."

Yaacov held Anna's hand and looked at Sam and Helen.

"This was not the Nazis," he said. "This was the British, who had power in Palestine, and who had agreed that a certain number of refugees could settle there. Everybody on that ship was stunned. They had travelled for nearly two weeks in appalling circumstances, thinking that when they arrived in Palestine they would be safe. Now they learned there was no homeland for them; no country, no respite. They begged the captain to continue into the harbour but he couldn't. It was too dangerous.

"He used a loud hailer to inform the authorities that there were a number of children on board. He said they were refugees from Nazi Germany, and that most of them were without parents, and he asked if he could land them.

"The answer was a firm, 'No', and furthermore, if they did not turn around and go back to their country of origin, they would be fired upon. The captain asked again if the children could be landed and again he was told, 'No'. He dropped anchor, and said he would wait to speak to someone else in authority. The people on the ship waited, and the British authorities waited; it was a standoff. Eventually, the British ship fired a warning broadside.

"There was a lot of screaming and several people jumped overboard. They were immediately picked up, and there was more firing. A large hole appeared in the side of the vessel, and the captain gave the order to abandon ship. The crew pushed as many children as possible into lifeboats, but remember – this was a cargo ship, and the number of lifeboats was not adequate for the number of passengers.

"Those who couldn't find places gave themselves to the mercy of the sea, hanging on to pieces of wood. Fortunately, the weather was warm, which undoubtedly saved many lives. Small dinghies were deployed to pick up people who were in the water, and they were hauled aboard dripping wet. When they all finally reached land, a head count was done and the only casualties appeared to be an officer who had broken his arm, and a passenger who had a great gash on his head. All the children were safe, and shivered together in fear as the British soldiers came among them.

"Anna seems to think that the British officers didn't believe the captain when he said there were little ones on board, and that is why he fired, but me...I'm not so sure. I know the British were determined that these people should not enter Palestine. I don't think they would have cared who was on board; they didn't want any more refugees in Palestine, children or not.

"There were about five hundred people on the cargo boat and when they had all been accounted for, they were told to get on a ship at anchor in Haifa harbour. They were being sent to Cyprus.

"Anna recalls that she hardly knew where Cyprus was. The frightened refugees were told they would be going to a camp and would be under British protection. There was a great outcry when they heard the word, 'camp'. The passengers on the Aurora had spent years in camps; most had lost relatives, many had lost their whole families. To be told they were going to be confined again was like condemning them to death.

"They couldn't argue and they couldn't fight. There was no resistance in any of them so they sat on the deck as the ship steamed away from the country they had all thought would give them a new life. Captain Hendry had asked for four officers from the Aurora to travel with him, as his intention was to talk to whoever was in charge on Cyprus. The rest remained in Haifa, waiting for a ship to take them back to Germany.

"The distance between Cyprus and Haifa is not much, less than three hundred kilometres, but it might as well have been three thousand. Only the children slept; the adults talked amongst themselves, trying to work out what was happening. There was a controlled panic, and a group of men sat together to try and work out some sort of escape plan, but it was impossible. Soldiers with weapons patrolled around the deck, watching for anyone who might jump overboard. The survivors realised it was futile when land disappeared, and they were far out to sea.

"Captain Hendry and his men went on to the bridge to try and plead the case of the refugees but to no avail. Nothing he said made any difference, not even when he spoke about the plight of the children.

"One of the crew came around with water, and they drank thirstily and were grateful for the small amount of food that was dished out. The children stirred when they smelled the stew, and ate hungrily before falling asleep again.

"They arrived in Cyprus in the early hours of the next morning – so near, yet so far away from their dream. The men who had been planning some kind of escape crowded together again, and there was a lot of furtive whispering. Anna says she wasn't near enough to hear what they were saying, but no one wanted to get off that ship and go to a camp in Cyprus. They waited to see what was going to happen.

"The men began to move around the refugees, whispering instructions. When they got to Anna they told her that they were going to refuse to get off the ship. They told everyone to sit down and not move and they asked Anna to make sure the children sat still.

"There was concern about the little ones; Avi, who had become the spokesman for the survivors, said that the soldiers would try to get the children off the ship first. He said that if that happened, everyone would follow. He suggested that the children sit in the centre of the group and keep as low as they could. He told the children it was an adventure and they were thrilled, because he also told them that pirates were coming on board and they had to resist.

"Captain Hendry was allowed to disembark, and he took Avi with him. They had asked to speak to the officer in charge of the British troops and they tried again to insist that the refugees should be returned to Palestine. Again, they were told it was not possible. They had to get off the ship and they would be escorted to the camp.

"They sat there, Anna says, for at least two hours, with no movement from either side, waiting to see what Captain Hendry might achieve. There was a total impasse, until eventually the soldiers came on board and started lifting the refugees off. They were put into smaller boats and taken to the shore, where they were guarded by the troops.

"Anna couldn't shout or cry but she says her heart felt as if it was broken. She had wanted to go to Palestine; she had wanted to make a fresh start and yet, once more, she was to be imprisoned.

"It took a long time before everyone was off the ship. They were corralled in a small area on the dock, with the sun beating down mercilessly on their heads. Some of the men took their shirts off and wrapped them around the heads of the children to try and prevent sunstroke. Avi asked for water to be given out, but there was no reply and some of the little ones started to cry. Anna did her best to comfort them but they were bewildered. The teacher had told them they were going to a new life with unlimited ice cream and chocolate and here they were, sitting in the burning heat without even water to drink.

While all this was going on, the ship was making preparations to return to Haifa.

'I am sure there are others who need to be brought to Cyprus,' the British commander said. 'Britain is in charge of refugees here, and I will see that orders are carried out to the letter. There is a quota of survivors who will be allowed into Palestine and I will ensure that will happen...but only when I receive orders that they may leave. They will have to wait their turn. In the meantime, they will be housed and fed at our government's expense; they will sail to Palestine at our government's expense, so my feeling is that they should be grateful for what we are providing.'

"The Aurora's captain shook his head despondently. He had volunteered to help camp survivors get to The Promised Land. He had not expected them to be turned away and placed in what looked like another concentration camp. He could see barbed wire fences in the distance and control posts at regular intervals around the perimeter of the camp. He asked why it was necessary for the refugees to be contained this way. He was told it was for their own safety. They would be protected by the soldiers.

"Anna remembers the ship's captain shouting angrily. He was speaking English, of course, so she couldn't understand but when a cheer went up from the refugees, she knew whatever he was saying was good. It seems he was trying to plead a case for the survivors but it wasn't making any difference.

"Avi stood up. He had some words of English and understood a little of what had been said. There was silence as he roughly translated the ship's captain's words and the answer he had received. Some of the survivors shouted,

'Nazis – all of you,' but the British commander was unmoved. He saluted Captain Hendry and told him if he didn't return to Haifa he, too, would be held in the camp.

He stood, legs apart, on the quayside waiting for the ship to leave. Captain Hendry had no choice. He boarded, and watched as the bedraggled procession moved off in the direction of the camp."

CHAPTER 23

Anna looked earnestly at Sam and Helen as Yaacov signed her words.

"Anna says she understands that you are British, but nevertheless she wants to tell you what it was like in the camp on Cyprus. She is worried it might upset you...or you might not believe it."

Anna tugged at his sleeve.

"She wants me to tell you that she understands how difficult it will be for you to learn how your country behaved after the end of the war but she needs you to understand. She wants to know if that will be all right."

"We are British, of course," Sam faltered a little, "but we are the children of survivors. In fact, I was born in Germany so we are able to understand how you feel. You know, in our synagogue every year, we remember those who were murdered in the camps. We mark Yom Hashoah with a special service, but I think what you are about to tell me will be new. I didn't know there were camps in Cyprus for people who were hoping to emigrate to Palestine. So, please, Aunt Anna, do not worry about our feelings. I just need to ask you if you would like a rest. We can always talk about this later. We will be going to the synagogue but we don't expect you to come. Should we continue when we get back?"

Anna smiled with relief. Her memories of the camp in Cyprus were not good and she felt a breathing space would be sensible. She and Yaacov went to their room and Helen put the finishing touches to the shabbat meal while Sam set the table, then they tiptoed out of the flat.

"Is it only a couple of weeks since we were last here?" Sam mused as they walked into the synagogue. "It feels like a lifetime ago." They were greeted familiarly by the rabbi and several members of the community, before Helen went upstairs. She sat near the railings looking down at her husband as the service began. Afterwards, as they walked home, they compared the synagogue in Haifa to the one they'd just visited.

"Of course, I am used to our traditional service but there was something very spiritual about last week." He appeared confused. "I never thought I would say that. I never thought I would feel that."

"Are you speaking as a rabbi or as a congregant?" Helen laughed. "I enjoyed it because we were able to sit together. I've never quite understood why men and women sit apart."

Sam started to speak – to explain, and Helen interrupted him. "I know the reasons, Sam, but inside my heart I think it's a good idea for husbands and wives to sit with the children and to be together. They're together at home, so why not in shul?"

Sam didn't reply, but he looked thoughtful.

Anna and Yaacov were waiting when they got back. Helen lit the candles and there was no comment from the visitors, who watched as Helen made kiddush and shared the wine and the bread.

Yaacov spoke Anna's words,

"She says she has happy members of her mother doing this on Friday nights. Her parents were not overly religious, she feels, but they had the most beautiful silver candlesticks – all lost, of course."

"Not lost," Sam said gently. "They were recovered after the war. Ma has them now, along with the menorah and even the shabbos tablecloth."

Anna's hands worked furiously, as she spelled out her delight, but she added that even the knowledge that her family's possessions had been saved, wouldn't encourage her to light candles on shabbat.

The dishes were cleared away, tea made, and Sam and Helen waited expectantly for Anna to resume telling her story.

"So! Okay! The five hundred people were gathered together and marched the short distance to the camp. British officers were at the front and rear of the column, with more soldiers at intervals down the side. Avi had made sure that he and his men were near the end of the column, in the hope that they could escape. However, the British soldiers were aware of this, and moved nearer to prevent it. They raised their guns threateningly, and Avi was completely deflated. There was no way they get away from the long line of refugees.

"As they approached the camp, several of the women started to cry, and it became difficult to walk at any speed. They could see that there was a perimeter of barbed wire, and high watch towers at regular intervals; they could see armed guards high above them, making sure that no one could escape. The whole column came to a standstill, until the guns were pointed again and the refugees walked through the gates.

"Inside there was a homemade signpost, written in German. It said, 'Dachau in Cyprus'."

Yaacov stopped speaking to ask if they knew about Dachau and Sam and Helen nodded silently. Yaacov told them that he had been there for a short while before he was marched to Auschwitz. He rolled back his sleeve and they saw the number tattooed on his arm.

"Only Auschwitz tattooed inmates," he offered. "Some people have had surgery to remove their tattoo, but I choose to leave it. It is a permanent reminder of what happened and very useful if people disbelieve that the Holocaust ever happened. But let's not talk about that now. Anna is getting impatient.

"When she walked through those gates it was as if she was back in the concentration camp. In fact, she was to find out that the conditions were no better. She wants you to close your eyes and listen. She wants you to imagine what it was like."

Obediently, Sam and Helen sat back on the settee and waited for Anna to resume.

"First of all, the person in charge of the camp tried to get people to tell them their names. There was a lot of resistance to this, as some of the refugees were frightened and others were trying to behave in as difficult a manner as possible – Avi was amongst the latter. He would not give any information at all, until the commander finally said no food or water would be given until everyone was registered. Faced with that threat, Avi instructed the refugees to be compliant. The children were beginning to suffer and snatched desperately at the hands of the men who were doling out water.

"Can you imagine what that was like? We knew all about camps – we were experts; why would this one be any different? We knew nothing about why the British had built a camp for Jews, and we didn't know about the orders the British had been given. Don't forget, we had been told we could go to Palestine but instead, here we were, facing the prospect of another prison."

'I need to know about families,' the commander went on. We will try and keep parents and children together. Any unaccompanied minors will be taken care of, and anyone who is unwell will receive medical attention. Would families please stand at this side, the children here, and the rest of you over there.'

"He urged the single people near to the barbed wire fence. The soldiers in the watch tower were looking down on them, and they were surrounded by men in uniforms, carrying guns.

"They had all been in camps where selections were done every day; when the nod of a head or the tap of a whip decided life or death for the inmate. When they were asked to separate in this way, most of them thought this was another selection, but this time by the British. Nobody wanted to be the first to move. They stood still, small children holding on to the hands of a parent. They tried, unobtrusively, to put the unaccompanied children with adults, so they would appear to be part of a family, thinking that, from past experience, any child without a mother or father would be disposed of.

"The commander became impatient, and barked out an order. A couple of camp inmates came running and listened as he spoke, translating his words to the five hundred."

Yaacov put his arm around Anna. "I was one of those men," he said. "I translated what the colonel was saying. Of course, not well. Even now, my English is not so good but it was enough for me to tell people not to worry."

Helen was entranced when she heard how Yaacov and Anna had met.

"So, was it a real romance? Love at first sight?"

"Not exactly! I thought Anna was one of the children. I didn't even notice her as a woman."

Anna affectionately swatted him on the head.

"She says it took a while before I noticed her but she had noticed me. But enough of that…I might tell you more later," he said tantalisingly. "For now we go back to that first day in the camp.

"Faced with the prospect of soldiers opening fire, the five hundred obeyed the colonel and dispersed into three groups.

"There was a lot of whispering amongst the refugees. They were appalled at what they saw in front of them." He looked earnestly at Helen and Sam. "Now, you must understand, concentration camps were not holiday camps. We weren't put there for our health, but at least we had wooden barracks to sleep in. Here, the refugees saw row upon row of tents. There were several camps on Cyprus and some had metal huts, but here there were only canvas tents. The camps had been built for ten thousand people but, by the time Anna and her group got there, there were many, many more.

"There was huge overcrowding; sometimes three families shared a tent. There was no privacy, not enough water to go round, and there were only basic hygiene facilities." Yaacov added as an aside, "you may remember how strict the Nazis were on hygiene. In the camps they ran we were regularly de-loused and even though most of us hated going to the showers because of what they could mean, we had water, at least to clean ourselves."

Anna interrupted him again and he watched her fingers again.

"Anna says she never thought that the conditions in a German concentration camp would be better than the place where the British were putting her. Even the watch towers and the guards to prevent them escaping were heavily reminiscent of where they had come from.

"The commander said that the children would be transferred to the youth camp as soon as possible but in the meantime they, too, were allocated space in a tent. They wanted to stay together and tugged at Anna's hands but it wasn't possible. There were too many of them. Anna herself divided them, making sure each little group had older children who would take care of the younger ones.

"Eventually, all the refugees were allocated places in the tents. They were able to find people who spoke their language. Anna and four of the children were placed in a tent which was originally meant for ten people. It had three families already living there; parents with children, and a couple of elderly women. Altogether, there were twenty people in a space meant for half that number. There was no privacy and when they first got there, no beds, although a couple of soldiers brought in some bedding later that evening.

"There was a large tent which housed the kitchen. The survivors stood in line for meals and then took them back to their tents. They didn't have tables or chairs but sat on the beds or the ground to eat. The food was only marginally better quality than the food they'd had in the concentration camps, but there was more of it.

"Without exception, everyone was at first afraid of the shower blocks; some people preferred not to wash at all until they saw friends going in and coming out safely. There was never enough water; not enough for drinking and not enough for keeping clean. Cyprus, as an island, is not endowed with an abundance of water, and it was strictly rationed. People made choices every day; whether to drink or wash. They were not living – they were existing.

"There were Hungarians, Poles and Lithuanians in the camp and a large number of Germans. Anna felt she was fortunate that the people in her tent were German because they were able to talk to her. She couldn't reply, of course, but she was learning to make herself understood. She was able to use the little pad of writing paper and the pencil she had in her pocket to write her name, although she continued to be evasive about her age.

"Because of her tiny stature, no one realised that she wasn't one of the children and she had no official papers to prove otherwise. She decided to keep her child status, especially when one of the families told her that the children would leave the camp first.

'We leave for Palestine strictly in the order we arrived but the young ones are sent whenever the quotas are opened and a ship becomes available. Some of us have been here a long time but we are happy to let the young ones leave first.'

'Our children are our future,' added another.

211

"Anna wanted to be a part of that future so she did everything she could to stay healthy."

CHAPTER 24

Anna nodded furiously and Yaacov smiled bleakly.

"She says she hadn't survived a concentration camp run by the Germans to die in one run by the British."

For a moment there was silence while Yaacov watched her hands.

"It was difficult to settle in Cyprus. She had expected to go to freedom in Palestine, not incarceration again in a different country. And make no mistake, she was imprisoned. There was no way out, even though people tried to escape. You remember she mentioned Avi? He was a real fighter! He did not want to stay in another camp and tried several times to disappear. There was a group of men constantly working out how they could avoid the watch towers and the menacing guns; they even managed to build a series of tunnels but, eventually, they realised that getting out of the camp didn't mean getting in to Palestine. They might manage to walk to one of the villages, but after that they would have to find boats and people willing to take them. They would also have to get through the blockade on the port.

"Daily life began to assume a kind of order for Anna. There was little to do because nothing was organised for the refugees, so the days revolved around food and queuing. There were queues at the kitchen tent, queues for water, queues at the showers. The children were bored and the adults became despondent.

"More and more survivors were arriving so the camp had to be enlarged. When the refugees realised that the men doing the construction were German prisoners of war, there was a huge outcry."

Helen looked at Anna in horror.

"How could that have happened? To use Germans to work in a camp where Jews were being held is out of order. What were the authorities thinking of?"

Yaacov shrugged his shoulders.

"I should imagine there weren't enough workmen on the island but, yes, of course, it was totally insensitive. And, however much the British tried to avoid contact between the Germans and the refugees, there was a high degree of animosity from each side. The only saving grace, if you like, was that they knew it wasn't a death camp. As long as they got enough food and water, and avoided illness, they would survive. I know that many babies were born in the camps on Cyprus." He smiled at his wife, as he thought back. "And, of course, they knew that one day, they would get to Palestine. Anna says that is what kept them going.

"She had been there a few weeks when a delegation came in through the gates. They were well dressed and obviously not destined to become residents. She managed to get near to hear what they were saying but none of it made sense – they were speaking English."

Yaacov shifted in his chair and asked Anna if he could take over and she signed 'yes'.

214

"If I speak my words, now, it will give Anna a rest and because I was there I know what to say. The delegation wasn't English at all; it was from the 'Joint' – the American Joint Distribution Agency."

"How strange," Sam started to say, until Helen shushed him, telling him to wait until later.

Yaacov raised his eyebrows and Sam couldn't resist saying,

"There is also a connection between my mother and the Joint but we agreed we'd leave that till later, so I shall do as Helen says and be quiet."

Yaacov went on, "I think the Joint was involved with a lot of refugees after the war. My feeling is if they hadn't helped, the death toll might have been even higher. They came into Anna's camp and assessed what was necessary. They were able to improve the medical services – they sent in supplies, extra food, soap and so on, and they established education for the children."

Anna's shoulders shook and they realised she was laughing.

"I suppose it *was* funny, darling," Yaacov said, amused also. "The Joint sent in teachers and, of course, there was Anna, a mature woman trying to remain as a child. She wasn't quite so skeletal but still very thin, and not so tall, so they assumed she was a teenager. There was no real way to assess what each child was capable of. Some of the kids had been in German camps for years and their education had been severely impacted. What the Joint did was start some rudimentary classes…"

Anna was laughing silently again, holding out her hands in the shape of an open book.

"Ah, yes, the stories! The children would sit on the ground in a circle and listen while one of the aid workers read stories. Anna had to pretend she was entranced by the fairy tales. That's why she is so amused. Some of the committee could speak German and for the rest, well, there were a few of us who helped with translation. One thing which they insisted on was that everyone, especially the children, should learn to speak Ivrit so they could start their new lives straight away in Palestine.

"The weeks went by and soon it was high summer, very hot and with little shade. The tents were uncomfortable, so people stayed outdoors as much as possible. There was little rain, so lessons were conducted out of doors. By now, we all knew that Cyprus was the last step on our journey to Palestine. We had overcome our fears that it was a death camp but still, we were impatient, just wanting to get to the Promised Land. We had to really concentrate on learning the language and I think that helped to bring Palestine nearer.

"Once a month, a ship would arrive to take the refugees to Haifa. There was always great excitement when this happened and groups would gather together to say goodbye. The children were given priority, then families and finally single adults. There was a great deal of generosity, because those leaving parted with clothing or kitchen utensils. They had been assured that everything they needed would be provided when they arrived in Palestine so gave away most of their possessions. As the time rolled by, and more people arrived, there were increasing shortages in the camp – of clothes and cups and plates and anything which could be passed on was gratefully received.

"Everyone made promises to meet up in the future and most of us do. We have a regular reunion every few years, and some of us have kept in touch with particular friends."

Helen was curious about how Anna and Yaacov had got married.

"Do you think you could share with us how you and Anna got together…now you're in the driving seat, as it were, and Anna is having a rest?"

The older couple exchanged glances and nods, and Yaacov said,

"Are you really interested?"

"Of course, we are. I think this is a true love story so please tell us."

"You must understand, I thought Anna was a child – a teenager, maybe, but not an adult certainly. Maybe not even now an adult," he said jokingly and ducked as Anna's hand came towards him.

"Anna, of course, knew I was a wonderful, handsome young man and she set her cap at me. I couldn't understand why this child wanted me to be her friend. Truth to tell, I was a little embarrassed by all the attention, and I hoped people hadn't noticed. They might think it was – how do you say…not right to be her friend?" He searched for a word, "maybe improper – a man in his twenties and a child getting so close.

"But my Anna is very resourceful. She decided that we should get to know each other better and that was it. How to do to this? I could speak to her, but she couldn't speak to me. In those days, she had to write everything down and so she did. When she told me her real age, I didn't believe her. I thought she had an attachment to me that a child would have, so I decided I should find myself a girl friend.

217

Anna would have to find someone her own age to be her friend.

"There were lots of very pretty girls in the camp." Again, Anna swatted him, "so I made it my business to find the prettiest. That meant talking to several," he said with a wicked twinkle in his eye. "Looking back, now, I don't think it was fair because I know that Giselle, the one I became friendliest with, became very attached to me."

Helen was laughing as she said,

"You sound as if you left a trail of broken hearts behind you."

Yaacov said modestly, "not exactly a trail but certainly one or two."

Anna made a face, and then urged him to finish his story.

"And then, one day, I was in the kitchen, helping to peel potatoes, when Anna came in. She had been given a new dress from the Joint and when I looked at her it was through new eyes. She had done something to her hair and it was on the top of her head. Somehow, she looked taller, more grown up, and she came and sat beside me, picked up a knife and began also to peel the vegetables. We didn't speak – Anna couldn't, and I didn't want to. It was a magical moment."

Anna signed again.

"She says that is why she has such a wonderful relationship with the humble potato. It was a potato which brought us together."

"Or maybe the Joint, with a new dress," and they all erupted into gales of laughter.

"I began to realise that she was older than I had first thought. I asked her again, 'How old are you' and this time I believed her.

"And then she explained why she wanted to remain so childlike. She wanted to get to Palestine as soon as possible. So many bad things had happened to her, and she needed to be out of camps and into freedom. I could understand this; this is what I wanted myself, but I realised I didn't have the same opportunities as Anna. We agreed that she would stay as youthful as possible, and that we would be cautious about our relationship. We both knew we wanted to spend the rest of our lives together, although I could see that Anna was more hesitant. She constantly said that no one knew what the future held, and we should take things slowly.

"I told her she was contradicting herself. If life was uncertain, we should seize any opportunity but she only told me that *she* knew what she meant, and I was stupid if I didn't understand. My Anna has always been a little – shall we say determined, to get her own way.

And then, the ship arrived which would take the next group of children, and Anna was on the list. Now she had a dilemma; should she go with the children or should she stay with me. There would be no pressure; no one from the camp would force her to leave, although they would be surprised if she said she didn't want to go. She would be able to take that decision herself.

"We spent a lot of time talking about it. One minute, she would decide to stay, and I would urge her to go – the next I would suggest she stayed, and she would say she wanted to leave. Our main concern was that we would find it difficult to meet up in Palestine. We knew the ship would dock in Haifa but after that – it was anybody's guess where we would be sent.

"The next day, Anna was told to go to the medical tent for a pre journey check up. They still thought she was a child, but were very sympathetic because she couldn't speak. They explained she would be taken to a hostel or orphanage, but her name and destination would be kept on file in case anyone was looking for her. This was such a relief to us and gave us more confidence, and so Anna made her mind up to go.

"The night before the ship left we sat together for a long time. I could sense that Anna had something to tell me but she kept shaking her head when I asked her what it was. She wouldn't say, but she told me firmly if we found each other she would tell me then. I had to be satisfied with that.

"The ships always left in the evening so they would arrive in Haifa the following morning. I walked down to the dock with Anna, holding her hand. No one noticed – many of the children were holding the hands of adults, but we didn't risk kissing goodbye. A mist was slowly coming in from the sea, spreading over the dock and it became difficult to see the passengers lined up on the deck waving. I couldn't see Anna but I hoped she could pick me out because of my height. I waved and blew a kiss and watched as the tall funnels faded away into the night air. The sun was sinking into the sea, the dark orange edges blurred as it slowly disappeared. I felt as if my life also was sinking as I walked slowly back to the camp, the ever present soldiers guarding us. I wondered if Anna and I would ever meet again."

CHAPTER 25

Helen instinctively put her arms around Anna.

"You must have been so worried, not knowing if you would ever see Yaacov again."

Anna straightened up and began to sign again.

"Worried, I was terrified!" she said energetically. "I had seen my sister die in front of me, and when I was liberated from the concentration camp I thought I was totally alone. Of course, there were good people who helped me along the way but no one close to me, no one who was my family. Even Sergeant Ben wasn't real family. There was no one like Yaacov; and then I had to say goodbye to him. It was awful. I stood on the deck, sailing to Palestine, knowing that the one person I loved and who I wanted to spend my life with, was not able to come with me.

"I had deliberately not said anything about what I'd had to do in the concentration camp; I was ashamed and I didn't want Yaacov to think about it when I wasn't there. I wasn't trying to deceive him. I knew if he really loved me, that my past wouldn't make any difference to him but there was a corner of my mind which was telling me…'wait until he comes to Palestine and tell him then.'

"There were cabins on the ship. I think before the war it had been a ferry, taking passengers to Palestine, so it was quite comfortable. Don't forget, I was still classed as a child by the Joint so someone came to me on deck and told me to go to bed. I shook my head firmly. I didn't want to. I wanted to see Yaacov for as long as I could. He is so tall, it's easy to see him in a crowd." She looked at him with such love, that Sam and Helen each had a lump in their throats.

"He was waving something – his white shirt, I think, so I saw him for a long time – until he was just a dark speck in the far distance. The Joint worker told me there was nothing left to see, and that soon I would have a new home. She told me they tried to find families for the children, although some would go into orphanages. A few would be sent to a kibbutz; the older ones, of course, where they could help on the land. There would be all sorts of activities and she knew I would be very happy. I would be able to put all the bad things behind me. She spoke to me as if I was a child, which of course she thought I was, and then took me down to my cabin and put me in a bunk, tucking the sheet around me firmly.

"I was feeling very deceitful now. I knew I was taking a place that belonged to someone else but I also knew that any longer in the camp on Cyprus would have sent me crazy. I couldn't sleep. Thoughts of Yaacov crowded into my mind. Already I missed him; his gentleness, his sense of humour and, dare I say it, his kisses."

Yaacov blushed and told Anna to stop giving away all their secrets, but she ignored him. He laughed and said,

"She says if I don't tell you accurately what she's saying, I'll be sleeping on the balcony tonight.

"She says that was the longest night of her life. Early in the morning, the sound of the ship's engine changed and she looked out of the porthole and saw the industrial buildings of Haifa port ahead. Now, she had another worry. The last time she had tried to disembark in Haifa she had been sent to Cyprus. Would this happen again? Would the authorities really allow the ship to dock?

"There was a steady trickle of passengers going on deck. Most had been refused entry before and were as apprehensive as Anna. The children raced around, getting under peoples' feet, their excitement infectious, until they were told sharply to 'sit down'. As the ship glided slowly into the harbour, some of the children begged to be lifted up, so they could get the first glimpse of their new country. Men and women lined the railings, some with children balanced precariously on their shoulders. They were excited; they were frightened, they were apprehensive. They waited with trepidation to see what was going to happen next.

"And then, suddenly, they were on dry land, being marshalled towards a tent which had a sign above it. 'Welcome,' it said 'baruchim ha'baim.'

"There were many, many people there to help, and the children were soon gathered together. Further back on the quayside, there were dancers and a choir singing. There was food laid out on long trestle tables. The atmosphere was incredible – relaxed and happy, so new to us.

"At this point, Anna knew she had to confess her age. The ship was still there and she worried she might be arrested and put straight back on it but she felt there was no alternative. When it was her turn to be registered she took her pad and pencil and scribbled furiously. At first, as usual, they thought she was deaf, but when she was able to answer questions quickly by writing down the answers, they knew she had hearing.

"Someone fetched a doctor, who looked into her throat. They seemed more interested in her lack of speech than how old she was, and she was grateful for that. There were plenty of interpreters around and many of the helpers spoke fluent German. The doctor invited her into the medical tent so they could discuss her problem in private.

"This was the first time she had been able to talk about her experiences during the war and she wept copiously, as she told the kindly doctor what had happened to her. His face was devoid of expression – no disgust; no criticism; nothing. She kept looking away from him and couldn't face him. He took her chin in his hand and turned it towards him, speaking clearly and firmly.

'What happened to you in the camp was not your fault.'

"Anna says by then she was almost hysterical. She began to beat her fists on the doctor's chest and he let her, waiting for her grief…because it *was* grief, as well as anger, to burn itself out. All the time, he was saying soothing words, until she had calmed down and was crying normally. He asked her if this was the first time she had been able to express her emotions and she wiped her eyes and nodded.

'This will happen again, my dear,' he told her. 'These feelings will continue to pop up, sometimes when you least expect them. You have every right to be angry with the men who did this to you, and sad because something was taken away from you.'

"Anna says when she heard that, she understood why she felt the way she did. The doctor went on,

'Your anger will get less as time goes on but do not be afraid of it. One day, I am sure, you will be free of it. And now,' he said, 'tell me your real age.'

"She says her heart sank at this – she had thought they were not interested in her age but she was wrong.

'It's all right, my dear. I will not send you back and your secret will be safe with me but I think you will not wish to be placed in an orphanage with the children.'

"Anna wrote again on her pad and the doctor laughed, tore the page out and pretended to eat it.

'There you are,' he said 'It's gone now. There is no record of how old you are.'

"Anna says her emotions were all over the place. When the doctor ate the piece of paper she laughed, then she cried again, then she shook and shivered.

'Reaction, Anna,' he told her. 'Be patient with yourself and all will come right.' He asked if she had any family, and again the tears fell, until he patted her shoulder, making some notes on his pad.

'I think the best thing would be for you to go to a kibbutz where you will be able to rest and recuperate. How do you feel about that?'

"By now, Anna was exhausted. She was still considerably underweight and looked very fragile. She sat very still on the chair as he sounded her chest and checked her over.

'You're extremely lucky,' he said when he'd finished. 'There is no sign of tuberculosis. Many of our refugees come here with advanced cases of the disease.' Anna says she scribbled again, telling the doctor that because she had worked in the brothel, the food ration was a little better than in the rest of the camp. 'So, a good thing you were there, if you look at it like that.' he said comfortably.

"Anna knows she was depressed because she told the doctor that she wished she'd taken her life, rather than submit to the men in the brothel. He learned over to her and wagged his finger.

'I do not want you to say that ever again. You should know that our most important commandment is the one which tells us to save life. That is exactly what you did. L'chaim, Anna, l'chaim.'

"The doctor completed his forms and gave Anna a sheet of paper.

'This is my recommendation: we have a kibbutz where there is a school for deaf children. I think it would help you if you were able to learn how to sign. That way, you wouldn't always have to use the notepad. You might also find work with the children. When you first get there, I want you to rest for at least a week. Enjoy the good food and fine weather, make friends, and when you are rested you will be able to properly start your new life.'

"She hesitated before she wrote again, thinking carefully. The doctor had seemed very helpful but she still wasn't able to trust anyone properly."

Anna signed again.

"She says the only person she could trust was me and, even then, she hadn't told me all her story.

"She decided she should tell the doctor about me and he was delighted.

'This is what you need, my dear. Someone who will care for you, and someone for whom you will care. What would you like me to do?'

"Anna explained how she and I had agreed to meet, and he said he would help. He knew where Anna was going, and he would give the address to me when I arrived. He couldn't promise how quickly that would happen, but he wrote all the information down.

'These details will be flagged up every time a ship comes in, and your Yaacov will be told where you are.'

"With that, Anna felt the doctor was a friend so she made no protest when she was taken to the bus. She slept all the way to the kibbutz, waking only when it arrived at the reception area. The passengers were helped down and taken to their accommodation. Anna says she just crawled into bed and slept for hours, waking only when she heard a voice over the loudspeaker system, welcoming the newcomers and telling them there was food in the dining hall. As if by magic, there was a knock at her door and a teenager stood there waiting to show her the way. She was stiff and grubby but the thought of a meal was the encouragement she needed to get out of bed.

"After years of deprivation, the sight of so much good food was overwhelming. The children were running to the buffet table, snatching bread and fruit and taking it away, only to come back for more. Eventually, worried that their stomachs would become overloaded they were sent to sit down properly and eat slowly. Even so, some of them hid food in their pockets. You know, even today, Anna cannot throw food away and she always has chocolate in her bag.

"There began a period of limbo for Anna. She was under strict instructions to rest to regain her strength, and found that was all she was capable of doing. She spent a lot of time sleeping, unless she was called to the doctor's office. The cause of her inability to speak was attributed to the trauma she had suffered in the first camp. She was sent to the kibbutz psychiatrist who explained it was her mind's way of dealing with the horrors. She told him about the brothel and he rubbed his chin before responding.

'It's possible you do not speak because you feel you would have to explain your actions in the camp. It's also possible your voice has disappeared because you feel you should have screamed or shouted more.'

"Anna says she became angry with the man, and insisted that she *had* screamed. She felt he was implying she hadn't screamed enough and she resisted all further attempts to make her see him. She told him she was used to not speaking and it was no problem. She was happy as she was.

"I arrived in Haifa one month later – not so long apart but for me it felt like a lifetime."

The fingers again.

"And for Anna too. The doctor kept his word, and gave me the address of her kibbutz. Once the paperwork was done and I was free to go, I hitched a lift on a truck. Anna was expecting me because the doctor had phoned to tell her I was on my way. She was standing at the gates as the bus drove through.

"I saw her there, her hair pinned on top of her head, wearing the shorts that everyone wore in the kibbutz. The child had disappeared and I saw in front of me a real woman. She waved as she saw me and I asked the driver to stop.

'That's my girl,' I told him. 'We're getting married soon.' The whole bus cheered and watched as I swept Anna up and kissed her. There were shouts of 'mazaltov' from those on board and Anna asked why there was so much excitement and why everyone was shouting congratulations.

'Because I told them we're getting married,' I said.

'Really,' said my Anna. 'And you haven't even asked me yet. Maybe I'll say 'no', but she had a beautiful smile on her face and I knew she didn't mean it."

CHAPTER 26

"Look," Sam began. "You've been very open about your experiences and I really appreciate it. I can sense how hard it was…"

He was interrupted, and waited until Anna had finished signing. She was telling him that she felt he was holding something back.

"Is it about Eva?" she asked.

"It's about Eva and me – the whole family, in fact. I do want to talk about it but I would like ma to be here. She's due to arrive next week. Could we leave it till then? I think ma would want that too."

Anna and Yaacov exchanged glances.

"From what you've said, I know that Eva went to work for Hoffman. I thought she'd gone to the ovens soon after we arrived but that's not right, is it? Is it something to do with him?"

Sam was amazed that she had picked up on this and stammered his reply.

"Yes, yes it is, but the more I think about it, the more I want ma here. I wouldn't want to wait if I didn't think it was really important."

Once again, the older couple exchanged glances and Yaacov cleared his throat before saying,

"There's nothing you can say that would shock us, but we respect that you want your mother to tell her own story. We'll leave it until she gets here. Enough for tonight, I think. Maybe tomorrow we'll tell you about our wedding."

Sam and Helen talked together after the others went to bed. The flat was quiet and there were long shadows on the wall, thrown there from the small table lamp. They had closed the curtains, but left the door to the balcony open. There was a slight breeze, which moved the drapes a little, and Sam got up to switch on the main light. Helen stopped him.

"I prefer this semi darkness, and I like seeing the lights outside in the square." Sam sat down again.

"I'm still having difficulty understanding that I have suddenly acquired an aunt – at my age." He rubbed his eyes and moved his hand across his face, trying to relax the tension he felt. "I can't help thinking about those wasted years."

"That's a bit hard, Sam. I'm sure the years weren't wasted – your mother became a doctor and Anna a talented artist, as well as a much loved teacher."

"That's not what I meant. I'm just thinking of all the years they could have had together. When you listen to Anna, it's pretty obvious that she's grieved for the loss of her family all her life, and ma is no different. And to think they were both in Palestine at the same time. I'll need to check with ma, but she was certainly there in 1947, and Anna would probably have arrived by then."

"That is a weird coincidence. They weren't at the same place though – each at a different kibbutz, I think.

"They must have been, otherwise they would have seen each other. It's just strange to understand they could have been in Jerusalem or Tel Aviv or Haifa, walking past each other in the street."

"I know, Sam, it sends shivers down my spine. Have you prepared ma for meeting Anna? I expect she's changed since they were last together – they've both changed, I'm sure. Anna seems quite a strong person, and before the war there's no doubt she was the gentle little sister. Maybe ma's in for a surprise!"

"I haven't said much at all. It was good Anna was happy to talk to us and, if she wants, I can tell ma the bare bones." He sighed. "It's not going to be easy. Anyway, will we go to shul tomorrow morning as usual?"

"How could we not. If we stayed at home, I think the wailing wall might fall down in shock!"

"What about those two?"

"I don't think we should ask them – they wouldn't come anyway, and I understand how they feel. They might like a longer sleep, or they might go out for a walk. I'll leave it up to them."

Anna offered to prepare lunch while Sam and Helen went to the synagogue and when they returned, the table was set with an assortment of salads, hummus and cheeses. The atmosphere was charged with emotion, until Helen said,

"Please tell us about your wedding. I can't wait any longer. Did you get married in the kibbutz?" asked Helen. "I think that might have been rather special."

Yaacov looked carefully at Anna and waited. She nodded slowly, signed a few words and then sat back, letting him speak.

"Before I tell you about the wedding I have to tell you that Anna really didn't want to get married. I had no doubt she loved me but there was something which prevented her from wanting to proceed, even though she had joked about it when I first arrived. We would walk in the evenings and sometimes I felt she was on the brink of speaking, but always the moment passed and I was none the wiser.

"One night we sat on a bench on the covered terrace overlooking the garden. It was raining – one of those downpours which sometimes happens and which stops as quickly as it begins. It was getting dark, and I could hear the crickets making that peculiar noise with their legs. A flock of birds flew overhead, and their raucous crowing interrupted my thoughts. Anna took my hand – I could hardly see her face in the fading light and then she showed me her note pad. We moved until we were under the outside light and I could see to read. On it she had written all about the horrors of the camp; she told me everything, and finished by saying that is why, although she loved me very much, she could never marry me. She took her pencil out and underlined the word 'never' so firmly, that the point of the pencil made a hole in the paper.

"When she stood up to walk away, I pulled her down beside me. I told her that what had happened made no difference to my feelings. She pushed the note pad into my face and shook her head violently. I could make out her lips shaping the word 'no', but it was soundless.

"And then she ran away. She just got up and ran. I was shocked; not because of what she'd told me but because she didn't think my feelings were strong enough. The night came down fast, and I continued to sit, pondering over what to do. I was hurt; I admit it. I knew I loved Anna more than anyone or anything in the world but it didn't seem to be enough for her.

"You know how Anna feels about God and religion. There was no way I could encourage her to talk to the rabbi but I felt that was the only way forward for me. The kibbutz had an elderly rabbi living there – he wasn't a war refugee, he'd been one of the early chalutzim coming from Russia, and he understood the survivors very well. I went to see him and I poured out my heart to him.

"He wasn't surprised at all that Anna refused to have anything to do with religion and when I told him about her experiences – what had been done to her, he shook his head slowly. He told me that in the camps many Jewish women had been forced to work in brothels. Some were unable to come to terms with what had happened and suffered mental breakdowns, others had taken their lives. It seemed that all had felt guilt and thought that what had happened was their fault. Without exception, they had all felt unworthy to be married.

"I began to understand how big the problem was and I begged the rabbi to find a way out. He told me that, although it was a subject rarely discussed, there had been a ruling which officially exonerated any woman for anything which had happened to her. He rummaged amongst his papers and showed me the document. I asked if I could take it to Anna and he agreed.

"I knew this was going to be the tricky part. Anna had refused to see me since we had sat together on the bench. I was in torment; I didn't know what to do. I didn't feel I could confide in anyone else; it wasn't my place to share her story, so I knew that I would have to make Anna listen to me.

"I found her in the kitchen a couple of nights later, and I stood in front of her and said I wouldn't let her leave until she had listened to me. She turned her back but, you know, she could still hear. I went through everything the rabbi had said, finishing with 'saving life is the most important thing.' You know that, Anna, and so you saved yourself for me.

"She was leaning against the table as I spoke and she sagged. I thought she was going to faint so I caught her…and the rest is history, as they say." He coughed and cleared his throat. "So now – here is our wedding…at last!"

Anna reached into her bag and pulled out an envelope of photographs. She pushed her plate aside and spread the pictures out.

"We can do better than tell you," said Yaacov. "We have lots of photographs for you to see. We knew you would ask us about our wedding so we came prepared.

"So! Here is what happened. First of all, as you can imagine, we had to prove to everyone that Anna was old enough to get married. She still looked very young but, when the kibbutz leader asked her age, she was able to convince him she was over twenty.

"Then I had to persuade Anna to let a rabbi officiate. Originally, she had said she didn't want to get married, we could just live together. No one would have had any problem with that in the kibbutz. And we wanted the rabbi to know we were taking the ceremony seriously; so many things were different after the war," he sighed, "but I wanted a proper wedding – a chuppah, a ketubah – the whole works. I think that has been the only time in our lives I managed to overrule Anna."

They both laughed comfortably. "Of course, I have never asked her if she regrets it." Anna just smiled enigmatically and let Yaacov tell the story.

"Neither of us had parents to stand under the chuppah with us; there was no mother to accompany Anna as she walked seven times round me. Our families were dead but, because of the wedding, we found that the kibbutz became our family.

"Before the ceremony, the women helped Anna get ready." He pointed to a faded black and white photograph. "She looked like a fairy tale princess when she came out of her room, dressed in a long white gown, with a circlet of flowers on her head. She was carrying flowers she had picked herself from the kibbutz garden – I can smell them still, jasmine and hibiscus and some roses. Wonderful, beautiful," Yaacov paused, reliving the moment.

"We, the men, that is, had fashioned a chuppah out of a tallit and I had been escorted there by all the men in the kibbutz. Here, look, this is a picture of me walking towards Anna." He was at the head of a long column of men, all wearing shorts and open necked shirts. "I stood waiting for my bride. I was still a little nervous; I wondered if she would come – she had been so adamant about not having a religious service and I thought she might refuse at the last moment."

"But she didn't," Helen said softly.

"No, she didn't. She came towards me, with all the women and girls following, all singing and I thought my heart would burst. She circled me seven times…I was so surprised; this was something I never thought she would do, and then stood quietly by my side. The rabbi was smiling so much he could hardly get the words out and we tried hard not to smile too much ourselves. We were making a solemn commitment but we couldn't keep the happiness from showing on our faces. Anna could only nod when she was asked if she agreed to the marriage."

Yaacov stopped as Anna tugged at his sleeve and he watched what she was signing.

"Ah! She says I spoke loud enough for the two of us. I had a slight moment of worry when it was time to put the ring on Anna's finger. She is so independent and I wondered if she would accept it. Not only did she let me put it on her finger, she had managed to bring a ring for me."

Yaacov stretched out his hand and showed Sam and Helen the ring on his wedding finger. It was made of silver and heavily embossed.

"She is so talented, my Anna. There was a small craft workshop on the kibbutz – now it is a very large one, and they export items all over the world, but in those days they were just starting to produce exquisite pieces of jewellery. She had found time every day to watch the master craftsman until she felt able to make my ring; so clever, so beautiful."

Anna made the sign of a thumbs up, and then pointed to her hand and laughed, signing again.

"She says she was happy to wear a ring because it meant she didn't have to explain to all the handsome young men who wanted to be her boyfriends that she was already married."

Helen and Sam laughed loudly at that but they could see that Anna must have been a real beauty when she was younger – she was still stunning, now.

"The kibbutz was such a cosmopolitan place. There were people from all over the world, mostly from the camps in Germany but many who were born in Palestine and some French and Greek also. Before the ceremony, I asked seven of my friends to make one of the sheva brocha in their own language. Avi was out of prison and he was delighted…"

"Prison?" interrupted Helen.

"Oh, Avi was often in prison. He really didn't like the British," Yaacov looked up apologetically, "so he did everything he could to upset their plans for preventing immigrants coming in. He was frequently on the beach when an illegal boat tried to land people, and he was often arrested as a result. He would serve his sentence, usually in Jerusalem, then come back and do it all over again. Avi was a character."

"Was?" asked Sam.

"Yes, was. On his last time on the beach, he was shot. He had been warned, the soldiers had told him to stop, but he carried on helping a young boy reach land. It's sad, but he died doing what he wanted to do. He is buried on the kibbutz and we visit his grave every year. Still, we should remember that the day we married was a happy day, and Avi was with us to share it.

"Of course, we drank the wine, and I smashed the glass and the crowd erupted into cheering and shouts of 'mazaltov'. And then there was a party. There was singing and dancing, and food and sweet wine. No champagne, but lots of wine. Someone had put twinkling lights along the roof line of our little houses and the whole kibbutz looked like a fairy town fit for my Princess Anna."

CHAPTER 27

Helen was so moved by this wonderful love story.

"It's amazing that such happiness came out of so much sadness," she said eventually. "How long did you stay in the kibbutz? You'll hear all about Eva soon, but she couldn't adapt to living within a community and that's partly why she and Friedrich came to England."

"Actually, we were happy enough. After all the horrors of the war, we enjoyed being in such an open space, with our own little house," said Yaacov. "We left for a completely different reason. So many of the holocaust survivors were living in the same place as us; many were affected badly by what happened to them. Others managed to start new lives but what they all had in common was a need to be together.

"They would ask us to join them as they talked over what they had experienced. We didn't want to keep talking about the past; we wanted to get on with our lives and we longed for a family."

A look of sadness moved over both their faces.

"We decided to leave the kibbutz and come here. My sculptures were selling well and Anna's paintings were in great demand. We had always sold them through the kibbutz before, but when we sat down and worked our finances out," they exchanged glances, "we realised that as long as we kept working, we would have enough to live on. Anna knew she would miss the kibbutz kids so she decided when the time came she would apply for a job at the school for the deaf, and they welcomed her with open arms. It wasn't often they had someone who could hear, but who was totally bi-lingual in sign language.

"We stayed at the kibbutz until 1953. By now Israel was well established as a country; we had joined in the celebrations for Yom Ha'Atzmaut and we go back every year to celebrate Independence Day. Of course, the 'birthday' celebrations are not as lavish as the ones we joined with in 1948. They were wonderful, but there were still tensions.

"Our kibbutz was not a particularly religious one, which as you can imagine, suited us very well." They both laughed, Anna silently. "Religion wasn't then, and isn't now, a part of our lives. We just wanted to get on with living in the present, not be held back by old traditions."

"You were telling us about Independence Day," Sam reminded Yaacov.

"Ah yes. You want to hear about it from someone who was there – a first- hand account, I think?"

"We celebrate in England, and I'm sure that Eva would remember the news reaching us from Israel on the day itself, but it would be wonderful if you would tell us what it was like to actually be there. I can imagine the excitement but I suspect there is more than that," Sam suggested.

"A whole lot more. We knew the announcement was coming. The Prime Minister, David Ben Gurion, had been in talks for a long time with the British but not everyone wanted Israel to exist."

"You mean…"

"No, not only the Arab states; some ultra orthodox Jews didn't want anyone to create Israel. They said it couldn't happen until the Messiah arrived."

Yaacov sat up. "We're still waiting for that, but at least we have a land for us, one where we have a right to exist. That was so important to all the Holocaust survivors so, yes, there was a big party at our kibbutz.

"The radio had been left on all day, and when Ben Gurion read the Declaration of Independence out…well, what a huge cheer went up. Anna and I were never ones for joining in things. We liked our privacy, but that night we connected with the rest. We hadn't been married very long and, even though Anna didn't speak, it was obvious she was very, very happy.

"There were huge snakes of people, weaving in and out of the walkways, hands round each others' shoulders; others were dancing the hora. Even the children were allowed to stay up late. No one had the heart to put them to bed. We all wanted them to have wonderful memories of the night we got our own country.

"There was food…there is always food, isn't there, and we ate and drank until the early hours of the morning." Yaacov watched Anna's hands and then added,

"There were fireworks, too. A huge display. How could I have forgotten? Every time a rocket flew into the sky, a great roar went up. These were friendly rockets, not the ones we had sometimes experienced from not so friendly fire!"

242

Anna smiled and signed again and Yaacov shook his head. She spread her hands out as if begging and, reluctantly, he agreed.

"Anna wants me to tell you that I fell asleep in the flower bed outside our house. She says I had too much to drink, but I don't think that was the case. I was tired; it had been a long day – the excitement and so on." He smiled sheepishly, and Anna shook her head. Yaacov continued,

"Well, I might have had a couple of beers, which would have made me more tired," and there was a burst of laughter. Sam clapped him on the back, and smilingly agreed, saying,

"It must have been very late so I am sure you were tired," and the two men grinned at each other.

Helen wanted to know if the decision to leave the kibbutz had been difficult.

"In a way yes, but in another way, no." Yaacov continued.

"We felt it was important to make independent lives for ourselves, but we didn't know how. We talked to the kibbutz leader and explained how we felt, and he understood. He suggested we concentrate on our work – sculpting and painting, to see if that would provide us with an adequate income. So far, we knew that what we produced was snapped up immediately by tourists in Jerusalem, but striking out on our own was a different proposition.

"We knew that as long as we stayed, we always had the kibbutz to fall back on if we didn't sell anything. There would always be a home for us and food; out in the real world we would have to provide this for ourselves. We

243

thought what Moshe said made sense and we decided to have an exhibition. We worked hard, but even so it took us a few years to build up a proper portfolio, and then we unleashed ourselves on the visitors. Not only did we sell most of what we had made, we also took orders for future pieces.

"Moshe was delighted for us, and we were delighted with ourselves. He promised to keep some of the work on display in the dining room and sell it on our behalf. He has kept that promise and even now, we get commissions from holiday makers staying there.

"There was another reason for us to leave the kibbutz; a very important reason. Even though Anna had been told she couldn't have children, she had always hoped that the diagnosis was wrong. We had heard there was an eminent doctor in Haifa who specialised in helping couples who appeared unable to have children. Many survivors went to see him and he had some considerable success. Over the years, there had been some times when we thought Anna was pregnant but our hopes always died. When we had enough money saved, we knew it was time to leave.

"We found our little house in Haifa fairly quickly. It had been damaged during the wars but we were young and strong and we knew we could fix it. Now it is beautiful, but in those early days we lived without water or electricity. It was slow work, so when there was a knock at the door one morning, and we saw a whole crowd of kibbutznicks outside, we were so glad. They helped us repair all the damage and made our house a home.

"We made an appointment to see Doctor Sherman. He was a survivor himself and very sympathetic. Anna was elated one moment, thinking her problems were over and the next moment in the depths of despair, thinking she would never be able to have a baby. Poor girl, she had so many tests. What, Anna?

"Oh yes, she says she felt like a pin cushion after all the blood tests she had."

Anna made a face and rubbed her arm.

"She can still feel it, even after all these years." But they were both smiling.

"All the tests proved that Anna would never carry a baby to full term. That was a bleak moment in our lives." He looked at Helen and Sam.

"It's one thing to *think* you can't have a child; in that case there's always room for hope. It's another thing to be told you *cannot* have a child. I think, after the final diagnosis, we had a very bad time. The doctor suggested that we adopt – there were a lot of children still needing homes after the war, but we both felt it wasn't right for us. We wanted children of our own – we had no family, no blood relations and we wanted to create our own.

"It took us a little time to accept this blow, but we did. Anna decided she would continue to work with children who were unable to speak, as well as creating her wonderful pictures, and I carried on with my sculpting."

He looked proudly at his wife. "She has done all sorts of training courses, and had great success with the young ones. Sometimes, at the weekend, our home is full of children who come to paint, or make pottery. I have a kiln at the back, and we encourage them as much as we can. In the early days, many of the children were orphans, brought out of camps in Germany or Poland. Now they are mainly children who were born deaf and benefit from Anna's teaching. We thought we had come to terms with what happened to us and were happy but finding you, or rather you finding us, has made us realise how much we have missed not having a family."

Anna spread her arms to encompass them and it was obvious what she was expressing. Sam stood for a moment, debating whether or not to start to tell her his story but, in the end, held back. This was a precious moment which he didn't want to spoil.

By now it was getting late, and Anna and Yaacov realised it was time for the bus back to Haifa. Helen and Sam went with them to the bus station. The shops were open after shabbat, and as they walked up Jaffa Street, Helen darted into the supermarket, coming out with a large bunch of flowers, which she handed to Anna.

"I know, something else to carry," she said, "but I want you to look at them and think of us during the week."

"We will see you the weekend after next," added Sam. "Ma will be here by then, and Esther and Daniel. You'll be able to meet them all. Will you come to Jerusalem again?"

"Maybe you should all come to Haifa," wondered Yaacov. "I think we have more rooms than you. Would you be able to do that?"

"I think that would be a good idea," Helen said, "although it might be difficult to keep ma from coming here straight off the plane. Sam is planning to buy a car to make getting around easier. Once we've settled ma in, we can fix a time to come."

"Aunt Anna, this is a difficult question for me," Sam said carefully. "Would you like me to tell my mother what happened to you? Would it be easier for you?"

Anna's face was wet with tears, and she brushed them away.

"Would you do that for me, Sam? I would be so grateful. Of course, I will talk to Eva and I will answer any questions but I don't think I can go over this again. It's been hard for me but I wanted to be honest with you."

The bus revved up and with a last hug, Yaacov and Anna boarded and found seats. Anna was by the window and blew kisses as the bus pulled out.

"Did you hear what Anna said as they got on the bus? She said she wanted to be honest with us. Why do I feel I've been less than honest with her? I have no doubt that there will be problems when she hears what ma has to say. Helen, what have I done, keeping all this to myself?"

CHAPTER 28

Helen was thoughtful as they walked back to the flat.

"You know, Sam, you made your mind up to wait until ma arrived before saying anything to Anna. A few days more and Eva will be here. And you still have to talk to Mr Morris at Yad Vashem. Be patient, darling. I know it's weighing heavily on you – you just need to hold back for a little longer. I'm glad you'll tell ma all about Anna before they meet, though. How do you think she'll react?"

"Knowing ma, she'll take it in her stride. I suspect the big problem will be when Anna learns about *my* link to Hoffman – and there's no way round that."

The phone was ringing as they let themselves in and Sam hurried to answer it. He was smiling as he replaced the receiver.

"The Levys and Steins have decided not to wait for me to talk to the rabbi; they did it themselves and they've arranged a small ceremony for Wednesday afternoon. They guessed I would be free. There's no problem with me conducting the service, now that my status has been confirmed. They don't care that I'm not a rabbi," he grimaced. "As you know, you don't have to be a rabbi to marry a couple…you just have to be Jewish, and I am definitely Jewish." Sam smiled with great satisfaction.

"They've already asked their kids to be there and then afterwards, they've booked a meal in a local restaurant – the two families and us, so no great affair, just 'simple and meaningful,' as Deborah said. It's amazing the way everyone, without exception, has accepted what's happened."

Helen opened her mouth to speak and Sam came across and put his finger to her lips,

"Don't say it, Helen. I know. Everyone loves me." He crossed his eyes and they both laughed out loud.

"This is going to be a very busy week," Helen remarked. "Have you made any plans for when Eva arrives?"

"Other than picking up a car?"

"A car! From where?" Helen demanded.

"From the cousin of your friend at school."

"Really, I thought you weren't too keen on that."

"I wasn't but I couldn't see anything anywhere else, so I called and explained what we wanted, and stressed we needed something reliable. He says the car's in good running order and he's only selling it because his family is growing and it's too small. I called to see it on the way home on Friday."

Helen interrupted,

"You didn't say anything."

"I didn't want to raise your hopes and I thought if it was any good, it would be a lovely surprise."

"It certainly is, Sam. When do you get it?"

"Tomorrow. He's collecting me from the yeshiva; I'll take him back to his home, and then you and I can have a run out to Abu Ghosh – they make the best hummus there and I know you've always wanted to try it. That'll give me time to get used to driving before we go to the airport on Thursday to collect ma and the kids."

"You've got it all worked out, haven't you darling," a smiling Helen said, going into the kitchen to fill the kettle with water.

Sam called Mr Morris at Yad Vashem, explaining the matter was urgent.

"My mother will be here on Thursday. I think if she saw her name on the wall it would cause her problems."

Mr Morris agreed. "I'll do what I can," he replied. "But I will need to see all her relevant documents. I already have her date of birth on record but she will need to sign something." He sounded worried. "I don't think we can do that part without her being present. I can see no way round it."

Sam was very thoughtful. "Maybe if we delayed taking her to Yad Vashem. After all, she will want to see her sister as soon as possible?"

"I'm sorry, Sam. She'll still have to sign a release. The best suggestion I have is that you talk to her and explain what happened, bring her in to see me, but avoid going in to the museum until the plate has been removed. She will have to know about it but she doesn't have to see it."

Sam had to be content with that, and he understood that the records needed to be accurate. His main concern was always Eva, and how she would react.

Helen was delighted when Sam arrived home, driving their newly acquired car.

"Raffi said it was ok and it is," she said. "I'm all ready for a ride out into the Jerusalem Hills. I guess it's not far to go for our first solo travel?"

"Probably about half an hour, depending on traffic. You know, Abu Ghosh is an interesting place. It has the highest number of hummus restaurants in Israel, and the one we're going to has been there about forty years. Arabs and Jews live side by side and co-operate in all ways. There's a lot of talk back home about the problems between Jews and Arabs; this place is a good example of harmonious living."

Helen wound her window down, hoping for some fresh air but the only air which came into the car was perfumed with the smell of petrol from the other vehicles on the road.

"Wait until we're clear of the city." Sam said. "Once we're climbing a little, you'll be able to smell the pine trees, maybe see some olive trees, too."

Abu Ghosh was fairly quiet. Most of the tourists had left, and the people enjoying meals in the restaurants were mainly Israeli – Jews and Arabs. Sam and Helen wandered down the main street, drinking in the atmosphere until it was time for them to go for dinner.

"We don't need a menu," they joked with the waiter. "We'll have hummus, please." He didn't look amused; he'd obviously heard this before! He brought out huge platters of freshly made bread and big bowls of hummus.

"How much?" asked Helen in disbelief after they'd eaten. "So very reasonable! I hope you left a decent tip?"

"The waiter wouldn't take a tip," Sam replied. "I don't think it's the custom, but I did tell him how much we'd enjoyed our food. He told me the Ibrahim family were the first to start a restaurant and their reputation for excellence grows every year. I told him we would recommend it to our friends and he said that was more important than a tip."

"Have you got plans for tomorrow, darling," Sam asked as they drove back.

"Not really," Helen said. "It's not one of my days at school but I need to call in to pick up some paperwork, and then I thought I would go to the Mahane Yehuda market to make sure we have enough food for when the family arrives. I may not have time later in the week, what with the wedding and so on. I'll be back before you get in, though, and in plenty of time to cook."

Helen saw Raffi rushing down a corridor at school the following day and she was able to tell her how pleased they were with the car, and that she knew it would make life easier for them.

"I wish you health to drive it," said the young teacher. "Enjoy! But now you're here, could you help out? We're a teacher short and it would be a great mitzvah. You could take another day off instead."

"That would actually work well. I have a wedding to go to on Wednesday."

"Settled, then," said Raffi, as she darted off again, dropping books in her wake.

Sam bounded up the stairs to the flat, calling Helen's name. There was a heavy stillness in the rooms and she was nowhere to be seen. He checked the back of the kitchen door and the shopping basket was missing. He groaned; where was she? The radio had been full of the news; a pipe bomb had exploded in the market, killing one person and injuring nine. The exact same market where Helen had planned to do her shopping!

There was nothing to do but wait, but he couldn't sit still. For the first time, he realised that Israel was not always a safe place. He had left the yeshiva as soon as he heard the news and the afternoon dragged on. There was no way of contacting Helen; all he could do was pace up and down. Those hours he spent waiting for Helen's return were some of the longest he'd ever spent.

He sprang to his feet when he heard the key turning in the lock and was in the hall as Helen came through the door.

"Where have you been? I've been going out of my mind with worry."

"Sam, I know you're always pleased to see me, but this welcome is a little excessive."

"Haven't you heard? A bomb went off in the market and I knew you were going there. Are you alright? Were you anywhere near it?"

Helen took off her jacket as she spoke.

"I stayed at school all day so I didn't get to the shuk. And we don't have a radio in the school office so this is the first I've heard about a bomb. Oh, darling, I'm so sorry you've been worried but I'm ok. I promise."

Sam held her tight and they stood together for a few moments, before Helen disentangled herself and went into the kitchen to start preparing the meal.

Sam was shaken. His mind almost couldn't cope with his feelings. To come all this way and nearly lose his wife…and then common sense prevailed. Helen hadn't been hurt; she hadn't been anywhere near the market; all was well, and there was no need to worry. His thoughts went to the family of the person who'd died; they would be grieving, he knew.

Over breakfast on Wednesday morning Helen asked,

"What time are we meeting this afternoon? I know it's the big day for the two families,"

"It's been arranged for six o'clock. Afternoon prayers will be over and the synagogue will be quiet. Rabbi Eliazar has arranged to have the chuppah outside in the courtyard and we are all meeting just before, so the ketubah can be signed. I'll go straight from the yeshivah and see you there."

Helen hurried through her day. She wanted to make sure everything was ready for Eva's arrival. She aired the rooms and put fresh flowers on the bedside table. Satisfied, she shut the door to the balcony and closed the shutters. Mrs Abelson on the next floor down asked her why she was looking so smart. Helen didn't want to tell her the real reason, because it was possible she knew the celebrants. She said she was going out for a special meal and the old lady was satisfied with that.

By the time she arrived at the synagogue, everyone was gathered. The two couples had asked if they could share the ceremony and, after some consultation, the rabbis had agreed.

"You can stand under the chuppah at the same time but we'll read the names out one after the other. This whole mishegas has given enough tsuris to us all, so why not marry two couples? All I would ask is that each bridegroom keeps the original bride."

Sam was very nervous. He'd conducted many weddings in his time. 'And I could probably name them all from memory, after all that's happened' he thought to himself. He looked at the four people waiting expectantly.

"This is a first for me," he said.

'And for me, also,' they chorused. 'Let's do it so we can be properly married. You don't know what it's been like these last few weeks,' Warren pointed out. 'Any thing I did wrong, anything I said to tease her, Natalie reminded me that we weren't properly married and she might just decide to leave. Please fix it so she can't.' This lightened the atmosphere and Sam went through the service with them, tailoring it to suit the special circumstances, while making sure it was done properly.

Once the traditional glasses had been smashed under the feet of the grooms and everyone had shouted 'mazaltov', there were handshakes and hugs. Later, Sam sat at the dinner table while the toasts were made, relaxing now his job was done. One of the Levy's sons stood up to speak.

'I have the great honour to propose a toast to my parents on the occasion of their marriage. And all I can say dad, is this; it's about time you made an honest woman of mum.' The room erupted into laughter and everyone clapped.

Sam leaned towards Helen,

"Now I know why there was no opposition to me doing the service. I guess no one else wanted to do it. It's probably the most difficult wedding service I've ever had to do and I'm glad it's done and everyone is satisfied. Another problem solved."

CHAPTER 29

"Should I make sandwiches today?" Helen asked as they prepared to leave for the airport to collect Eva and the twins.

"I don't think we'll need them, but we should take water. Ma will find it very hot and the twins, too. Once they're through immigration, we'll get them back here as quickly as we can. I need to talk to ma as soon as possible."

The airport was crowded. The regular Thursday night flight had been full of passengers who wanted to get to Israel before shabbat. Sam and Helen stood by the barrier, impatient to see their family and delighted when they saw Esther and Daniel pushing a loaded trolley towards them.

"Good flight, ma?" Sam enquired.

"Good? Yes, I suppose so, if you don't mind cold food, turbulence and having to listen to these two talking constantly, when all I wanted was to sleep." It was said with a smile, though, and not taken seriously.

"How do we get to Jerusalem," asked Esther. They had been walking briskly, avoiding the queue for taxis.

"Wait and see," said Sam, as he paused to locate the car keys in his pocket.

"A car? Dad, you bought a car? Wow!"

"It seemed sensible, especially now you're here. We'll be able to see more of the country, without having to depend on buses. Ma, are you ok?"

"Ok? Listen Sam, I very nearly cancelled. The only thing which made me get on that plane was seeing Anna again. And you two, of course," she added hurriedly.

"Why would you cancel, ma? You should be getting used to planes by now."

"Planes I'm getting used to. Bombs I am not!"

"Bombs? Oh, bombs! You mean what happened on the beach in Tel Aviv yesterday?"

"Yesterday? No I was talking about the bomb in the market. Was there another bomb yesterday? What kind of a country have I come to? I would be grateful if you started up this car of yours and got us out of here as soon as possible.

"So, tell me, Sam. Why are you not bothered about bombs? I left Israel *because* of bombs and fighting and I've landed straight back into the middle of it."

"I don't think what happened on the beach was a welcome back gift for you, ma. It just happened, and no one was hurt. The papers said the terrorists were intercepted. It's possible that the military knew there was going to be an attack. As far as I know, the targets were supposed to be tourists, so the beaches were cleared.

"It's awful that a man was killed in the shuk but we have to accept that these sorts of incidents are part of life. Even in the short time we've been here, we've got used to it. We're also used to seeing armed soldiers everywhere – men and girls. In a way, it makes us feel safe."

Eva's head was drooping as Sam turned out of the airport on to the Jerusalem road and within a few minutes she was asleep, waking only when they arrived at the flat.

"You didn't tell me about the stairs," she said as she puffed her way up the three flights. "I'm not sure this will do me any good. Still, you two look well on it." She cast a critical eye over Sam and Helen, who did indeed look better than they had in England. They had both acquired light tans and Sam was more relaxed than he had been the last time Eva had seen him.

"I think Israel is agreeing with you – despite the bombs," she said reluctantly. "But for me, the fact that you are here is one more thing to worry about. I don't like wars and fighting."

Sam looked over at Esther and was about to speak but she shook her head.

"Later, dad," she mouthed, so Sam concentrated his words on Eva. Before he could say anything, though, his mother was asking questions, finishing with,

"When do I get to see my sister?"

"We're going to Haifa tomorrow. Anna has a spare room but I've booked the rest of us into a small hotel nearby. We thought you would like to spend time alone with Anna and we can show Esther and Daniel around Haifa. And find out what on earth is going on with our daughter." Sam added grimly to himself.

"But, we need to talk. Anna has agreed that we can tell you what happened to her in the camp. In some ways, she's still traumatised."

Eva looked very thoughtful.

"I can understand that, and it will be good to know what happened to my little sister. We used to call her

'Little nightingale', you know, because she had such a beautiful voice. She was always singing – I know mama thought one day she might be famous."

Sam took a deep breath. This wasn't going to be easy.

"Before I start, ma, there is one thing you need to know, and I think you will find it very hard to come to terms with. Anna has no voice. She is unable to speak."

"What do you mean? She can't speak?"

"No one really knows why. After she was liberated, she never spoke again. She was taught to sign and that is how she and Yaacov communicate. When she's with people who can't understand sign language, she writes everything down. It's laborious for her but she manages."

Eva was visibly shocked.

"Can she hear?" she asked.

"Her hearing is perfect, but what happened in the camp has left her with an awful legacy. She's seen all sorts of specialists, and had all sorts of treatment but she has resigned herself to the fact that she will never speak again. She has worked for many years with the children from the school for the deaf – they all love her and you will, too."

Eva rocked herself back and forth.

"What dreadful things happened to my little nightingale to affect her in this way? She was such a bright child; much younger than me, and timid in many ways, but with a wonderful personality."

"Oh the personality is still there, ma, but I think you'll find now she's very feisty! She is an extraordinary woman – an accomplished artist and very talented. She and Yaacov love each other very much. They met each other in a camp in Cyprus."

259

"You mean the Germans had concentration camps in Cyprus?" Eva was incredulous. "I had no idea."

"Not the Germans, ma. The British built displaced persons camps there, and Anna spent some time in one." Sam went on to explain how Anna had finally managed to get to Israel.

"Or Palestine as it was in those days."

"When was she there?" Eva was remembering her own time in Palestine. "Your father and I left in 1947. Please don't tell me Anna was also there and I didn't know about it."

"She arrived in Palestine at the end of 1946, so yes, you and she must have been there at the same time."

At this, Eva broke down completely.

"I can't believe it," she sobbed. "I can't believe that we were there and we didn't know about each other. I was told both my sisters had died..."

"And Anna was told by a kapo that you had died, so there was no reason for you to assume that wasn't true."

Helen looked at Sam and raised her eyebrows. Sam knew what she meant.

"Ma, you asked me to go to Yad Vashem to get the family names included among the lists of those who were murdered in the Holocaust. That was how we found Anna."

"I'm confused, Sam. I'm not thinking straight and I don't know what you mean."

"We went to Yad Vashem and we saw that the names were already on the wall," Sam paused, omitting to say it was the Wall of the Dead. "We saw our family name, and then we saw that Anna's was missing but yours included."

Eva was aghast.

"My name is amongst the dead?" she whispered.

Sam and Helen had known this would cause heartache for Eva and tried their best to explain. It was Daniel who intervened and said,

"Granny, your name on the wall is a mistake, but you have to look at it in a positive way; dad wouldn't have found Anna if it hadn't been there."

Eva searched in her bag for a handkerchief and wiped her eyes.

"So Anna put the names there; our parents' names, and Leah's and Reuben's. Does she know they are definitely dead?"

"Sadly, yes." Sam explained.

Eva accepted this.

"But I can't leave my name where it is. It has to come off."

Eva was getting more and more distressed.

"You don't have to see your name, ma. I've made arrangements for it to be removed but I'm afraid you *will* have to see Mr Morris. He's the man who is the Keeper of the Names. All you have to do is to confirm who you are and sign a document. Then they will take the plate down and engrave a new one…without your name on it."

"Learning about Leah and Reuben has only confirmed what I already knew. Poor Anna; for her to think all these years that she was the only survivor. You're right, Daniel, I have to see it as a miracle. Oh Sam, when can I see my sister?"

Sam knelt in front of her chair.

"There is something else you need to know. Anna couldn't bring herself to tell you. I tried to say that you knew some of it but I couldn't find the right moment, and I'm finding this increasingly difficult."

"Sam, I know she was sent to the officers' brothel. Is that what she couldn't tell me?"

"Partly, but what you don't know is that…" Sam was overcome and couldn't carry on.

Helen took his hand and continued.

"What Sam is trying to say is that Hoffman was the first officer…" she also stopped and Eva, with dawning reality voiced the words they couldn't say.

"What you are trying to tell me is that Hoffman had his way with Anna first."

The room became heavy with feelings. Only the sound of Eva's sobs and their breathing intruded into the atmosphere.

Sam laid his head back and let the tears fall. Helen saw that Esther and Daniel were also crying.

"We haven't told Anna and Yaacov the real reason why we're here. She's curious, but said she would wait till you arrived. We didn't know how to tell her about Hoffman and his relationship to Sam."

Eva looked at her son.

"I will tell Anna," she said. "I will explain what happened but, from what you say, it is not going to be an easy conversation. I need to sleep now. I don't need to eat; I just want to be on my own. You can tell me the rest tomorrow."

Eva walked slowly to her room. This bombshell was not what she had expected and, as she undressed, her thoughts turned to what she would have to say to her sister the following day. How could she tell her that Sam, her son, was really the birth child of the Hoffmans?

In the living room, Sam was waiting for Esther to speak.

"Let's leave it for tonight, dad. Don't you think we've had enough shocks for one day?"

"So there is something wrong, Esther. Your mother and I have been thinking about what it could be. We thought perhaps you might have met a nice young man?" Sam tried to lighten the mood.

"And then we thought you might have met a young man who was not nice! We thought perhaps you were ill – all sorts of things have been going through our minds so, Esther, put us out of our misery and explain."

Daniel smiled at his sister.

"Go on, Esther," he said. "Tell them."

"Ah, I understand. I see you're in on this great mystery. Esther, please…"

Esther saw that her parents looked really worried. She decided that she couldn't keep her decision to herself any longer.

"You know I've done well in my exams..."

"Esther," her father said sternly. "Don't prevaricate. Tell us what the problem is."

"It's not a problem, dad. It's actually something I've been thinking about for a while. I just wanted to tell you face to face."

"Esther!" Sam said again, "What is it?"

"I've made a decision about my future. I've applied for a place at Leo Baeck College and I've been accepted. I plan to become a rabbi."

CHAPTER 30

Sam sat bolt upright.

"For a moment there I thought you said you were going to be a rabbi." He looked at Esther who was blushing.

"Did you want to tell me you were going to marry a rabbi? I've always thought you'd make a good rebbetzin." He paused as Esther took a deep breath.

"You were right the first time, dad. I start at the college this coming autumn."

Sam looked at Helen in consternation before speaking.

"A rabbi? How can that be? There aren't any women rabbis."

"Actually, dad, there are. The first women rabbi in England was ordained in 1975 and there's been a few each year ever since."

Sam interrupted, "are you talking about reform rabbis? Certainly, there are no orthodox women rabbis. Women can't even go on the bimah, or touch the scrolls. How could they be rabbis? I don't understand any of this Esther. You've lived all your life in an orthodox house – what's made you decide to take such a radical step."

Esther chose her words carefully.

"At university," she began, "there's a synagogue which accepts all Jewish denominations. I've been going there for some time."

"But you've never said anything – never discussed it with your mother and me. I've heard of this synagogue; it's been around for a while but it never occurred to me – to us, that you might have gone to services there."

"One of the things that university teaches you, dad, is to keep an open mind and explore all your options. I've always had a bit of a problem with orthodoxy – you know that."

"I'm not sure that I do, Esther. You haven't been attending services so frequently, but that's often the case when children leave home for university. There's a lot to see and do, and sometimes religion gets pushed into a corner. I had no doubt that once you'd got your degree you'd pick up again. Perhaps Oxford wasn't the best university for you. And why," he added, "have you always had a bit of a problem with orthodoxy?"

"I didn't want to get into all of that," Esther said wearily. "I just want to let you know what I'm doing."

"I can see what you're doing. You're turning your back on everything I thought you believed in."

"Calm down, Sam," said Helen. "That's a bit harsh. Does it really matter what branch of Judaism we belong to? After all, we're Jews whatever our divergences."

"Of course it matters," Sam responded. "We follow the Torah, we keep the commandments, we do the right thing."

"Really, dad?" Esther shouted angrily. "Is that so? What about those people who park their cars around the corner from the shul because it's forbidden to drive on shabbat and they don't want the rabbi to see. Reform Jews think it's more important to join together; some synagogues even open their car parks. They leave it up to members to decide and some people would rather drive and join in, than stay at home because they live too far away from shul to walk there." She stopped, out of breath.

Sam stood up jerkily and caught the corner of a cushion. It fell on the floor and he picked it up and stuffed it back angrily on to the sofa.

"What's got into you, Sam," Helen asked. "I've never seen you like this. I've never even heard you raise your voice." She looked directly at Esther.

"We need to keep the noise down. Granny's gone to bed and we shouldn't disturb her. Sam, sit down and tell us what is really the matter."

Sam considered his words.

"All my life I've never questioned my background. I never had to. I had Jewish parents, I lived in a Jewish house, I went to shul, I *was* Jewish. For the last few weeks I've been in turmoil, not knowing whether or not I would be accepted…"

Helen snorted, "As if you wouldn't have been."

"Helen, I'm telling you how I've been feeling. Please don't interrupt – just let me explain. I've had to convert before I could be recognised as Jewish. How do you think that made me feel? Even after that, my future as a rabbi is hanging in the balance. Who knows what will happen at the end of the six months here?

"And now my daughter tells me that she's always had a problem with orthodoxy and prefers the reform way of life. I can't believe I'm hearing this. There are rabbis at the yeshiva who don't think I should be allowed to resume being a rabbi because of my birth father. How do you think they'll react when they hear I have a daughter who wants to become a Reform rabbi?"

"I can't work out if you have a problem with reform or with me becoming a rabbi. Or are you just worried you won't be allowed to be a rabbi again?"

Sam gasped, shocked his daughter could speak to him that way. She went on, "dad, I'm not saying *you* should have a problem with orthodoxy, I'm telling you that *I'm* the one who's had the problem. Would you rather I told you I wanted to leave Judaism altogether?"

"Maybe that would be better."

There was a cry from Esther and Sam looked shamefaced.

"Essie, I didn't mean that. Of course, I want you to continue to be Jewish. You'll always be Jewish…It's just that I wonder if you've thought this through."

"What's to think through, dad? She wants to be a rabbi and she can be one in the reform movement." Daniel contributed.

"I see," Sam said coldly. "Everyone has known about this except me." He turned to Helen, "I suppose she told you first?"

"No, she didn't, but I do know there have been many things Essie's not been happy with."

"Such as?"

"Okay, dad, how come Daniel had such a wonderful barmitzvah and my batmitzvah was a very low key event? Why couldn't I leyn from the Torah? Why couldn't I stand on the bimah? Why couldn't you put a tallit around my shoulders and welcome me into the community as an adult?"

"Is that what this is all about? You're jealous of your brother?"

"I thought you knew me better than that. I can't believe you've said that," Esther said sadly. "I've never been jealous of Daniel – we're twins, how could I be? I've always been proud of him, but I don't understand why men and women are treated so differently in an orthodox synagogue. The Reform community has been a real eye opener for me. But I don't suppose you've ever been in a progressive synagogue, have you dad?"

Helen spoke quietly. "As it happens, your dad and I went to a reform synagogue in Haifa when we stayed with Anna. It's linked to Leo Baeck college in London – you may have heard of it. Your dad and I were very impressed with it, actually. Sam, tell her what you thought."

Reluctantly, Sam described their visit.

"We both enjoyed the service and we could see many similarities between our shul in London and the Haifa one. The siddur was different – more English was said during the service but, yes, I admit I did enjoy it. I liked the atmosphere and the decorum."

"So why are you being so difficult? I'm twenty one years old, dad, I don't have to ask your permission to become a rabbi, but I would like your blessing."

"There are so many things you'll have to overcome, Esther, and I fear for you," Sam said slowly. "There may be women rabbis in the reform movement but I can't see it happening for orthodox women. You won't be accepted…"

"Dad, I'll be accepted by the reform community."

Sam conceded that. "But you won't be orthodox. What about your children?"

"Any children I have will be Jewish. Does it matter if they're orthodox or reform or liberal or whatever?"

"It could matter to whoever they may want to marry. It might matter to the man who asks you to marry him"

"Dad, that's all for the future; I haven't met anyone I want to marry yet. I may never meet anyone, but I know that above all else, I want to be a rabbi."

Esther tossed her head back and her eyes flashed.

Sam made one last attempt to make her think.

"Could you not find a nice rabbi to marry, and then you would be a wonderful rebbitzin?"

"How many times do I have to tell you both? I don't want to be a rebbitzin. I want...no I intend, to become a rabbi." Esther ventured daringly, "and you have only yourself to blame, dad. I've seen how much being a rabbi means to you. Even when you're arguing with me, like now, and since you never argue, I know this is really important. Your example taught me that I want to have what you have; a community – a congregation."

Helen, ever the voice of reason, said there was food for anyone who wanted it. Daniel, as was to be expected, went into the kitchen to forage and came back with a plate piled high. Esther followed with a more modest amount, but Helen and Sam felt they couldn't eat. They decided an early night might help tempers cool and told Daniel and Esther to be quiet. "Esther, you'll have to creep into granny's room" said Helen. "Daniel, everything you need is here in this pile. Just fold out the settee and we'll see you in the morning."

Daniel and Esther sat side by side, enjoying their supper.

"I've never seen dad like that," said Esther worriedly. "Do you think he's having some sort of a breakdown?"

"No, I don't, Essie. I think he was shocked to hear what you had to say. I could see him and mum were worried about what you were going to tell them, but I don't think either of them had considered this. Maybe you should think of dad a bit more."

"What do you mean, think of dad. This is my life we're talking about."

"There you go again. I know it's your life, but think of what dad's gone through recently. From what he says, I think he's fighting to remain a rabbi, and here you are, swanning around, telling him *you're* going to be a rabbi – no questions asked. You are challenging everything he believes in. As far as he's concerned, the orthodox way of life is the only way of life."

Esther was thoughtful.

"I hadn't looked at it like that," she said.

"That's your trouble, Essie, you don't look at anyone else's point of view but your own. Dad's already had a lot of explaining to do and now this. Can't you see how stressed he is. Dad never raises his voice, never argues. He always says that the voice of reason is quiet. Granny said he looked relaxed, but I don't think she noticed the worry lines across his forehead. He's having a really hard time and we should be helping him, not making it worse."

They sat silently, lost in their own thoughts and then Essie stood up, shook the crumbs from her skirt onto the plate and said,

"I'm off to bed. See you in the morning, and thank you, little brother."

"Hang on, Essie, I'm only ten minutes younger than you."

"Ten minutes, ten years, it's all the same to me. I'm the big sister!"

Daniel finished his meal and then hunted for some fruit before unravelling the sofa bed and crawling in.

His parents were talking in whispers.

"That was a very severe reaction to Esther's plans," Helen started. "Are you really so against her joining the rabbinate?"

"If it was Daniel…" Sam didn't finish because Helen sat up in bed and stared at him.

"I can't believe I heard you say that. You're against Esther becoming a rabbi because she's a woman? Sam, you have always treated everyone with respect, and helped them fulfil their dreams. What's happening to you? What difference does it make if it's Daniel or Esther?"

Sam also sat up and pulled the pillow behind his head.

"I don't know what's happening to me. One minute I'm happy, the next minute I'm not. I'm enjoying the extra studying but at the back of my mind, always, is the thought I won't be good enough. Maybe the rabbis won't accept me. Maybe I'll have to look for another job. I have no idea what is going to happen and I feel very insecure. Helen, you know the rabbinate is my life and I can't think of anything else I want to do."

"Sam, that's exactly what Esther said. She can't imagine a life unless she becomes a rabbi. We should support her, darling, not criticise her decision."

"But Helen, we don't have orthodox women rabbis. There's no way round it. I can't change it."

271

"So she'll train as a reform rabbi? She'll be good, I'm sure, because she'll take after her father. Be happy that she's found her vocation and support her in her choice. Whatever she does, she'll still be our daughter."

CHAPTER 31

There was a strange atmosphere in the flat the following morning. Esther was withdrawn, not talking to anyone and avoiding her father as much as she could. Eva was distant, speaking monosyllabically and sometimes not answering. Helen was flustered, aware of the different problems and unwilling to say anything which might upset anyone. She was finding this especially difficult because there had always been harmony in their home.

Sam was trying to be jovial, and failing miserably. The only one whose behaviour resembled any kind of normality was Daniel, who didn't speak at all, mainly because he had his mouth full of food.

"Have you decided what you're going to say to Anna?" Sam asked his mother after a long silence.

"No!" said Eva. "How can I decide which way to tell her? I need to see her first. You've already told me she can be a bit…what was the word you used? Ah, yes, feisty. She might throw us out."

"I hardly think so. You're the only family she has – and us, of course."

"And that, Sam, is exactly the problem. Of course, I'm her sister and nothing can change that but, strictly speaking no one else here is related to her at all."

"You can't mean that, ma," Helen protested. "Sam is your son and that makes Daniel and Esther your grandchildren and Anna's great nephew and niece."

"It sounds so simple when you say it like that. Of course *we* know that Sam is my son but, in reality, his birth parents are..." she stopped, finding it difficult to continue. "There is actually no blood link at all between Sam and the twins, and Anna. It might be difficult for her to accept him as her nephew."

"There's no point in worrying about it now, ma. We should wait until we see Anna and Yaacov and take it from there. It's about an hour's driving to get to Haifa so let's leave as soon as we get our things together."

Sam looked at the twins and asked them if they were ready. Daniel shrugged his shoulders and Esther went back in to the bedroom without speaking. They heard the sound of a case being zipped shut angrily. Eva asked what was the matter and no one replied, until Daniel remarked laconically,

"Tired, I expect," and Eva seemed to accept that, saying she also was still tired.

In Haifa, Anna was in the kitchen, clattering pots and pans. She was opening drawers and banging cupboard doors shut.

"What is the matter?" asked Yaacov as he came in to the room, just as Anna was tipping the contents of a drawer out on to the table. "You're making a dreadful mess," he remarked mildly.

Anna turned around so he could see her fingers. "Why is it that I can never find anything in this place? All I want is a rolling pin and it's not here – gone – unless you've been using it to roll out clay."

"Don't be ridiculous, darling. What would I want with a rolling pin?" He rummaged around the pile of utensils.

"Look, here it is. Anyway, why do you want a rolling pin?"

"Because I want to make strudel. I want Eva to come in and smell strudel, just like mama used to make." She burst into tears.

"Ever since I was liberated from the camp I have wished I had someone of my own." She shook her head violently. "Don't say it, Yaacov, I know I have you, but you know what I mean. I wanted someone who knew me as a child; someone with shared memories of what I was like as a little girl; someone who can remember mama and papa and Reuben and Leah. Now that moment has come, I'm terrified. I don't know what Eva will think of me. Maybe she will think I would be better off dead, after what I had to do."

Yaacov looked at his diminutive wife and said dryly, "And maybe you should make strudel. It will give you something to do. Come on, I'll help you slice the apples."

Anna stared at him. "Why aren't you telling me that what happened in the camp wasn't my fault?"

"I don't need to tell you; you should know already. You're getting yourself into such a state, and I can't believe it's necessary. Calm down and bake, and then I'll benefit too. We haven't had strudel for a long time…at least a week!"

Anna smiled weakly at him and with a swift movement, swept all the kitchen tools noisily back in the drawer. She cleared a space on the table and started to make pastry. They worked in companionable silence for a while until Anna lifted her head.

"Do you at least understand why I'm worried?" she signed.

"Darling, I do understand but you need to be positive about it. No one will blame you or think anything bad of you. Ask yourself this; did you sense any difference in Sam after you told him? No! See, you don't need to worry."

They heard the car pulling up outside just as the strudel was coming out of the oven. The sweet smell of apples and cinnamon permeated the little house and Anna pulled off her apron. She was standing at the door as Eva climbed stiffly out of the car.

Anna turned to her husband and signed rapidly,

"Yaacov, she's an old lady!" and her tears fell unchecked.

Yaacov whispered to her, "What did you expect – it's over forty years since you last were together. Did you think she would look as young now as she was then? We're all older but inside she'll be the same sister you grew up with."

Eva, too, looked shocked. She also had expected to see a young woman, and the Anna in front of her looked remarkably like the face she saw in the mirror each morning; the thick white hair – even the laughter lines.

Sam and Helen hung back a little, giving Eva the opportunity to greet her sister. There was a brief pause and then Eva moved towards the other woman.

"My Anna," she said. "My little nightingale. I thought I had lost you and now you are found," and the two sisters put their arms around each other.

Yaacov stood by, waiting for Anna to sign.

"She says she is now a nightingale without a song but she will use her wings to speak. Her hands are very eloquent." He smiled at the two women who were standing so closely together.

Yaacov pushed the door wider so they could go into the house and Eva sniffed appreciatively.

"Mama's strudel," she said. "Oh how I've longed to smell mama's strudel again. Anna we have so much time to make up – a lifetime, nearly. Sam has told me what you had to do in the camp…"

Anna tried to move out of Eva's embrace but Eva wouldn't let her.

"There is nothing you could have said and done that would stop me loving you. But I worry that you may feel anger towards me when I tell you my story."

Anna's eyes were wide,

"You mean…you, too?"

"No, Anna. I have a quite different problem to talk about. I asked Sam to keep my secret but it is time now, I think, for you to know all about me…and my family."

Anna was so relieved by Eva's response that she hardly heard what her sister was saying but when she looked at Eva's face she could see the gravity of the situation.

"I don't know where to start," Eva said. "It's all such a mess."

Helen, practical as ever, had gone into the kitchen to make tea. She brought a laden tray into the living room and set the cups and saucers out, sniffing, and saying the strudel smelled so delicious. Daniel's eyes lit up at the generous wedges and reached his hand out to take a piece.

"Wonderful, Aunt Anna," he mumbled through a warm, fragrant mouthful and his genuine enjoyment broke the ice.

"Would you like us to go while you talk? I can always run our things over to the hotel?"

"No, please stay, Sam," said Eva, and Anna nodded in agreement. The two sisters were sitting side by side on the settee until Eva got up and moved to an armchair.

"What I am going to tell you will, I think, be very painful. You may decide you don't want to see any of us again, and I could understand it but, please understand, that I didn't plan any of the things that happened to me, anymore than you did.

"So, back to the beginning. I watched you being taken away – you and Leah, and I begged to be allowed to go with you. Hoffman wouldn't let me. I think he enjoyed separating families so I was glad that you two were together. After that, I didn't see you again."

Anna's hands moved rapidly.

"Why didn't you look for me after the war?"

"I could ask you the same, little nightingale. I was told – the same as you, that all my family were dead. I had to accept it. Of course, it was a miracle when I saw Friedrich and we were lucky to have time together, and then I lost him, too. All I had left was my baby."

Anna smiled at Sam and, Eva knowing what was to come, felt as if a knife was being plunged into her heart.

"I worked for Hoffman, in his house."

"He was a monster," Anna interjected.

"Yes, he was. It's because of him I lost my teeth and I have a finger missing on my left hand."

Anna gasped in horror,

"Sam never said."

"No point – nothing can be done, and now I'm used to it."

"But the piano…"

"I don't play. I'm sure I could, even with a finger missing, I just don't want to."

She looked at Anna,

"We're a pigeon pair, aren't we! You don't sing and I don't play. What a legacy we have from that damnable man." Both women took deep breaths before Eva continued.

"Shortly before the end of the war, there were constant bombardments. I'm sure that the Germans knew the end was near and they began to organise their departure."

"It was in one of those bombardments that Leah was murdered," Anna signed, "but I thought you had died long before then. I know our parents went to the ovens almost immediately after we arrived."

"No, I suppose I was lucky. Do you remember Mina, from our village?"

Anna looked perplexed.

"She was my age…we were at school together? No matter. She was hanged because she ate the scraps off a plate, but before she went to the gallows she said I should try and work for Hoffman."

Anna got up and was visibly trembling.

"Like *I* worked for him? Tell me it's not true."

"No. I looked after his children."

"What do you mean, you looked after his children?"

"Just as I say. I was expecting Friedrich's child and I managed to deliver my baby secretly. By then, I thought Friedrich was dead, along with all my family, and so all I had left was my unborn child. And then, the night the Allies tried to destroy the camp, Hoffman came to me and said he would help me get out of the camp. He would also let me take my baby."

Anna, by then was extremely agitated. Yaacov tried to calm her but she wouldn't listen.

"Why would Hoffman help you? What was in it for him?"

"At first I wondered if he thought I came from a wealthy family which would help him once the war was over. It wasn't until he drove me to Berlin and left me that I realised what it was he really wanted. I found a room which was almost demolished and I dragged in all the things Hoffman had left me with: the food, the baby clothes and the money."

Anna signed furiously, and smacked her head with her hand.

"She wants to know why he would do this. Not just help, but leave you with things to ensure your survival. She doesn't understand. The man she knew was a monster, with no compassion. The person you are describing is not the same man."

Sam and Helen were holding their breath. Anna's reaction so far had been worse than they had expected; not just anger, but trauma.

"I have to tell you this, little nightingale. The baby Hoffman left me with was not the child of Friedrich and me. My child had died and Hoffman saw that a way of saving one of his children was to help me escape."

"You mean you and Hoffman…!

"No, Anna, not me and Hoffman. Frau Hoffman was the child's mother."

"I don't understand. What happened to that baby? Realisation slowly dawned and Anna looked straight at Sam.

"You mean Sam is…" before she could finish signing she choked and slid to the floor.

Yaacov rushed to pick her up, saying over his shoulder, "Is this true. Hoffman is Sam's father?"

CHAPTER 32

Esther ran into the kitchen for a glass of water, while Yaacov laid Anna tenderly on the settee. Helen found a blanket and covered her but they were unable to rouse her. After ten minutes, Yaacov decided to call the ambulance. He described what had happened and was told someone would be there immediately.

Almost as soon as he'd replaced the receiver, he heard the sound of the siren. Sam went outside so that the ambulance driver would know where to stop. Two paramedics rushed in and did their best to revive Anna.

"I can't say what's wrong," the older one said, "and I don't wish to alarm you, but she may have had a heart attack. Her pulse is racing and she has an irregular heart beat. We need to take her to the hospital."

He looked at Yaacov, "Would you like to come in the ambulance, sir? It would be good for her to see a familiar face if...I mean when, she wakes up."

"Shall I put some things together for her in case she needs to stay in," asked Helen. "We can follow on in the car?"

Suddenly, Yaacov looked like the old man he was. His face was grey and drained and he was grateful when Esther hugged him and told him not to worry.

"It's just shock, I expect," she said. "What with seeing her sister, and then all the talking," she added diplomatically. "I'm sure she'll be all right when she wakes up."

The ambulance kept its siren on, and arrived at the hospital in record time. Two nurses were waiting and Anna was gently lifted on to a trolley. Yaacov was keeping tight hold of her hand and had to almost run to keep up with the trolley's speed. The nurses pushed through the double doors of the accident and emergency department, telling Yaacov he had to wait outside.

"I cannot stay outside," he said firmly, "My Anna will not be able to communicate if I'm not there."

"I'm sure that's not true," said a formidable looking sister, "we will take good care of her. Please, take a seat in the waiting room and we'll call you when we've assessed the situation."

"You don't understand," Yaacov's lips were trembling. "My wife is unable to speak."

"Ah, she is deaf," said the sister.

"No, she's not deaf. She just cannot speak. If I tell you she is a survivor from the camps, perhaps then you will understand."

The nurses exchanged glances, then the sister took over again.

"I'm so sorry, sir. Please come with me. We'll get you a comfortable chair and some paper and pen ready for when your wife is able to tell us what happened."

"She won't need that," Yaacov replied. "She can sign and I understand sign language but, in the meantime, I can tell you what happened." He went on to explain that Anna had received disturbing news but, other than that, was in good health.

Anna's vital signs were checked but there was no change.

The doctor came to talk to Yaacov. "As you can see, I've checked her over and I cannot find anything organically wrong. She is unconscious but, apart from that, appears to be in good health. Her heart rhythm has settled down and all I can say is that it is a waiting game. You will need patience, as she will decide herself when she will come back to us."

He smiled comfortingly at Yaacov. "Some would say she is in a coma but I don't think so; her level of unconsciousness is not as deep as I would expect for that. You said she had disturbing news and she was a camp survivor. Perhaps those two things are linked. It may be that her body wants to shut out this bad news.

"We should let her rest and see if she wakes up of her own accord. Sister has explained the exceptional circumstances and we think it would be good if you could stay. Do you have anyone who could take a turn at watching her?"

Yaacov told him that her sister would be coming to the hospital and the other man agreed that she could also sit with Anna.

"But, no one else, please. And it would be good if you would talk to her. I have heard that people who have lost consciousness can still hear speech. Only talk about good things, though, and don't mention what upset her."

Yaacov took Anna's hand again, stroking her fingers before pressing them to his lips. He smoothed her hair away from her brow and kissed her forehead.

Eva came into the room, and told him the doctor had spoken to her and she knew what she had to do.

"I mentioned to him that I'm a retired GP, and so he has no worries about me being here. We just wait and talk a little to her. The others are in the relatives room but they will go soon. They have to check in at their hotel."

She handed Yaacov a bag. "Some things Helen thought Anna might need."

The waiting room was empty; Esther took the initiative, "Dad, we can't do anything here. It looks as though Aunt Anna will have to stay overnight at least. We should go to the hotel, and after that I'd like to go to the shul you told us about – the progressive one."

Sam was about to speak but Helen silenced him.

"I think that's a good idea. Even though we've only been to this synagogue once I felt very comfortable there. We will be able to sit together and I think that will be good for us."

They walked out into the late afternoon sunshine and climbed in to the car. The hotel wasn't far from Anna's house and, by now, Sam was beginning to know his way around. The building was small but welcoming, with a sign saying there were vacancies hanging over the door.

The receptionist gave them the keys to their rooms and told them the restaurant was closed but breakfast would be available after seven in the morning. She recommended several nearby good places to eat, and added,

"If you go now, they'll still be open but they will close soon as it will be shabbat shortly."

There was a falafel shop almost next door, and they ate, leaning against the counter. They suddenly realised how hungry they were – no one had eaten lunch, and the filled pita was just what they needed. Sam was reluctant to go again to the synagogue.

"The first time we went, it was an accident. We didn't know till we were inside that it was not orthodox. I can't do this again knowingly."

Helen took his hand. "What do you think will happen if we go again? She asked. "Look, Sam, I don't know about you but I need a synagogue right now, and this is the only one within walking distance. If you prefer not to come, I'll go without you."

Sam could see she was determined and said he would walk with her. He remembered the way to the synagogue, and they arrived just before the service started. Reluctantly he followed his family inside and found seats at the back of the sanctuary. Sam secretly watched his daughter's face, as she moved effortlessly through the prayer book. She was aglow with content – even the shock of Anna's collapse couldn't prevent the happiness that was so apparent on her face.

Afterwards, as they mingled in the kiddush room, Sam saw Esther speaking animatedly to the rabbi. She brought him over to where her parents were standing and introduced him.

"Esther tells me you are a rabbi but orthodox. What did you think of our service?"

There was a pause as Sam tried to collect his thoughts.

"Don't worry," said the rabbi. "I know there is a certain degree of…shall I say reluctance, to accept other branches of Judaism. However, this is not your first visit here I think, so something must be interesting you."

"My daughter," Sam tried to say the words. "My daughter is thinking, considering..."

Esther broke in with a smile.

"I've already told the rabbi my plans. He's very enthusiastic, dad. He's even suggested I do some voluntary work here when I have my study year in Israel."

There was nothing Sam could say. He shook hands with the rabbi and ushered his family out into the street for the walk back to the hotel.

Evening drew in. The curtains were closed and a soft light was switched on at Anna's bedside. Nurses came and went; they sponged her face with cool water and her sheets were straightened. Sister looked in at intervals but there was no response; Anna lay like the dead in the narrow hospital bed.

Yaacov wanted Eva to go back to the house to rest but she refused.

"I've travelled a long way to see my sister. I want to be here when she wakes up," and there was no argument.

When dawn started to break, the bedside light was switched off. The sun gradually lightened the room and they heard the early morning sound of bird call. A trolley moved on squeaky wheels along the corridor and a cheerful head popped itself round the door.

"Anyone for tea?"

Yaacov and Eva gratefully accepted the offer. They stood up, stretching their cramped limbs, and folded the blankets they had been using. Anna slept on serenely, her white hair like a halo around her head, one hand resting on the blue bedspread.

In the hotel, the Goldmans were doing justice to the breakfast buffet.

"Very different from cornflakes," Daniel joked, as he dived in to the salads. "Whoever thought of having salad at breakfast was inspired."

"If things had been different, I could have shown you Haifa. I know you've been here before but I expect it was too long ago for you to remember. You were very young."

"I think we should go to the hospital, dad. I can see you're on tenterhooks. There'll be plenty of time for sightseeing later. And, of course, in the future I'll be living here for a year," Esther couldn't resist adding.

Sam's face closed but he didn't say anything. He understood that Esther was trying to get him used to the idea of her entering the rabbinate.

Nothing had changed when they went into Anna's room. Eva left Yaacov, and beckoned to the others to come with her to the relatives room.

"I've got my 'doctor head' on now and I'm getting more and more concerned. I've asked if Anna can have a brain scan – I'm worried she may have had an aneurism and they've agreed. Actually, you've come at the right time; they're about to take her down now.

I think they're humouring me," she added wryly, "but all possibilities need to be considered." As she spoke, Anna was wheeled out of the room and passed them in the corridor.

"What do you really think, granny?" asked Esther.

"I don't know what to think. She's had a severe shock and that could be enough to precipitate all sorts of things. The longer she stays unconscious, the more the likelihood will be it's a serious problem. I can't help feeling it's my fault. Yaacov and I have been talking and he doesn't blame me, but I know that before she found out about Hoffman she was all right."

"You can't say that, ma," Helen replied. "You don't know if anything was wrong with her – this could all be a coincidence. She could have some sort of underlying health problem. Come on, though, we shouldn't leave Yaacov on his own."

Anna wasn't away very long and when she was settled back in her bed, the Sister spoke sternly.

"I can only allow two people in the room. Decide who that is to be and I would be grateful if the rest of you could leave."

Yaacov had resumed his seat and was again holding Anna's hand. Sam offered to stay while Eva went with the others to the cafeteria.

"I don't know what to say, Yaacov. It was never our intention to upset Anna. Maybe we should have kept this Hoffman stuff a secret?"

"No, you were right to tell us. I expect we would have found out anyway, and it was better coming from you. So have you any more revelations? Anything else you want to tell me."

"The whole story of what happened to me…and how I became a rabbi."

This was not something Yaacov was expecting to hear.

"A rabbi? How did that happen? And are you still a rabbi?"

Sam flinched at the question before taking a deep breath. He explained and finished with why he was in Israel.

"So you see, Yaacov. I don't know whether I will be able to continue as a rabbi. It's all I ever wanted. What else could I do?" He risked a look at the older man.

"And yesterday my daughter informed me she also wants to become a rabbi."

"Is that possible?"

"Yes, but only in the reform movement, which is so very different to all I'm used to. I don't know where my life's going at the moment," and Sam rested his head on the bed.

"So, is different wrong?" Yaacov probed. "Are we not all Jews?"

"That's what Esther keeps telling me and, of course, we are all Jews…but reform and orthodox…they're poles apart."

"Poles can be shifted," said Yaacov delicately.

"You know, Yaacov," said Sam. "You're making a pretty good case for religion, for someone who professes a dislike for it."

The rain had stopped and the windows were streaked with water. Yaacov shifted his chair and it scraped on the floor. Anna moved her head and they saw her eyes were open. She signed weakly. Yaacov immediately pressed the bell for the nurse.

"What is Anna saying?" asked Sam impatiently.

"She said could we please make less noise as she's trying to sleep. She's been awake a while but we didn't realise because we were busy talking. She's heard everything you said, Sam, and she wants to go back to sleep now. We can talk later."

Anna's hands moved again.

"She wants to know what will happen to you because you didn't go to the shabbat service. Is it the first one you've missed, and are you likely to disappear in a puff of smoke?"

Yaacov and Sam laughed with relief and Anna covered her ears with her hands before making a shooing gesture. The nurse came into the room and told them to leave and Anna waved goodbye. They left her to rest.

CHAPTER 33

The doctor intercepted them on the way to the waiting room.

"I think it would be advisable if Mrs. Brendel stayed another night, and I suggest it would be a good idea if she saw our psychiatrist."

Yaacov bristled at this.

"What are you saying?" he asked stiffly. "My wife does not have any mental health problems."

The doctor beckoned to him.

"Come into my office and we can have a chat about this." He held open the door and ushered Yaacov in. "Please take a seat. Perhaps you would like your sister-in-law to come, too. I understand she is a doctor."

Eva nodded and said, "Retired, of course, and a GP, not a psychiatrist but I am happy to come with you if I think I can be of any assistance."

The rest of the family continued into the waiting room. Their advice had not been sought!

"Now," Dr Halpern began. "I think this is the first episode of fainting your wife has had. Is that right?" He looked at Yaacov, who nodded. The doctor directed his next question to Eva.

"I also understand that Anna thought you had died in the Holocaust and this is the first time you have met since you were separated in the camp. That alone would have been enough to cause her to faint, but I suspect there is more to it than that? Did she faint as soon as she saw you?"

Yaacov and Eva were uncomfortable. They didn't want to elaborate and the doctor didn't press them. He accepted their silence as a negative response.

"I also understand," he went on, "that Anna has not spoken since she came out of the camp. Dr Goldman, was Anna's speech normal when she was a child?"

"Not only normal, she had the most beautiful singing voice. The family called her 'Little Nightingale' and she often sang at concerts in our village, while I accompanied her on the piano."

"And her personality, Dr Goldman; introvert? Extrovert?"

"I don't understand why you're asking me all these questions. That was a long time ago; what relevance does it have to Anna's predicament now."

"I'm trying to build up a picture of Anna."

"I see. She was a very engaging child; bright and sociable, always happy to meet people. She was quiet most of the time but when she sang, she really came out of herself. She was so pretty – like a little angel and everyone loved her. She was able to chatter to anyone."

"So, her early life was happy; it seems that whatever happened in the camp has had a lasting effect and I'm not sure she has addressed the problem." Turning to Yaacov, Dr Halpern asked,

"Was she able to see anyone after the war? A specialist, I mean? Was she ever diagnosed, I wonder?"

Yaacov leaned forward thoughtfully.

"As far as I know, she saw several doctors before she went to Cyprus; this is where we met. She seemed to be managing without speech; she writes things down but she has also learned sign language, as have I, so we can talk together very easily. I know she didn't pursue any further investigations in Israel because all the doctors had said she was a puzzle, and there was no reason why she couldn't speak. They all said that she would start to speak again in her own time but, as you can see, time has gone on and nothing has happened. I believe she is content and has accepted she will not speak again. She works with the children at the school for the deaf and she is a great asset to them."

"Mr Brendel, I will be honest with you. Anna interests me very much. She is in excellent physical health and, considering what she went through during the war, this is amazing. As you know, she had a very intensive check up yesterday and I could find nothing wrong with her physically. Mentally, of course, I think this is not the case."

Before Yaacov could protest, the doctor stopped him.

"Please listen to me. I am not suggesting that Anna is mentally ill. You must believe that, but I do think the trauma she experienced has caused her speech to disappear. We need to find a way to unlock this. Do you agree, Dr Goldman?"

Eva didn't answer. She had seen patients in her practice displaying similar symptoms; people who had lost the use of their legs or hands – she had worked with them, and usually they regained the use of their limbs. However, she had never seen a patient who had lost the ability to speak.

"It's possible," she said after deep thought. "I have had patients who stopped walking after intense trauma. I always recommended that they saw a psychiatrist. After I'd eliminated all physical problems," she added hastily. "It wouldn't hurt to try, Yaacov, would it?"

"Anna is so precious to me. I would be concerned if she felt there was some sort of conspiracy going on, and we were implying she was suffering from a breakdown. I suspect you may be right in what you say but we need to approach this very carefully. At the moment, Anna is recovering from a fainting attack. Once she's home, I will talk to her."

Dr Halpern felt that progress had been made.

"We'll keep her here for another night, then, and make an appointment for her to come back in a week or so. Why don't you go home and have some rest. You've been here all night. Strictly speaking there is no visiting until this evening and it'll give Anna time to have a sleep, too. Thank you for talking with me, we'll keep in touch."

Outside the doctor's room Yaacov asked Eva directly,

"Do you think Anna's lack of speech is a mental problem?"

Before answering she considered her reply.

"I do think Dr Halpern is right. Anna suffered exceptionally during the war and I think this is how she has dealt with it. Her lack of speech means she has never actually spoken about those awful days."

"I don't agree, Eva. She has signed what happened."

Eva looked squarely at him.

"Yes, she has but she hasn't actually spoken. Sometimes, things seem worse when you say them out loud. Anna's signing has probably kept many of her memories hidden. I am worried because I suspect if Anna could speak, there would be worse horrors to tell. In the end, though, it must be her decision, and I think you are right to wait until she's at home and recovered more before you even try to talk about this. Why don't you go back to her room and tell her she's to stay another night and you'll be back to see her this evening."

Sam jumped to his feet as Eva went into the waiting room. He felt she had been away a long time.

"What's happening," he asked. "Is she all right?"

"They think she should stay another night, just to make sure she's okay but yes, she is all right. Yaacov's telling her she's to stay in, and then we'll go back to the house for a shower and a rest."

They waited for Yaacov to return. His face was glum.

"She said she won't stay. Now she has found her sister she doesn't want to lose her, so she told the doctor that she was going home and Eva, rather 'Doctor Goldman,' would be able to care for her. I tried, but nothing I said made her change her mind. She's getting dressed and…here she is."

Anna looked very fragile in the large wheelchair, as she was pushed into the waiting room, but she was smiling happily and motioned to Eva to come to her side to hold her hand.

"I think you should stay," Eva said and Anna signed frantically.

"Apparently," Yaacov said grinning, "you were always the bossy sister but this time you're not going to get your own way."

Anna signed again.

"I'm sorry about this. I did get a shock but I've had some time to think. I'd like to get home and then we can talk."

Sam was standing uncertainly, listening.

"You, too, Sam," she said firmly. "There is a lot to talk about and there is no doubt you are at the centre of it all. Yaacov can call a taxi and you can come with us."

Sam shook his head and said "not on shabbat, we'll walk."

Anna looked at him piercingly before continuing, "Esther and Daniel can walk also, unless they would rather see a little bit of Haifa and come back later."

The twins, who hadn't said anything at all, looked at each other and said almost together, "we would like to be part of this family conference."

"Good. That's settled. I just have to sign some papers because I'm discharging myself and then we can be off." She took the house keys out of her handbag and gave them to Daniel. "You will probably get back before us so make yourselves at home."

Esther and Daniel walked slowly back, discussing the latest developments.

"It looks as if she's ok physically but she's made an unconscious decision to stop speaking. Do you think a psychiatrist might help?"

"Listening to granny, I think it's possible. The biggest obstacle to overcome will be that Aunt Anna has to accept there's a psychological problem. I don't think she'll find that easy. Anyhow, what is encouraging is that she might be a bit more accepting of dad. She could have told him to leave her alone and she didn't."

Daniel unlocked the front door and a wall of heat rushed at them.

"We need to get some fresh air in," and Esther went around, unlatching the windows and opening the back door. There was a small, stone built building at the bottom of the garden, and they were curious. Peering through the glass, they saw various sculptures balanced on a long table.

"Yaacov's studio – perhaps he'll show us his work later. Look, there are some paintings stacked against the wall. I bet they're Aunt Anna's. From what granny said, she had a wonderful voice; I think she's transferred her artistic ability into painting instead of singing."

"We shouldn't pry. They'll be back soon – time to find something to eat. I'm hungry."

"Daniel, you're always hungry," laughed Esther, as the sound of voices heralded the return of the family.

"You need to rest," Yaacov was saying but Anna was disagreeing, waving her hands to say 'No'.

"You heard what the doctor said," Yaacov persisted but Anna sat herself firmly on the settee and shaped the letter 'T'.

"Of course, Aunt Anna," said Esther. "It's just coming."

Anna waited until everyone was settled before looking at Yaacov. She seemed even smaller, sitting against a pile of cushions, her feet barely touching the floor.

"Let's begin," she signed. "There's so much to sort out and I want to go first," Eva subsided back into her seat. She had intended to speak before her sister but, looking at Anna's determined face, she gave the younger woman the floor.

"I was shocked when I learned who Sam's father was. Of course I was. He was the main person in the camp who had degraded me, who had killed my sister in front of me, laughing as he did so. When I first met you, Sam, I thought of you immediately as my nephew. I was thrilled that Eva had been able to have a child. As you know, I was never fortunate enough to be in that position. And to find out who you really were was more than I could take."

Sam interrupted.

"Who I really am, is the son of Eva and Friedrich, not the son of Hoffman. The Hoffmans are not my parents and never have been. My parents are the people who brought me up, who encouraged me in everything I did, and who are the grandparents of my children. Surely you must see that."

Sam refrained from calling Anna 'Aunt', even though she had suggested it originally. He didn't want to upset her even more.

"On one level, I understand what you're saying, Sam, but on another level it is difficult for me to accept that my sister has reared the child of a monster."

Eva couldn't stay silent any longer.

"I agree that Hoffman was a monster, but Sam has none of the characteristics of that odious man, He has all the attributes of a rabbi."

"Yes, I find that ironic, under the circumstances. Hoffman wanted to destroy all the Jews and his son became a rabbi."

Sam was heartbroken.

"Please do not refer to me as Hoffman's son..." and he left the room, Helen following him.

Anna started to get up. Eva hesitated, not sure whether to go after Sam or stay with her sister, but realising that Helen would comfort Sam, she put her arms around Anna.

"Why can't you understand that from the moment I saw Sam, he became my son. He has inherited only good from Friedrich and me."

"I don't know if I can accept any of it, Eva. Why did you not give him to the authorities? None of this would have happened if you had."

"That's true, but Sam would probably not have survived. He would have been a victim of the war like the rest of our family. With us he has had a life and, until recent events, a good one. All this is difficult for him, too, but he is doing his best to work through it."

CHAPTER 34

Eva decided to take a strong stand.

"Anna, we've just found each other after over forty years. We haven't had the opportunity to be together, to know each other as adults. I don't want to lose you again, so please don't make me choose between you and Sam.

"You have to look at him as an individual, one who has grown up with the sister *you* grew up with. How could he be anything other than a good man?"

"I wasn't asking you to make a choice," Anna signed, visibly distressed.

"But you were. If you cannot accept Sam, what hope is there for us to see each other, be close to each other?"

Yaacov shook his head as Anna told him to tell Eva what she'd signed.

"I'm not prepared to ask her that."

Anna signed again, and Yaacov reluctantly gave in, saying first to his wife,

"That's none of our business," and then to Eva, "if I don't tell you what she said, she will only write it down. Anna wants to know if you told Friedrich about Sam."

This was the question Eva had been dreading. There was no other way to answer; she had to tell the truth.

"No, Friedrich never knew that Sam wasn't his son."

"And why was that? Why didn't you tell him?" Anna pursued the question.

"All sorts of reasons. When Friedrich arrived at the kibbutz, he saw Sam for the first time. Of course he thought Sam was his son! The last time we'd been together I'd been pregnant; why would Friedrich have any doubts?"

"But you could have told him. Were you frightened he'd make you give the baby up?"

"I don't know what was going through my head, but when I saw Friedrich's tears, and when I saw Sam reach out to him, I made a snap decision to keep Sam's background to myself. I don't know what I was thinking – perhaps I knew that keeping the secret would be a kind of punishment for me. There was also the possibility that I might never be able to have another child – Sam might have been the only child I could ever have. I couldn't know, and I couldn't take away the joy Friedrich felt when he saw Sam. They bonded immediately."

"But then you had Rachel!" Anna said thoughtfully.

"Yes, I had Rachel and there was no difference in the way Friedrich treated Sam. I had wondered if he would bond more with the baby because he had been there when she was born, but he treated them the same. He loved them both."

"But Eva, did he never comment there was no family resemblance?"

"Why would he?"

"Because, despite having a beard, I can see that Sam doesn't look like anyone from our side of the family."

Eva was stricken with guilt. Had Friedrich known all along that Sam wasn't his son? And then reason prevailed.

"Friedrich didn't question anything. He was just happy to have a healthy child."

Anna appeared to accept this but, even though it was true, Eva was now filled with doubts. Had she kept this awful secret all these years when, in fact, Friedrich was aware of it? Now, there was nothing she could do, but at least she was confident that Friedrich had loved the boy.

"I was listening, you know, when you were talking to Sam," Anna signed to Yaacov. "I heard what you were talking about. For a man who says he's not interested in religion, you seemed very focused on Sam being a rabbi."

Yaacov looked a little shamefaced. "I was interested, not because of Sam's parentage, but because of his total conviction that he wants to resume being a rabbi. Maybe you should look at this through Sam's eyes. It must have been an awful shock for him to learn about Hoffman, and in such a dreadful way. I think he's still trying to come to terms with it. I can see how distressed he is, even though I don't know him well and, Anna, if you were thinking straight, you would see that too."

"Sam told me that there is doubt about whether or not he'll be able to continue. There are a few rabbis at the yeshivah who feel the same as you, Anna," said Eva. "They are having difficulty in considering Sam as Jewish; they think because his father was a Nazi he must have similar traits."

"But the yeshiva rabbis didn't know that monster. For them it's an abstract thought. The reason I'm having a problem is that I remember what he did. I don't want to find myself in a situation where every time I look at Sam,

I see Hoffman." Anna rubbed her eyes as the tears started to flow again.

"I agree the rabbis didn't know Hoffman, but they knew *of* him; they know his reputation and they will have heard about his trial."

Yaacov fidgeted a little in his chair.

"Anna was asked to testify at Hoffman's trial," he said eventually. "Once he'd been identified, the war trials tribunal got in touch with anyone they could find who'd ever been in a camp run by him. They were asked to appear in court as witnesses for the prosecution. Did they not get in touch with you?"

Things were getting very complicated for Eva but she bravely spoke up. "They did but I refused."

"Because of Sam?"

"Because Hoffman had been blackmailing me for years until eventually I contacted the Nazi hunters and told them where to find him."

This stopped Anna and Yaacov in their tracks, and then the questions came thick and fast.

"He was blackmailing you? Because of Sam? How long did it go on? And where did you find the money to pay him off? And then you informed on him...even though it might have meant a death sentence? You would have had Sam's birth father hanged?"

There was a moment's silence and then Eva said impatiently,

"How many times do I have to tell you that Hoffman only gave life to Sam. He was never his father. Hoffman's sentence was handed down by a judge, not by me. It was right he was caught, and right he was prosecuted. Anna, did you go to Berlin? Did you testify?"

"I gave a written testimony. I couldn't see the point in travelling; I wouldn't have been able to speak so why not write my deposition here, in the safety of Israel."

"Oh Anna," said Eva tearfully. "We've had so many missed opportunities; we missed each other in Israel; we missed each other by not going to Berlin for Hoffman's trial and we missed each other because I didn't put the family names into the records at Yad Vashem. Can't you see that we have to resolve this?"

"Yes, I can. When I first met Sam and he told me you were alive, I was shocked as well as thrilled. I never doubted I had found a nephew as well as a sister. The latest revelation is even more overwhelming, but I can see where you're coming from. Maybe you keeping Sam is retribution for all of that beast's misdeeds."

Eva spoke angrily.

"There was never any question that I kept Sam as revenge. I kept Sam because from the moment I saw him, I loved him."

There was a little chink in Anna's demeanour. She paused and then signed,

"I can see he's a good person...let's leave it for now, while you tell me all about your life. There are so many things I want to know. Maybe the first thing, though, is that you should tell me how long you're staying in Israel."

"I have an open ticket so I don't really know. I need to be back for when Rachel has the baby – her first, and she's not a young mother to be."

Yaacov was looking tired. The constant translating was taking its toll on him.

"I'm not such a young man, now," he joked and Eva looked a little worried at that.

305

"But you're in good health, aren't you?"

"I am," he risked a look at Anna who didn't appear to be listening. "I do worry about Anna because if I wasn't able to watch her sign and then tell people what she's saying, she would have to write everything down. I suppose now it's too late for her to try and regain her speech."

Eva realised what Yaacov was trying to do, and answered him carefully.

"It's never too late to recover anything. From what Dr Halpern said, there is no physical problem with her vocal chords. A visit to the psychiatrist might unlock her voice."

Anna didn't respond; there was no movement from the hands on her lap. She was staring out of the window as if oblivious to the conversation, but Eva was pretty sure she was taking it all in.

"Dr Halpern suggested Anna make an appointment, didn't he, but that will depend on whether or not Anna wants to speak again. She could be happy as she is; she seems to have adapted well."

At this, Anna turned her head and signed furiously. Eva didn't need anyone to translate for her. She looked directly at her sister but addressed her words to her brother-in-law.

"It's ok, Yaacov, I can guess what she's saying. Just make that appointment for her and she can take it from there. And now, Anna, I'm going outside to see how Sam is."

Sam was sitting on the low wall at the bottom of the garden. Haifa was beginning to get busy. He could hear the traffic noise and smell the petrol fumes but nothing could detract from the beauty of the rainbow in the distance. The iridescent colours shone in the day's fading light and he stood up as his mother approached.

"I've been looking at the rainbow and praying; it means so much! A reminder that the almighty has made a covenant with the Jewish people and it's also a symbol of hope. I need some divine help because this is more difficult than I thought. To be truthful, I didn't expect Anna to fall into my arms with joy, but she really has a problem with me. I don't know what to do."

He looked so woebegone, that Eva was taken back to when he was a little boy and wanted something she wasn't able to give. She wished it was in her power to make everything perfect for him.

"I've been speaking to her, Sam, and there is a softening of her attitude. I can understand what you're going through, but I also understand how she must be feeling. I'm sure that once she gets to know you, she will love you as I do. It will need time and patience and one good thing has come out of this. She's going to see the psychiatrist."

Sam's ears pricked up and he said bitterly,

"I'm glad something good has appeared, because as far as I feel, nothing could be worse than this."

Eva tutted, and told him that Anna had agreed to Dr Halpern's suggestion. She went on,

"That's progress. Yaacov will make an appointment, and Anna will take it from there. In the meantime, I want to stay here in Haifa. There's a lot of catching up to do. Esther and Daniel can explore Jerusalem and maybe the weekends will be a time when we can all get together. I've realised that the twins will have to go home before me."

"Not at all, ma. They're on vacation so they can stay as long as they wish. I'm sure Esther has plans and I expect that Daniel will want to try every restaurant in Israel." Sam was more cheerful and he and Helen decided to make a start back to Jerusalem as soon as shabbat was over.

Yaacov came out of the house waving a piece of paper.

"It's amazing! Anna has an appointment tomorrow with a Doctor Stein. Apparently Robert Halpern is a friend of hers and rang her after Anna left the hospital. She's very interested because she's done some work with people who have psychosomatic illness – even some who've lost their voices, but she's never had a patient who has been unable to speak for over forty years. Between you and me, I think she sees Anna as a challenge."

"And is Anna comfortable with this."

Yaacov moved to Eva and hugged her.

"I think what you said – about her not wanting to speak again, made her think. Maybe it's a little bit true…I never thought so, but it's certainly a way of avoiding the issue. She told me she'll go, but not to expect a miracle. There's no doubt about it, Eva. Even though we're in the middle of an emotional mess, your being here has given Anna the incentive to move on, and for that I thank you.

"We have been in a rut; we've made a comfortable life, with no unpleasantness and we've adapted to Anna not having a voice. We are settled here, and our life is very smooth. That is going to change. There may be difficult times ahead but I think now is the time to welcome that change."

CHAPTER 35

Esther and Daniel arrived back, flushed with excitement at how beautiful Haifa was.

"I know you love Jerusalem, dad," said Daniel, "but Haifa is great. There are lots of young people here and the place is alive."

"Well, shabbat is over so I expect all the kids are coming out," Sam said mildly.

"I think it's more than that. There's a wonderful atmosphere – not so solemn, like it is in Jerusalem."

"Do you mean, 'not so religious'?" signed Anna, who was at the kitchen door wiping her hands on her apron.

"Not exactly…well, sort of…"said Daniel, grinning. "Maybe Jerusalem *is* a bit too religious for me."

"Before we go, ma," said Sam, "we should talk about Yad Vashem. I've been in touch with Mr Morris and he told me what documentation he needs to prove you survived the Holocaust. I must tell you that he was absolutely thrilled. He said it's rare for a survivor to be found, especially so long after the Shoah, but it's wonderful when it happens.

"He already has the ID number of your listing in the book of Shoah victims' names; as soon as he gets proof you're alive, he'll have it removed."

"Will I need to go?" Eva asked. "I don't think I could cope with seeing my name on the wall commemorating the dead." She shuddered. "It's an awful thought."

Before Anna could sign, Eva told her that she didn't blame her – she knew that Anna had been making sure the family was remembered, but she would feel better when she was no longer listed. Sam pressed on.

"Okay, ma. First of all, you need to fill in a survivor's registration form. Actually, I can do that for you. They also need details to prove you are alive – passport, photograph, that sort of thing. They've asked for five separate things but I don't think that's a problem."

Eva opened her handbag and handed a folder containing several sheets of paper as well as her passport, to Sam.

"I think everything Mr Morris needs is there, and I've included some information about Friedrich and his family. We should also get their names included. If you could see to that, darling, I'd be very grateful. If I have to sign anything – well, I guess I'll cross that bridge when I come to it."

Anna had gone back to the kitchen while Sam and Eva were talking, emerging only to give Helen a parcel of food.

"Anna has never been known to let people leave without a 'care package'," Yaacov laughed.

"Ma's exactly the same," said Sam, chivvying everyone into the car. "I think she wants to feed the world."

Helen and Daniel were sitting in the back of the car. "Maybe this wasn't a good idea," Helen said. "The way Daniel is getting through Anna's food, there probably won't be anything left by the time we get back to the flat."

Helen's comment lightened the mood, and Daniel passed the bag forward to Esther, once he'd finished eating.

"What plans do you have for the week?" Sam asked. "You'll have to entertain yourselves. Your mother will be at the school and I'm teaching and then studying. You might prefer Haifa for the easy going way of life, but there are so many museums and galleries to see in Jerusalem."

"Don't worry, dad, we'll find plenty of things to do."

In Haifa, Yaacov and Anna were talking over the visit and the doctor's suggestions for Anna.

"What worries you most?" asked Yaacov as they ate.

"Learning about Sam's background was a terrible shock, but I can put that to one side for a while. The thing I'm most concerned about is seeing the psychiatrist tomorrow. I don't know what will come out of the woodwork."

"Even so, you've always been able to tell me what happened. Why should there be any more to find out?"

"I think there is something in my past that I have unconsciously hidden. The psychiatrist might be able to get it out of me but I'm so scared, Yaacov. I've managed to live pretty well after what happened. Maybe I don't want to discover any more. Maybe there's something really bad my brain has shut out." She placed her knife and fork neatly on her plate before signing again. "I'm worried in case you stop loving me."

311

Yaacov looked at her in horror. "How could you think that of me?" he asked, and Anna hung her head and wouldn't sign any more.

He persevered and went on cautiously,

"You said you would go – I think Eva needled you a little. If you find you don't want to continue, don't go back. One session only, Anna, please. Try it and see what happens."

Neither Yaacov nor Anna slept that night. The humidity was high and the sheets felt damp, but that wasn't the real reason. At two am, Anna went downstairs and opened the fridge to get some ice water. Yaacov padded behind her and they took their glasses to the kitchen table.

"You must sleep, Anna. There's no need to worry. I'll be with you all the time; I'll stay with you and when you've finished, we'll go to Barzinsky's and have cheesecake and cappuccino."

Anna turned on him.

"I'm not a child you can bribe with a sweetie, Yaacov. I know I have to go, but it won't be because you'll buy me cake and coffee afterwards," and she flounced back to bed.

They were both heavy eyed in the morning, and neither could face breakfast. They drank some juice and arrived early for the appointment at the mental health centre.

"I wish it wasn't here," Anna said. "Anyone could see us, teachers or parents from the school; friends; anyone. They might think I'm crazy."

"Or they might think I was," said Yaacov.

"You're crazy to put up with me," Anna signed but she was smiling.

Dr Stein was waiting for them in the reception. Tall and slim, she had a coloured kerchief tying her hair back and tanned feet peeping out from under her flowing skirt. She wasn't at all what Anna expected, who had thought she would be seeing an old doctor wearing a white coat over baggy corduroy trousers, wire rimmed glasses covering his eyes.

"This hospital is a rabbit warren so I thought it would be good if I met you. Let me introduce myself. My name is Rivka Stein. I will be your doctor while you attend the centre."

As she spoke, they were walking along a carpeted corridor, which had prints of the Carmel beaches fixed on the walls. There was a pleasant smell of lavender and the doors on either side were painted soft green. Altogether the ambience was calm and reassuring.

The doctor's office was comfortable, with soft seating arranged around a low coffee table. The desk in front of the window was small and neat and the whole appearance was one of a relaxed sitting room.

Dr Stein saw them looking around.

"Do you like it?" she asked.

Anna nodded and signed. Yaacov started to tell the doctor what was said but she stopped him with a smile.

"I understand sign language. I learned because I have several deaf patients and it really helps confidentiality, because I don't need someone to interpret. So, our discussions can be totally private; no one else needs to be in the room. There is a coffee shop in the basement; why don't you wait there. Anna will be about an hour and then she'll join you."

Before he realised it, Yaacov found himself on the other side of the door, wondering how he'd got there. He and Anna were inseparable, and he worried that she might not be able to deal with any intensive conversation. He raised his hand to knock on the door, and then thought better of it. He realised that the next hour was going to be the longest of his life.

"Is it okay if I call you 'Anna'?" the doctor began. "I like to be as informal as possible."

Anna signed 'Yes', and sat back waiting.

"Okay. I have your notes here from Dr Halpern. I'm pleased he did a thorough medical, because it shows that your vocal chords are intact. I can see you had a sudden unexpected shock, and that you have a very supportive husband. Your sister explained that, as a child, your speech was perfect and you had a beautiful voice. Do you agree with the notes?"

Anna signed 'yes' again.

"In my professional career, Anna, I've taken a great deal of interest in what used to be called 'war neurosis'. Now we call it PTSD – post traumatic stress disorder. So many Holocaust survivors, even years after the war, are affected, but you are the first I've met who has never spoken for such a long time. It seems to me, that as all the physical signs are good, there is some kind of a psychological blockage which is preventing you from speaking. Now, I'm going to ask you some questions and I'd like you to answer honestly. You can just say 'yes' or 'no' but if you can expand, it would be better. How do you feel about that?"

Dr Stein took Anna's nod to be assent.

"I don't know what you know about PTSD but it is very common in survivors of trauma. However, to make such a diagnosis I need to know about your behaviour –

your feelings, if you like. For example, how is your sleeping pattern?

Anna shrugged. "Not wonderful," she signed. "Sometimes I don't get to sleep for a long time and then other times I wake up early and can't get back to sleep. And sometimes I have awful nightmares."

"What about feelings of anxiety?"

"Yes," admitted Anna. "I'm often frightened that people will find out what I did during the war. I blame myself because I know I could have ended my life, and I didn't."

Dr Stein was busy scribbling notes as she asked another question,

"Do you ever feel suicidal?" She watched Anna's face closely as she signed.

"Not really, but I do sometimes doubt why I let myself live."

"Do you often get angry for no real reason?"

"Not often. But sometimes," she added thinking back to when she'd told Sam she never wanted to see him again.

"I suspect you were faced with violence during the time you spent in the camp. Can you tell me about that?"

Anna shook her head, and again Dr Stein wrote on her pad.

The doctor looked up and said slowly,

"Based on what you've just told me, I think you are very definitely suffering from traumatic mutism caused by PTSD. We need to find out why it has robbed you of your speech."

Anna got up and went to the window. Her shoulders were shaking and the doctor couldn't work out if she was laughing or crying as there was no sound.

Sitting down again, Anna signed the words carefully.

"I was laughing because I have never heard anything so stupid in all my life. Of course, we know what happened to make me lose my speech. The war happened; the camps happened and the brothel happened. I don't need a psychiatrist to tell me that."

With infinite patience the doctor spoke again.

"Of course we know you survived the most awful atrocities, but I think there is something else which stopped you speaking. You have been able to describe much of what happened, but somewhere inside your memory there is an additional problem, one you have not been able to recall. Would you like to try to access it? Whatever we find will be between you and me. You will not need to tell anyone, unless you want to – not even Yaacov."

At the mention of Yaacov, Anna jumped up again before signing. It was clear she was agitated. Dr Stein paused a moment and then said,

"Yes, I know he's wonderful but maybe that's part of the problem. As long as he is able to translate what you say, there is no real reason for you to ever speak. And, I assume, you *would* like to speak again? And, before you tell me you can write things down if people don't understand sign language, I want you to think how easy that is.

"Wouldn't it be better to say the words out loud; to have a proper conversation with your sister without Yaacov translating; without having to write things down? Come once a week to see me and together we'll try and bring out into the open whatever is hiding from you.

"However, I don't want you to feel pressured into anything. I suggest you find Yaacov and discuss our proposed plan with him. Give me a call if you want to proceed and we'll set it up."

Anna left the doctor's office determined not to go back. She found Yaacov sitting at a white table in the cafeteria, a cold cup of coffee in front of him, the skin congealing on its surface.

He almost knocked his chair over as he stood up anxiously. Grasping her hands he sat her down.

"So, what did she say?"

"She wants me to see her once a week. She thinks there is something in my past which I haven't acknowledged and, if we can find out what it is, it will bring my voice back." Anna was surprised she was saying this, and even more surprised when she said she was going to do it.

"Are you sure?" asked Yaacov worriedly. "What if there is something you can't come to terms with?"

"Do you know, Yaacov," Anna said with sudden confidence. "I think she's right. Signing or writing everything down as I have done all these years means I'm ok to talk about some things, but my silence seems to mean there are others things I don't want to talk about. You have been a tower of strength, but the time is right for me now to say my own words without your help. I have faith in this doctor. I *will* see her and I *will* learn to speak again."

CHAPTER 36

Eva was eager to hear what had happened in the doctor's office but Anna refused to say, so she didn't pursue it. There were a lot of other things for them to talk about. They had a lifetime of being apart to catch up on, and so much to share, which meant the meeting with the psychiatrist paled into insignificance. The most important thing was for the two women to become sisters again. Patiently, Yaacov sat with them day after day, as they exchanged information about their lives. They never tired of talking, although initially they avoided subjects which each thought the other might find upsetting and, as the days went on, they became close.

Anna showed Eva her paintings. Some were dramatic, mainly mono-chrome, depicting scenes from the camp; faces pressed against wire fences, some without eyes and many without mouths, all wearing striped uniforms. Yet still, the effect was startling. Wherever you moved in the room, it seemed that you were being watched.

Anna proudly told Eva that they sold well.

"In the beginning, when I painted, it was just after the war. There was a great deal of interest from tourists, mainly Americans, who had never seen anything like them. Without exception, they wanted to know if I was a survivor until, in the end, I wrote a little bit of background and included it with their purchase.

"Not all my work is about the Holocaust," she went on. "There came a time when I felt I was becoming burnt out. There are only so many wire fences you can paint; only so many sad faces. I discovered I had a talent for landscape and now I concentrate on that. Sometimes I take my canvas and easel outside and work."

She showed Eva another corner of the studio where paintings were stacked against the walls. There was a pleasant smell of oil paints and linseed; several colour streaked rags were piled on the table, and an oversized shirt had been flung casually over a wooden chair.

"I haven't done much recently," she told Eva. "I think I need to start again. I have several commissions to fill and customers waiting."

Eva wanted to know about Anna's work at the school.

"I worked there as a teacher until I officially retired. Now I'm a volunteer, which means I can choose my hours."

Yaacov chipped in,

"What that really means, is that Anna's hours haven't changed at all. It's just that now she doesn't get paid." They both laughed and it was clear that money was not a problem.

Eva decided the time had come to talk about Hoffman and Sam. She began to speak at the same time that Anna was signing. Yaacov laughed.

"You really are sisters," he said. "You're both saying the same thing at the same time. Anna, too, feels that this problem has to come out into the open. Her sessions with

Dr Stein have made her see that she has to confront her demons, not try to hide them."

Eva opened her mouth to speak, but again Anna shook her head. Even in the short time they had been together, Eva had managed to pick up some sign language and she knew that what Anna had spelled out meant she wanted to continue.

"I admit I have a problem," she stopped to correct herself, "*had* a problem with Sam – and maybe with you, too. I couldn't understand why you kept him. I understand it wasn't your choice to leave the camp with him, but when you found out he was Hoffman's son, I couldn't work out why you just didn't leave him somewhere." She held her hand up to keep Eva quiet.

"I see now that Sam has none of Hoffman's characteristics. He is a warm, kind man and I'm so sorry that I was ungracious when he first arrived. You know, Eva, one of my worries was that every time I looked at Sam I would see Hoffman. But I don't. I see you and Friedrich. It's funny, but when Sam was here I watched him peeling an orange. He carefully scored the peel with a knife, pulled the skin off then separated the segments and arranged them on a plate. I remember Friedrich doing that for me, before you were married, when I was very young." Her eyes stared into the distance. "Sam is very like Friedrich, isn't he?"

Eva nodded. "In so many ways."

"When Sam speaks, I even hear you sometimes; your voice, your expressions, the way you say things. I just wish I could reply," she said wistfully. "All these years, I never worried about the fact I couldn't speak. Now I would do anything to tell Sam I love him, because I do, and you, too," she added hastily.

Eva responded by hugging her sister and saying,

"I also wondered at first if Sam would become like Hoffman as he grew. I never doubted that I loved him. I couldn't bear to have parted with him but, at the back of my mind, was a worry that he would somehow develop a sadistic streak. Of course, that's nonsense and, as the years went on, at least until I was contacted by Hoffman, I completely forgot about his background. I paid blackmail money to Hoffman so that Sam would never find out and look what's happened as a result."

The sisters looked at each other, realising how intertwined both their lives had been with Hoffman.

"We don't need to worry about him any more – he's gone and we have the rest of our lives together," and they hugged again.

"How many more sessions do you have with Dr Stein?" Eva asked, as Anna got ready the next morning. "You've been seeing her a lot lately."

Anna was sitting on her bed, peering into the dressing table mirror. "I know. I have a feeling she's going to say we've gone as far as we can. I still can't manage to find the memory which could unlock my speech. Maybe I never will." She looked downhearted. "She suggested hypnotism at my last appointment, but I'm not sure I want to do it. I don't know if looking into my brain while I'm unconscious is a good idea."

Dr Stein was ready for Anna when she arrived. She patted the couch, inviting Anna to sit, and passed her a warm blanket.

"Have you thought any more about the conversation we had last time you were here? I think we've gone as far as we can in these sessions if we keep them as they are. You've been honest and open so I don't think you are deliberately keeping things back but I would have thought, by now, that we would have made more progress. We talked about hypnosis – it can be a wonderful way of bringing things out into the open and I promise to stop if you become upset." She looked searchingly at Anna, waiting for her to sign.

"I have thought about it and I really do want to speak again but I don't know if I'm ready for any more revelations. So far, it's been a rollercoaster of emotions for me. Do you think I'm mentally strong enough?"

"To be honest, Anna, I don't know."

Anna began to tremble; her hands were shaking and she clasped them tightly in her lap.

"That doesn't give me much confidence," she said, trying to smile and failing miserably.

"I promised you the truth; I can't say what effect any disclosures will have on you, because I have no idea what they might be, other than I'm convinced they have to do with whatever happened to you in the camp."

Anna bit her lip, trying to calm herself. This was probably the most difficult thing she'd ever had to deal with.

Dr Stein left her to think; she felt that any pressure could mean that the hypnosis wouldn't work. She knew from experience that a reluctant patient might be unable to fully explore her problems.

The clock in the background ticked the minutes away as Anna debated with herself, and then she sat up and said,

"I have to do this, don't I? I realise I'll never be free until all my ghosts have been laid. What do I have to do?"

"First of all," said Dr Stein, "I think you're being incredibly brave. Tell me, is Yaacov with you?"

Anna shook her head.

"In which case, I think you should call him. It would be a good idea if he was here when the session finished. You might be glad of his comfort if he's here afterwards."

Anna looked alarmed and her hands told Dr Stein she didn't want Yaacov in the room.

"Don't worry, my dear. He can wait outside." She pushed the phone across the desk and busied herself with paperwork, so that Anna had some privacy while she made the call.

"He's on his way. Can we get started now, please? I think the waiting will worry me even more."

"Would you like to lie down on the couch and get comfortable? Use the blanket if you feel cold and I'll talk you through what will happen."

"I feel shivery," said Anna.

"I expect that's apprehension. Nevertheless, pull the blanket over you and try to relax. I am going to ask you to look at my necklace."

Dr Stein was wearing a large amber pendant which had flecks of brown and gold in it. She took it off and showed it to Anna.

"I want you to lie still and watch the pendant. Follow it with your eyes," and she began moving it from side to side.

Anna did as she was asked and listened to the soothing tones of the doctor, who was telling her she was to relax, empty her mind and let things go. She wasn't aware of the

323

doctor telling her she would go deeper and deeper into sleep; she wasn't aware of the doctor telling her to count backwards from ten. She was aware of a delicious heaviness in her limbs and of feeling warm and comfortable.

Dr Stein began her questioning gently, asking Anna to talk about her time in the camp. She wasn't surprised that Anna was able to speak. Her voice was young, like a teenage girl's, as she described her life. She spoke of how she and Leah had been so close; how Leah had been the protective older sister and how Leah had told her what would happen to her in the brothel.

"How did you deal with that?" the doctor probed.

"Oh, I managed because I thought of happy things. I decided that I wasn't there; I was in a beautiful place. Sometimes I felt as if I was flying, or I was hovering on the ceiling looking down. It was someone else doing those things and when Leah and I were back in our barracks we forgot all about it."

"Can you tell me about the worst thing that happened?" Dr Stein asked carefully.

Anna shifted on the couch, moving her head from side to side. The blanket slipped onto the floor and the doctor picked it up and covered Anna again.

"Deep breaths, Anna! Take deep breaths," she suggested and waited until Anna was calmer. Then she repeated the question.

"The worst thing that happened to you," she prompted.

"It was when Leah died," whispered Anna. "We were crossing the parade ground. There were bombs falling," she cowered against the arm of the couch, "bombs everywhere, and people falling. We were running and then something hit Leah. I don't know what it was – shrapnel or a piece of wood from one of the barracks? She fell and I could see blood on her stomach, and something sticking out. She was bleeding and bleeding and there was nothing I could do to help her."

Anna's distress became palpable; her face was pale and there were beads of sweat on her forehead. Dr Stein had to consider whether or not to continue. She decided to take a risk and said again,

"What happened after that?"

"Hoffman came! He was wearing his uniform and it looked clean. How could it have remained so clean amidst all that carnage? His boots were polished and his hat was firmly on his head. He walked across to where Leah was lying. I was holding her – she was half across my lap, and my dress – my stripy uniform, was covered in blood." She looked at her hands. "There was blood everywhere. I didn't know people had so much blood inside them."

"You've already told me that Hoffman shot Leah…"

"He took out his pistol and said,

'Sie nützt nichts mehr…she is no use any more,' and he shot her in the head. But she didn't die. The bullet took part of her head away but she was still alive. Hoffman just laughed and walked on. I was holding Leah's hand and she said…she spoke to me…and she said, 'do it, little nightingale. Finish what Hoffman started. Please, help me.'

"She was begging me to kill her and I couldn't. I couldn't. And then she cried – big fat tears mingled with her blood and her eyes begged me. I leaned over her and put my hand over her nose and mouth and she didn't struggle. She died in my arms but her eyes were smiling. I killed her." Anna's voice was rough and hoarse and full of anguish. "It wasn't Hoffman who killed her. It was me. And then the soldiers pulled me away, and they were laughing too. One of them said 'one less Jew in the world,' and I couldn't do anything. I had to go back to the brothel and work."

Dr Stein spoke soothingly. "When I count to five you will wake up and you will be able to speak. You will remember what caused you to lose your voice but you will be calm."

Anna came to, slowly, and then sat up and gave a great shout. "I killed my sister," she cried. "I killed Leah."

CHAPTER 37

Dr Stein handed Anna a glass of water and pressed the button on the intercom. She asked the receptionist to send Yaacov in. Anna was shaking and wouldn't look at her husband. She shrugged him off as he tried to put his arms around her. He stroked her hair, trying to calm her and the doctor observed the couple.

A dry croak emerged from Anna's throat as she told Yaacov,

"All these years, the reason I haven't been able to speak was because of the dreadful thing I've kept inside me. I was the one who killed Leah, not Hoffman."

Dr Stein didn't intervene. She watched Yaacov's reaction to Anna.

"You're speaking! How is this? It's a miracle! Is this why you didn't…couldn't speak? Oh, my darling, what a burden you've carried all these years. Are you able to tell me what happened?"

Falteringly, and with frequent pauses, and many sips of water, Anna related what had happened, with Yaacov listening carefully as she voiced the words. She stopped, exhausted, and he reassured her.

"I don't think you had any choice, darling. From what you've described, Leah would have had a very painful death, lying outside amidst the bombing, terrified and alone. There was no way she could have survived – not with a head wound like that. She asked you to help her and very bravely you did, and you were with her at the end. So many of us didn't get that opportunity; so many of us never found out where our families died."

He turned to Dr Stein.

"I can't thank you enough," he said emotionally. "I never thought this would be possible. My Anna has her voice back and it's thanks to you. I have never heard her speak and she has such a beautiful voice." He shook the doctor's hand and then impulsively kissed her. She looked pleased and then urged him to sit again.

"This isn't the end, you know, Yaacov. This is only the beginning." She turned her gaze to Anna.

"You will have to take things slowly at first. Not too much speaking and," she added with compassion, "no singing for a little while. Your voice has been asleep for over forty years so you should give it time to wake up properly."

She handed Anna a prescription.

"This is something to help you get a good night's rest. Take one of the tablets thirty minutes before you go to bed. This is just a precaution, to stop you going over and over what you've discovered today. I'm only prescribing enough pills for one week. After that, you'll come for a further appointment and we'll see how you are. I'm very proud of you, Anna," she went on. "You've faced up to your past so well, but you need to be cautious and not overwork your vocal chords. You can always sign a bit to

Yaacov until your voice returns to a more normal state." She glanced over at him,

"There's one more thing. I would advise that you keep questions until later. Let Anna say what she wants when she wants to, and don't pressure her into giving you more details."

"Don't worry, doctor. I'll make sure she follows your instructions," Yaacov said as he helped Anna on with her jacket. Despite the heat, she was still shivering as she slid her arms into the sleeves.

"Wait until we get home before you say anything else. Save your voice," he continued. "This is going to be a complete surprise for Eva. I can't wait to see her face when you say 'Hello' to her."

Eva was relaxing in the garden when they got back. She was lying on a sun lounger, one hand resting on the grass, the other holding a magazine. A floppy hat was obscuring her eyes a bit, but she still saw the couple coming through the gate.

"How was it?" she asked, getting up cautiously, her hand in the small of her back. "I was thinking of you all the time."

Anna had composed herself on the way back from the centre and she sat down beside her sister, took her hands and looked directly into her eyes.

"It went well," she said, waiting for Eva's reaction. She was not disappointed. Eva shouted in delight and then burst into tears, before wrapping her arms round her sister.

Yaacov intervened, "We should wait for Anna to talk when she wants to. It's important she doesn't strain her voice, so some of the time I intend to encourage her to sign."

"You just don't want to be made redundant," Anna responded, and even though her words were hoarse, she spoke with a happy lilt in her voice.

"True," said Yaacov. "Soon you'll be able to tell people anything you like. You won't need me to translate any more, but I'll always be here for you. Always! In the meantime, I'm going to phone Sam. We haven't seen them for a little while so maybe they could come up this weekend?"

Sam was incredulous when he heard the news, and immediately said they would all come up on Friday afternoon. Helen was listening at his shoulder and sat down abruptly.

"I can't believe it. Do you think ma coming was the catalyst? Her visit has certainly started things off."

"I don't know how the doctor managed it, but we may have seen a miracle. They want us all to go for the weekend, so I'll need to get on a bit with this thesis I'm writing. Rabbi Eliazar has asked me to see him next Monday to discuss my progress. It's strange, really. When he told me to come to his office I felt like a child at school again. I thought rapidly to see if I'd done anything wrong and I couldn't think of anything. When he said he wanted to talk about my work I was so relieved."

"Oh, Sam!" Helen laughed but not unkindly. "I think you're regressing. You'll be wearing short trousers next."

"Not with my knees," Sam shot back.

"Will you tell the twins about Anna regaining her voice?"

"I hadn't thought about it, but no, I think we'll let it be a surprise."

"What's a surprise?" asked Daniel as he let himself into the flat, Esther close behind.

"I think the biggest surprise would be if there was no food in the fridge."

Daniel accepted the good natured teasing but asked again.

"The surprise is that Aunt Anna has invited us all for the weekend. Do you feel like another visit to Haifa?"

"Absolutely," they said together.

"That's good, then. We can leave early on Friday morning and be there well before lunch. Mum doesn't work on Fridays and I can leave the yeshiva after shacharit. Maybe we could take a small detour and go and have a look at the beaches. Hof HaCarmel is one of my favourite places."

"Swimsuits, dad?" asked Esther. "I love the flat and I love being in the centre of Jerusalem but it will be so great to see the sand and the sea."

Esther and Daniel had been systematically exploring Jerusalem and they spent the next couple of days visiting a couple more museums and doing some essential shopping.

"Essential?" joked Daniel. "New swimsuits? Essential?"

"Swimsuits and flip flops and some sun glasses," Esther replied firmly.

Sam was getting so familiar with the road to Haifa and the early start meant the roads were fairly quiet. The car purred along, performing well, and in no time at all they saw the signpost to Dado Beach and turned off. They parked on a gravelled area, behind a low wall.

"Wow," said Esther. "That beach is magnificent. Are we ok to stay a while before we go to Aunt Anna's?"

"I told Yaacov that we'd be there mid afternoon, so you have time for a swim and then we can walk along the promenade and find a restaurant for lunch. Your mother and I will have a coffee and enjoy some peace and quiet without you."

"You would think we were five and not in our twenties," said Daniel as he raced towards the sea. He scooped up some water and threw it over his sister, who responded by making a face at him and shouting,

"Some of us behave as if we *are* five, Daniel," and then ran off, shrieking as he chased her into the warm water.

"Let's walk for a while," said Helen. "And, by the way, did you tell ma about your meeting with Mr Morris?"

"Only that everything is in order. To be honest, she's been more interested in Anna these last weeks, and I can understand that. It's been hard for her since dad died and I think she's got a new lease of life. I'm more bothered about how Anna will be with me. It's been hard talking to her via Yaacov. Now she has her voice back she'll be able to have a proper conversation with me. Of course," he said somewhat gloomily, "that might be worse. She's already told me once that she didn't want to see me."

"And she changed her mind."

"Yes, she did," said Sam brightening up a little.

They stopped at a restaurant overlooking the sea. The menu was stuck on a board outside and Helen laughed that there was enough on it to feed her hungry son. They ordered coffee and Sam went to the terrace to wave at the twins. Daniel did a 'thumbs up', by which they understood they would be joined as soon as the twins had had enough of the water.

The scene was idyllic. It was too early for the weekenders to be there and the beach was almost deserted, apart from a few small groups of youngsters. The waves came rushing in, leaving white foam behind as they receded, and Sam and Helen felt the tension, which had become a part of their daily life, drain away. They were sitting very still until Helen suddenly jumped in her chair, then bent down to the floor. A small tribe of cats had appeared under the table, obviously waiting for tit bits.

"Careful," urged Sam tolerantly, as Helen stroked the animals. "They might have fleas."

"I don't think so," was the indignant reply, as a particularly curious tortoiseshell cat wound itself round her legs. The waiter came over and shooed them all away before telling his customers that he liked the cats, he just didn't want diners to be bothered.

Replete with good food – even Daniel declaring he couldn't eat any more, they piled back in the car and drove the last few miles to Anna and Yaacov's house. Eva waved as they came up the path and Anna came out, smiling enigmatically. She directed her first words to the twins.

"I'm so pleased to see you, Esther and Daniel," she said, watching their astonishment with great satisfaction.

"Dad, did you know?"

"Yes, but I thought a surprise would be good for you. Just take it easy. Aunt Anna needs time to get her voice working properly." As he said this, he glanced at Anna through lowered lids to see if she was upset he'd called her 'Aunt'. She didn't seem to be showing any reaction so he continued. "There will be a lot to talk about but we'll take it easy."

"And tea first, I think," said Yaacov passing around glasses full of the hot liquid. He'd set a table under a large tree at the side of the garden, and they were glad of the cool shade as they sipped their drinks.

Eva cleared her throat. She knew the announcement she was about to make would not be popular.

"Now we're all here, I need to tell you of my decision. I've made up my mind to go back to England soon."

Anna couldn't believe what she was hearing.

"Because of me? Because of what I've told you about Leah?" she asked with a quiver in her voice.

"Not at all! I've just realised I've been here longer than I intended. I've been speaking to Rachel on the phone and, although she's not complaining, I can see she needs some extra help. Ivor can't take time off work to look after her and he's worried because she's not a spring chicken and it's her first baby. It might be her only baby, so she needs special care."

"What about us, granny?" asked Esther. "Does this mean we have to go home, too?"

"Of course not, darling. That's up to you."

"But you don't like flying."

"No I don't, but I suspect I shall have to get used to it. With Anna here, and the rest of you in England I have no doubt I'll be travelling back and forth a lot. I can't always expect someone to be with me so I intend to do this next flight on my own. However, I won't say 'no' if you decide to come," she finished with a twinkle in her eye.

CHAPTER 38

"For a moment," Anna hiccoughed, "I thought you were going back to England because of what I told you. I'm so relieved, Eva. We mustn't lose each other now."

"And we won't, but I need to help Rachel. She and Ivor have been married a long time and I think they'd given up having children. This little one is a wonderful surprise for us all."

Daniel waited until his grandmother and great aunt finished their conversation and then said,

"I think you'll be pleased granny, when I tell you I'll fly home with you."

Eva looked extremely surprised, and Daniel went on,

"It's all right for Esther; she has university terms and won't start at Leo Baeck until October but I have to do my rotation. I've already been away longer than I planned, and I had a call from my supervisor who pretty well told me to 'get back or get out'."

"Would this week be too soon for you?" asked Eva. "Perhaps Thursday?"

"No problem, gran," said Daniel. "The only problem will be mum and dad having to cope with Esther, without me here to help." The twins had always enjoyed sparring gently with each other so no one took any notice of his comment; they just laughed, including Anna.

"It's so good to hear you laugh, my darling" said Yaacov. "Until now, I've only seen you smile…and a beautiful smile it's always been. But this laugh! It seems as if it's coming from your toes!"

"Plans for the week then! Will you come to Jerusalem on Wednesday Aunt Anna, and we can have a special meal before ma and Daniel get their flight."

"A wonderful idea," answered Yaacov. "In the meantime, we have another surprise for you." All attention was turned on him.

"We are having a party on Sunday. The children from Anna's school are coming to tea, with their teachers and some parents. They don't know that Anna's found her voice. I can't wait to see how they respond to a sound coming out of her mouth. Now, I expect you want to go to the synagogue. We'll eat when you get back."

Sam asked Anna tentatively, "would you like to come along? It's a very relaxed progressive shul and despite my initial reluctance, I'm comfortable there. We've always felt very much at home."

Esther couldn't hide her smile but wisely, didn't comment.

Anna fixed her piercing eyes onto Sam and said quietly but firmly,

"I'm very grateful that I've got my voice back, but my gratitude is to Dr Stein, not to God. I've been silent for forty years – where was God then? Where was God when I needed him? When Leah was dying? When I was in the camp?" Her face was flushed with the intensity of her words and she looked defiantly at Sam.

"I know you're a rabbi...or will be again soon, and I suppose it's your job to see as many people as possible return to their Jewish roots, but when I told you I wanted nothing else to do with God, I meant it. I don't want to hear another word about it."

Anna's words seemed to have more gravitas now that she was actually voicing them out loud. Somehow, there had been a small lack of emphasis when she was signing so Sam knew there was no point in trying to persuade her. He agreed not to tell anyone she'd regained her voice.

"Some of the parents are members of the shul and I want it to remain a secret until after Sunday."

"I'm beginning to feel like a regular," he said to Helen, embarrassed, as they found their seats in the synagogue. The rabbi smiled over at them and Esther raised her hand in acknowledgment.

The words flowed over them, the singing uplifted them and the kiddush after the service, fed them – but only lightly. They knew they would need to do justice to Anna's cooking when they got back, so held back a little.

"Do you have plans?" Yaacov asked Daniel, as they sat at the table. "Any idea what branch of medicine you want to go into?"

"I've always liked listening to granny's stories about her patients," Eva blushed and muttered,

"No names, of course; all very confidential," and Daniel winked at her.

"Of course, granny! Your secrets are safe with me, so I'm thinking I'd like to go into general practice."

Eva looked thrilled. "It would be wonderful to see the name 'Dr Goldman' outside a surgery again," she said emotionally. "Your grandfather would be very proud of you."

"Of course I'll still need to do all the rotations, but I've already been approached by a doctor who would be pleased to have me in his practice. Assuming all goes well and I pass all my exams, of course," he added hastily.

"What's happening about the names at Yad Vashem?" asked Anna. "Have they been changed?"

"They have," Helen spoke comfortingly. "It took a bit longer than expected which is why we haven't said much, but all the paperwork was completed yesterday and a new listing and plaque will be up soon. Certainly, by the time you come back, ma, it'll all be done."

"And what about you, Sam? How are you getting on?"

Sam shrugged and then asked, "what is this? Twenty questions?" but he was smiling.

"Things are going well and I'm enjoying the teaching. I'd forgotten how good it is to help shape young minds and they're all eager to learn. The afternoons are a bit more challenging. I'm back in the classroom and that's not so easy, but I'm getting there. In the evenings, when I get home, I'm working on my thesis and once that's completed to Rabbi Eliazar's satisfaction there'll be a meeting to discuss whether or not I will resume as a rabbi." He looked pensive, as there was a general outcry of,

"Of course you will."

"I shall tell you what I've been doing before I get interrogated," said Helen, smiling. "I'm very happy at the school. I don't have a job title as such, I just help out when needed and I'm enjoying being with the little ones."

Yaacov turned to Sam.

"Have you thought of making aliyah?" he asked. "It would be wonderful to have you near us."

Eva held her breath because it was obvious that Sam and Helen enjoyed living in Israel, and were very contented with what they were doing. In gaining a sister, would she be losing a son and daughter-in-law?

"We have," said Sam slowly. "Of course we have, but we won't settle here. Our lives and families are in England. One thing, though, we shall be visiting regularly, especially when Esther's doing her study year here."

Esther could hardly believe her ears. It seemed as if her father was coming around to the idea of her being a rabbi. She didn't speak – there was no need.

The party on Sunday afternoon was amazing. With the help of Eva and Helen, Anna had cooked enough food to feed a multitude of people. The twins had placed tables and chairs in the garden and set the food out on a long trestle. From two o'clock onwards, people started to arrive and Anna smiled at each of them but didn't speak. By around three o'clock, there were over a hundred people in the garden, all enjoying the afternoon but wondering why they'd been invited.

Yaacov tapped on a glass and invited everyone to find a chair or to sit on the grass. He waited a few moments for people to settle down and then introduced Anna who was going to give an address. The children were silent, the parents' expectant and the whole group waited for Anna to sign. Instead, in a clear voice she welcomed them all, and spoke briefly about how she'd regained the use of her voice.

"Of course," she said with a catch in her throat, "I wouldn't suggest it was easy to learn to speak again but it is worth it." She sat down amidst a roar of applause. So many people wanted to talk to her – and listen to her talking to them, until eventually, Yaacov had to ask people to let Anna's voice have some rest.

Anna knelt on the grass as one of the little ones tugged her skirt. The child signed a question to her, and a look of sadness crossed Anna's face.

She held the little girl's hand and signed back very carefully.

"I only got my voice back because I had a very serious problem when I was young which caused my brain – the part of my brain which controls talking, to shut down. Until then, I could speak like anyone else. It's different for you, Ellie; unfortunately, when you were born your ears didn't work properly, and so you never learned to speak with your voice." The child's eyes filled with tears.

'So I will never speak,' she signed.

"No, it is not possible for your voice to come back, but you will always be able to talk with your fingers, and I will talk to you with *my* fingers. We will always be able to understand what the other is saying."

There was a sigh, then with the resilience of childhood, the little girl stood up, and ran off to join the other children from her class.

"I can see why the kids love Anna," said Helen who had been watching this little cameo. "She is wonderful with them. I'm so glad she has decided to carry on at the school. She would be a big loss."

The last few stragglers left after five and Anna looked around happily. For the first time since the war ended she had a family she could call her own. She had delighted in introducing her sister, and her nephew and niece, and her great - nephew and great - niece to her friends.

Eva was lucky. There were seats available on the flight to England on Thursday and she wasted no time in booking them. She decided to spend the last couple of days with Sam, Helen and the twins, apologising in case they thought she'd been neglecting them. She was reassured when they said they understood.

"It's not every day you find a sister you thought was dead, and it's not every day your sister speaks again after forty years of silence."

Daniel was very thoughtful on the drive back to Jerusalem. He helped Eva up the stairs to the flat and took her case into the bedroom.

"Can I have a word with you, granny? I intended to become a GP as you know, but I've been amazed at how Aunt Anna has been able to find her voice, thanks to the efforts of Dr Stein. What would you think if I did some additional psychiatric training?"

"I think any extra training would be good for you, but you need to consider why you would want to do it. I was a doctor for a long time and I don't think I've ever seen a recovery as dramatic as Aunt Anna's. Most of the time, this kind of work is a hard slog with not always a lot of results. However, I rather think asking my advice is a courtesy, isn't it. I guess you've made your mind up."

"I'll finish my exams first, I think, and see how I get on; but yes, it's something I think I could do."

Eva ruffled his hair and, as usual, he shrugged her off and ran his own fingers through his hair to restore order.

Sam and Helen left for their respective jobs early on Monday morning. The others slept on unaware of their

341

departure. Sam dropped Helen at her school and continued on to the yeshiva. Rabbi Eliazar was waiting for him in his office. The desk was piled high with folders, and the draught from the open door blew some on to the floor. There was a great deal of muttering as the rabbi gathered the papers up again and told Sam to push the door to, then sit down.

Sam was extremely nervous; he knew he was there to defend his thesis and he waited for the opening question.

"Why did you decide to choose this topic?"

Sam cleared his throat.

"I had always thought of conversion as something a proselyte should consider carefully. Most of the people who came to me," he paused, "in a past life, were about to marry a Jewish partner. Sometimes, I have worried if that was the real reason why they were converting, rather than a religious conviction.

"My own circumstances told me differently. I didn't have to think about why I wanted to become Jewish; I had always thought I *was* Jewish. I've done considerable research, and I can find only one case even similar to mine; where someone who had been raised as Jewish suddenly discovered he wasn't. He was a rabbi, also, and the ramifications were truly awful.

"I felt if I wrote about this – the procedure, the knock on effect, it might offer some understanding as to why I want to remain a rabbi."

Rabbi Eliazar looked impressed with this explanation.

"You're right, Sam. We have also done extensive research. There was little precedence for your situation and I think we will be pleased to read what you have discovered. How near to completing your thesis are you?"

"The research is almost done. Then I need to put it into some sort of order and write it up."

"In that case, I wish you luck. Try and get it finished in the next two weeks, make three copies and I will meet with my colleagues to discuss your work. We will notify you of our decision."

Was it going to be as easy as that? Sam somehow doubted it, but he would follow the instructions to the letter. It was his future that was waiting.

CHAPTER 39

Anna was silent on the way to Jerusalem. Originally, she had been happy with the idea of a meal the night before her sister and Daniel flew home. Now she was not so sure.

"You keep calling it a 'Farewell Dinner' – it's as if we're never going to see Eva again."

Yaacov started to speak, then gave up as Anna continued.

"We're not so young any more. You know that Eva is much older than me. If she goes back to England, she could get ill. She might die. Anything could happen. I want to keep her in my life."

"The only way you can guarantee that, would be for us to go and live in the UK. Could you do that?"

"Are you trying to say we should live in England? Are you saying Eva won't come here because she has Sam and Rachel and their kids? You know how much I wanted a family, Yaacov. I feel as if I'm being penalised because I couldn't have children."

"I'm not saying that, Anna, but it would certainly be easier for us to move because we have fewer ties."

The bus was eating up the miles and they were not far from the bus station.

"I don't think I could leave Israel, it's been my home for too long. Perhaps Eva will come and live here," she added hopefully.

"I think that's unlikely. She has her children and grandchildren near her."

"What you're really saying is that because we haven't any family here, we should be the ones to move."

"Darling Anna, I'm not saying that. I'm just pointing out that it would be harder for Eva to uproot herself. You need to be positive, sweetheart. Travel is so much easier now. We can visit them in England; they can visit us here and don't forget – Esther will be here for a whole year as she studies. How would you feel if she stayed with us?"

Anna's face lit up.

"I'd never thought of that; it would be wonderful – we just need to ask her. As usual, my dear husband, you're right. We'll just wait and see what happens," but there were still worry lines on Anna's face.

The bus pulled smoothly into the bus station, and Yaacov looked over the heads of the other passengers to see if Sam was waiting. It was Esther, standing on the kerbside, who spotted him first and she waved furiously.

"I'm the welcome committee," she said beaming. "It's so lovely for me to have you here and to be like others who are meeting their families. It's a joy."

Anna was touched by these words and she embraced Esther, who kissed her great aunt on her velvety cheek. The smell of face powder lingered in her nostrils and she knew that whenever she smelled it, she would be reminded of Anna.

"Are you okay to walk down to the flat? Dad's booked a table at a restaurant round the corner."

"It would be good to drop our things off and have a wash," said Anna. "We decided we'd stay over, and go to the airport with your grandma and Daniel. That way we get to see them for a bit longer."

"Dad will be pleased, because he was worrying about them going on their own. He has classes all day and it would have been difficult for him to get the time off. I can tell you, Aunt Anna, he's working his socks off."

"His socks? He has to take his socks off to do his work? How strange!"

Esther laughed out loud. "No, it's a saying – it means he's working very hard."

"Oh, I see," replied Anna doubtfully, but she still looked baffled.

Impulsively, Esther stopped and hugged her great aunt.

"I'm so, so happy we found you. It's like having another granny. Daniel and I are very lucky."

Anna was pleased to hear this and told Esther that she, too, was lucky to have found them.

Eva was at the door of the flat, waiting impatiently.

"We're just about ready. Sam booked the table early so we could get a good night's sleep and you could get your bus back to Haifa."

"Not necessary, now," and Yaacov explained.

Eva, sitting next to Anna, looked around at her family. This meal was tinged with sadness for her, and she could see that her sister felt the same. They were together at the end of the table and somehow, Anna's small hand had found its way into Eva's.

"I can't bear the thought that you'll go home, and I won't see you again," she whispered.

"There's no need to worry about that; of course you'll see me again. As soon as Rachel's ok after having the baby, I'll be flying out."

Anna's face was wet with tears.

"You promise, Evalli," she begged.

"Of course I do, little nightingale. Time will go by quickly, I promise, and you'll have Sam and Helen here, as well as Esther."

"I know you're right and I have grown to love Sam and Helen, and the twins, but they're not you."

"We can talk on the phone; we can write, and I'll send pictures of the baby."

Anna had to be content with that. She tried hard to compose herself, knowing that the goodbye at the airport would be even more difficult.

She was right. By the time Eva and Daniel had disappeared through the gate, both women were in floods of tears. At one point, Eva even considered missing the flight and staying in Israel, but the thought of Rachel needing her spurred her on.

Daniel had the window seat but once she was settled, she looked across him and tried to compose herself.

A compassionate voice from the man sitting next to her asked if she was frightened of flying.

"I am," she said, "but that's not why I'm upset." By the time the plane was in the air she had told her new friend all about seeing Anna again. When she looked out of the window she could see clouds and, far beneath, the city of Tel Aviv.

"Goodness," she said. "I didn't even know we'd taken off," and the young man laughed with her. Daniel patted her hand, saying,

"Well done, granny."

Ivor was at the airport and bundled them into the car.

"I can't thank you enough for coming home like this. Rachel's okay, I guess, but she's finding these last couple of months difficult. She's always been slim, and now she says she looks like an elephant. I tell her she's a very beautiful elephant, and she bursts into tears. I don't know what to say to her; I think I'm a bit out of my depth."

Eva saw he wasn't his usual immaculate self. There was a button missing from his shirt and a spot of something on his tie.

"Don't worry, Ivor. Women can get very emotional during pregnancy, and Rachel is possibly worried that something might go wrong."

"I'm worried too, but I don't want to worry her by telling her."

"Perhaps each of you should tell the other your worries. She might be thinking you don't care. This is maybe not the time for keeping things to yourselves. Share your concerns and it will be better."

"Ma," said Ivor affectionately. "You've only been back for five minutes and already you're solving problems."

"There is one problem you can solve, Ivor. I hope the house is warm. After coming from a hot country, I'm absolutely frozen." They all laughed. Eva's intolerance to the cold was legendary.

Rachel was, indeed, very large. Eva ran her 'doctor eye' over her daughter, and saw shadowed eyes, with dark circles under them and a pale skin.

"Are you anaemic?" she asked.

"A bit; I'm just tired all the time."

"We'll soon sort that," said Eva decisively. "You can rest as much as you like and I'll do whatever is necessary."

"Oh, mummy, you don't know how pleased I am to see you."

Eva noted Rachel's use of the word 'mummy', gauging that she was even more exhausted than Ivor thought.

Once they'd watched the plane take off, Anna and Yaacov took the bus back to Haifa. Anna was in a sombre mood and Yaacov decided that action was necessary. Unlocking the front door he said,

"You haven't done any painting for a while," he said. "How about doing something for the baby? Something bright and cheerful for his room. Or her room," he added quickly.

Anna took notice of what he'd said and agreed, and within a short time she was engrossed in sketching something on the canvas. Yaacov tip toed out of the studio and left her to it.

In Jerusalem, Sam was debating a contentious part of the Torah in his class. The other students had, at first, deferred to what they thought was his superior knowledge, but it hadn't taken long for that attitude to disappear, and now he was shouted down as much and as frequently as the other students.

The weeks passed, with regular phone calls to England. Eva reported on Rachel's progress and, since her return, she could see a great difference in her daughter. Anna and Yaacov became 'anxious great aunt and uncle to be', despite never having met Rachel. When the call came to say the baby had arrived, everyone was in Haifa. They were not expecting to hear so soon, so there was no urgency for Anna to answer the phone. This was still a novelty for her. Before, when she had no voice, Yaacov had always been in charge of the phone; now she raced to be the first to pick up the receiver.

They were all lethargic from the sun, and there was a relaxed ease when Anna spoke. She gave a great whoop of delight which was heard in the garden and she came rushing out, shouting, "It's a girl; mother and baby doing well, granny's exhausted!"

They each took it in turns to speak to Rachel, who insisted it had been a very easy delivery and she was fine.

"We're calling her Leah," she said, and Anna found it difficult to put into words what she was feeling. Eva came back on the line and said they had to go; they had used up their telephone time but she promised to call as soon as she could, with all the information about the baby.

"Champagne," Yaacov said and busied himself with opening a bottle and pouring it into glasses.

"Mazaltov to Rachel and Ivor," Sam toasted and they raised their glasses saying,

"Le'chaim to baby Leah."

"I'm so relieved all is well," said Sam on the way back to Jerusalem.

"Were you worried?"

"Not exactly, but Rachel's not as young as you were when you had the twins. What did worry me was her asking ma to help – she's always been so independent."

"It won't be long now till things are back to normal. Once you've presented your thesis, we'll be able to go home and you can get back to the community."

"And I've been asking myself if that's what I actually want."

"Are you saying you want to stay in Israel?"

"No, I'm not."

Esther, sitting in the back seat, was holding her breath.

"I'm just not sure I want to go back to the same community."

"What?" Helen was shocked. "East Lane shul is a wonderful community, and everyone loves and respects you."

"One thing I've learned from being here is how much I enjoy teaching."

"So you want to teach?"

"I'm not sure, Helen, but this has been a wake – up call. Our community is wonderful but when I stopped to consider, I realise just how big it is – how impersonal it's become. Do you know that we have over three thousand members? Of course, I know many of them but I don't know all of them. The regulars, the ones who come every shabbat – they're the ones I know well. The rest, the members who come on high days and holy days, I know less.

"In fact, at the last shabbat service at home, I went over to a man who was taking off his tallit. I welcomed him to the shul and he told me he had been a member for the last twenty years. To be fair, he didn't seem put out that I hadn't recognised him, but I was embarrassed. It was an awkward moment. I mentioned it to the chairman but he didn't seem too bothered. He told me that if people didn't come regularly, they shouldn't be surprised if the rabbi didn't know who they were."

"I can see this has been bothering you, darling. What conclusion have you reached?"

Sam looked excited as he outlined his thoughts.

"All this started because I was in the running for Chief Rabbi. I've come to realise that I don't want to be a Chief Rabbi – indeed, I don't want to be a chief anything. I don't want to have to be an administrator – I want to be the rabbi of a community I can help grow; one where I know everyone."

"That might be difficult, Sam. Most of our shuls have a large number of members – even if they don't all attend services."

"As it happens…" he started carefully. "The Chief Rabbi has mentioned that a new synagogue is being developed in Essex. There's been an influx of Jews – well," he corrected himself, "about fifty families. Rabbi Hershell says that no one wants to take up the position of a small town rabbi, and when I was talking to him last week about my future, he suggested I should think about it. He also said there's a part time teaching post available at the college in London and he thinks the two jobs together would work. I could travel in to town a couple of days a week. What do you think, Helen? Would you be prepared to move and live on a reduced salary?"

Helen looked at his face, alight with enthusiasm, more animated than she'd seen for a long time.

"Sam, you know I'd go anywhere to be with you. It doesn't matter where we live, as long as we're together. There are a couple of things to think about but yes, of course, I'm with you. But I need to ask; is this anything to do with Esther wanting to be a rabbi?"

CHAPTER 40

They had been so engrossed in their conversation, that they had forgotten Esther was in the back of the car.

An indignant voice called out,

"Don't blame me for this, please. If dad wants to change direction it's his choice," and she subsided back on to her seat.

"You're right," Sam replied. "This is something I've been thinking about for a while, although in a way it does have something to do with you. We've been to the progressive synagogue a few times and I've seen how great the atmosphere is. I'm thinking that a smaller shul might have more of that kind of feeling about it."

"Perhaps you're thinking about really changing direction and becoming a reform rabbi" Esther said wickedly.

"I think that's a step too far," Sam replied tolerantly, thinking back to the big argument they'd had when Esther had declared her intentions of becoming just that. He followed through what he had been saying before Esther interrupted.

"Rabbi Hershell wasn't surprised when I told him my thoughts. He confirmed what I already knew; even in the future, I would have little opportunity to become Chief Rabbi. 'People have long memories', he said and I agree.

"However, he did say something that interested me; he would recommend me to take up a position as 'consultant to the Chief Rabbi'. He feels that I could do this as well as the other things I'm planning."

Esther looked impressed and then she said more soberly,

"Tomorrow's your big day, dad. Have you got everything ready, enough pens and pencils, and is your revision done?"

"None of that," laughed Sam, "even though you sound like me, when I was helping you prepare for an exam. All I have to do is hand the folder in, and then I'm free. I expect it'll take a couple of weeks before the decision is made but then, after that, your mother and I will start to make plans for returning home. I presume you'll be coming with us?"

"I start at Leo Baeck in five weeks, so yes, I guess I'll come back with you. There'll be books to get and so on. At least I won't have to find somewhere to live – or will I mum? Is dad serious about this move?"

"Yes, he is. I suppose we could commute from home to Essex but it would be more convenient to find a house there. That could take a bit of time, which will give you the opportunity to look around for a flat. Maybe you could share with another student?"

"Worth thinking about." Esther yawned and closed her eyes. A short nap would be good before they arrived back in Jerusalem.

The next morning, Sam was as anxious as a child on its first day at school. In the end, Helen offered to walk with him to the yeshiva and wait while he handed his thesis in.

"And after that we'll go for coffee. There's nothing you can do until they call you back so let's make the most of a free morning."

Rabbi Eliazar was waiting. He motioned to Sam to sit, and took the blue folder from his shaking fingers.

"It's understandable you're nervous. We'll read through this and let you know our decision as soon as possible."

Sam cleared his throat.

"I think you know already how much this means to me. Being a rabbi is all I've ever wanted to do…"

Rabbi Eliazar interrupted him.

"I know that, Sam. When you did your study year here, when you were first studying for the rabbinate, it was clear you were an outstanding student. I hope what I'm about to read substantiates that. But what I can't do is make any allowances for you. We'll let you know our conclusion in due course. In the meantime, take a couple of days off and have a rest. My secretary will call you as soon as we've reached a decision."

Sam had to be content with that and he and Helen spent a lazy morning drinking coffee and making plans for the future.

"I'm going to ring ma," he said eventually. "It's about time she let us know when she's coming back. Anna's desperate to see her again and it would be good to spend some proper time, all together. We may not get another opportunity once I start my new job." Helen smiled to herself. Sam had been so up and down; one minute thinking he would never have a congregation again, the next moment planning his first sermon.

Eva was very decisive about her plans.

"I was about to call you," she said. "I'll be back in Israel next week. Rachel's absolutely fine now and I'm so looking forward to seeing you all." She gave Sam the flight details and he said he'd collect her.

"Don't worry about that," she replied. "I'll just take a taxi and go straight to Anna's. You can come up at the weekend. Is that okay?"

Sam replaced the receiver.

"This whole episode has been dreadful but in a strange sort of way, it's given ma a new lease of life. She's already organised the flight and she says she doesn't need me to collect her."

"Good," Helen said happily. "That means when we return home we won't have to keep accompanying her here. Once she's done the journey by herself, she'll manage in the future."

Sam wasn't so sure, but didn't say anything.

"It's all very well for the rabbi to tell me to have 'a holiday' but you're still going to the school."

"Only three days a week. There's plenty of time to explore more of Israel. Why don't you plan out some things to do while I'm there, and we can get organised." She turned to her daughter. "You can help dad, can't you?"

"Probably not," Esther said cheerfully. "I'm going up north to stay at one of the kibbutz's. I'll be back when granny's here but, until then, you two are on your own."

When Helen got in from school the following day, Sam was already sitting on the balcony with a pile of leaflets on the table in front of him. He looked up and answered Helen,

"These are all the places we can visit. I picked up the information at the tourist centre near the Jaffa Gate, and the young man in there suggested we do a couple of organised trips."

"Good idea," Helen said, "especially a visit to the Dead Sea and Masada."

"It's on the list. In fact, I've already decided we should drive there and I've booked us into a hotel."

"Can we afford it?"

"I think so. We check in on Thursday."

Helen was pleased. They'd both settled in to Israeli life – studying, teaching and so on, but she wanted a bit of 'tourist time' before they left, realising that it could be a while before they were able to visit again.

The Dead Sea was incredible. They behaved like two teenagers, covering themselves in the thick, black, viscous mud, before rinsing off under the showers on the beach. They floated in the sea, with Helen taking the inevitable picture of Sam leaning back in the water, reading a newspaper.

The hotel was small but the back doors led straight onto the beach and they sat for hours, planning where they would go next, watching the fiery orb of the sun go down.

Masada was spectacular. They decided to walk up the narrow pathway, and set their alarm for three am so they could watch the sunrise. Sitting close together on a flat rock, they ate the packed breakfast the hotel had made for them. Sam laid his arm across Helen's shoulder and said,

"Can you believe we are walking in the footsteps of those who preferred to die than submit to the Romans? That's our heritage, don't you think?"

They took trips to Tiberius, and visited the tomb of Maimonides; they went to Akko and marvelled at the excavations which were uncovering Templar sites. On the way back from Akko they visited the Museum of the Warsaw Ghetto fighters at Kibbutz Lochamei HaGeta'ot.

"The kibbutnicks here are all amazing," Sam told Helen. "This kibbutz and the museum were founded by survivors. Like Anna, they arrived after the war and most of them have stayed ever since. They've had their children here and, in fact, the museum was founded before Yad Vashem."

"And, talking of Yad Vashem…"

"Yes, I know. We'll take ma and Anna there when she arrives. She'll want to see the plaque and I know Mr Morris wants to meet her."

"When we get home, Sam, it will be wonderful to talk about these places. I can tell the children in my school, and the ladies guild."

"And the cheder kids; except they'll all be different now we've decided on the big move."

"True," said Helen, "but the principal is the same."

The day before Eva was due to arrive, Sam was sorting out his papers. The phone rang.

He answered it and his face became grave. He listened for what to Helen seemed a long time, and then thanked the caller.

"What?" asked Helen. "Tell me. What is it?"

Sam's whole demeanour changed.

"It's ok, Helen. The rabbis decided I could retain...or should I say be awarded my semicha. As from now, this minute, I am a rabbi again." His shoulders shook as reality struck him.

"I can't believe it. They liked my thesis. They said I had described the conversion process in a way they had never considered before. Rabbi Bendell, the rabbi who wasn't convinced of my sincerity, even said they would include it as essential reading for the yeshiva students."

He was overcome and held Helen tightly.

"This means so much to me. Even though I hoped it would be all right, there was always a feeling in the back of my mind that they would reject me.

"I need to tell ma. I know she's been worried. This will put her mind at rest because all along she's been telling me that what happened was her fault."

"You need to tell Rabbi Langer, too. And the family and so many people."

"Yes, but not the press. There's nothing wonderful about being re-instated. It was just essential so that I could continue being a rabbi."

Practical Helen made tea, and sat Sam down with the telephone.

"You just get on with it," she said. "I'll start dinner."

She listened as he told his mother what the Rabbi had said and learned he would receive semicha on the shabbat before they returned to England. He had been invited to lead the service, pretty much the way he had when he had received his conversion certificate. That had been a low key event and he wanted this to be the same.

Sam was on the phone a long time.

"I called the Levy's and the Steins, and Bernie and Karen," he said. "I think it was only right they should be there. They were delighted and wanted to make a big event but I told them, 'no'. It's just a continuation of my life."

"All my life, ma's often said things were 'bershert' – fate, call it what you like. How about this for fate? The portion I will read is the same one I read for my barmitzvah. Can you believe it? I couldn't have planned it better if I'd tried, and I feel that life has come full circle, especially as ma will be able to hear it. Last time, I think she cried all the way through the service."

"I should imagine she did," Helen said dryly. "I did the same with Daniel."

"So you did," Sam remembered. "Well, now ma will have a second chance to hear it, maybe without tears."

"I wouldn't be so sure," Helen said as she went into the kitchen to take the food out of the oven.

Eva's plane was on time and she called Sam from Anna's.

"All's well. I managed the flight fine and I'll see you with Anna and Yaacov on Friday afternoon."

Sam was very surprised.

"After all Anna's said about 'synagogue going', I assumed she wouldn't want to come."

"This is different," Eva said. "Look, talk to her," and with great pleasure she passed the receiver to her sister.

"So, Aunt Anna," said Sam, "you're coming to shul this week. After all you've said," he joked, "I'm astonished."

"Don't get excited," was the response. "I'm not going to the synagogue to worship God. I'm going because my

360

nephew is taking the service. Probably, I'll never go again," she said loudly.

Sam was touched; not because she was going to the synagogue, but because she had referred to him as her nephew. He said 'goodbye' and put the phone down.

"Things are coming together," he told Helen and she just smiled.

When Anna, Yaacov and Eva arrived, Anna seemed to be bubbling with excitement. Yaacov kept looking at her, as if to keep her quiet, and Eva had that all too familiar look in her eyes; the one he remembered from his childhood, gently warning him to behave. Try as he might, he couldn't discover why everyone was so buoyant, and he had to do with Eva telling him it was because things had 'turned out all right in the end'.

They were all in bed when they heard Esther's key in the lock. "Of course I'm coming back from the kibbutz for dad's big day," she had told her mother. "Just a pity Daniel can't be here."

Breakfast was a hurried affair. Sam wanted everyone in the synagogue early and, although Anna took a deep breath and hesitated a little before going up the steps, she allowed the other women to encourage her up the stairs to the Ladies' Gallery.

By the time the service was due to start, the synagogue was crowded. Helen whispered to Esther,

"That looks like Daniel and Ivor, and is that Rabbi Langer?" She looked up from the siddur to see Rachel coming through the door, with baby Leah firmly clasped in her arms.

"I can't believe it. Is everyone here?"

"Not everyone, mum, Just the ones we love," said Esther.

Sam took his place on the bimah and his eyes widened as he saw all the members of his family. He led the service almost in a dream, and then paused for breath before he gave his sermon. He had written a dvar Torah, and the papers were in front of him on the bimah. Decisively, he laid them aside and spoke from the heart.

"Today's portion is parashat Noach, and it takes me back many, many years. It is the portion I read when I was barmitzvah. It tells us that Noah was a righteous man and was supported by God; it says that he walked with God. I cannot compare myself to a man such as Noah but I feel that I wouldn't be here today if God had not supported me in my journey.

"Over recent months, I have had a series of problems and difficulties; there were times when I thought a day like today would never happen but, here I am, surrounded by my family and some old friends from England, as well as new friends from Israel. Their love and support has helped me become what I am today and my thanks go to them all."

Sam looked up and saw the tears raining down his mother's face. Once again she'd missed him reading the portion.

GLOSSARY

Aliyah	Emigrating to Israel: being called up for the reading of the Torah
Baruchim ha baim	Welcome
Beth Din	Jewish court of law
Beshert	Fate
Bimah	Raised platform, where the reading desk is in the synagogue
Boreka	Savoury pastry
Brit milah…brit	Circumcision
Brochah	Blessing
Cardo	Jewish quarter in the old city of Jerusalem
Challah	Plaited bread, eaten on shabbat
Chalutz/im	Traditional way of learning the Talmud, in pairs
Chumash	Printed Torah, rather than a scroll
Dayan/dayanim	Judge[s] at the Beth Din
Dvar Torah	A talk on topics relating to a section of the Torah
Dybbuk	Malevolent wandering spirit
Get/gittin	Religious divorce

Glatt kosher	Stringent adherence to kosher laws
Golem	Artificially created being
Hashem	Jewish reference to God
Hatafat dam brit	Procedure for men wishing to convert, who have already been circumcised
Hora	Jewish dance
Kaddish	Prayer said regularly in synagogue
Ketubah	Marriage contract
Kichel	Cookie
Kiddush	Literally, 'sanctification' over wine or grape juice but also a light repast after the service
Kippah	Head covering for men
Kotel	The Western Wall in Jerusalem
L'chaim	To life
Leyn	Chanting of the Torah
Ma ha'matzav	What's up? What's the situation?
Magen Dovid	Star of David
Mahane Yehuda	Jerusalem's famous market
Mazaltov	Good luck
Mea Shearim	Ultra orthodox area in Jerusalem
Meshugah	Crazy
Mishegas	Silliness
Parashah	Passage in Jewish scripture
Peyot	Sidelocks, sideburns
Plotz	Explode, burst
Semicha	Rabbi's ordination
Shacarit	Morning service
Shakshuka	Traditional Israeli breakfast dish of onions, tomatoes, peppers and egg

Shalom	Traditional greeting: peace
Sheva brocha	Seven blessings recited over a bride and groom at a Jewish wedding
Shoah	Holocaust
Shuk	Market
Shul	Synagogue
Siddur	Prayer book
Souk	Market
Tallit	Prayer shawl
Torah	The first five books of the Hebrew Bible
Tsuris	Troubles, worries, aggravation
Tzitzit	Specially knotted ritual fringes on a garment, worn by Jewish men
Yad	Ritual pointer, used to follow the text on the Torah scroll
Yad Vashem	Israel's official memorial to the victims of the Holocaust
Yarmulke	Head covering
Yeshivah	Academy of Talmudic learning
Yichud	Time the newly married couple spend alone together immediately after the wedding
Yom Hashoah	Holocaust Memorial Day